The Masterpiece

A Unique Heroine an Intriguing Mystery
Is it a **TURNER ORIGINAL** people are dying for?

Bob McCabe

New Generation Publishing

Thanks Helena, Carolyn, David
and the love of my life, Pat

The view across the Vltava River to Prague Castle with all its romantic beauty in no way could ease the troubled mind of Sir Geoffrey Fletcher as he stood at the dingy attic window, hands crossed behind his ramrod straight back.

At last, turning to face the three men at the small table he spoke quickly and with some reluctance.

"Susan Macken is her name, she's an Irish citizen, living near Dublin. The painting is in her possession and I believe she has no idea of its potential value apparently having purchased the work simply because it provoked memories from her childhood. All relevant information is contained here." He held up a small computer memory stick before placing it in front of them.

At seventy years of age, a diminutive corpulent man his unimpressive appearance belied his achievements in life, fifteen years into retirement he was appalled to find himself under a compliment and beholden to such people. Sir Geoffrey wore his Knighthood proudly insisting on being addressed by his full title on all occasions.

"I am aware of your source of information." He continued.

"I am also aware that the information may have become corrupt by exposure to the worldwide web and contributions of an unreliable nature, casting some doubt on its validity." He paused to gain composure before continuing.

"Should this painting eventually prove to be the original masterpiece, as claimed, it must be offered to the Tate Gallery to take its place amongst the artist's other great works. I insist that this be a condition of my co-operation and that Susan Macken or members of her family should not come to harm."

"Of course Sir Geoffrey," The response came glibly and easily.

"We are grateful and full of admiration. We know about Mrs Macken, in fact we know the person in question even better than she knows herself."

About to reply Sir Geoffrey was stopped by a raised hand.

"You may serve us better by concentrating on more important matters."

There was no mistaking the edge to the voice, which in an instant changed becoming polite again.

"This is Vaclav Janacec, Sir Geoffrey, he will be accompanying you back to England." The retired Knight of the realm instinctively accepted the proffered hand as the youngest member of the trio stood up and leaned across the table.

"It's a pleasure to meet you Sir,"

The smile was disarming, the handshake firm, the voice cultured without a trace of an accent. The Windsor knot of the Etonian tie beneath the perfect white collar matched his own. Sir Geoffrey looked up into a pair of startlingly dark eyes. Mesmerized by their intensity he felt momentarily disorientated. For a fleeting moment he imagined the knot of the familiar tie below the handsome face had transformed into, of all things, a white mouse. He blinked and the image disappeared.

Leaning forward in the passenger seat Susan Macken studied her reflection in the vanity mirror, Jane, taking her eyes from the car in front, with amusement and genuine affection quizzically looked at her mother as they waited in the city-centre traffic.

"You persuaded the busiest advertising executive in town to take precious time off mid-week, to attend O'Reilly's auction?" She said incredulously.

"Well not quite," came the matter of fact reply, I explained to your father that I was being taken to lunch for my fiftieth birthday and told him about the painting.

Susan flicked up the vanity mirror as she characteristically and expertly readjusted a wayward strand of blond hair before continuing with a wide smile.

"It's that painting in O'Reilly's, the one I was telling you about. I just can't stop thinking about it. You know when I told Paul he actually offered to go to the auction. It's today. The bidding should start about 2.45."

The fate of the bunk beds was of no consequence to the man waiting for Lot 216. Paul Macken shifted his position slightly in anticipation, ensuring he was in auctioneer O'Reilly's field of vision.

In spite of an extremely busy schedule his magnanimous offer to attend the auction had been motivated by the fact that he had totally forgotten his wife's birthday, a crime of some magnitude in the family orientated Susan's eyes.

Paul knew he was paranoid, well mildly paranoid. He would claim the condition to be an advantage in life giving him an edge over others, particularly in business. He had convinced himself, based on his own theory, that being mildly paranoid made him more sensitive, aware and therefore one step ahead of the opposition.

Arriving far to early for lot 216. He had immediately suspected several individuals of being potential bidders for the painting. As the auction had proceeded each of the would-be art buyers had fallen by the wayside. A woman in a moth eaten fur coat, he had decided was an eccentric millionaire art dealer from the city, had just purchased the bunk beds.

"Make sure you don't miss it, lot 216." Susan had said, it will come up at about 3.30." Paul watched as the auctioneer offered each lot with the gravitas and expectation one would attribute to a great masterpiece at a Sotheby's sale.

Auctioneer O'Reilly from his lofty position viewed the attendant bargain hunters with a calm eye. "Is that a bid madam or are you just waving to a friend." The lady who was indeed waving to a friend and had no interest in the lot whatsoever dropped her hand, with a half-smile and in some confusion. Satisfied that he had embarrassed the woman enough he completed the sale.

O'Reilly's Fine Auction House situated approximately 10 miles from the city centre of Dublin, the Thursday afternoon auction was now in full swing dealing in everything from cardboard boxes of kitchen ware to the odd piece of nice furniture.

"Now," glancing down, "what have we? Lot 216, fine painting this." *Deal- Hobblers going out to a wreck.* He scanned the bargain hunters with a practiced eye disappointed to see that none of the top art buyers he had instructed Sheila to notify had in fact turned up, their loss.

He sniffed his disdain for those who did not normally attend his fine auction rooms and shot a glance to the far corner of the large crowded room over the heads of the bargain hunters to where the beleaguered Sheila stood clasping the very important white dockets in a chubby bejeweled hand. The very important pink copies had been carefully separated and stowed away in their appropriate files in the back office. She returned the look with assumed nonchalance and hefted her ample bosom with folded arms.

"Fine painting this, unsigned, excellent quality, attributed to Nash," He repeated. "Have I got a start?"

Susan's description had not prepared Paul Macken for the impact of the painting. As an artist of some note and creative director of an advertising agency in the city Paul had been dealing with the graphic image and creative solutions for the most part of his 53 years.

He could feel the power of the work. Not a superfluous stroke, spontaneous consistent treatment throughout, definitely the work of a master craftsman, signed or unsigned. He could understand why Susan felt so strongly about it.

Hovellers going out to a wreck, what a fantastic turbulent sea merging with the wild sky, a wonderful feeling of light, two boats, square cut sails, russet red, wallowing and driving in a race to a distant wreck, a glimpse of buildings on a shoreline quite close, painted at a slight angle adding movement and drama. D2, the letter and number could be made out on the nearest boat, three figures crouched and leaning into the gale, the glimpse of a faded blue shirt and a red cap. *The Cutter dragging her anchor bowsprit and main mast gone was in deep distress. The year was 1825 and the notorious Goodwin Sands was about to claim another victim.*

"Do I hear five hundred?" Paul, transfixed by the painting was jolted back to his surroundings....

Mr O'Reilly gavel poised, cast about expectantly for the next bid. Without hesitation Paul indicated approval with a raised hand.

Expertly and confidently, O'Reilly restated. "A very fine Nash ...surely more than five hundred," glancing left and right the auctioneer's keen eye sought a further bid. Paul's eye flew to another woman in a fur coat.

"I will let it go for only five hundred. No further takers...then?" ... the gavel dropped. "Sold for five hundred euro. Now then, Lot 217, a very nice wardrobe, needs some repair, an excellent reminder of fine living in Georgian Times, will someone start me with fifty euro?"

"That will be five hundred euro plus the usual 12%." Sheila Markey glanced at the computer screen as she selected a white docket and pushed it across the surface of the Formica-covered desk.

"Cheque or cash please, we don't take cards."

The Auction over, the Thursday afternoon speculators queued to collect their purchases. Paul anxious to make up for the lost time having left immediately after his successful bid for the painting had returned to collect Susan's birthday present. He carefully leaned his purchase against the shiny green painted wall and reached for his chequebook.

"If I might say a very nice painting, you did very well there,"

Mr O'Reilly making his way along the queue of purchasers that had formed at the pay counter stopped with exaggerated casualness, hands in pockets. Hand tailored three piece suit just about coping with the girth of a figure nurtured with good wine, dining out on the proceeds of a reasonably successful business, and the ruthless pursuance of the main chance.

Quick eyes glanced to the painting and back to Paul Macken.

"Sure the frame alone is probably worth that. I see there's some slight water damage at the edges."

He peered closely at the painting, his interest no doubt fuelled by the fact that Paul Macken, a fellow member of the Borough Council and an astute businessman, had made the purchase. In reality 500 euro was quite a high figure for a painting at O'Reilly's Fine Auction House.

"Pity it's not signed, a signed Nash of this quality would fetch a pretty price," he continued, with a sympathetic expression.

"You know, I could put you in touch with someone who could, like, take it off your hands for about €700 should you so wish."

"No thanks," Paul declined the offer pretty sure that the generous "someone" would turn out to be the good Mr O'Reilly himself who was having second thoughts about the "Nash."

"No, I really like the painting, I'm pretty sure it's not by Nash, though, style doesn't fit. I reckon this is much earlier," he continued. "Nash was born in 1893 and was not particularly famous for seascapes, well not like this one anyway."

"The customer's always right." O'Reilly stooped, putting further strain on his already stressed waistcoat, looking even closer at the painting.

"M... m...," he murmured stroking his chins in contemplation. "It's a pity about the water damage. Well, if you change your mind then.... probably worth a king's ransom, we'll never know?"

Standing up he turned to the next in line with a last glance at the work of art.

"Hello- Mrs Galvin...two lots is it? A fondue set and bunk beds."

"That will be Twenty Six Euro and sixty cents...Yes - We can deliver," Then with a narrowing of his bushy eyebrows,

"Sheila, You didn't put Mr Macken's pink docket in the wire tray, do that before you serve Mrs Galvin," he admonished with some irritation.

"Yes, Mr O'Reilly," the pink docket found it's way propelled with some agitation and tightening of ruby red lips as the long suffering Sheila complied.

Paul Macken headed for his car. He and Susan lived approximately 2 miles from the auction house outside the village on the coast. The house with its lovely aspect just inland overlooking the wooded landscape to the beach had been Susan's family home for many years. In Paul's opinion a town house in the city would have been more appropriate but there was no moving Susan.

Looking at his watch, 6.15, deciding to take the coast road he contemplated with eager anticipation arriving home and Susan's reaction to his success at O'Reilly's.

Yes ... The painting...originally he had been somewhat sceptical but now it was a different matter. Stopping at the traffic lights on the outskirts of the picturesque village he couldn't resist an intense urge to look behind him at the heavy gold-framed picture leaning upright against the back seat. The early evening low sun cast a golden glow accentuating the rich russet colour of the sails of the two boats. The skill of the artist had caught the power of the rough sea, the sense of drama, the nearest lugger plunging into another wave and rising.

Michael Wakeley, Hoveller, hands gripping the tiller shouted instructions to his two sons. "Make ready to come about, we'll get them on the next tack." He watched Walter and Matthew, nimble and quick, go about their business. The tiller bucked and jumped in his grip. "I'm getting too old for this." Michael, at 39 years of age was strong and determined, capable.

Nobody knew these waters better than him. The Goodwin Sands were like an open book, but he lacked the quickness and stamina of his youth. My time here is nearly finished, my mission nearly accomplished. Almost as soon as the thought formed in his mind it was dashed away by the challenge of the task at hand and the manoeuver that would take him past and ahead of the other Hovellers.

The foundering cutter loomed larger and ever closer. Get a rope on board, first come first served, the law of salvage, the rule of the Deal Hovellers.

Michael could see the vessel was in great distress her foremast and bowsprit torn away. It was blowing a terrific gale. She was dragging her anchors and would soon be in the jaws of the breakers closer to shore.

Get a line on her port side, board her, slip her starboard chain and haul her away Southward to calmer waters. But he'd need the help of the others. There were enough luggers out but they'd never pull together.

The Cutter Renown, captained by George Stewart on His Majesty's service, was bound for London. Off Deal a terrific gale blew up, NNW and a very heavy sea. Her anchors couldn't hold her to ride out the storm. She was being dragged towards the Goodwin Sands and the massive breakers. Captain Stewart's thoughts were for his crew and for his cargo but mostly for the essential business of the King entrusted to him.

Should he cast off anchors so the ship might be manoeuvred? With the bowsprit and mainmast gone survival would be down to luck. Through the gale he could see the luggers of the Hoveller's approach. He had heard of their bravery and their piloting and rescuing skills. He had also heard of smuggling and thievery, of desperate characters resorting to piracy and false claims to enhance salvaging rewards.

He reached for the leather valise emblazoned with the king's Crest.

The vessel was steadily drifting, the mountainous sea wallowing over her deck.

As she began to break up the hold filled through her hatches, brave souls were swept away as the Helmsman was thrown by the spinning wheel. She rolled, no sanctuary, no rope strong enough, no man could swim, tossed down beneath, screams filled with salty liquid, deep green and silent then the burst of clamouring chaotic noise, lungs gasping for life itself. The fate of the cutter's crew was at the mercy of the storm and the Goodwin Sands.

Michael Wakeley shouted against the wind, "She's breaking up lads there'll be precious little to salvage here. Bring her about and cut our losses. Cast about we'll see what we can save."

The water was a churning soup of debris,

"Keep a weather eye out for a long boat. They may have had time to get one away, little chance." Amongst the debris could be seen the odd poor soul floating and battered, none moving or crying out now.

The D2 now been joined by the other Hovellers, all with the same purpose in mind salvage what they could, maybe save a life.

Michael looked across at the nearest Hoveller Lugger.

The storm was increasing in its intensity the sou'wester howled in the rigging. The Dutchman looked back and raised an arm signalling his intention to return to the safety of the Downs. The luggers in turn began to come about and head for shore.

One more pass Michael decided. He waved his intention and the Dutchman acknowledged with a shake of his head, "You're crazy Wakeley," he shouted through cupped hands but the words were whipped away by the wind.

The mighty sea lifted the D2 high and she was alone as she plunged into the trough and rose again. "Starboard!" Michael looked as the boat dropped again to rise on the crest of the next wave and there through the spray following his son's pointing arm he saw the man clinging to a bundle of rope and tarpaulin arm raised, waving.

The manoeuver took all Michael's skill. As they approached it would be easily done for the heavy bough to swing late driven by the turbulent sea and crush the helpless man in the water, but at last they had him where they wanted him close astern.

Michael reached out and the boat hook caught first time in the binding of the tarpaulin. He dragged the bundle in close. It was bulky and lashed tightly as it rode the waves with the pitch of the lugger.

Michael could see a hand the wrist entwined in the lashing. Then another hand holding a vicious bladed knife reached over the bundle and he was face to face with the man he had saved. Michael expecting to find a half drowned unfortunate nearing exhaustion recoiled in surprise.

The knife hand moved. It was an unusual looking weapon with the handle held in a fist, a vicious blade protruding from one side and a needle sharp stiletto at the other, the lashings on the wrist parted under the blade. Michael reached to help but it was hardly necessary as the man came across the back of the lugger dragging the bundle after him.

It was an extraordinary feat of athleticism and strength under any circumstances, never mind the pitching of the boat and the fact that the man had been in the water for some time and should have been near to exhaustion.

"Thank You," the accent was unfamiliar to Michael's ear as the man crouched on the boards extending a hand. Penetrating black eyes looked deep into Michael's as with the first feelings of unease he took the strong grasp of the stranger's hand.

The Copper Kettle in the village with its "Fine Italian Cuisine." Well, that had been the boast in the early days. Over the years due to demand and the astute observations of its owner, the menu choice had become somewhat blurred at the edges. The sign over the door boasted authentic Italian cuisine but Antonio the original chef had long since departed Ireland's shores for his native Italy where no doubt, today, some fashionable eatery could make the proud boast with a better conscience.

Warm and cosy with a touch of gingham, blue and yellow, the Italian ambiance prevailed, pasta, spaghetti, mingled with leg of lamb, garlic and rosemary, posh fish and chips and Irish stew, now the order of the day. The solitary window alongside the glass pane door offered a view up the narrow main street of the Heritage village.

Susan and Jane having completed their shopping trip had returned along the coast making their way like homing pigeons to their favourite haunt in the village. Having done justice to a very nice tomato, goats cheese and onion tart followed by apple pie, they sat in deep cushioned chairs and shared the last of the Chablis, another latte on its way, all part of Jane's day out.

"Happy birthday mum," Jane savouring the moment raised her glass but Susan did not respond, she was gazing past Jane and seemed in another world. Judging by her expression not a very pleasant one.

"Mum, Happy birthday, Mum!" She reached anxiously across the table for Susan's hand. "Mum, what's wrong are you alright?"

"Of course," Susan replied vaguely and then more positively as her mind and her eyes returned to focus on her daughters face. "Yes, yes I'm fine," but welling tears betrayed the attempt at a smile, she looked down at the table, hands clasped together.

" No… Jane, that was the strangest thing,

I suddenly got this terrible feeling of dread."

With a shudder, she looked up,

"It was really strange."

Recovering her composure, she smiled a more natural smile.

"It was as if I was being gripped by a strong compelling force. I know it's ridiculous. I can't explain what just happened but somehow it had something to do with the painting … for a moment I felt lost, abandoned, frightened."

Unused to seeing her mother so distressed, Jane rose to her feet to comfort her but Susan raised a hand.

"Stay where you are it's ok," she laughed brushing the incident aside, back to her normal self.

"Too much wine and rushing around I'm afraid, a touch of the hot flushes."

She laughed again and quickly changed the subject.

"So how are the spotty teenagers?" She deflected, referring to the sons of Jane's partner Simon.

The spotty teenagers Jerry aged fourteen and Vincent thirteen typical of the species, could be considered to be a responsibility well outside the scope of a young inexperienced woman. This fact had not escaped Susan who, liked Jane's partner Simon and generally approved of the union, based on the, as long as she's happy syndrome, worried about her daughter and her ability to cope.

Simon, at 45 years of age, 20 years Jane's senior, had two children. Their mother had died tragically leaving Simon to care for them on his own. He and Jane had met two years previously and one year later, Jane, against her mother's advice, had given up her well-paid job and they had moved in together. Whenever the Simon subject was broached Jane would be somewhat evasive but not today.

"The spotty teenagers are just fine," like all young lads they're full of contradictions, they love football, have opinions on everything."

She fluttered a hand dismissively and frowned her concern peering intently for a clue to her mother's uncharacteristic discomfort.

"Are you ok, you really looked weird for a moment there, mum?"

"Of course I am, hot flushes, menopausal me, not a word to Paul!" The now fully composed Susan raised an admonishing finger.

"On with the story," she commanded.

Jane hesitated for only a moment then reassured, she continued enthusiastically.

"The other day Jerry, the older one, had a very earnest conversation with me about Vitruvian man and Leonardo da Vinci's ability to write in mirrored hand, quite impressive, I thought. Then he went outside and kicked a ball through the kitchen window." She laughed. "As for the other lad, Vincent, he's a bundle of tricks, some of the things he says, he's picked up on this "contradiction speak", where you say the opposite to what you really mean. His dad finds it irritating sometimes but its harmless stuff when you get the hang of it."

Jane chatted and Susan listened, fascinated.

"You really like the lads don't you?" She eventually interjected with an understanding smile.

"Of course, they're great lads. Simon's done a great job since his wife died."

"What about you Jane?" Susan looked earnestly at her daughter.

"What about you? I worry. You're only twenty-five. Is this really what you want?"

13

"I couldn't be happier and you know me better than anyone. Do you see someone under pressure, someone who can't cope? Simon is the best thing that ever happened to me and I genuinely love him and the spotty teenagers, so stop worrying and cop on."

Then with a mischievous smile she peered into her mother's face.

"What were you doing at my age?" She asked, mischievously, answering before Susan could form a reply.

"You were married with two kids and living in an apartment not knowing where the next penny would come from."

"Well your father had prospects he was very creative and was starting the partnership." Susan defended weakly.

"In advertising, a Creative in advertising? The most volatile and insecure business of them all!" Jane countered.

Susan, smiling looked at her radiant animated daughter.

"Jerry and Vincent, I don't know them very well. Why don't you bring them for Sunday lunch, and Simon of course?" She added. "Richard and Geraldine are coming with the kids." Jane's momentary hesitation was not lost on Susan.

"Why not? Sounds good to me Mum, I'm sure they'd love to come, I'll check with Simon."

"You can have a look at the painting. I know exactly where I'm going to put it. That is if your father managed to get it."

"I bet he did, you know Dad, he probably paid over the odds, there's no way that painting is not going to end up in your possession."

Talking of Dad," Jane pursed her lips. "He doesn't approve of Simon."

"Of course he does!" Susan attempted to brush the point aside.

"No Mum, he doesn't!" Jane would not be deflected.

"He thinks Simon's too old for me. I suppose I can't blame him, he and Dad are almost the same age." She raised an eyebrow unable to contain a wry smile. "But Simon's so much younger, you know, he wears nice clothes and makes me laugh and messes around with the lads, Dad's always in trousers with a crease and suits and in control."

Susan couldn't help a smile at the image Jane portrayed of her busy father.

"Your Dad loves you Jane and he works very hard, he wasn't always like that, he's a good man. He does lots of fun things." Susan defended, realizing as she spoke how middle class and boring it sounded.

"Yes, I know Mum he's a great Dad, no one could have better. I suppose he'll come round."

"Give him a bit of time Jane. Don't forget you're still his little girl and he sees this "old fella," like himself, getting all the attention from you. You know Simon is a bit on the tactile side. Maybe when you're around your Dad you could ease off on the touchy feely stuff."

Jane amazed, "touchy feely stuff"? She laughed. "Ok," she agreed with a smile, "though it'll be hard. Simon's a bit of alright Mum," she teased, "isn't he?"

Susan couldn't help being amused by Jane's playfulness.

"Yea, he's a bit of alright, alright," she laughed.

"Wouldn't kick him out of bed on a cold Saturday night?" Jane retorted and the two women laughed together. Susan dabbed at the corner of her eye with a napkin.

"Oh, if Paul could hear us he wouldn't approve."

There was quiet at the table in the Copper Kettle Bistro as the two women, mother and daughter attended to their repairs, each harbouring their own private thoughts not quite sure where the hilarious exchange had taken them.

"Now, I'd better be off, the lads will be home from school soon." Jane called for the bill with a warning look at her mother who was reaching for her bag.

"Don't you dare," she admonished. "This is my treat."

15

The silver Mercedes nosed into the driveway of the Macken Home.

The hedge could do with a bit of a trim, Paul noted. If only Susan didn't insist on doing the garden herself. With an employed-gardener the place would always look ship shape.

To the satisfying crunch of wheels on gravel the large car came to a halt alongside Susan's Volkswagen Golf.

A glimpse of the sea and some white sails with the distant sound of seagulls and the putt-putt of a motor mower greeted Paul as he emerged into the evening twilight before turning to retrieve the painting from the back seat. O'Reilly was right about the frame he observed as the deep leather upholstery slowly regained its shape relieved of the weight of the heavy gilt framed picture. In the 1820's hand crafted expensive frames like this were reserved for only the very best paintings.

With a feeling of excited anticipation he let himself into the tiled porch way and headed through the open plan bungalow to the back of the house and the large garden, the sound of the lawnmower growing louder. He could see Susan through the high window that stretched the entire width of his studio.

Still wearing her "going out to lunch gear" she strode purposefully behind the mower totally concentrating on the job in hand. He watched as, stooping she bent her tall angular figure to detach the full grass bag, looking towards the house, her face slightly flushed from the effort as she straightened up.

At the large sliding glass door he hesitated and leaned the painting in its heavy gilt frame against the wall out of Susan's view.

"How did the lunch go, how's Jane?" He called

Having emptied the grass box, silhouetted by the now setting sun she was making her way to the house across the lawn. Behind her in the distance the curved line of the horizon divided a darkening sea from the faintest pink of the sky. Her face in shadow he could not make out her expression but he knew by her voice that she was smiling. "Good, good," her beautiful face emerged as she joined him in the shade of the tiled patio that ran the length of the house.

"Where is it?" They hello kissed.

"The painting, where is it?" She enquired, smiling expectantly, her face still close to his.

"Did Jane have any news, kids OK?" He teased as releasing her he headed back in through the door.

"Never mind Jane," she followed him.

"You didn't get it did you. Someone bid an enormous price?" She assumed, "I'm not surprised it's a beautiful painting."

Paul turned in the middle of the studio and contemplated his wife's barely concealed look of disappointment.

"How much did it go for?"

"Five hundred euro," he said, shaking his head matching her look of disappointment.

"Well you could have afforded that," she fired back her face showing anger and disappointment in equal proportion. "We agreed we'd go to more. I should have gone myself. I knew it. I can't believe you didn't get it Paul, you're useless."

Susan strode angrily past her husband and headed for the kitchen. At the door she turned, hands on hips, flushed, "I really did want that painting, it means a great deal to me personally! I suppose you did go to the auction, did you?" She enquired suspiciously.

The impressive painting leaning against the wall just inside the door caught her eye. She looked back at the now grinning Paul.

"Why didn't you say?" Indignation turning to amused delight, relief and surprise.

"You never gave me the chance, Happy Birthday," he said crouching down in front of the painting, looking up at her his grin widening.

"What do you think? Good, isn't it?"

The painting leaning against the wall looked magnificent in what was left of the natural light filtering through the large skylights of the studio. Captivated, they gazed in wonder.

"It's even better than I thought," she clutched his arm.

They looked at each other and then back to the painting, transfixed.

"O'Reilly tried to get me to part with it, no way. He offered seven hundred euro, implied he could get me a buyer. I think he feels this one slipped through his fingers." Paul said happily revelling in his successful purchase.

"Pity it's not signed," Susan peered at the bottom right of the work hoping to see initials or some indication of a signature.

"Why do they think it's by Nash?"

"It says so on the back."

Paul grasped the heavy gold frame in both hands and turned the picture around leaning it carefully against the wall revealing a large piece of plywood nailed in place and covering the entire back of the painting.

"There,"

He pointed to some blue biro lettering written with a rather clumsy hand.

"BY NASH - Deal, Hobblers going out to a Wreck 1895 Great Exhibition Belfast"

Susan read the lettering aloud and then made the observation.

"If it was exhibited in 1895 that puts John or Paul Nash out of the frame, so to speak unless Paul Nash painted it when he was four. John was born in 1893. What does Deal mean and that's a weird word Hobblers?" Susan queried all curious concentration, head to one side as if by looking from another angle somehow the answer would be revealed.

As she examined the work a sudden feeling of Déjà vu struck her, so elusive, images too quick to grasp, a cat looking at her, white hands, flashed across her mind. She shuddered slightly. "I'm so glad you managed to get it, Paul, thank you, I love it."

Unaware, Paul continued,

"Deal is a fishing Village in Kent and Hovellers were local boatmen or something like that. They were pilots, lifesavers, and fishermen. Someone once referred to them as Warriors of the sea." He looked at his watch.

"I've got a council meeting tonight."

But Susan wasn't listening, the feeling had returned, somehow the painting was familiar, a little child, a white haired woman, she tried to hold on to the memory but it eluded her and was gone. Surprised at the intensity of the feeling she was left knowing that now this painting had returned to her life she would never part with it.

"Take off the plywood. I want to see the back of the painting. You never know, maybe the artist left a clue."

She was met with little resistance from Paul who was equally anxious to have a look. "I'll get something to remove those nails."

He rose up from his position on the floor where they had been examining the painting and headed to the Kitchen.

On the way he made a quick call to apologise for the possibility of being late for the borough meeting that evening. He didn't mind as he held most of the information on the new development currently being discussed so they'd have to wait for his input.

When he returned hammer, pliers and screwdriver in hand, Susan had turned over the painting and was examining it closely. It was now lying flat on the Studio worktable

"Odd, there's no signature."

"Not really," replied Paul. "Lots of famous artists didn't sign their work. Turner for instance and Leonardo Da Vinci."

"I rang Des and told him I'd be late for the meeting."

"I'm sure that went down well," Susan looked up from the painting.

"They can't do much without my report so they'll just have to wait." Paul said dismissively.

It took a few minutes to remove the firmly nailed plywood. Paul carefully moved it to one side anxious not to disturb what was concealed underneath, revealing an old label pasted to the back of the frame, top centre, faded and a bit torn.

Strickland
Frame Maker Belfast

"Well there's our Belfast connection."

Within the frame was a sheet of light shiny tin obviously relatively new, protecting the back of the picture. This came away easily to reveal at last the reverse side of the painting. Susan running her finger over the surface of the paper observed that it was smooth to the touch unlike modern watercolour paper.

In a beautiful flowing script, slightly faded graphite, protected by the backing of the picture for the best part of Two Hundred Years was revealed the legend.

Deal - Hovellers going out to a Wreck

"Look at the spelling. This says Hovellers. The other says Hobblers. It must be the old spelling."

They looked at each other sharing the moment, then back to the lettering for further examination.

Whenever a collector removes the backing from an old painting there is always the expectation of something interesting, a further clue to origin or value of the work.

This beautiful script, obviously written as the title to the picture would be by the artist. They both knew the value of this further piece of information, pretty sure handwriting experts could prove provenance by making a comparison should they find the original artist. Further examination of the reverse side revealed nothing more of interest. The water damage was evident but could be repaired.

Carefully removing the exposed artwork from the frame Susan turned it over and gently laid it flat. The picture looked brighter than it did behind the glass, the entire image more defined. Paul could not find a blemish in the work. Everything seemed so right, no over-painting, utterly spontaneous. He did not consider himself an expert, just a pretty competent artist who had confronted the various obstacles within his own style and had conquered most of them.

"This looks good," Susan whispered, transfixed by the image.

"Abigail!" the name flew into her mind. "Her name was definitely Abigail,"

" Who?" Paul looked puzzled,

"The girl in the picture her name is Abigail the little girl, I told you!"

"Susan, what are you talking about? There's no girl. Well I don't see any sign."

He looked closely at the painting.

"There is no way she was here and someone painted her out. You're remembering a different painting or maybe she was swept away by the big waves."

He laughed. Then seriously stated,

"I smell money, this is a good painting, and I'd say it's worth a lot. That glass covered a multitude. Forget all this little girl stuff." He said with a dismissive gesture. "We need an expert opinion. I reckon the next move is to put all this back together again and then start a bit of research on the Internet."

But Susan wasn't listening she was remembering.

When she was five years old she had listened to the sea and played with Abigail, the girl in the picture. Now forty-five years later here it was in front of her, but where's the little girl and her mother? There had been a little girl standing on the wharf in the picture, her name was Abigail. It's the same painting, the same ornate old gilt frame with the bit missing at the corner, her eyes flew to the corner of the frame and there it was. A small section of plain wood exposed where the gilt had come away.

"Money… money… money…" Paul chanted quietly, taking charge, carefully modulating the words as with exaggerated delicate movements, using only the tips of his fingers, lips pursed, he began to carefully put the picture back into its frame.

Suddenly he stopped, clicked his fingers and said,

"We should photograph everything, then we can E-mail elements to various sources and get some answers. I'll get the camera."

Excited and impetuous he rushed from the studio totally unaware of Susan's silent, stunned bemusement as she sat on the floor, her mind in turmoil.

When he returned, camera in hand, she was securing the backing board in place.

"What are you doing?" He said. "Don't put it back in the frame we need to photograph each element and the glass is dirty."

She calmly surveyed the over excited Paul.

"It's done now." You can photograph it some other time I want to see what it looks like on the living room wall."

"It's not done, you haven't put the nails back in," Paul retorted, reaching for the painting.

"It'll only take a minute Paul I just want to see how it will look,"

"Yes! Yes! And you'll take another picture down and you'll hang this one on the same hook and it'll be too low but you'll leave it there anyway without attaching the back properly"…. Paul, keeping a firm grip on the heavy gilt frame chanted the words sarcastically wagging his head from side to side in a manner designed to ridicule.

Susan grabbed the frame, incensed by his tone.

"Don't be such a prat Paul, it will only take a minute and then you can take your precious photographs!"

"No! I have the camera, the nails aren't secured in the frame, and it's here now! You're just being impatient and childish, it'll only take a few minutes!" He tugged the painting but she didn't' let it go. Right where he was holding the frame a sliver of gilt detached itself and dropped to the floor.

"Now look what you've done!"

"You tugged it!" Paul shouted

"You stupid woman! That's an expensive frame!"

"Don't call me stupid!"

Incensed Susan spat out the words.

"You're the stupid, childish one here Paul. All you see is money, money, money in everything, the frame's worth a fortune, the picture's worth money, O'Reilly made a financial mistake, Paul's going to make a fortune!"

She held the painting tightly in both hands leaning forward glaring in frustrated anger. "Look at it Paul! Have you actually looked at this fabulous painting without at the same time thinking of what it's worth?"

"I'm off to the meeting. Do whatever you want!" He strode to the door furiously turning to deliver his last word.

"Well at least I don't imagine I'm seeing things, Abigail, was it? Maybe Abigail will pay for the frame you just ruined."

"Paul!"

But he was gone through the living room to the front of the house. Susan waited for the door to slam, bang! Somehow the slamming of the front door was more of an irritation than the argument itself. With a sigh she listened to the crunch of wheels on the gravel. The picture was heavy and she lowered the corner of the frame to rest on the floor.

What a pity, she reflected, angry with herself because she had become angry with him and angry with him because he had walked away.

Leaning the picture against the wall she retrieved the piece of gilt from the floor. It was about two inches in length, wedge shaped with a jagged point. It fitted perfectly into place but tiny pieces of filigree had flaked off leaving a slight exposure of the plain wood. No big deal, super glue and some gold leaf and it would be hardly noticed.

She hefted the heavy picture with both hands and carried it into the living room. One of Paul's paintings had pride of place over the fireplace. The powerful colours, the vigorous brush strokes, the image of the man playing the saxophone encased in its simple white frame, a complete contrast to the traditional style of her seascape. In fact she suddenly realized something she had not really thought of before. All the paintings in the house were Paul's.

Tempted to replace the Saxophone player with the seascape Susan hesitated, that would be seen to be an act of war when Paul returned later, especially after their argument. Anyway the picture was quite heavy and she was not sure she could manage to get it in place. So Susan returned to the studio and placed it on the large worktable.

About to nail the backing in place Susan spotted the camera where Paul had left it. Putting down the hammer she carefully removed the old picture pins and placed them to one side, taking the back off she then carefully removed the painting.

It would be important to get a really accurate photograph of each element. The label on the back of the frame, the overall painting, a close-up of the russet sailed luggers. She photographed the artist's handwriting and then zeroed in for a close -up of the buildings of Deal right in to the narrow streets running down to the beach and the misty figures watching the luggers from the shoreline.

Grace Wakeley, shawl wrapped around tightly folded arms watched, her 9 year old niece by her side standing amongst the group gathered at the waters edge, awaiting the return of the Luggers.

The Women of Deal shared a common bond, their fears for the safe return of husbands and sons. Though the rewards for salvage were considerable the risks of injury and survival were high.

The Hovellers would ride the high seas out beyond the Downs. Watching constantly to compete in the race to provide their piloting skills to all Vessels requiring guidance and a good wind to reach the Thames Estuary.

Hard working, skilful sailors, they built their own craft and took pride in their achievements. They lived close to the waterfront in wooden structures some two storied, some mere hovels. Competition for survival and the spoils was rife, survival of the fittest the order of the day.

Deal was described as an open port without the need of a conventional built harbour. Between the treacherous sands and the coast many ships could wait at anchor in the Downs, a vast stretch of safe water, a natural haven. These craft needed servicing and maintenance, many trading ships after a long voyage, man o' war, and of course those wrecked and run aground on the treacherous Goodwin Sands. So Deal had become, arguably the most important town along the south coast of England.

The town was growing fast with the influx of various nationalities and those attracted to the opportunity of the spoils.

A great problem was posed for the authorities by the complexity of alleyways, storage sheds and makeshift structures running down to the coast along a four-mile stretch. After salvage a large number of luggers, as many as twenty, could beach at the same time and the entire contents of a trader, canvases, ropes and cargo could disappear rapidly without opportunity of a tally.

After a wreck the beach could be strewn for miles with debris and all kinds of valuables. Hoveller families would scavenge and there would be much dispute and argument.

The town of Deal in 1825 had a notorious reputation and its inhabitants were well versed in the ways of illegal activities. The number multiplied to about 400 Hovellers, all skilled and watchful along the coastline.

Deal, was also the nearest point to France. On a good day you could see Calais.

The activities of these people, their boating skills and their bravery had not gone unnoticed by those in Whitehall.

The Napoleonic wars not that long over, it was still necessary to keep an eye on the French and here was a readymade means of doing so.

Mobilize the Hovellers. There was not much that happened in the Channel that escaped the eyes of the Deal Boatmen.

Grace Wakeley held the child's hand as she anxiously watched the return of the Luggers, shielding her eyes from the driving spray as the storm grew in its intensity, but there was no sign of her brother and his sons and the D2. One by one the boats returned appearing out of the spray and the running sea making the complex manoeuvre beyond the breakers. Beaching these craft was a difficult and dangerous business. Wait the moment, get the bough high and ride the wave in to shore where many willing hands waited to haul her up the shingled beach to be secured ready for the next run. Mistime the approach and the stern would come too high driving the bow deep and losing the impetus with disastrous consequence, as the following huge breaker would come crashing in.

Twelve boats made the landing. Exhausted crewmen and helpers alike stood in groups, the women now joining their menfolk.

Grace and the child scrambled on the shingle from group to group. Snatches of conversation reached Grace's ears. "We had her, the D2 was nearly alongside… The cutter broke up and disappeared in a thrice."

Grace had never spoken to the Dutchman. He was not exactly approachable particularly by a young single woman.

A group led by the Dutchman had lighted a fire, their intention being to wait all night if necessary on watch for the missing Lugger.

One of the Hoveller women offered to take the child up to the Inn where Grace lived and worked so she could join the watchers.

Recognising her as Michael Wakeley's sister a place was made for her beside the blazing fire, one or two nodded but no one spoke, their conversation interrupted by her arrival started up again after a few minutes.

The fire was welcome she could feel herself warming. The waves still pounded on the beach but with somewhat less force. "He'll come," The Dutchman was standing beside her. He smiled a wolfish smile through his sparse beard. "No fear, Michele strong, good," He nodded his head vigorously.

Surprised at the source of such comfort Grace started with an instinctive apprehension.

She looked at the man who carried such a notorious reputation; some said he had killed men in fights. He looked back candidly. His eye was steady and his expression conveyed nothing other than sympathy.

Grace nodded and the Dutchman took a step back from her side and turned to the men who chorused words of encouragement, "Don't worry Missus he'll be fine, there's no better sailor."

Some women had arrived and there was soup. Grace took a bowl gratefully and some bread.

And so the night progressed while they watched. The storm abated and a fiery dawn streaked with long black clouds filled the sky. Some of the men having gained a few hours sleep returned to launch their boats for the search.

The Dutchman already on the beach was the first away, his men crouched and leaning forward as they released the Lugger and it flew down the rollers timed to ride the wave as it began to recede dragging the cumbersome craft through the shallows into deeper water.

Grace made her way up the beach towards the Inn weary after the nights watch, though she had slept in spite of herself.

The russet sails of the luggers caught the dawn light as turning she watched for a while at the waterfront. She could see the Dutchman close to the beach heading west the other boats ranging in an arc to the farthest boat heading east, if there was anything to find they would find it.

The seagulls wheeled and screeched. "Starboard!" The Scrambler Cruikshank in the bow was attracted to activity beyond the headland. The spit of land that signalled the end of the beach concealed the object of the seagulls' attention. It was still a distance off but nonetheless the concentrated activity was worth investigating. The Dutchman trimmed the sails as with a good wind the lugger heeled and drove towards the cove beyond the outcrop. As they neared, the Scrambler with the aid of the telescope sighted the top of a mast. The D2 was beyond the headland and in the cove. All hands, surefooted and capable, expert in the manoeuver, made ready. The Dutchman set a flare high into the morning sky the signal for all boats to assist.

The D2 lay in the quiet cove, still, in a slight swell. The seagulls wheeled, whirled screeched and dived covering the deck in a frenzy of white splintered activity.

Nosing forward in the shallow water they approached, each man fearful of what they were about to find, the seagulls telling their own story. "Scare them off first then we'll board her," came the quiet order as they closed. Three rifle shots sounded and the white blanket rose splintering into the sky revealing a sight that no man should ever have to clap eye upon.

Wakeley lay across the tiller face up, sightless eyes to the sky, one of his sons in the bough lay half in and half out of the water, the other son was lashed to the mast, everywhere blood, even the sea close to the boat had a ghastly pinkish hue. The men had been brutally butchered. The seagulls had completed the work.

Aboard the Dutchman hardened sailors all averted their eyes, each reacting according to his faith.

Sir Geoffrey Fletcher checked his seatbelt as he looked down on the welcome sight of London as the flight BA 378 from Prague made its approach to land at Heathrow.

"Do you always travel business class, Sir Geoffrey?"

Vaclav Janacec leaned over to share the view.

"Not so much these days," came the reply

"You know it wasn't necessary for your people to go to the expense,"

"Not at all, you're a very important person and entitled," Vaclav smiled.

Sir Geoffrey, in spite of his prejudices had come to like this polite educated young man. However he was not enjoying the role he had to play as conspirator in the plans with the Prague Group. It was all a bit "cloak and Dagger," for his liking. Also he knew that the man beside him was travelling under an assumed name.

"Please fasten your seatbelts," The stewardess collecting the debris from the on flight meal, stopped. "I'll just put up your table for you." She smiled at Sir Geoffrey as he swiftly rescued his double Brandy.

Then turning to Vaclav Janacec, "everything all right, Mr Grant?" She enquired.

"Yes, Thank you very much."

What a hot looking man, she thought.

Vaclav contemplated her wide-eyed open friendliness, his thoughts of a sinister nature. He was pondering on those beautiful blue eyes and how they would gradually fade in death if he were to take her life.

"Good morning Richard I enjoyed the sermon, pepper seeds will never be the same to me again." A warm handshake followed.

Richard Macken, Auxiliary Minister in the parish of Glencarrick, at the door of the small country church, smiled at the reference to his sermon as he took leave of the last departing member of his congregation. Standing in the church porch doorway he watched the local attendants of St Kevin's make their way to their various means of transport. Away to Sunday lunches, the local beach, picnics or whatever took their fancy on a beautiful sunny Sunday in Rural Ireland.

Well, he thought to himself that went well. This was Richards's fourth service, flying solo, so to speak.

With a feeling of goodwill and some satisfaction he turned and headed for the sacristy. In the small dressing room he began to remove his vestments, the white surplus felt crisp and clean against his face as he lifted it over his head. Carefully he folded the garment patting it contemplatively.

Though working with a local government authority was a very fulfilling occupation and a full time job for Richard, all his life he had been attracted to the church. Now in his twenty-ninth year Richard had realized an ambition. It had been a long hard road, not without it's sacrifices. Studying in the evenings and assisting at various services and with the support of Geraldine and the kids he had reached the status of auxiliary minister. This allowed him to officiate at Sunday service entirely on his own. He felt fulfilled and optimistic this Sunday.

Geraldine and the two kids ready at home, the four of them would be heading to Richard's parent's house to share Sunday Lunch. Today's lunch would be special, it being his mothers 50th birthday.

After service Richard loved to sit in his favourite place at the back of the ancient church. Today the sun streaming through the solitary stain glass window showed this small house of worship at it's best, a sturdy structure quite unpretentious and simple save for the magnificent bronze eagle lectern which held the large bible, a gift from a local dignitary and landlord, no doubt languishing in the indulgences gained by his investment.

The walls of totally unadorned natural stone reached to the beamed raw wood ceiling high above the well-worn family pews. A survivor of Ireland's troubled history this small church of God maintained a wondrous air of peace and tranquillity.

The young minister knelt alone head bowed in his own time for reflection, silence pervading, save for the quiet whispering of his prayers. Eventually he sat back allowing his mind to become occupied with day-to-day matters and the impending visit to the family home.

Susan, Richard's mother, issued the invitation a week in advance and they would be expected to turn up en famille. He smiled as he thought of Susan and the sacred Sunday lunch.

"We'll expect the lot of you at 1.30 for 2.00. Don't forget to bring dessert, one of Geraldine's Pavlova's will do nicely and tell the children not to forget their video games. I don't know whether your sister and that Simon fellow are coming."

Susan had mixed feelings about their relationship. "She's only a child and he's forty five and he's got teenaged children. She could be throwing away her best years."

Jane had introduced Simon to the family and announced her undying love for him, "we're going to move in together."

31

Richard, at the time, had some misgivings about this smooth talking successful businessman with the readymade family. He did however know his sister and with a smile and a handshake had offered Simon his commiserations.

Misgivings disappearing over the ensuing year, Richard had developed a liking for his sister's partner and had met the spotty teenagers. He hoped that they would come for lunch. In spite of her continuous protestations he felt his mother approved and was looking forward to one day being the Mother in law, a roll she played to perfection.

Later, as Richard and the family approached the outskirts of Dublin Sunday traffic was all heading southward out of the city to the coast it was nearing 1.30.

Being late was not an option for him. He always arrived on time, just a habit he had grown into. Memories of previous Sunday lunches invading his mind, a little smile of anticipation played around his lips.

He sometimes wondered about his confident strong willed mother. As with most resourceful characters there was a soft spot lurking, a vulnerability, which very seldom showed itself, but was there nonetheless.

He had no reservations about the bond and strength of his parent's partnership of 30 years. Though there had been that glitch a few years ago when Paul had transgressed. It had something to do with a younger woman. There had been an implication of Paranoia. This had been dismissed as having no significance in fact Paul had pronounced the condition as being an asset in business. "Gives me an edge, I never let the guard down, always one step ahead." He would nod his head sagely as he propounded the theory. "Knowing, being aware that you're mildly paranoid. That's the trick."

At the time his mother had been very much in charge and his Dad had ended up attending a special Clinic. It was all a bit vague in Richard's mind as his parents had not shared all the details and he had been preoccupied with the move to the country house at the time.

Things had settled down. Richard had not thought much about the matter until now. He knew how fiercely possessive Susan was of her beloved husband. He knew how vulnerable Paul could be in spite of his business success and his air of superiority. Susan was the glue that kept the family together and Paul on the straight and narrow.

Glancing to the left at Geraldine his wife of seven years sitting in the passenger seat of the family saloon he smiled contentedly. There was not a sound from the kids in the back totally engrossed in their Nintendo's.

Geraldine's thoughts were her own as she cradled the pavlova perched on her enlarged tummy. The imminent arrival of child number three was not however uppermost in her thoughts, it was the pavlova she was thinking about.

Why did Richard's mother always ask her to do a Pavlova?

Sometimes the competitive Susan really irritated her. She would reason to herself that Susan really had a good heart and did not mean to put her down all the time and after all she is Richard's mother.

Geraldine over the duration had produced on request the dessert for Sunday lunch with varying success. Always greeted by Susan with a jaundiced eye, perused carefully and if flawless not commented upon but dutifully and without ceremony set on the table after the main course for the delectation of all. However should the slightest flaw be detected, "Oh what a beautiful dessert. You really are improving. Everybody, look at this beautiful dessert Geraldine has created for us. Richard, can you see if there's some cream in the fridge. You know just a wee bit more cream whipped to the right consistency and we'll have it absolutely right."

Then, inevitably, "I've done one of my special apple crumbles as a backup, just as well, I suppose," and the dessert would be whisked off into the kitchen for some running repairs.

This morning Geraldine, in a bit of a rush on using the oven had neglected to notice the proximity of the top shelf in the oven to her perfectly prepared pavlova.

Of course every well-behaved Pavlova rises dramatically in cooking. This one was no exception, with quite an effect. The merengue in rising had managed to squeeze itself through the bars of the shelf above and solidify.

"This has got to be a first, maybe we should bring it with the shelf attached," Richard, while Geraldine was changing, had been requested to remove the Pavlova from the oven.

She joined the amused group, Richard and the kids peering into the open oven. The rescue operation had been a total failure. The best job possible was done on the unfortunate dessert with all willing hands and a huge amount of whipped cream, the result now resided on Geraldine's lap.

She couldn't help smiling to herself at the image of Susan wearing it all over her face. The thought provoked a slight chuckle.

Richard, taking his eyes from the road glanced at her.

"Come on, I know that look. What are you thinking?" he said, looking back quickly to the road and then back to his wife who fixing him with a wide eyed stare said in a serious tone.

"You know the way your mother greets us? She always does that big hug thing." Richard, aware of Geraldine's discomfort with overt demonstrations of affection looked back to the road again not quite sure what she was going to say next.

"Go on," he said, "there isn't much I can do about it you know. I can't say stop this hugging people."

"No, exactly that's the thing," Geraldine still wide-eyed and serious.

"Today I want her to come at me,"

Richard detecting the hint of humour in her voice offered a tentative

"Yes?"

"Well I was thinking...This pavlova is going to get the works from your mother. I mean she's going to really go for it, no holds barred, it's going to be a massacre,"

She paused, "What if… ?"

A gleeful look came on her face as she continued, savouring the thought.

"What if, when she goes for the big hug I manage to get the pavlova trapped between us, cream side on Susan's side, so to speak, and quite high up, about face level?"

She looked enquiringly at her laughing husband as she spoke.

"It makes glorious sense, I destroy the evidence and get revenge for all the previous pavlovas in one go. What do you think Richard, are you with me?"

She swivelled in her seat to face him.

"I could make it look like an accident. Just say yes Richard...I really want to do it ...please. I'm not a bad person, really."

"Go for it", Richard laughed. "Can you imagine it? Pavlova everywhere."

"It would be so beautiful."

Geraldine sighed longingly, the image still in her mind. There was a pause while they contemplated the prospect.

"It's not going to happen is it?" She sighed wistfully.

"Well maybe I could drop it as I'm getting out of the car,"

Richard offered sympathetically.

"No way," Geraldine shook her head in mock aggression.

"Either it's right in her beautiful fifty year old face or nothing."

She looked down at the pavlova on her lap.

"It doesn't look that bad, in fact its' got character. I'm going to name it Pavarotti."

She began to stroke the pavlova making little love hearts in the cream.

Richard, who loved her sense of humour and zany personality drove on to the lunch, seriously considering the idea of accidently dropping the pavlova.

"I got it in O'Reilly's for 500 euro. What do you think?"

The lunch near completion, Pavlova being dished out in tandem with the usual backup, this time a spectacular fruit coulis with a tincture of amaretto and specially imported mango fruit inspired by Susan's "Cooking For Special occasions" evening classes.

Paul had produced the latest acquisition from O'Reilly's Auction, now propped up close to the dining room table on display for all to see. "We haven't had much time to research, Nash and Hovellers and Deal..."

"Your father is convinced we have found an unsigned masterpiece,"

Susan interrupted. "Tell them what Sheridan's Gallery had to say."

Turning to the family gathered round the table. Paul stood up proudly beside the painting and in his best presentation voice began...

"You know that chap you went to school with Richard, Graham Roach."

Immediately Susan interjected, speaking rapidly. "His parents separated, you remember, he was interested in art, did a degree in Trinity College. I think there was another woman involved and his mother walked out, silly woman, you should never walk out, make the man do it," Susan demonstrating her ability to talk about two subjects at the same time.

"He has an important job with Sheridan's in Dawson Street. You know they're one of the leading art experts in Ireland, he's an Art Auctioneer. Paul told him about the painting and he called last night. He lives in Meadow Lawns, those nice red brick houses with the bow front windows. I think they were built in the Thirties, he's not married but he has a dog. Tell them what he said Paul."

She turned to the impatient Paul, just too late to catch his eyes to heaven expression. Paul took up the story and in his precise manner explained how Graham Roach had expressed a very keen interest in the unsigned painting and how it, in some respects resembled the work done by the famous artist Turner.

"J.M.W. Turner, The last Turner found fetched millions of pounds at Christie's," Susan interjected dramatically, "and Graham wants Paul to bring it in to their Gallery for a further examination and a discussion with their team of experts."

"Thank you Susan," Paul couldn't contain his irritation.

"Is there any more Pavlova Mrs Macken? I don't like that jelly stuff." One of the spotty teenagers proffered an empty dish and was ignored by all except a smiling Geraldine.

"Do you reckon he really thinks it's a Turner?" Simon, sitting across the table beside Jane enquired, his business mind doing cartwheels.

"Well Paul, we need a new extension and you can throw in a new car as well," quipped Richard's auntie Laura with a wide smile. "Don't we Tony," she turned to her husband. Uncle Tony contemplated his wife, his slightly florid face, eyes betraying no particular emotion, well used to her over the top and sometimes-hilarious reactions.

"Give the kid some Pavlova," he said.

"What are you going to do about it?" Richard asked, leaning over and spooning the remainder of the Pavlova into the waiting dish.

Paul now the centre of attention, the advertising man, addressed the expectant faces.

"No he didn't say it's a Turner."

Susan about to speak this time was hushed by his upraised palm and a fierce glance.

"He did say that it's an extraordinarily high quality painting in a style similar to Turner's and he thinks it's worth pursuing. He also said that many other contemporary artists in the 1820's came to admire Turner's work and tried to emulate his achievements, copying his style, and from time to time these paintings turn up. In their own right, they can be quite valuable. So either way we'll get a pretty good return on our investment. We're going to find out all we can and see where it leads us, and then, we'll let you know about the extension Auntie Laura."

"The only way you'll get a good return on your investment Paul is if we sell it and that's never going to happen, it's my painting, don't forget," Susan announced heading for the kitchen with the unfinished coulis to get on with some pan rattling. Geraldine followed with the empty Pavlova dish.

"What age is Nana Susan?" The beautiful Becky, Richard's eldest, suddenly enquired. "On my birthday we had a cake and presents and we sang happy birthday?" Under the impression she had come to a birthday party Becky could no longer contain her disappointment.

In the adjoining kitchen overhearing the clear voiced enquiry Susan and Jane looked at each other.

Paul immediately fielded the question.

"Grown-ups, grown-ups don't sing happy birthday and have cake, it's really just for children," came his ill-considered reply.

"Auntie Jane had a cake when she was twenty five and we sang happy birthday," Becky was not going to be deterred.

Paul immediately retorted,

"Well she's younger," and then with a flash of inspiration

"She's my daughter, you see, my child."

Becky seeming satisfied with the explanation was silent for about thirty seconds during which time Paul congratulated himself on a situation well handled.

Susan and Geraldine in the kitchen waited expectantly.

"Ga Ga Paul?" Becky looked at her granddad across the table and asked

"Is Simon Aunt Jane's boyfriend?"

"Why don't we get into some research on the painting," Richard proposed.

"That's enough questions Becky."

"Yes Becky he is her boyfriend," with a generous smile in Simons direction the confident Paul stated firmly and "She is my daughter,"

"Then you could be Simon's Daddy,"

Paul laughed, "No, no, Becky, Simon's far too old, I'm too young to be his Daddy."

"But you've got skinny hair and its grey and Simon's got lots of hair and he plays football and he's funny."

"Happy Birthday to you, Happy Birthday to you, Happy Birthday dear Susan," Geraldine sang coming into the dining room holding a lighted candle, Susan following on her heels.

All joined in, Rebecca clapped her hands and Paul smiled weakly.

As was the custom all hands helped in the after dinner clean up with the exception, this time of Richard and Simon, who picking up the "Turner" headed for the studio at the back of the house and the waiting broadband assisted Apple Mac. The Internet would prove to be a mighty research weapon.

Paul followed, calling after them, "be careful of that gilt frame it's a bit delicate!"

Jane Macken sitting on the garden seat could feel the warmth of the summer sun. She ran her hand on the wood, smooth, worn and familiar. How often as a child had this bench been involved in their play as a house, a ship but mostly as a place to sit and chat with Granddad Mac, Pauls father, when she was little.

She could recall his face so familiar and kind, his soft voice and how he made the eleven year old, Jane, feel so grown up.

This was her favourite place in the garden. The large sliding door from the studio was open and she could see her Dad at the computer. For a moment as he turned and leaned forward to peer over Richard's shoulder he was the image of his father.

"Your father's gorgeous looking, like George Clooney." One of her schoolmates staying for a sleepover, confided, it was generally agreed by the rest of her classmates that Jane Macken had the best looking parents in the school.

Jane's attention switched to the two teenagers, Vincent and his older brother Gerry. A makeshift goal had been arranged on the other side of the garden. Jane's niece the beautiful Becky had been placed between the posts.

As Jane watched Susan appeared round the side of the house summer skirt swinging, straw hat on the back of her head, some stray hair catching the sunlight.

Somehow her mother always looked good no matter what she wore Jane couldn't help thinking as she watched the tall figure stride across the grass.

"Hi, Mrs Macken, do you want to play three and in?"

Gerry, eldest of the spotty teenagers, ball juggled towards her and proffered the ball inviting her to kick it. Susan stopped, adjusted her position and swung a foot at the ball. With a laugh the boy moved it at the last second making her miss. He flicked it to his brother. Vincent trapped it. As Susan turned he flicked it back in the air to Gerry.

The gangly youth was standing on one leg when Susan's shoulder charge caught him square in the middle of his scrawny chest. Caught completely off balance he ended up in the flowerbed. The ball bounced free. Susan shuffled into position and hitching up the summer dress she booted the ball past her granddaughter goalkeeper.

"One nil," Jane heard her mother say as she helped the crestfallen Gerry to his feet before turning and heading to join her daughter on the garden seat. A slight limp could just be detected as she walked across the lawn but there was no indication of discomfort on her now slightly flushed face. Kicking footballs was not part of the, Birkenstock Designer Sandals, claim to fame.

She sat down on the bench beside her highly amused daughter.

"Well the little shit tried to make a fool of me," she protested gently massaging her foot.

Jane glanced at her mother's profile and noticed the slight smile of amused satisfaction.

"You really are a menace," she admonished. "After me bringing them specially, you know they really didn't want to come. Jerry said you were a poshie," she laughed.

"Well I didn't really mean to knock the poor child into the flowerbed, I got a bit carried away. It was a fair tackle. They said so on Match of the Day. Shoulder to shoulder is a fair tackle."

She looked across at the two lads who were now sitting on the grass, heads together in deep discussion, the smaller of the two with a bright grin on his freckled face.

Arising from the seat, the birthday girl headed back across the lawn. Both boys scrambled to their feet at her approach. The taller one, a handsome boy, she noted for the first time.

"I'm sorry for knocking you into the flowerbed Gerry it wasn't a fair tackle, anyway you'll be glad to hear I hurt my foot when I kicked the ball."

"That's all right," he smiled back. "It didn't hurt."

"He's afraid I'll tell them in school that he knocked for six by a toe poking granny." Vincent roared laughing.

"I'll toe poke you up the backside if you don't stop laughing," she made as if to attack him, at the same time unable to keep from laughing herself. Vincent backed off ready to run for it, fully aware of her amused expression.

41

The ball was on the grass close by. Susan picked it up and bounced it a few times. "Here Gerry, show me how to kick it properly."

He caught the ball when she threw it to him. For a moment he hesitated, unsure.

"Go on," she encouraged,

"Then you can show me how to dribble.

Come on Jane," she called, "it's three and in,"

Jane looked across at Gerry, the ball at his feet, demonstrating how to use the instep instead of the toe, whilst Susan watched intently.

Jane joined the footballers and Geraldine, who, hearing the laughter, had abandoned the Turner pursuit, took part in a hilarious game of three and in. Geraldine pleading pregnancy was the referee. The game lasted until Susan, attempting a penalty kick broke the strap of her expensive designer sandals.

Taking refuge on the garden seat with Jane Susan ruefully examined the sandal. "Beyond repair, I'm afraid, but in a good cause. I'm not a toe poker anymore."

"That was quite a performance you put on, I appreciate it, thanks, the lads enjoyed themselves," Jane looked at her mum, "You really are something else it's a pity about your shoe."

"I enjoyed myself," Susan laughed. "I haven't played football since you and Richard were kids."

The sound of voices from the house suddenly increased obviously at the unearthing of some further revelation.

"Poor old Dad, he walked into that one with Rachael, out of the mouths of babes…"

"I know," laughed Susan, "You wouldn't mind but he's quite paranoid at the moment about getting old and his looks, especially his hair,"

Susan looked across at the studio window.

"Sure he looks great, I think he looks great for his age. I'm always saying it to him." Both heads turned towards the house and the three intent figures at the computer.

"Dad's really into that painting, what do you think?"

Susan looked at her daughter considering the question. Since the row she had not mentioned the little girl or the painting to Paul, though her feelings had intensified. The feeling of Déjà vu persisting, she was convinced that it was the same picture she had seen as a child. Her memory of the picture was a happy one though strangely tarnished by a feeling of foreboding. However no possible explanation offered itself as to why the little girl was missing.

Susan with some hesitation explained to Jane her feelings about the little girl and the painting carefully leaving out mention of black cats and her unexplained feelings of dread. "It's probably just my imagination Jane, I'm not sure what to think."

"I may have the answer to the mystery,"

Jane smiled and leaned forward.

"While you were talking I was remembering,"

She looked excitedly at Susan.

"When I was little, Richard and I used to stay with Aunt Laura. There was a box, you know, one of those wooden boxes, big with a lid, black with old lettering on the outside, it was full of old papers and photographs, you know those sepia ones. Aunt Laura showed us the pictures and told us stories about when she was young and living here in this house."

"Yes, I remember the box it belonged to your granddad he used to keep all his papers in it, it used to belong to his mother, I haven't seen it in ages we weren't allowed to open it when we were children."

"Go on," Susan prompted.

"There was a picture, a painting of a little girl in a frame." Jane continued, "Her name was Abigail, it was printed on the gold card, you know the way there's a gold card with an oval cut-out on old pictures."

"Abigail, that's the name I keep remembering," Susan exclaimed.

"Well there's your explanation," Jane patted her mother's knee. "You must have seen the picture when you were a child so long ago that you can't remember the details."

"Probably," Susan said not completely convinced but it was a pretty good explanation. "I wouldn't mind getting hold of that box all the same."

She looked at Jane,

"I'll ask Laura about it,"

"So what do you think?" Jane enquired

"Of what?"

"The painting, the Turner,

What do you think of it apart from mysterious little girls, that is?"

"I think it's a really good painting and I know that that chap Roach from Sheridan's thinks so too. Now whether it's a Turner or not is another matter."

Susan turned and looked earnestly at her daughter.

"To tell you the truth I'm not sure I care whether it's worth a lot of money. I love the painting there's something about it that makes it very special to me and I'd never sell it but I want to find out everything I can about it."

With a glance to the studio, "of course your Dad's convinced it's worth millions and eventually we'll all ride off into the sunset, our pockets bulging with money."

She said with a laugh.

Jane laughed at the image. "Well I wouldn't say no, I'll settle for two million and another couple of million for the spotty teenagers."

"And I'll pay to get my shoe fixed."

Preoccupied with their own thoughts the two women sat side by side for a short while content in each other's company.

Susan eventually broke the silence, "I'll make sure Paul makes that appointment with the gallery. It's not signed, but there's that title on the back in the artist's handwriting. You know Turner didn't sign many of his paintings."

Turning to her daughter, index finger raised, she wiggled it to indicate that she was thinking things out, a characteristic all too familiar to Jane.

"If we could get a sample of Turner's handwriting for expert comparison and if the writing matched then it's got to follow Turner painted the picture." Susan got to her feet. "I'm going to ring Angie Foley. She'll know someone."

Angie and her husband Zack, friends of the family for the best part of thirty-five years, Angie, a barrister, would be the very person to advise about forensic handwriting experts.

Jane followed leaving the kids in the back garden.

"Have a look at this,"

Paul turned from the computer as the two women came in from the garden.

Jane stopped to look at the screen as the purposeful Susan continued into the living room.

Uncle Tony was there on the sofa, head back, and mouth agape in deep slumber watching the cricket on Sky 2. Auntie Laura, tray in hand emerged from the kitchen,

"I was just going to join you in the garden with some nice cold drinks. Is Geraldine with the young ones?"

Susan stopped and enquired about the black box.

"I think it's in our attic, wake up sleepy head." Laura vigorously shook her slumbering husband, "it's a lovely day." With a jerk, Tony awoke and struggling to a sitting position, spluttered.

"What is it woman, can't you see I'm watching the cricket." He glared; his normally red face a slightly darker shade.

"Susan wants the black box,"

"What black box?"

"The one in the attic that belonged to your Mother," said Laura before continuing on her way towards the back of the house.

"That woman would try the patience of a saint." Tony looked up at Susan rubbing his eyes with the back of a beefy hand.

"There's a box alright I put it in the attic a good while ago. To tell you the truth I never looked inside it. You're welcome to it Susan. Jasus! England have collapsed one eighty-five for nine!" He rubbed his hands together and leaned towards the telly.

"Yes, I'm just going to make a phone call. I'll be with you in a few minutes."

Susan headed for the phone resolving to get her hands on the black box as soon as possible.

In the studio Jane had joined the enthusiastic group at the computer looking at a painting of Deal, a town in Kent displayed on the screen of the apple mac. It didn't mean much to her at first. Then looking at Paul's newly acquired purchase and comparing the two pictures there was no mistaking the similarities.

The picture on the computer was of a rough sea and a beach with boats well drawn up from the waves. The edge of the town ran along the beach with some people gathered at the boats.

The sky was thunderous, dark clouds with a light translucence emerging from the horizon. The remarkable similarity lay in the colouring of both pictures and the style of the painting.

"Look at the boats closely," said Richard, "Especially the one on the left."

Jane looked closer, fascinated, very definitely the same kind of boat on the computer picture, russet colour square-cut sail at half-mast.

Richard turned the picture around so Jane could read the legend on the reverse side

"Hovellers going out to a wreck – Deal"

Richard explained, "Deal is a town in Kent. In Dad's picture you see Deal in the background and the Hovellers racing out to the wreck. Now look again at the picture on the computer." Jane with mounting excitement looked and then she saw it, in large letters above the picture. She read the words,

DEAL, KENT BY J.M.W. TURNER 1825

"It's early days yet," said Paul, "but a bit of a coincidence. The expert says it looks like a Turner, and here we have a painting by Turner of the same location with a similar boat in it and look what it says here." Scrolling up the picture her father pointed and read out, "Turner in 1826 visited his friend in the Isle of Wight, who commissioned two paintings from him, a certain John Nash. That could explain the Nash connection."

Auntie Laura, tray in hand, "How is my extension coming," headed out to the garden without waiting for a reply.

The sun shone for most of that Sunday afternoon but it went unnoticed by the researchers. The Internet gave up its information readily and in much detail. Those who relaxed in the garden were plied from time to time with new revelations and the story began to unfold.

Turner was born in born 1775 and during his lifetime, unlike many painters, made a great deal of money, dying in 1851 a wealthy man. In spite of being arguably England's greatest painter and all the documentation of his undoubted genius, his life held many mysteries. He was secretive, quick witted, highly intelligent and of a garrulous nature. He managed to stay aloof and much of his life remained a mystery in spite of his fame.

A prolific artist he produced astounding masterpieces that are acclaimed to be amongst the greatest paintings in the world. He bequeathed most of his estate to the Nation and the Turner Gallery was born. Significantly 300 of his sketchbooks are available today on the Tate Gallery Website.

As a great artist he fraternised with the higher echelons of society. Though many details of his life were revealed when he died not one of his associates, family or friends was aware of his 18 Year involvement with Sophie Booth. She had been widowed in 1833 and they had become companions, their relationship lasting until his death in 1851. Significantly Sophie came from Deal in Kent where Turner frequently painted.

"Imagine, nobody been close enough to know about their devotion to each other for 18 years." Jane said. "That's really sad."

Paul had just updated the group in the garden on the latest developments.

"You miss the point, Jane, Deal, she came from Deal in Kent,"

"What about the Tate London?" Susan interjected. "Three hundred sketchbooks left to the nation. You said earlier something about them being accessible on the Tate website. Surely there must be samples of his handwriting in 300 sketchbooks. We might even find a preliminary sketch of our painting done when he was sitting on the beach with Mrs Booth." To Susan this seemed very logical. She looked at her husband and realised that he was not listening to her.

Paul was preoccupied with the possibility of the painting being a Turner masterpiece. The information received so far all seemed to point in the right direction.

"Sorry Susan, I wasn't listening. We know that he lived with a woman for 18 years who came from Deal. He painted the sea, he painted wrecks and rescuers, everywhere I see his paintings I see dramatic seascapes with wonderful skies. He must have returned to Deal with her at some time during those 18 years. He always carried his sketchbooks. You know, he actually had himself lashed to the mast of a ship during a storm for four hours so that he could experience the effects of the elements and somehow get close to the power of the sea."

Paul brandished the sheets of laser prints he had spent the afternoon compiling with the help of Richard and Simon

"You know in 1825 he painted Deal as part of a series of English towns. There is no way he just painted one picture and then walked away. In those days most artists were poor. Turner wasn't, he was very well off. He travelled around the place.

You know after the Napoleonic wars when things quietened down he travelled around Europe, Switzerland, Germany and Italy. There are the most amazing paintings of Venice. They all look like the painting we got from O'Reilly's."

"It is a sad story though, eighteen years a secret," Jane shook her head

"I couldn't keep something like that a secret for eighteen years,"

Paul looked at her for a moment wondering what she meant.

"She's still thinking about the romantic bit," Susan explained with a smile.

"Now Paul," she looked at her husband, "I reckon we've had enough Turner for one day. Go in and talk to Tony, you've been neglecting him."

"Dad, are we going soon?" Simon and his two spotty sons were left in the garden with the football. "This is a bit boring and they don't have computer games."

Simon feeling guilty for spending almost the entire afternoon on the computer, looked at his watch.

"Look I'm sorry, I should have spent more time with you two but I got carried away with the picture and the time slipped by. I'll have a word with Jane and see if she's ready to go. I know you didn't want to come but I'm glad you did."

Gerry who didn't really care where he was at any given time as long as he had his phone in his hand lifted his eyes from the latest received text.

"That's ok dad, I quite enjoyed it, Jane's Ma is mad. She says she's a Man United fan, and she knocked Gerry into the flowerbed, wimp," Vincent jeered.

"Did she?" Simon laughed,

"She took me by surprise, it was a foul tackle," Gerry defended, feeling his ribs, "She's got bony shoulders and she caught me off balance, anyway she told Vincent she'd kick him up the arse," he laughed and they joined in.

"What's so funny?" Jane came into the garden.

"I was thinking maybe we should be going. What are you laughing at?" She confronted them.

"Your Mother told Vincent she'd kick him up the arse,"

Simon put his arm around her as he delivered, what he considered one of the funniest lines he had heard in a long time.

"Why did she say that?" Jane quizzed with a half smile

"Vincent called her a toe poker."

"Well then he deserves a kick up the arse," she rejoined. "Now come on in and say goodbye," She herded the two laughing youths towards the doorway leaving Simon to follow.

Initially Simon had been apprehensive about bringing Gerry and Vincent to the Sunday lunch and they had resisted strongly, especially Gerry. "No dad we don't want to go, they're really old and there's no kids there," they had protested.

Bribery and corruption had prevailed in the end and also because they really liked Jane. Simon had also employed the sympathy angle.

"Look you've met them before and they're not bad. For Jane's sake I'd like to make a go of it. I'll have a word with Jane and see what the story is." The ploy had worked.

Simon sometimes thought that she had a better relationship with his two sons than he had. She's twenty years younger than me he reasoned. They probably see me as a Dad and her as more of a big sister. He followed the threesome with a feeling of relief and some elation. She had her arm around Vincent's neck and was poking Gerry in the ribs.

"Don't forget to say thank you," he overheard the words delivered like a mother. It was one of those moments when everything seemed just right and Simon knew he was going to marry her.

Fitzwilliam Sq., Dublin, the ivy covered Georgian structure housed Macken, McCarthy and Aylward, Advertising and Public Relations. Ideally situated at the heart of the Capital, the agency occupied the entire building. Moderate in size, they laid claim to some important accounts.

The careful balancing of creativity and good marketing sense had been the policy of the agency since its inception. Preoccupation with creative solutions and neglecting good marketing sense had been the rock many aspiring businesses had foundered upon.

Fran Aylward, partner and Doyen of the public relations fraternity in the capital was responsible for a large percentage of new accounts. At sixty-five years of age Fran, with no intention of ever considering retirement cut an extraordinary figure, old style, he had come in and out of fashion many times in his career but had remained consistent in his undoubted skill and effectiveness.

The epitome of sartorial splendour, every morning a rose adorned his lapel, plucked he maintained from his own garden. A bow tie in a complimentary shade with a perfectly prepared shirt, often with a light stripe and hand tailored suit completed the picture. That is save for the most beguiling smile reflecting an outgoing effusive personality.

Fran Aylward strode the boards of the Public Relations Business as one of its undoubted stars. Behind the obvious flamboyance was a keen mind fuelled by impressive academic qualifications. Very few occasions on the Press calendar featured without some reference to Fran Aylward who had a great gift for being in the right place at the right time, especially when the cameras were around.

Getting on in years, instead of the man slowing down he seemed to have increased in his vigour and hunger for even greater success.

Fran had some reservations about Paul and was aware that he would never be a close friend but successful businesses were not built on friendship. Mutual respect and a blending of diverse talents were far more important. He found Paul to be a bit precious and defensive on occasions.

Certain members of the board however, while appreciating Fran's usefulness and recognizing his contribution to the mutual benefit, found him hugely irritating and impossible to deal with wishing that he would reserve his talents for the clients and leave them out of the boardroom.

Confrontation and criticism rolled off Fran like water off a duck's back often to the particular frustration of Stella McCarthy, fellow director and a highly qualified accountant. Their conflicting views leading to many heated debates normally ending in an agreement to agree to disagree.

Shelly Holmes, Creative Group Head, looked up from the grocery list she was typing on her high-powered Apple Mac computer.

Divorced mother of 3 kids under the age of 10 years and no immediate relative in Ireland, New York born Shelly combined a very creative and demanding job with some busy and pretty hectic domestic demands. An achiever with a powerful, outgoing nature she took life in her stride.

With a more than ample figure and quick wit coupled with a very direct gaze from eyes that challenged every man she met, Shelly had a formidable reputation especially amongst the younger male staff.

Having dropped the kids to school and play school, uncharacteristically, this Monday morning Shelly was feeling under pressure.

Monday mornings, before the 10am production meeting presented a chance for her to deal with the grocery list and some other chores.

On hearing Paul's voice greet the other occupants of the large studio, with a feeling of some irritation she cancelled out of the grocery list.

Normally she had this time to herself and was rarely interrupted by one of the directors, not that Paul would object to her extra curricular activity. The extremely talented Shelly was indulged and her involvement with family matters was considered an asset to a greater understanding of the average consumer's needs.

Paul Macken, having entered the department through the door leading to the back stairs greeted the occupants of the studio individually with his usual jovial comments relating to the weekend activities, as he made his way through the open plan office to Shelly's section of the partitioned space.

Leaning both elbows on the glass partition he reached out and dropped a small memory stick on the mouse pad in front of Shelly.

"See what you make of that. It should interest you, it's how I spent my week end."

Shelly cancelled out of her shopping list, she would forward it later, and curiously reached out a well-manicured hand for the small USB connection.

"What's in it?"

She looked at Paul sensing his enthusiasm.

Rounding the partition he reached behind him retrieving a chair and sat down.

"Remember when you worked in London and there was that fraud business involving your husband?" He enquired in a confidential tone.

"Ex husband," she corrected, "Go on."

"You mentioned some forensic company that was involved in the court case,"

Shelly had been quite open about her past life when she had joined Macken & Aylward.

In fact Paul had been a great help in all the logistical matters surrounding her move from the London agency. She liked his sometimes-casual style and friendly manner, which never seemed to waiver no matter what the circumstances.

Slipping the memory stick into the USB port on the computer and clicking the exposed icon, suddenly remembering, "Kathryn Thorndike," that was her name.

She looked at Paul, "Kathryn Thorndike" she repeated reflectively, "Forensic expert specialising in Calligraphy. She's one pretty formidable lady.

My ex husband Tim never knew what hit him."

Forgetting the screen, Shelly cast her mind back to the traumatic time of her life.

"Yes the whole affair hinged on her judgment," she continued, "Tim's lawyer tried every trick in the book but he couldn't shake her. Kathryn Thorndike stood firm. She was quite amazing really."

"Yes I remember you referring to her before." Paul prompted.

"It's her track record, her reputation from previous cases, her opinion is held in great esteem. She worked as a group head of forensics with Scotland Yard even though she's quite young. Thanks to her I won the case and my beloved husband ended up in jail."

She laughed at the memory.

"My only regret," she said ruefully, "is that he had no money and since the divorce his support for the kids has been sporadic to say the least. He dotes on his daughter from his previous marriage. She spends a lot of time with him in London."

Shelly studied the pictures revealed on the screen with great interest assessing rapidly. "So if it is anything to do with proving authenticity of handwriting," she continued, taking note of the *"Hovellers going out to a wreck,"* as it was displayed before her. "She's got to be the best."

Paul stood up, "Sounds good, thanks, I'll contact her, interesting lady."

Shelly clicked on the icons in turn as Paul went on to explain, in a low voice, to a very attentive listener, all about buying the painting and the Turner possibilities.

"I really think I could be on to something quite big. What do you think?"

Before Shelly could reply, Paul, looking at his watch said, "I'd value your opinion, we can talk about it again after I've had a word with the famous Ms Thorndike. I'll see you at the production meeting. Major developments on the beer front, everything's on hold, apparently there's to be a re-brief."

Shelly recoiled at his words

"What? I don't believe it!"

Shelly and her entire creative team had been working for two weeks on the pitch for the new major beer account. The information so casually delivered by Paul was not exactly what Shelly Holmes needed at that moment.

She sat back in her seat open mouthed shaking her head from side to side, glaring at Paul in angry disbelief.

"A re-brief? You mean all the work accomplished so far could be for nothing, scrapped, a re-brief! When is the launch date? Don't tell me it hasn't changed."

Paul looked calmly into the furious face of the normally composed woman in front of him. Then, with a shrug, hands held out palm upwards,

"See you at the production meeting." he said and headed for the door.

Full of frustration and anger, outraged Shelly looked after the retreating back as her boss left the room. His unshakable calmness infuriated her.

Lately things had been getting on top of her. She could feel the pressures invading her from all sides, money, kids, school fees, one income and the demands of her job, now this. She and her team would be burning the midnight oil to make the deadline.

Sitting at her desk screened from the rest of the creative staff she could feel the tears beginning. The tissues had had a fair amount of use during the last few weeks.

Blinking rapidly she composed herself and through misty eyes started to rearrange things on her desk, grocery list forgotten for the moment. She saved out of the "Turner" files one by one.

Paul, heading for his office, was pretty sure that Shelly and her team would cope with the problem in hand. Anyway everything was on hold now until the re-brief. He knew the launch date would be put back. No need to share that with the "Creatives" he thought, perhaps he should have told Shelly. Better to keep them under the bit of pressure though, I might need some leeway later on.

Putting the matter behind him he headed for his office unconcerned about Shelly and her predicament, all in a days work, in a good mood, anticipating some good "Turner" news his step quickened as he neared his spacious office on the second floor.

Fran Aylward was already there when he arrived. Fran as usual smartly turned out in his "George Melly" pinstripe with yellow rose and matching bow tie standing at the high window overlooking the beautiful Georgian Square. He turned briskly to greet his fellow Director.

"Just the two of us today, our Ms McCarthy has an early meeting with the bank people."

Fran for some reason found it difficult to refer to his fellow director using her Christian name. There were those who subscribed to the idea that Fran had a soft spot for Stella in spite of their confrontations.

"She'll be back for the production meeting."

Paul intercepted the older man as he headed across the grey-carpeted area between him and the inviting leather chairs and low coffee table. Fran had a habit of making himself comfortable for a prolonged chat punctuated with cups of coffee, especially on Monday mornings and especially without the presence of the persistent, pedantic Stella.

"We should put the meeting off till eleven. I'll inform the others, I've got a lot to sort out anyway, lets get together in the boardroom before the meeting say 10.45 okay?" Paul redirected him towards the door.

Having despatched the slightly reluctant Fran he turned to the business at hand.

Sitting down behind the large curved desk he turned on his computer. The Agency Logo sprang into view on the huge monitor mounted on the wall opposite.

Paul's large office functioned as a conference room equipped with all the necessary presentation equipment. Working quickly he accessed the Internet and immediately found what he was looking for.

Kathryn Thorndike Consultants, Forensic *Scientists*, *Expert Witnesses,* with a London address. He scanned the impressive credentials.

Specialist areas of work Forensic Document Examination, Handwriting impressions, Forgeries.

Then followed a list of associated experts past experience etc.

From the information provided he deduced that she could be only in her early thirties. What had Shelly said? "A pretty formidable lady."

Paul scrolled through the nicely designed website and came across a news picture featuring a group of people. He scanned the caption for her name curious to see what she looked like. He zoomed in on the rather low-resolution picture.

Her image filled the large screen on the wall opposite, quite bitmapped and blurry, slim figure, cropped blond hair, hard to make out the features. What really caught his attention was the fact that, all the people in the picture, with the exception of the one woman were wearing dark business suits. Kathryn's spectacular red suit and black blouse made a very powerful statement.

Resolving to contact her later he reached for the phone.

"Could you get me Graham Roach of the Sheridan Art Gallery please?"

Leaning back in his chair as he waited for the call to be put through he absentmindedly perused the bitmapped image of the woman still enlarged on the big monitor imagining how her face would look in reality.

Paul Macken had more than a weakness for beautiful strong women he had married one. His was more of an obsession, certainly not just a normal penchant for the ladies. The people at the Clinic had likened Paul's condition to the same irresistible attraction an alcoholic might have for a bottle of whiskey, a condition that needed controlling. The last time he had transgressed the lady in question also had short blond hair.

As a result of an infantile infatuation that had invaded him at the time he had jeopardised everything, his marriage and his business.

Ignoring the warning signals Paul studied the picture, eyes, mind and imagination, devouring the image of the youthful spectacular figure.

In his imaginings the close cropped blond hair sprang into focus, white oval beautiful face, lips as red as the dress. She looked across the room at him. Transfixed he imagined her lips parting as she spoke...

"There is Mr Roach for you now," a pause. "Hello Paul. Hello!"

Startled back to reality Paul answered, controlling his voice as best he could. Graham at the other end responded enthusiastically without the normal polite preliminary chat.

"I've been talking to some of my colleagues about the painting. How is your research going or did you pursue the matter any further?"

Paul, having recovered his equilibrium answered smoothly.

"Yes quite a lot of info on Turner clicked into place, some of it quite compelling, especially the handwriting. The Tate Modern website allows you access to all Turners Sketchbooks and notes. I found very definite similarities between Turner's handwriting and the writing on the back of my picture. I also found references to Nash and sketches of boats identical to the one in my picture." He paused to allow the information to sink in and was not disappointed.

"Sounds good," Graham Roach intending to play down his interest and enthusiasm found it difficult to keep his voice casual.

"I'm available to show all the evidence to you right away how are you fixed, Graham?"

"What about Wednesday at 11.00?"

Paul checked his diary. The beer re-briefing would be Friday.

"Great I look forward to it."

"Look Paul I don't want to get your hopes up too high, you know I'm not a Turner expert but I will have my colleague Declan Traynor attend. He's an authority on early 19th century watercolours. He'll have a pretty good idea if it is a Turner or not."

Completing the call Paul returned to the Kathryn Thorndike web site. During his conversation with Graham, so compelling had the image on the wall opposite been that he had lost concentration several times.

Locating her email address he attached the Turner information, mainly featuring the lettering and his home address and telephone number, with a short explanation inviting Kathryn Thorndike to contact him if interested. He pressed send, resolving to get to London as soon as possible.

Before leaving the website Paul relocated the picture of the lady in the red dress. Relaxing in his chair stretching his legs out in front of him, fingers interlocked behind his head, he allowed his imagination to run free completely giving in to an urgent desire to get as close to her as possible.

With a compelling urge to hear her voice he reached for his mobile and keyed in her London number. The dial tone was interrupted by an answering recorded message. The voice fulfilled his expectations, warm, precise and confident. He waited for the intake of her breath at the finish of the sentence.

Later that morning Paul used the production meeting to re-arrange things so that he could have the entire week free, his intention to meet with the gallery and then get to London and the exceptional Kathryn Thorndike.

Angie Kiely, larger than life, paused for effect at the entrance to the chic Bistro. When she was sure she had the attention of all she made her way towards the table where Susan was sitting, on the way greeting real and imaginary friends. With some amusement Susan watched the approach of her audacious friend.

Plonking a couple of designer bags on the chair beside Susan, with a, "The usual" to the waiter she carefully arranged her ample figure into the chair opposite.

"I really meant to ring you for a get together but Zack and I have been away for a while and I have been so busy since we got back. You know how time goes so fast, you're looking great but then you always do. How's Paul, still as beautiful as ever? You know you two are so lucky, and Jane, how's she getting on with that fellow Simon, he has grown up children hasn't he?"

Angie had a tendency to prattle in a loud voice on social occasions. Susan had decided long ago that this was Angie's release from her normal formidable and precise delivery as a barrister presiding in the Dublin courts.

After a short time during which several of their mutual friends had been discussed, the state of the world economy had been solved, more or less, and the availability of "Designer Fakers" aired, along with the consuming of several cream cakes, mostly by the large proportioned barrister, Angie, courtroom face in place, eventually got around to the business at hand.

"After you called I did some thinking on a person to help you with that Turner business. There are quite a few companies in London with specialists in Calligraphy forensics, all very professional. There is however a good one I worked with about three years ago; she came to Dublin for a case, very competent. She was initially in newspapers and then Scotland Yard, great organising abilities and an astute mind."

Angie paused collecting her thoughts.

"Yes she's got a practice in London for about four years and has really emerged as one of the leading experts. Her opinions are most respected in the forensic field especially calligraphy. She has worked on a few cases in Dublin."

Angie then lapsed into usual vernacular

"Fair play to her. She has got something. She's about 35, now she is not stunning no you couldn't say stunning."

Angie looked at the ceiling for the right word.

"Young, spectacular, she looks young. Far too young for such a highly technical and responsible job," she continued, "no make up, well maybe a bit of eye shadow, good figure, very tall. It's her manner, almost naive, innocent. She's a really nice person, which makes her even more infuriating." Here Angie smiled knowingly. "She has a knack of making men feel as if they're in control. You know what I mean."

"Is she married?" asked Susan listening to the description of this paragon of some kind of perfection.

"No she's got a partner, or she had last time I came across her."

"Really," Susan smiled, "lucky man,"

"Not a man a Woman actually, her partner is a performer, quite well known, musicals and that. "

"Formidable!"

"She really sounds like a remarkable character and you'd recommend her for this Turner thing we're into?"

"Yes, I would and I'll tell you why,"

Angie in barrister mode continued,

"Very few cases identifying in favour of a notable work of art succeed on the basis of an art expert's opinion alone. You could have one expert in favour and one against. They cancel each other out. All kinds of factors kick in, paper or canvas, carbon dating, brushwork, style, repetitive characteristics, always a matter of opinion in the absence of a signature. Handwriting as approved by a recognised authority can be conclusive."

Angie, now speaking in more normal tones continued,

"Now you say there is a handwritten title on the back of the picture?"

Leaning forward for emphasis Angie poked the tablecloth with a well-manicured index finger, "Prove that's Turners handwriting and the picture is then accredited to Turner.

It comes down to the credibility of the forensic evidence. That's where our formidable young expert comes in and she is the current best."

The general chatter and noise of morning coffee partaken by the well heeled brigade frequenting one of Dublin's more trendy suburban bistros continued as Susan contemplated the information.

"And what is this amazing young lady's name?"

"Kathryn Thorndike," came the reply.

Shelley Holmes having completed the grocery list, anticipating a busy day phoned the child minder.

"Can you hold on to Derek for an extra hour please and give him something to eat at about five o'clock?" On getting a reluctant and not very enthusiastic, "Ok, then." She rang the apartment number. It was a while before the phone was answered.

"Hello," said the sleepy voice.

"Are you still in bed? I thought that you would be gone by now."

Jaric, Shelly's Polish partner who ran a successful painting, decorating business had a propensity for lying in most mornings and compensating at the other end of the day, working till late at night.

"I left a list of calls you need to make on the dining room table." Mrs Murphy called again about her windows," Shelly prompted.

Jaric, in spite of his laidback style was hard working and thorough and much in demand. It was becoming a major part of Shelley's day keeping track of his business for him.

"Don't forget Jackie and Sandra. You are collecting them from school today and I asked the child-minder to keep Derek for an extra hour and feed him. I'll be home about seven thirty."

These instructions were greeted with a snore from the other end of the phone.

"Jaric! Jaric ! Wake up."

"Just joking," came the reply. "I will do everything. Have a nice day."

The year old relationship with Jaric seemed to be working out, pity he had to send so much of his earnings home to Poland to support his wife and kids.

Shelly's mood had not improved since the production meeting, a pretty hectic timetable for the next couple of weeks would tax her and her creative group to the maximum. Putting down the phone she reached for the mouse. The decks would have to be cleared to make way for the imminent work because of the postponed beer account briefing, the presentation date not having been put back.

Paul had a nerve, she thought, announcing his departure for a few days on personal business. Off to London, typical!

The Turner Icon caught her eye. She clicked on it and a picture filled the screen, another click and the pencilled wording, *Deal-Hovellers going out to a wreck* came up followed by about eight examples of very similar handwriting, under the heading "From Turner's sketchbooks."

Her attention was captured by a piece of information that stopped her in her tracks. In 2006 a Turner painting was discovered and was subsequently sold at auction for several millions.

She looked at the picture of Paul's possible Turner purchased for five hundred euro and then at the picture of the actual recognised Turner.

Her hand strayed to the phone. Hardly able to take her eyes from the screen, she dialled a London number.

Inserting another memory stick into the mac she dragged the entire contents of the "Turner" onto it and downloaded. Removing the device from her computer she dropped it into her handbag.

"Hello Tim Holmes Agencies," answered her ex-husband's familiar voice.

Shelly hesitated for a moment collecting her thoughts, the memories flooding back, maybe this is not such a good idea she thought. A quick glance at the screen prompted her to continue.

"Hello Tim,"

"Bim a Bam Bim a Boom it's the mother of my kids, how ya doin, dis better be good, it's been a while," came the over- the -top response.

Shelly couldn't resist a smile.

"Cut out the messing and listen,"

"I'm all ears Noddy,"

Five minutes later she finished an earnest conversation with a much more serious sounding and efficient Tim Holmes.

*F*rom the rocky cliff face further up the coast dark eyes watched the discovery of the D2. Vojta Matej Janace smiled his cold impersonal smile. He felt at home here in this rugged coastal terrain. Thinking of his nights work he dwelt on some details to savour more so than others. The man and two boys on the boat had witnessed his arrival so they had to be silenced. He wished to come to Deal in his own chosen manner, unannounced. There is no such thing as life without death, it's how the last hand is dealt that *counts whether it be by the hand of God or by the hand of Vojta Matej Janacec.*

For a while he watched the activity of the Dutchman. Out to sea he could see the approach of the other boats in response to the flare, time to move inland.

Whilst aboard the ill-fated Renown he had had access to detailed maps of the coastal area. The surrounding moorland drew him like a magnet. Here he could survive comfortably in isolated surroundings similar to his homeland. It would suffice to keep a low profile until things had quietened down. The Town of Margate was within striking distance by coach to Deal. When the time would come to join the Deal community this would be how he would approach the thriving town, a town where a foreign accent was not uncommon, vessels coming and going, cargos unloading, people on the move.

Grace Wakeley was a well liked, well set up woman with an astute independent disposition who proved to be a great asset to the running of Sofia Booth's guesthouse. Hard working and reliable she made it possible for Sophie to remain most of the time in Margate, her main dwelling and Hostelry. Grace' s primary concern was for the welfare of her brother's child now orphaned by the events of that terrible night six weeks previously. All Michael's possessions had come to her and the girl. The D2 and a small house on the waterfront now belonged to her. Michael had been thrifty enough and there was some money too. The Dutchman had proved to be a good friend supplying a crew for the boat now plying its Hoveller trade, the proceeds coming to Grace, the Dutchman taking a generous percentage, rightly so, Grace could not sail the boat and having someone trustworthy to help her was of supreme value.

It was confided to Grace, very much to her surprise that her brother had been on very important business for

Whitehall, business that concerned the community of Deal. As a result of his untimely death Deal drew the attention of the authorities and there was unprecedented activity.

Now one of the Kings ships rode at anchor in the sound. It seemed that her brother had been working secretly for the government for the best part of two years. A murmur of expectation rose from the large crowd gathered on the beach as a longboat pushed out from the side of the man o' war and headed for the beach.

It had been a good 28 hours since a party of four men from the town had been taken aboard.

The word had spread in the town that Michael Wakeley their fellow Hoveller was in fact a high-ranking officer in the Kings employ.

During the 28 hours Michael Wakeley's followers amongst the Hovellers, a group of 26 had shown their hand. Specially recruited they represented all the various trades in the town, men of influence and well respected.

Wakeley had done his work well and had picked wisely. The word had been spread and committees were being formed. The movement within Deal to avail of their resources as a cohesive group was gaining impetus by the hour. A newfound pride amongst their leaders showed in their bearing, they were ready for something to cheer about.

A welcoming committee waited on the waterfront for the return of the four men closest to Michael, his right hand men so to speak. There was the Dutchman Van Klaasen, Michael Ellis, a local butcher who owned two luggers, James Wholesworth and Jake Mitchell, all Hovellers Michael Wakeley had been influencing and guiding, advising and recruiting during the previous year.

Mobilise the Hovellers, organise a formal Salvage Company structured for the benefit of all, life boats to work side by side with the Pilots, all in demand by the seafaring fraternity. At any given time there could be up to 700 ships at anchor on the safe haven of the Downs between the treacherous Goodwin Sands and Deal, all awaiting the right conditions to make the Thames Estuary and London. These ships needed repairs and provisions and continuous servicing. Deal had the resources, butchers, bakers, rope makers and sail makers, all the local produce would be needed for supplies.

The town of Deal was fast becoming one of the most important ports in England. Opportunities for right minded men abounded.

The committee waiting on the beach, all Wakeley's men consisted of members of all the various services Deal could provide.

As the longboat neared the beach the noise of the gathering grew into a great cheer.

Beaching in the surf through the breakers was always a hazardous business at Deal, but many willing and experienced hands made light work of it.

Certain formalities followed as the four men alighted from the longboat.

A good lot of boisterous good-natured backslapping ensued as the rest of the Hovellers fell in behind to parade up the town. Children skipped, dogs barked and the odd fight broke out. The crowd grew bigger as they made their way to the Weigh Office.

There were speeches from the Politicians and accolades to Michael Wakeley who in his absence was represented by his sister, Grace Wakeley, who graced the occasion admirably and with a great presence.

Amongst the crowd a foreign gentleman strode, newly arrived off the coach from Margate his dark eyes taking in everything especially the striking Grace Wakeley.

All Luggers conducting the business of salvage and piloting would be numbered and officially registered. The D2 would be reserved in the name of Michael Mallory Wakeley of Her Majesty's Senior Service, ex Hoveller.

In time Grace Wakeley would prove to be a good businesswoman, at first employing the Dutchman, a true and fine asset. With the new thinking and sense of fair trade opportunities came her way and she increased her fleet to four fine Luggers. The foreign gentleman was very much in favour and she could often be seen walking out with him around the town sometimes with her friend Sophie Booth.

Eventually she and the foreign gentleman married and she became Mrs Grace Janacec.

The power shower drilled cold water flattening the close-cropped blond hair. Capable strong fingers combed and scrubbed quickly in water cold enough to catch the breath, cascading, teasing the skin.

Boyish features lifted into the icy deluge. Why do I do this to myself every morning? She stepped from the shower her body tingling. The feeling of vitality and utter cleanliness was an essential part of Kathryn Thorndike's working day.

The white grandfather clock chimed once, 5.30am. Engulfed in an incongruous floral housecoat she prepared scrambled eggs, too early for the papers, the radio voice advised of the affairs of the world.

Crossing the room she plonked a small tray with her breakfast on the smooth top of the computer station.

Scan her emails, part of her routine, consume a good breakfast, then zip across London in the early hours for a controlled workout at Jimmy's, then back to her apartment for 7.30. Well that was her intention.

Today would be spent working at her apartment, after a day in the courts, a good space without the constant involvement of phones and staff. The Thorndike office nearer central London could become hectic at times though it was an essential front to her business.

Sitting down at her desk she reached for the keyboard and quickly scanned through yesterday's E- mails. The previous day had been pretty hectic. On arriving home late her bed had beckoned.

Having been away from her apartment all day she had not had time to check her e-mails. With only a passing glance at her computer Kathryn had headed for the bedroom knowing that a precious five hours sleep would prepare her for tomorrow. Curiously opening the email with the Irish address the word *wreck* swam onto the screen the beautiful longhand script immediately appealing to her special talent and interest, calligraphy. She noted the graphite rendering, the mottled paper background yellowed and aged.

All things save the email fled from her mind as she quickly opened all the attachments. Her interest and excitement rose as her eyes devoured the images presented to her, JMW Turner, the possibility of discovering a masterpiece by the great artist. The ascenders and descenders of hand written script offered a world of intrigue to Kathryn Thorndike now completely absorbed and losing all track of time. This script sent out immediate messages, artistic hand, regular consistent slant, generous, confident, beautiful and spontaneous.

Sometime later eating cold scrambled egg and toast washed down with hot coffee, still wearing the flowered housecoat, all rituals were forgotten for the day.

Kathryn Thorndike decided to phone the Dublin number on the e-mail.

Ireland such a short way away, so many Irish people in London. She had been to Ireland on business a few times, now unstable economy, always fun, sometimes got in the way of business. Her clock showed, 7.51. The phone was answered immediately,

"Hello," a woman's voice answered.

Paul, in the shower when the phone rang immediately thought of Kathryn Thorndike. All the previous day his thoughts had been interrupted with her image. He had found it difficult to maintain concentration. Distracted during that Directors meeting it had been quite embarrassing. Fran was talking at length about some staffing problem and Pau's mind had slipped away. It had not gone down very well with the other Directors when his apparent lack of interest in the proceedings was exposed.

Turning off the shower he could hear Susan talking on the phone.

"No, No. That's ok I'll get him for you now, Paul," she called "It's for you."

He appeared from the bathroom with a towel around his waist.

Susan handed him the phone with a grin accompanied by a remark about Kathryn's apparent power over the opposite sex.

He was hardly aware of Susan's light-hearted comment as he took the phone from her hand and waited for her to close the door before speaking, his words tumbling out hastily.

"Hello, thanks for calling. I rang yesterday but you weren't there. I was going to ring you later today in the hopes of catching you....," his voice trailed off as he heard the cultured tones quietly interrupting his slightly overanxious flow.

"Mr Macken, could you perhaps give me some idea on how you would like to proceed. The content of your e mail is quite interesting."

Stopped in his tracks Paul paused listening to the voice, imagining the red lips close to the mouthpiece. Raising his hand he rubbed his fingertips on his forehead as if trying to smooth the small furrows caused by the confusion in his mind, slight beads of perspiration appeared on his brow. Controlling his voice with some effort, "Yes ...good... thank you.... sorry ...m...m," then unable to collect his thoughts... "I'll ring you a bit later, at a more convenient time," He ended the conversation abruptly.

Sitting down on the nearest chair quite amazed and confused at his own reaction to the sound of her voice, his logic told him to be prepared the next time, compose himself and control the conversation. What kind of a fool must she think I am?

"Well that was a quick," Susan curious to know what had ensued entered the room. "Your breakfast is ready," without waiting for a reply she headed for the dining room.

Still sitting in the chair the towel around his waist Paul assessed the situation calmly, smiling slightly, ruefully, as he remembered the last occasion when he had indulged himself in such a fantasy.

He stood up and headed for the bathroom resolving to ring Kathryn back as soon as he finished his breakfast. What must she be thinking? Next time I will not be taken by surprise, I'll be ready. Ms Lady in Red sounded very tasty.

He dried himself quickly promising his reflection in the mirror, "You can have both, Paul, You can have both."

What an extraordinary phone call! Kathryn held the phone in her hand not quite believing what she had just heard. Well, it's pretty early. Perhaps he was just waking up she thought, the wife sounded pretty ok, efficient, business-like. Perhaps I will send an email outlining my conditions.

Looking at her watch she headed for the bedroom located at the back of the apartment. "Wake up, Sleeping Beauty don't you have an audition this morning?" All she was greeted with were the crumpled sheets of the empty bed.

Kathryn's partner, as unpredictable as ever was nowhere to be seen. When Kathryn had awakened at 5am, Christina had been sleeping like a baby.

She sometimes envied her talented partner's casual attitude to life. How nice it would be to take a whole month off and do absolutely nothing, for a change. She quickly rejected the idea. It may be glamorous and exciting to be a West End star but in the past three years living with one had given Kathryn an insight into the life. The key turned in the front door heralding Christina's return.

"You were at the computer in deep concentration when I was going out earlier. I said hello, I took Mamuska to the park to see her pigeon friends. You didn't raise your head," Christina held up the large blue Persian cat in evidence as she came down the hall and swept past.

Kathryn following her into the kitchen watched with some amusement as, cat on hip like a baby Christina bent her athletic dancers frame to reach out for a bottle of milk from the fridge. Flicking the top open with a long ruby red fingernail she coaxed the plastic kitty bowl into position with her foot, stooped and about half filled it.

Then looking Kathryn straight in the eye she held the cat at arms length.

"This is the last time I'm going to babysit this bloody animal," she said and dropped her current producers prized blue Persian.

The phone rang in the living room, the cat hit the floor in a perfect four point landing and started to lap the milk. With an amused glance at Mamuska Kathryn went to answer it. A much more controlled voice now greeted her, business like, friendly and apologetic.

"Hello Kathryn, it's Paul Macken, Thanks for ringing, sorry about earlier, a minor domestic crisis but everything's fine now. How is London? I always like getting to London, capital of the world."

It was always there with the Irish, the free and easy way with words, the soft brogue the superfluous and most times entertaining banter. Still amused by Christina's antics with the cat Kathryn accepted the informality with a light-hearted retort, "Well Mr Irish Macken perhaps you should get over here a bit more often." As soon as the out of character sentence was uttered she regretted it. It was her unwritten rule, polite, mannerly concise, to the point and strictly business.

Paul, expecting a more frosty response was encouraged.

"We have this most amazing painting Kathryn. What do you think about the handwriting? I know you have to do all kinds of research before making a judgment. But, what's your initial reaction, you know, your gut feeling. Do you think it could be Turner's?"

Kathryn, in an effort to retrieve the situation and her lack of professionalism took a more frosty approach.

"You know I can't answer that question Mr Macken. In the business of proving or disproving authenticity initial reactions can be misleading." She responded.

"Well do you feel it would be worth my while pursuing this. Could the handwriting on the back of the picture be Turner's?"

Kathryn, who generally trusted her first impressions when confronted with handwriting, gave the professional answer.

"There is a possibility, there are, on initial inspection similarities to Turner's hand. I would have to see the original of course. Also the samples of the handwriting you sent are not quite clear enough. I would need to see the originals at the Tate."

This mixture of professionalism and light heartedness struck a note with the already smitten Paul. To him the comment referring to more frequent visits to London could be interpreted as an invitation, however the fact that Kathryn Thorndike seemed to agree that the caption on the back of his painting could possibly be in Turner's handwriting was very exciting news indeed.

"What happens next?" He said. "When do I go over to meet you? Or do you come to Ireland?"

Hesitating, Kathryn sensed the voice on the other end of the phone was slightly too familiar, eagerness detected that made her feel slightly uneasy. Perhaps I should step away from this one.

It was only a fleeting thought. Kathryn Thorndike had no reservations in her ability to cope with the over enthusiastic male.

Looking across at the image still displayed on the computer screen, this is exactly the case I've been waiting for. She felt a surge of interest and excitement, considering the enormous implications of a Turner discovery

"I could take on the case should you wish. It would not be necessary for you to come over yet. I would not need the original until I had explored the matter further. Of course should you decide to come I am sure you would find it very interesting."

Again Paul's imagination took over as he mistakenly sensed an invitation in her words. He listened, seduced by the silken tone of her voice.

"The Tate Gallery in London can supply me with all I need for the moment. There would be a preliminary stage with a minimum cost. This would cover initial research and a report relating to the possibility of a positive or negative discovery. You would then decide if you wanted me to continue or not."

Every word resounded on Paul's receptive ears, the honeyed tones, and newscaster like delivery. The subtle invitation, come over I would make it interesting.

Urged to keep her talking, he asked.

"I'm curious to know can positive proof of identity be supplied from hand writing?"

"In some cases yes, in most cases it is accepted without dispute, depending, of course on the person who is doing the assessing," came the honeyed reply.

"After the initial cost, can you give me an idea to completion or do you do it for the love of it? What about a no foal no fee arrangement?"

"That is something we could talk about when we reach that stage. Every case is different Mr Macken. I will give you an assessment on the possibilities, after which you can make up your mind if you intend to pursue the matter. My first impression is positive. There are similarities, but I will need better samples. I have contacts at the Tate Gallery and could do some comparisons from the originals should you so wish. Of course there is no guarantee that the foal will be to your liking."

"I wish very definitely Kathryn, please go ahead with the initial stages," Paul responded, "and I will get over as soon as you need me."

"Fine I'll get on to it right away. Goodbye for now Mr Macken, and of course I look forward to seeing you in London."

"Or perhaps you could come to Dublin, you know you'd be made very welcome."

"Actually I do go to Dublin quite frequently, on business mainly. Some day I'll get there for a holiday I really like Irish people, very charming."

Paul fulfilled the charming Irish man image for a while longer managing to elicit a gentle laugh and some light banter from a more relaxed and personable Kathryn Thorndike, business momentarily set to one side.

Well she sure is some piece of work, he thought as he put down the phone, resolving to get a plane ticket as soon as possible.

Kathryn placed the phone on the receiver unaware that she had sent out signals, which had been totally misconstrued by the misguided Mr Macken.

The Irish always had so much to say. They played so lightly with words and the brogue was pleasant enough to her ears. It was a change from the usual cut and thrust of business.

"That was a long one?" Christina draped on the sofa opposite, looked across at her partner, a spoonful of muesli hovering "Very cosy, so when are we off to Ireland?"

Kathryn smiled, "No that was strictly business." The big Persian cat hopped up onto her lap. Stroking its soft fur, she explained about the Turner possibility and the slightly weird attitude of Paul Macken.

She felt, though the lettering looked a lot like Turner's in 1825 those who could write, wrote very similarly. There were some obvious discrepancies; a Turner hand of 1825 could be considerably different to one in later years. The consistent characteristics would have to be whittled out.

The evidence proved and all professional paths having been pursued, eventually the truth would be revealed without prejudice.

"Well how did it go?" Susan enquired of her husband. "From what Angie says Katherine the Great can be a bit of a man eater?"

"Nothing like it," came the easy reply "To the contrary, more of a boring academic, pleasant enough. She was pretty positive about the lettering but needs to see the originals." He went on to tell Susan about his conversation leaving out bits and pieces here and there eventually casually stating that the only way to proceed was for him to go to London as soon as possible, before Friday's beer re-brief meeting.

"I'll go tomorrow - get the red eye at 7.15 and back on the 6.30".

Susan looked at her husband sceptically, something amiss here, she thought, searching his face for clues. 30 years of marriage with many ups and downs had made her an expert on Paul Macken.

He looked back wide eyed; eyebrows slightly raised "What?"

"Look that painting could be worth millions and this woman can help us prove it. Of course I want to get over there as soon as possible. If I go tomorrow morning I'll be back tomorrow night."

"What about the meeting?" Said Susan

"What meeting?"

She looked at him calmly and in a quiet voice replied,

"The very important meeting with Graham Roach that you organised, at the Gallery, surely you haven't forgotten. You said you'd arranged a meeting with the gallery team to discuss the painting."

For a second Susan saw a flash of the reckless Paul, "You go," he said impulsively.

So unlike the thorough calculating mind she understood and admired so much. Liar, liar, pants on fire, she thought to herself. You've got the hots for Kathryn the Great.

With feelings of anger and sadness combined, rising to her feet she looked down at her husband, who, preoccupied with his thoughts failed to detect the change in her attitude. To conceal her feelings from him Susan walked to the window and stood looking out at the garden before she spoke, when she did her voice was quiet and controlled.

"You mean you would like to go to London and let me handle the Gallery? But we've collected all the evidence together surely you would like to know first hand what they think."

She turned, Paul was sitting there his mind elsewhere and she was not sure he had even heard what she said. She took two quick steps towards him to crouch down on one knee and looked into his eyes.

"You can go to London the following day, you'd still be back in time for the Beer re-brief. Or better still, I'll go to London and see that woman Thorndike and we both keep the Gallery appointment. It's far more important."

She was giving him every opportunity to change his mind. Again she searched his face.

"No", he said suddenly, "I have to go, I forgot to tell you Fran Aylward wants me to meet some of the UK connections, its essential. I might even have to stay overnight and get an early flight home the following day. You deal with the Gallery, ring me in London and fill me in, you'll enjoy it." He stood up, "I'll ring Shelly and let her know she can advise everyone." Jumping to his feet he walked briskly out of the room to the phone in the studio.

Susan followed quickly, trying desperately to get his attention, "Jane phoned she's coming for lunch to morrow she has something important to tell us about herself and Simon," she said. "She particularly wants you to be here."

But Paul was on the phone making his arrangements. When he was finished he turned with an apologetic smile, back to his usual self.

"Sorry Susan what did you say, something about Jane?"

"It's nothing," she said in a firm voice shaking her head.

"'Go to London!" She stared into his eyes her jaw set, the warning signals obvious, but Paul did not take heed or was too preoccupied to notice. The moment passed. Susan abruptly walked out the door leaving him standing with the phone in his hand.

With a shrug he closed the door behind her and dialled Kathryn Thorndike's number. He let the phone ring for a while but there was no answer, disappointed not to hear her voice he decided to leave a message.

The phone was ringing as Christina let herself into the apartment. Dumping her parcels in the hall she was too late to answer it. There was a handwritten note on the table propped up against the fruit bowl. With a smile she read.

Gone to the Tate on spec, locked the cat in the bathroom. If my Irish weirdo rings tell him I'm already spoken for xxx Kathryn.

She pressed the message button and listened to the Irish weirdo's voice.

"Hello Kathryn, This is Paul, thanks for the nice invitation, I'll be in London tomorrow for a couple of days arriving at 9.15, I'll call when I get in to Heathrow, looking forward to seeing you, I'll be staying at the Regent Palace."

Christina listening to the tone of the voice, the way the message was phrased, detected what Paul had in mind. Typical man, jumping to all kinds of conclusions just because someone's friendly and polite, she considered deleting the message.

Tim Holmes was intrigued by the content of the conversation with Shelly, his talented wife. They had had some contact since their separation mainly over the kids. It had been an amicable enough separation.

She had been very strong at the time of the break up and the court case. Even the scam over the forged cheques had been detected and he had ended up doing some time at her majesty's pleasure. An experience he was not prepared to repeat. He felt no hard feelings and bore no grudges towards Shelly. In fact he still harboured a hope that some time in the future they could get together again.

Tim Holmes like all natural con men was an optimist. In Tim's world all things were possible. It did not take him long to decide how to use the information he had just received.

For some time he sat with his laptop and his mobile, forwarding the contents of his wife's email carefully deleting any reference to the owner of the painting.

He watched the screen until it registered everything safely downloaded and sent. All the time his sharp brain working, scheming and planning assessing opportunities.

One year as a guest in her majesty's prison had not dulled Tim's ambition and desire to exploit the main chance. It had just strengthened his resolve to be more careful the next time. His wits had served him well.

Sharing a cell with one of the prison's toughest inmates for some could have been a very harrowing experience.

"The man" had power and contacts, running all sorts of illegal activities from his cell and backing up most of his dealings with indiscriminate violence administered either by him or by one of his cohorts of which there were many. Tim quickly insinuated himself into a position of usefulness to "The Man" thereby gaining respect from all.

Wherever "The Man" was there was Tim alongside cleverly adding a word or thought, accepted as a stroker, a clever dick. There were many who envied him his position and would have gladly "done for him" but Tim was under the protection of "The Man" and therefore considered untouchable.

With promises to keep in touch and be of assistance from the outside Tim had walked away from the prison armed with a list of contacts and information useful beyond his wildest dreams.

The reduced sentence he received was a mystery to most but some had their suspicions. Being so close to "The Man" seemed to be contradictory to good behaviour and model prisoner status.

Tim never looked back, he used the knowledge from time to time but always kept "The Man" sweet.

In a previous life Tim had supplemented his reasonable earnings performing as a stand-up comedian, old style comedy, Tommy Cooper, Morecambe and Wise. The latest alternative stuff left him a bit cold although he could see the humour he couldn't perform it. What happened the good old Joke, the one-liner? "

Did you hear the one about the Irish Cowboy?..... Rick O'Shea Ha! Ha! Got them every time.

Now, here was something special. This Turner Deal had all the makings especially the bottom line. Eventually, having considered all points, checking and re-checking, satisfied with his plan he made some phone calls to London numbers.

Yes nice, very nice that should do it. Now just relax sit back and wait for the phone to ring.

Shelly's phone call had interrupted his morning ablutions so he returned to the bathroom to survey his corpulent image in the full-length mirror.

Lifting his fists and crouching in the stance of a prizefighter he grimaced menacingly at the mirror.

The chubby five foot four figure with the cherubic face and receding hairline grimaced back. "Rocky Balboa- Eye of the tiger," he jabbed with his left lead and swung a right uppercut, the motion stretching his soft midriff only for it to fall back into place with a bouncy wobble.

Laughing, he reached for the electric shaver on the glass washstand.

Half way through shaving the phone rang. Now that didn't take long, he smiled and humming, "Eye of the tiger diddum de dum," he answered the phone. "Timothy Holmes Agencies, how can I help?"

When Audrey Langton, stern faced, grey haired, PA to one of the world's most successful businessmen accessed the email from Tim Holmes, a name she did not recognize, it didn't take her long after viewing it's content to come to a conclusion. Without hesitation she rang through to inform her Business Celebrity Boss in the palatial office next door.

Immediately the quick abrupt tones of the voice familiar to Television viewers and radio listeners alike came on the line. "Yes, Yes I see it."

The Dragon, in spite of having the valuable Audrey Langton as his PA usually opened his own e-mails. On this occasion the Tim Holmes information had hit home.

Greed and power feeding one off the other, working together, combined to be a formidable force in his pursuance of all ambitions. From an early age he had realized success, gaining huge wealth, respect and fame arriving now at a stage in his life with little else to achieve even a knighthood appeared just a matter of time.

Never admitting to failure or weakness of any kind he did however harbour great regrets concerning his appearance. Plastic surgery may have improved things somewhat but he regretted his lack of inches, considering himself, with brutal honesty, to be an ugly little man in elevator shoes. Being obsessed with JMW Turner since his first sight of the masterpiece "The Fighting Temeraire" he had studied the great painter absorbing all the information he could find. He now considered himself to be a foremost authority on the master.

His was no ordinary obsession. To him there were great parallels between himself and Turner.

Turner was also a genius becoming extremely successful at an early age and very wealthy during his lifetime, undoubtedly one of the greatest artists that had ever lived. He was also about the same height and no oil painting.

The prospect of securing an original, previously undiscovered work, by Turner appealed to the obliteration of all else. Astute intellect quickly assessing the possibilities offered, scrutinising the other pictures in the file, calculating, considering, he then spoke to his PA.

"Audrey I will see whoever sent this information this afternoon, 2.30, at the office and Audrey, I want to see a profile of the party before the meeting."

"You are committed for 2.30, it's the patents people," the ever-efficient Audrey informed

"Tell them I'll be 15 minutes late and make my apologies."

"Mr Holmes, concerning your communication," Tim listened razor poised, his face half covered in shaving cream, to the precise voice of Audrey Langton as she continued, suggesting to Tim that he should present himself at a certain location at 2.30 sharp.

Audrey Langton went on to say, however, that he would have to provide her with considerable information about the proposal and about himself personally before confirming.

Sensing by the sound and attitude of the caller that nothing of his personal life would remain unexplored, Tim Holmes, for the first time in his life told the truth the whole truth and nothing but the truth.

It was a pretty gruelling interview. The time and location were confirmed, a very upmarket establishment in the centre of the city, "2.15 sharp Mr Holmes."

Eye of the tiger....dum...de...dum dum, punching the air, moonwalking, Tim swivelled and reversed out through the bathroom door and then back in to continue shaving.

The "Turner" in its gilt frame, now well protected with padding and a secure canvas bag had been placed in the back of the Volkswagen Golf.

Susan, leaving the coast behind her headed for the city centre and the Gallery her mind coping with the prospect of a very busy day. She was in two minds how to handle the evidence supporting the "Turner" claim. Having e-mailed all the information ahead the copies now encased in an A3 folder were on the passenger seat beside her.

On an impulse, she had also e-mailed the information to Sotheby's in London although an opinion is rather invalid without them seeing the actual painting.

As she drove along the familiar route through Donnybrook Village she mused on the unlikely choices her husband Paul had made.

After thirty years of marriage there were very few surprises left between them yet she was completely taken aback with his choice to forgo the cut and thrust, the intrigue of discovery that the Gallery meeting offered. Then there was his complete dismissal of any suggestion that he could go to London at a later date. But most of all was his expression, the look on his face, that total preoccupation with his own wishes. Why? Why? Why? The old familiar suspicions and anxiety crashed into her mind now with total conviction. The very intriguing youthful and amazing "Kathryn the Great."

Surely not, no, not again, remembering the last time Paul had transgressed Susan was filled with sadness and anger, the apologies, the pleading and the appeal.

"I don't know what came over me. It will never happen again, forgive me."

Paul, like a recovering alcoholic had agreed to counselling.

The gradual and eventual repairing of the rift was mainly due to the professional help and the admission by Paul that he had a psychological weakness.

A very strong feeling began to replace Susan's good mood, a feeling deep rooted and unshakable. This time there would be no relenting.

How dare he put all their happiness in jeopardy to satisfy his own stupid needs whatever they might be, what had the experts said?

Paul had not matured in some way and in certain circumstances still saw himself as a young man. The emotion caused him to act in a reckless manner towards those he loved most. In this case his family. Or that was the gist of it.

Susan failed to grasp the subtlety of the argument. She didn't understand it. At the time the young Psychologist was quite convincing and Susan had craved for and accepted the explanation. Well not this time, 'the little Shit'.

He wasn't even interested in whatever news Jane and Simon had to share. Sadness and fury and the feeling of injustice all coming together, tears sprang suddenly to her eyes.

The back of the red car came rushing to meet her wrenching Susan from her reverie, she jammed her foot down on the brake pedal, too late. Blind instinct propelled her grasp as she wrenched the steering wheel; wheels locked the car spun out of control. The car in front moving forward just avoided the rear bumper of the golf as it whipped around to end up facing the wrong way across two lanes blocking the progress of a large articulated truck.

Susan, white-knuckled hands grasping the steering wheel, wide eyed in shock at the near miss looked up at the truck driver who from his lofty position, looked down into the ashen face of the woman below and made a patronizing-eyes-to-heaven, women-drivers, expression. Men! His expression provoked her to such an extent that all normal behaviour momentarily forgotten, incensed she uncharacteristically glared, uttered an obscenity and gave him the two-finger salute.

This was road rage, she would admit at a later date, with a new understanding of the term. The fiery Susan managed to resist the temptation to ram the front of the truck. Good sense prevailed. Instead, crashing the gearbox into first gear she did a humiliating, very angry and jerky four-point turn. Looking in her rear view mirror she imagined the lorry driver grinning from ear to ear.

Arriving in Kildare St. none the worse for her experience, in actual fact thankful that it had only been a near miss, she parked the car and sat quietly composing herself.

It had been a lucky escape and thankfully no one had been hurt. Though her pride had taken a bit of a knock she did treasure the moment of giving the lorry driver the two fingers.

Thoughts of her unfaithful husband seeped back into her mind. What an absolute eejit. This is going to end in tears and they won't be mine, she resolved.

She was surprised by the fierceness of her expression reflected in the mirror. The expression pleased her. I wouldn't like to tangle with someone like that. She allowed herself a little smile. Getting out of the car, she retrieved the painting from the back seat and placing it on a small-wheeled trolley stretched the elastic holders and hooked them in place.

With the A3 folder in one hand she grasped the handle just above the painting in the other and strode purposefully up Kildare St towards the Gallery and the waiting experts. "Probably a horde of men she speculated."

The gallery building, situated in a fashionable part of central Dublin was well guarded by a large impressive black Georgian door, the gallery name discreetly displayed on the window alongside in gold letters.

Susan rang the bell and pushed the door at the sound of the buzz signal. The spring-loaded mechanism resisted and she leaned harder towing her precious cargo with her, aware that she was probably being observed by a host of security cameras. The troublesome door wanted to close behind her making it difficult to hold open to allow passage for the small-wheeled trolley and the bulky painting.

Following a bit of a struggle and a few choice words under her breath most of them relating to the absence of her husband, she managed to get herself and the Turner through the doorway.

Pausing for a moment to get her bearings, galleries are so quiet like libraries and always empty she thought. High heels making an exaggerated clacking sound on the very nice Junker's wooden floor, shattering the silence, Susan towing the trolley made her way towards the swirly black shiny desk and the bent head of the receptionist.

"There is nobody available to look at your work at the moment you will have to phone and make an appointment." The perfectly coiffured head remained in position. The voice was devoid of any warmth, cold impersonal. The first defences of the gallery were not likely to be easily breached manned by an empowered ogre who took pleasure in her position. Susan and her trolley had been mistaken for an aspiring artist hoping to have her work displayed at the reputable Sheridan's Gallery. The head remained lowered as the very important work on the desktop was completed.

Susan stood there slightly flushed from her encounter with the door and contemplated the possibility of delivering a well-aimed blow with the A 3 folder. Instead her eyes fixed on the door behind the desk. PRIVATE stated the gold letters. The receptionist unaware of the danger sharply lifted her head as Susan swept past and pushed open the door.

"You can't go in there, Stop! There's a meeting!" She swung around and stood up. Too late Susan was already through the door and confronting the group of people at the large table.

"I'm sorry, she just barged in I couldn't stop her." Then to Susan,

"Please leave immediately and take your work with you."

"I would like milk and two sugars in my coffee, thank you." Graham Roach standing up coming round the table was in time to hear Susan make the demand to his over zealous secretary.

Turning she put out her hand, "Hello Graham nice to see you again."

Graham smiled a welcome, Susan had always been spectacular, and all the kids at school had fancied Richard Macken's good-looking Mum.

"Yes, good, I've got some people here who are dying to see it. Is Paul with you?" He glanced out into the reception area. "No," said Susan with a slightly dismissive wave of her hand. "He's off in London talking to the calligraphy people."

Smiling she turned towards the other people in the room. Graham did the introductions.

"This is Susan Macken, she and her husband own the very interesting painting that I am sure you are going to confirm is a Turner Original."

He turned briefly to the forgotten receptionist who was still standing at the door. "That'll be coffee for all and see if there are any chocolate biscuits Sally, thanks." He turned back into the room.

"Now, I'd like you to meet Desmond Sheridan our chairman, Declan Traynor watercolour expert, and Annette Fitzroy, curator of the National Art Museum.

Susan shook hands with each in turn.

Lastly, Annette Fitzroy, a very small woman in her mid forties with penetrating black eyes, stretched across the table and shook hands with Susan.

"When Graham rang about your painting I decided to come straight away, you know that we have several Turners at the National."

"I believe the last one discovered was about five years ago."

Declan Traynor meanwhile was making his way from the other side of the table. A tall skinny man wearing corduroy trousers and a green and red spotted dicky bow Susan noted with some amusement.

He reminded her of someone on television she couldn't think of his name, he was on quiz programmes. "May I?" He proffered an open hand in the direction of the trolley by Susan's side. "Of course, please."

"Thank you, lets get it up here on the table where we can have a good look at it."

In a moment he had the elastic stretchers unhooked and the painting with its protective covering removed and carefully placed on the table, revealed for all to view under the Gallery's perfect lighting conditions.

"My oh my, how wonderful, we have something special here!"

In his 55 years Declan Traynor had handled many fine paintings. Very seldom had he been so taken at first sight of a work.

Immediately resting his palms on the table each side of the painting, forgetting those present, lost in the study he bent his elbows bringing his face close, the sleeves of his tweed jacket riding up to reveal his skinny wrists. Quiet prevailed as the expert plied his trade, now close, now further back, muttering and making little sounds all the while.

Eventually he stood back apologetically rubbing his hands together, smiling and gesturing at the painting.

"Sorry, sorry, Please Ann what do you think?"

Annette Fitzroy the Curator of the National Gallery was already close along side. He moved to one side allowing her to get a closer look.

"Definitely high quality she murmured to herself, that section," she indicated with an outstretched hand, fingers splayed, "The waterline and the town, very definitely Turneresque, there are many things that are right about this picture. May I remove it from the frame?" she enquired of the expectant Susan.

There was a knock at the door and Sally came in with the coffee and biscuits. She made an extra effort with Susan who smiled and nodded her thanks.

"Sugar and milk Mrs Macken and would you like a chocolate biscuit?"

The interruption giving Susan time to take in her surroundings, she sat down at the highly polished boardroom table. The arrival of the tea gave her an opportunity to size up the people in the room. Declan Traynor was obviously very knowledgeable and devoted to his subject. He and Ann Fitzroy, now both wearing protective white gloves were deeply engrossed examining the painting, looking at the reverse side, checking the ornate frame, even the cord for hanging the painting, their coffee ignored.

It was Desmond Sheridan the Chairman that intrigued her. Very charming, dressed immaculately, a big man who looked as if he was used to getting his own way. Apart from the introduction at the beginning he had not uttered a word.

It surprised Susan that as the owner of the gallery he had made no attempt to examine the painting or even view it face on.

He sat at the end of the table and watched everybody including Susan. On one occasion on catching her eye he had glanced away to examine his fingernail minutely.

Susan now took the opportunity to have a good look at the man to whom she might be entrusting the painting, a painting that may very well be worth a fortune. She sat back and sipped her coffee.

Desmond Sheridan, without excusing himself stood up from the table indicating to Graham Roach with an almost imperceptible movement of his head, "A word" he mouthed and headed for the door. Already standing, Graham who had been engrossed in the painting followed.

Suddenly remembering his manners Desmond Sheridan turned his head glancing casually over his shoulder. "Excuse us I need to discuss a matter with Graham here. I'll leave you in their capable hands Mrs Macken, just for a few minutes," with a large hand slightly touching his elbow he guided his young colleague out to the reception area.

Susan watched the departure of the Gallery Owner with interest. He had seemed preoccupied, detached. She couldn't understand how a person in his position could sit in a room with a potential newly discovered masterpiece and not get off his feet to examine it, most odd.

The painting now removed from its frame and no longer covered by glass looked vibrant.

Appearing to be unaware of the Gallery owner's departure Declan Traynor was holding the 180 years old painting very delicately with white-gloved hands viewing it from varying angles.

Eventually he looked across the table. "What we can tell you at this stage is that many things are right about it. Turner did paint in a very similar style to this around 1825."

"We are reasonably sure the painting was done around then also the paper is smooth and hand pressed in five layers very typical of the time, very possibly made by Whatman in London."

"Turner lived in London as you probably know from your intriguing and pretty comprehensive research." He smiled as he indicated the hand written samples, sketches, all the information she and Paul had been collecting to support the Turner theory. "Perhaps we could offer Mrs Macken a job in the National as a researcher."

Ann Fitzroy looked earnestly at Susan,

"Mrs Macken, It's possible that you could have a Turner original here."

She looked down at the beautiful painting lying flat on the table. "The subject is right, the dramatic merging of sky and rough sea, the ship wreck, the coastal scene. We know he painted the sea around Deal in Kent we also know he had connections with the town of Deal. There are many factors that connect this painting to JMW Turner. Mind you I only say it's possible you could have a Turner in all probability it's not."

Anne Fitzroy who really loved the work of Turner and was the guardian of fifteen original Turners, the proud possession of Ireland's National Gallery looked into the composed face of the woman opposite.

This person is responsible and level headed, Susan decided. Pleased, that if it did prove to be a priceless masterpiece it would be in good and capable hands.

Anne decided to continue. "This is a high quality piece of work rendered by an extremely competent artist. At the time when Turner was painting in this style he was immensely successful and many of the leading artists attempted to emulate his work. This painting is likely to be by one of these artists. They come up from time to time and are often considered masterpieces in their own right and valuable. Now there is the matter of the handwriting on the back of the painting."

She carefully turned over the painting to show the title, Deal_ *Hovellers going out to a wreck.*

"I am no handwriting expert, this writing and Turners handwriting look very similar but I must point out that at the time when this painting was completed people who could write, wrote in a very similar fashion one to another. If we can prove this is Turner's handwriting then it would become difficult to deny the painting as a Turner Original."

Sitting down she looked up at Susan. "The repercussions of that discovery would be enormous for the art world."

Susan thought of Paul over in London. What would he think of this? He really should be here. Though, it would seem, the proving of the handwriting is crucial. I wonder how he's getting on? She resolved to ring him immediately after finishing here.

Through the slightly open door leading to the reception area Susan could see Desmond Sheridan and Graham Roach in conversation. The owner was talking earnestly. Graham's body language, arms folded right hand raised to his chin, eyes downcast indicated a resistance to the older mans words. Susan felt she and her painting to be the subject in question. Maybe I'm wrong she second-guessed herself. They're probably talking about something completely different. But there's a lot about that Sheridan fella I don't like.

"Of course we do not have the final word. Proving provenance, especially in something as paramount as this, will require extremely specialised skills and of course the Tate gallery in London will have a huge influence in the final outcome."

Susan switched her attention back to Anne and Declan Traynor as the two men returned from their discussion in the reception area.

A smiling, genial Des Sheridan followed by a slightly more serious Graham Roach.

"Well Mrs Macken what do you think of our experts?" He placed a familiar hand on Anne the Curator's shoulder and with the other, palm upwards made an all-embracing generous gesture. "Have we got white smoke?" Looking down at the painting on the table and clasping both hands together in front of him he solemnly moved his head from side to side.

"What wonderful work, a masterpiece, probably worth a very large amount of money, but not a Turner."

He looked at Susan with an apologetic smile, "That is in my opinion, he added, of course time will tell and I could be proved wrong. I hope I am. Of course all avenues must be explored. We will take great care of it for you. It is essential to make the right moves. We have a very good relationship with the Tate Modern in London and the curator is a personal friend of mine. Graham will be looking after you He will travel over personally to London and bring the painting with him. With your permission of course," he added hastily. "Graham tells me your husband is over in London with a certain Kathryn Thorndike." Pursing his lips he gravely shook his big grey head from side to side. "Of course," looking slightly condescendingly at Susan, "the decision is yours and you must be happy in your choice. Ms Thorndike would not be our choice however, no real depth, a bit on the young side. Now on the other hand there's Austin Medford, very well established, superb reputation highly recommended in the art world."

"And married to your Sister,"

Susan interrupted bluntly, deciding to slow down the process and not that enamoured by Mr Sheridan's attitude.

"Yes, Mr Sheridan we did consider Austin Medford amongst others. However every path led to Kathryn Thorndike, it would seem that the calligraphy aspect of this case is crucial and she is considered to be the current best."

Delivered in a measured tone accompanied by an equally level gaze this statement took the confident Mr Sheridan completely by surprise.

"Yes of course I'm sure she will be perfectly adequate but the matter of the painting itself. I suggest we take action right away."

"What do you suggest?" Susan turned to Annette Fitzroy, "I would be very interested to know what the Curator of the National Gallery would recommend."

Declan Taylor was in the process of carefully returning the painting to the safety of its frame his white gloved hands moving with expert ease. Anne who was helping him continued at her careful work for a few moments, head down.

Susan was sure she could detect a flicker of amused satisfaction in those dark eyes as the Curator then looked at her.

"It is very early days, why don't we wait for a reaction from your husband's visit with Kathryn. She will give him an instant assessment of the possibilities. I know her quite well and the way she works."

"Then we will talk again. The resources of the National Gallery will be at your disposal should you wish to continue. Susan, it will take time proving provenance of this magnitude and will involve a great many people. The implications of a positive outcome are enormous. All art lovers would want to see a new Turner."

"Yes, yes, a good plan," Desmond Sheridan nodded sagely. "Make haste slowly. You must leave the painting here with us at the Gallery, for safekeeping. We could make some further enquiries on your behalf, keep the ball rolling, so to speak."

Susan had already made up her mind.

"Thank you so much Mr Sheridan. I really am very grateful for all your help. I don't think I should return home without the painting. Paul and I will have to consider what to do next. I'm sure we will all talk again quite soon."

She turned from the rather disappointed gallery owner. "I have a question for you Mr Traynor."

"What might that be?" The expert enthusiast's head bobbed and he peered at her intently.

"Could the painting have been altered in any way?"

Susan explained about the little girl and mother she remembered and indicated the area where they had stood looking out at the boats."

"Mm…" The delicate hands, fingers splayed, hovered over the area. There are a few brush strokes here that would indicate a slight over painting. But it would be impossible to eliminate the image of two figures already painted. This painting is as it always was. It has not been tampered with in any way. You see with a watercolour, because of the transparency of the medium being water based, once it has dried any over painting would be easily detected."

Declan Traynor bobbed again. About to get into his stride he checked himself with a smile. "I hope that answers your question Mrs Macken you need no further opinion on that one. This painting is as it was the day it was painted."

"Thank you," said Susan, no more the wiser on the mystery of Abigail.

Anne Fitzroy proffered her business card. Susan taking the card felt that the Curator was someone in whom she could have confidence.

"Thank you Anne perhaps I could visit the other Turners in the National," She said. Further handshakes followed and Graham saw Susan to the door offering to wheel the little trolley to Susan's car.

On the way the "Turner" hardly got a mention He enquired about Susan's family especially his old school friend, Susan's son Richard. He was quite surprised about Richard's vocation to the church. "Wow, I'd never have thought that."

Such a likeable chap Susan thought, deciding to take him into her confidence.

"Look Graham, I'm not that keen on your boss, you probably gathered. However I am grateful to you for getting the National involved. Anne Fitzroy seems really clued in, you and I will talk again about this, I really do value your opinion."

Graham looked slightly relieved. "Des can be a bit forceful at times. I think you were a bit hard on him Mrs Macken." The memory of Susan's performance in the gallery seemed to amuse him greatly, he laughed, the rather serious business face transformed.

Susan couldn't resist a smile herself. Graham continued, a broad grin on his boyish face,

"In a way I kind of enjoyed it, I don't want to appear disloyal but he really is a pompous ass."

Quite enjoying the exchange with this handsome young man she joined in the humour of the moment. "That was a good one about his sister been married to what's his name, did you see his face? I thought he was going to self destruct on the spot."

Graham shook her hand looking into her face

"Thank you, Mrs Macken that was a fairly entertaining meeting."

Susan returned the handshake. For a moment the freshness and vitality in his grasp took her by surprise in a pleasant way.

"Susan," she said I hate all that Mrs Macken stuff.

"What?" Still holding her hand.

"Susan, call me Susan."

"Of course Mrs Macken, yes, ok then Susan, Thank you."

He looked down at the painting. "I understand your reluctance to leave it with the gallery, Des can be a bit patronising. But it could be worth a lot of money and it should really be somewhere safe."

"I'm sure you're right," Susan flicked back a wayward strand of hair as she spoke. "What can happen to it? Who knows of its existence? Sure we only found out its potential today. Maybe a gang of international art thieves led by Ann Fitzroy and Declan Traynor is going to break in and steal it." She joked.

Noting Graham's concern she decided to reassure him. "I promise to do the most sensible thing when Paul comes back. I'm sure it will be perfectly safe at the house for a day or two, we have a very good alarm system."

"Of course, well I look forward to our next meeting, Susan," the young man smiled. "May I suggest you contact the National Gallery and ask them to take the painting into safe keeping, they have all the security required and I'm sure they would be pleased to do so." Susan, in the process of releasing the elastic stretchers paused and glanced at Graham.

"Thanks I'll take your advice" she smiled, "I'll ring Ann at the National tomorrow."

"Perhaps it would be just as well if you didn't mention my suggestion to Mr Sheridan," Graham confided with a

96

smile as he helped stow the work of art onto the back seat of the Golf before heading up the street and back to the gallery.

Susan, observing the youthful stride as he departed allowed herself a gentle wolf whistle before getting behind the wheel and pulling out into the busy city traffic.

The fact that the painting was not likely to be a Turner original did not worry Susan as she headed for home, she was happy that the experts all agreed that it was a painting of great quality. They could have dismissed it completely, she thought. Instead they were talking about Sotheby's and the Tate. If only they could get good news on the handwriting now that could change things.

Well that's up to the redoubtable Kathryn the Great and her reaction to the evidence when Paul meets her.

Well anyway, she thought as she keyed in his mobile number he can't get up to much mischief in the few hours he'll be in London. His flight home is at 6.15.

The perfectly tailored white cuff flashed exposing the large gaudy gold Rolex watch. "Is this all you've got?" his voice was truculent as he tapped the page with a bejewelled index finger and fired an intimidating glare in her direction.

"That's all" came the calm response.

"Key elements, aged 57, well educated, some form, petty fraud, divorced relatively recently, four children, one from the first marriage a female aged 24, exited prison, good behaviour, fairly lacking in any noteworthy achievements."

The grey head of the Dragon bent over the page, eyes scanning, brow furrowed absorbing the information. "What's this, a stand up comedian?"

"Yes," with a smile Audrey acquiesced. "He has from time to time performed humour, - the Comedy Store in Dublin and that sort of thing."

"Blimey! A bloody comedian wants to sell me a priceless Turner. I must be going mad," The Dragon exclaimed with a mirthless smile, his assumed air of sophistication honed to perfection over the years, forgotten momentarily.

"He's waiting in the reception,"

"Give me 15 minutes and then wheel him in."

Audrey left quietly closing the wood panelled door.

The Dragon, a formidable entrepreneur and one of the richest men in the world sat back in the big leather chair, allowing himself a small smile. Incapable of a genuine version full of generosity and mirth, the Dragon's smile at best resembled a leer. This was due to his facial structure rather than his ability to be amused.

The dragon scrutinised the single page of information headed

TIMOTHY ANDREW HOLMES.

Audrey Langton PA and staunch associate for over thirty years stood back and awaited a response from the man sitting behind the big desk.

Those close to the man could relate occasions of mirth and genuine humour. He generally did not find a great deal to smile about being of a serious disposition. Low in stature without the benefit of a handsome visage he wallowed in the power allowed to one with a huge fortune in money.

When the Dragon first encountered Turner's famous painting of the Fighting Temeraire being towed to its final resting place after a major role in the battle of Trafalgar, the picture sparked the beginnings of an obsession, a fascination appealing to the man's sense of patriotism initially and later, as his knowledge grew, to an affinity with the artist.

The more he learned of the great Turner and his work, particularly in descriptions of Turner physically, he could see himself, an ugly garrulous, rotund, little man with a big nose and a great fortune. The Dragon's giant ego allowed him to assume that he had become one of the foremost experts on JMW Turner having studied the great artist and his life collecting where he could. Yes, if this Dragon could admit to a weakness it would be his weakness for the greatest artist that ever lived, JMW Turner.

That morning the Dragon had opened his emails little expecting to come across such a spectacular discovery. The name had caught his attention first and then incredibly the painting.

Familiar with all Turners works, intimately aware of how he used colour and form; to see these familiar skills displayed in a picture he had never witnessed before stopped the Dragon in his tracks. Shocked by the impact and the magnitude of the discovery he could only stare in amazed incredulity. Eventually, having studied every minute detail of the picture he finished reading the email, which outlined exactly how he might gain possession of the masterpiece.

Not for a moment questioning his own ability to identify the painting as Turner's, convinced he was looking at a masterpiece which would end up in his possession and blissfully ignoring the fact that so many people had tried to emulate the master, he set the wheels in motion to achieve the ambition of a lifetime, ownership of an until now undiscovered work by Turner.

The Dragon seldom failed to exploit an opportunity generally manipulating circumstances to his own advantage. Never outside the law he sometimes precariously skirted its edges to achieve an objective.

Deal- Hovellers going out to a wreck. The now familiar image of the painting swam into view on the desktop computer.

Not a gambling man, that was for morons. He reassessed the evidence, captured again by the power of the painting. No doubts, it's Turner he concluded.

The palms of his hands beginning to itch, his heart raced up a notch in anticipation of the confrontation, the deal, the winning. Very few powers on earth could stop him.

One of the richest and most powerful men in the world touched the computer screen on his desk.

"Wheel the little blighter in," he said.

Audrey Langton looked grimly across the expanse of carpet at Tim Holmes, lazing back, stubby legs in creased trousers stretched out in front of him under the glass coffee table, his air of casual indifference betrayed by the sheen of perspiration on his brow. From where she was sitting Audrey could detect his discomfort.

"You may go in now, please knock before you enter."

Tim Holmes, ever the comedian swivelled his head from one side to the other as if someone else had been addressed then pointed to himself, "Moi?" he enquired.

The deep cushioned lounge settee posed some difficulty for him as he struggled and bounced into an upright position.

Standing up he tucked in a wayward shirt tail and strode across the carpet with an imperious, "Thank you Miss Moneypenny," knocked on the dark wood panelled door and without waiting for an answer entered the Dragons Den.

Total silence struck Tim Holmes as the heavy door swung closed behind him. Silence like he had never heard before or never hadn't heard before. The deep, deep pile of the carpet, the dark lush leather button-back furniture, the subdued lighting, eyes adjusting to the darkened room he began to find his bearings.

"Take a seat,"

Soft, gravelly commanding, the invitation came from somewhere to his left.

Tim turned to look in the direction of the voice and came face to face with the dragon. It's him, him from the telly, all Tim's rehearsed tactics, plans, words fled from his mind as he sank into the huge deeply cushioned high backed armchair, his toes just able to reach the pile of the luxurious carpet as he sank deeper.

The Dragon's penetrating gaze coldly surveyed the comedic figure sitting in front of him. It seemed like an age to Tim Holmes. He did everything to avoid those cold grey eyes. Surveying the room, he pressed his lips together, made a tent from his fingers, and examined his fingernails. Somehow his glance inevitably slipped back to the Dragon who remained unmoving, a silent staring predator reading his every thought. No funny stuff here, eye of the tiger is right thought Tim uneasily.

Though the Dragon's face was quite familiar to him none of the media resources, TV or high definition, could have prepared him for the impact of that stare and the prolonged silence.

"Tell me Mr Holmes why I should do business with you." The voice when he eventually spoke was surprisingly soft without the aggression Tim expected.

Tim's eyes flew back to the source of the soft tones. He felt nervous and ill at ease, knowing that any attempt at trickery would be detected. He tried to remember his plan but for once his normal filibustering confidence had deserted him.

Abandoning all his personal rules of negotiation, never show all your cards, keep your trump until the last, put your brain into gear before opening your mouth, the nervous con man blew the lot.

"I know the guy who owns the painting,

I know where he will be tomorrow morning,

I can stop him going to the Tate,

I know all about him. My ex-wife works for him in Dublin.

The right money offered at this time will clinch it, but we have to move fast.

The more confident he gets the higher the price." The words tumbled out.

He abruptly stopped speaking and looked at the Dragon expectantly.

Nothing, he examined the face for some kind of reaction. Was that a flicker of contempt?

"Good Bye, Mr Holmes."

The expression on the face had not changed and the words were spoken softly.

"I have an American contact in New York you know"...... Tim's voice trailed off. The Dragon appeared to no longer be aware of his presence.

"Mr Holmes, please," Audrey Langton was standing silhouetted in an open doorway at the other end of the room.

"This way if you don't mind," she beckoned.

If the chair in the reception area had proved difficult to negotiate the present one was a nightmare, but Tim eventually managed to extricate himself leaving a fair amount of his pride behind as he obediently and dutifully did as he was bid.

"The back door for me, Elvis has left the building."

He walked through the door expecting to be greeted by a fire exit or stairs. Instead he found himself in a very pleasant room, conservative and a bit old-fashioned. He looked around half expecting to see a cat curled up before a fireplace.

"Please take a seat Mr Holmes."

Audrey Langton PA to one of the richest men in Britain preceding him into the room sat down behind the antique oak desk and gestured to a vacant chair.

I'm still in the game thought Tim.

"They called him George. Bring on the dragon," he said quietly to himself, taking the offered seat. Once again he looked across a desk. A very similar set of eyes to the Dragon's looked back. But did he detect a slight smile?

Audrey Langton opened a folder in front of her and removed a sheet of paper. She looked across at Tim. This little con man is in control of a possible fortune. If only he knew.

She looked down at the sheet of paper that the Dragon had dictated earlier. "Mm... Perhaps he is being a bit generous, she thought, most unlike the Dragon to act in this manner, in fact very much out of character. But then her boss very seldom made mistakes when it came to the money game.

"I am authorised to offer €123,000 for the unauthenticated "Turner." The original must be viewed before the money is exchanged.

You, Mr Holmes will receive €12,000 for your services. This is not negotiable Mr Holmes. The fee will be paid in cash at completion of the deal. The money will be paid directly in receipt of the painting. Should the painting prove in time to be a Turner the seller will receive an additional €100,000. You Mr Holmes must bring the seller to us and we will conduct the final negotiations. As you know the person you are dealing with is a public figure, his word is his bond and the price is a fair one. You will come to this office and be paid in cash. You have exactly 4 days to deliver. If it comes to our attention that you are negotiating with another party there is no deal and we will step away. Do you understand and do you accept the conditions?"

Tim, a wheeler-dealer by nature had expected a more prolonged negotiation. He looked across the desk at "the Dragon's Dragon". Her face betrayed no assistance. Tim was not particularly sure of the actual value of the painting. He did know that it would be some time before the painting was declared a "Valuable Turner" or a relatively worthless copy.

She continued, "It is felt, taking all things into consideration, the painting not being a proven Turner, it is a fair offer."

Audrey Langton expected the little fat man to accept.

Tim felt it was a good start. I may have some room for manoeuvre at the other end of the deal and twelve grand is not bad for starters, he thought to himself. Who knows, binga bam binga boom, I might scoop the whole pot in the end.

Standing up, he proffered a chubby hand "You're a princess, smile you're on candid camera, it's a deal."

Looking out the fifth storey window a panoramic view across London also had a view of the car park. The Dragon and his PA watched the diminutive figure leave the building and saunter across the tarmac.

A few minutes later they observed Tim Holmes drive away in a tired looking Coupe. "Whatever plan our little fraudster had in mind he never got it off the ground and by the way, you owe me a fiver." The Dragon held out his hand.

"I got the car right."

Tim Holmes drove from the car park his mind racing, his great plan to wrest huge money from the Dragon in tatters.

Driving straight to the car dealer he surrendered the coupe handing over the keys to the salesman. "Thanks but no thanks, she doesn't suit my super star image. I reckon I'll stick with my Lexus."

On the subway heading for central London he resolved to meet up with Paul Macken and make him an offer on behalf of the Dragon. After all twelve grand is twelve grand. Better than "a slap on the belly with a wet fish" as me ould granny used to say and some of his plan was still in place, he consoled himself.

Go with the plan Tim, see how the cookie crumbles, eye of the tiger de dum de dum.

Neither The Dragon, his P A, nor Tim Holmes noticed the very tall powerfully built man who watched Tim's every move as he left the car park. They did not notice him as he slipped behind the wheel of the high-powered saloon and address the man in the passenger seat beside him who responded in a thick foreign accent.

The Very Tall Man spoke quickly and with an aggressive tone.

"In Prague I would not expect you to follow my instructions but in London you have no option."

He set the big car in motion and followed in the direction Tim Holmes had taken. The inability of the car to accommodate his large frame was not the cause of the

Very Tall Man's irritation. It was the foreign bloke in the passenger seat. This one smelled of garlic and stale cigarette smoke, he sniffed frequently and was inclined to make a noise at the back of his throat. The Tall man retrieved a small packet of tissues from his pocket, a purchase at the corner shop opposite to the Dragon's building.

"Here," He held up the pack.

Surprised, the smaller man nodded his gratitude and fumbled to extricate a tissue. "Take the pack I bought them for you."

"Danka" the pack looked bigger in the slimmer, smaller browner hand. The big Man noted the group of warts clustered around the knuckle close to a gaudy gold ring with a dull looking gemstone. He sighed. The foreigner blew his nose and settled back into his seat. One minute later he sniffed and made the throat noise.

The big car passed the Car Sales sign and pulled in about fifty yards from the entrance. The big head stooped slightly lower and steady eyes watched the rear-view mirror checking the comedian's emergence and where he might be headed. The foreign bloke sniffed again.

At Dublin's airport amid hundreds of holidaymakers Paul stood in front of the touch screen of the automatic self - check in. Not inclined to queue, the automatic service accorded Paul quick access to the departure lounge and the Aer Lingus flight to London.

This was a very familiar activity for a successful executive in the ad business. Take the red eye, the earliest morning flight, get into London in time for a 9.30 meeting, possibly a working lunch and then the 4.30 flight home, absolutely essential for business but not a very enjoyable day, and of course, a complete waste of London.

Today would not be like other days. He would arrive in London and immediately contact Kathryn Thorndike.

His mind did contented cartwheels at the prospect. He smiled to himself. They would talk about the "Turner" have a nice leisurely lunch, perhaps a glass of wine.

I wonder does she like a glass of wine? He speculated, the Tate in the afternoon, maybe back to the Regent Palace, a walk in the Green Park, exchange thoughts, ideas, get to know each other, a bit of romance, evening meal, theatre. Becoming lost in the fantasy her face swam close up to his, he closed his eyes and imagined what it would be like to hold her.

"It's very simple sir just start by touching the screen,"

Kathryn's exotic image evaporated to be replaced by a pleasant looking woman wearing a cap. Paul, his eyes coming back into focus for a moment was confused.

The Airport attendant whose job was to assist those appearing to be confused by the relatively new check in system continued to explain.

"You need your printout from the online booking, Sir."

He didn't respond immediately.

"Are you alright, Sir?"

Paul, perplexed, distracted, reality merging with his fantasy, lifted his hand to his forehead

"Fine, fine thank you. You're very kind I'm alright."

He reached inside his jacket and producing the document proceeded to efficiently check in and select his seat aware of the close scrutiny from the attendant who had been watching him for some time, her curiosity aroused by his immobility in front of the machine and the fact that his eyes were closed, very odd behaviour for what seemed to be a businessman on the move.

"Could you please help me with this goddamned machine!" the exasperated American woman with the blue hair, at a nearby machine, called to the attendant saving Paul from any further close scrutiny.

He hastily removed his boarding card from the machine and heading for the departure area and gate A22 speculated on the incident. Security had become such an issue these days it was not a good idea to attract any kind of negative attention.

The attendant now fully occupied with the aggressive American woman appeared to have lost interest in him.

Having negotiated the security procedure he was threading his belt around his waist and replacing his shoes, just about to put on his jacket, he noticed the very zealous attendant walking by with some other officials.

Out of the corner of his eye he watched their progress as they chatted appearing quite casual, but had he noticed a glance or two in his direction? Paul's paranoia had clicked in. He quickly retrieved his small bag and after checking his pockets to make sure he was not leaving anything behind casually left the security area and walking into the Duty Free began to examine wine labels he had no intention of buying, a slight sheen of perspiration disturbing his brow.

The group of officials now out of sight he began to relax. Get a grip Paul, what are you thinking?

"You are mildly paranoid." He recalled the words of the specialist at the clinic on his final meeting some years previously. At the time he had dismissed the idea as indeed he had dismissed everything the young guy had said, including that poppycock about him having some sort of condition to do with getting older and not accepting the fact.

Well, he reassured himself, being mildly paranoid is good it gives me an edge. Because I'm mildly paranoid I'm always on the watch out for pit falls and problems. I see the problem quicker than the average person, that's probably why I'm successful in business. Knowing that I'm mildly paranoid is the trick. If I know that I'm *mildly* paranoid I won't get paranoid about it.

By the time Paul had reached the departure gate A22 he had convinced himself that his paranoia was a great benefit and an advantage in life.

Half an hour to take off he sat along with the other travellers in the departure, area. "Departure to London now boarding," the flight number was announced. Paul stood up and joined the queue moving towards the desk.

The cap caught his eye and then the calm ordinary looking face, the over zealous attendant he had met earlier was standing at the gate checking the boarding cards.

I'm mildly paranoid he reassured himself giving her a smile. The fact that she was twenty feet away and totally unaware, concentrating on the other passengers as she checked their boarding passes completely eluded him.

Take the card, tear off the stub, look up, and smile, the attendant preoccupied with getting everyone on board became distracted by a man who as he approached seemed quite agitated.

On nearing the desk he seemed ill at ease smiling broadly and rather unnaturally, at first she thought perhaps he might be an acquaintance then she remembered the man at the automatic check in.

Taking the card from him she looked at the name,

"Everything alright now Mr Macken?"

She smiled tore along the perforation and handed him the stub.

Paul unnecessarily considering he had had a near escape took the card with a mumbled, "Yes thanks," and hurried through the boarding gate congratulating himself on his handling of the tricky situation.

Today Paul Macken, successful advertising man with charm, brains and good looks, money in his pocket and the world at his feet was single and free. He looked around at his fellow passengers, mostly businessmen off to London for the day, poor sods.

Two rows up the aisle on the opposite side sat an acquaintance, Jerry Long, younger than Paul, manufacturer hardware products, hard pressed. *You'll never sell your stuff in London, stop manufacturing and start buying off the Chinese. They'll sell it to you cheaper than you can make it.* Paul knew them all and their stresses and strains.

Jerry Long had just secured his seatbelt over his ample midriff and was in the process of retrieving a carefully folded white handkerchief from the top pocket of his jacket when he received a tap on his shoulder. Mopping the beads of perspiration on his furrowed brow, he turned handkerchief poised, to be greeted by a rolled up Irish Times and the smiling face of Paul Macken someone he knew vaguely.

"Hi 'ya Jerry, good to see you, usual business thing I suppose?"

Jerry Long who was in no mood for an over the shoulder chat answered briefly with a half smile and a nod.

"Ok, and you?" Turning away to resume wiping his brow.

"Well not exactly," came the persistent voice from behind.

"I'm off to London alright but not on business more should I say to do the business."

Jerry turned round just in time to catch Paul smiling and tapping the side of his nose followed by a knowing look and a wink.

To Jerry Long who knew Paul Macken by his reputation more than from personal contact, this behaviour seemed out of character. He had met Paul at various functions particularly to do with the Marketing Institute, where he had often addressed the gathering on major issues. Jerry had found him to be particularly astute and quite impressive.

"Oh yes." He responded with an unenthusiastic half smile, considering the possibility that Paul Macken must be a nervous traveller.

They're all losers Paul summed up looking around at his fellow passengers.

"Get a life," he wanted to shout out, "Enjoy yourselves, life's too short smile for god's sake."

The hostess moving down the aisle from seat to seat appeared to give him a special smile. He also imagined she leaned a little closer to him than was necessary as she checked to make sure all seat belts were fastened and seat backs in the upright position in preparation for take off.

His stewardess was now going through the safety demonstration. Transfixed by her every movement Paul watched as if she were performing an erotic dance just for him as she leaned forward to secure the safety vest behind her back and then demonstrated the inflating valve. Definitely she made eye-to-eye contact and gave him a little smile.

Resolving to make the best of this time to himself, knowing that his thoughts would not be interrupted for the next 45 minutes, the duration of the flight, he closed his eyes and relaxed intentionally letting his mind wander making room for images of Kathryn Thorndike.

I wonder what Susan is doing now? I should be with her for the Turner meeting.

The thought popped into his consciousness. There it was, taking him by surprise driving all elaborate fantasies from his mind. His eyes flew open. He looked around, closed his eyes again struggling to recapture the feeling of elation that now seemed determined to avoid him.

At last he managed to force the thought away replacing it with the purpose for his sudden headlong visit to London, Katherine Thorndike.

Conjuring up her image, the smooth voice, the astute mind, the independent confidence, her look, all were triggers feeding Paul's fantasy. Letting his imagination take over he could feel the urgent obsession, a compelling force. It eliminated caution rendering him exposed to reckless action.

In spite of this, thoughts of Susan persisted. She had spelled it out for him in no uncertain terms. He could see her face strong, beautiful. She had not changed over the years. She was still the remarkable woman he had married and of course he knew how much his family loved him. I'm a lucky man... the thoughts persisted... so what's the harm? A little flirtation, nobody gets hurt.

The fantasy image flooded his mind and he let it happen. As the powerful plane surged away from the tarmac he felt free. He was a young single man again, carefree and alone. The mirror told him this morning that he still had it, the looks now even better. Paul believed his own propaganda, an advertising man who could sell himself anything.

As soon as the wheels touched the tarmac Paul reached for his phone. They taxied towards terminal one at Heathrow. As the plane came to a standstill he activated Katherine Thorndike's number and headed down the aisle. Oblivious to the other passengers, he pushed past Jerry Long and the other businessmen preoccupied with their own plans for the day and did not take kindly to being jostled. Paul blundered on.

The dial tone was sporadic, intermittent. He could hear her answering but could not make out the words

"How are you?" he said. "I'm in London...."

Paul made his way along the plane, one finger in his ear, elbow held high making contact with the back of some clean cut heads as he made his way to the exit door.

"Sorry, yes I am in London," he repeated, "what did you say?"

He could make out the now familiar tones, it sounded nice to his ear, he still couldn't make out what she said but to Paul it sounded very inviting,

"I'll ring you when I get to the terminal," he said

The open door of the aircraft presented itself.

"Thank you for travelling Aer Lingus, have a nice day sir."

Oblivious, Paul launched himself through the door and down the steps moving quickly. He practically ran through the baggage area and into arrivals terminal.

About to ring Kathryn again he saw the little fat guy with the sign.

MR PAUL MACKEN it said in big letters.

Slowing down he put his phone back into his pocket and approached the man curiously, "I'm Paul Macken."

The little guy who had been looking past him started, looked him in the face and said with mock seriousness.

"Are you sure?" Then, "I'm only kidding I *am* here to meet you."

"Miss Thorndike must have sent you, very nice thank you." Paul assumed.

The small fat man with the jovial face indicated the way and strode ahead without looking back, through the entrance and down the stairs towards the subway. Moving quickly, he descended the escalator, Paul hurriedly followed. On the platform amidst the hurly burly of people and trains coming and going the fat man turned and handing Paul a ticket pushed him towards the stile.

"Wait, wait this doesn't seem right," Paul stopped, "Who are you?"

Hands palm upwards gesticulating,

"Danny De Vito, Miss Thorndike's lost cousin, the Shah of Iran, it don't matter who I am. Look, Turner, Thorndike, take all the T's. I'm here to make a deal. Just follow me please, Mr Macken."

Without waiting for a response he headed through the stile and onto the platform, looking back as he quickened his pace.

"Here comes our train, the blue line, Chelsea and the heart of town."

Stopping, arm out, palm upwards with an exaggerated bow he indicated for Paul to "BOARD PLEASE" as the train came to a stop and the doors opened.

The fast-talking, amusing character had mentioned a deal, he had also said the Thorndike word. Hesitating for only a moment Paul boarded the train, found a seat and sat down. His rotund companion quickly following sat beside him.

The Tall Man stood on the platform and watched the unlikely duo board the train together. His huge hand dwarfed the slim mobile phone. "Viking," he stated before quietly barking instructions that were repeated word for word by the quiet voiced recipient. Satisfied, he contacted another number on the international exchange only having to wait a short while before an accented voice answered. This time the Tall Man spoke in a quieter less commanding tone.

As he took his seat in the crowded carriage Paul reached for his phone to ring Kathryn Thorndike. A chubby hand grasped his wrist in a surprising strong grip.

"Don't ring anyone. I am about to offer you a very substantial sum of money for an unproven Turner."

Astonished, Paul looked into the very serious face. All the humour had disappeared.

"I assure you Mr Macken in all earnestness, listen to what I have to say and you will arrive in Piccadilly a very rich man."

Paul looked at the man sitting beside him,

"What are you saying?"

"I am saying that I have a buyer for your "Turner" whether it is a Turner or not Mr Macken, now, this minute, big dinero."

"How do you know about the Turner and who are you?"

"Timothy Montague Holmes at your service, Mr Macken. I believe you are acquainted with my beautiful and talented ex-wife Shelley."

"You are Shelley Holmes husband?" Paul took another look at the fat man.

"You're a bloody fraudster." He laughed in the little man's face shaking his head in disbelief. "I've heard about you Mr Holmes. No deal, thank you."

Just then Paul's mobile rang. He retrieved it from his pocket.

"Hello Mr Macken this is Kathryn Thorndike."

Turning his shoulder to the little man he spoke into the phone.

"Hello Kathryn I'm sorry for not getting back sooner. What are your plans for the day?"

"Tomorrow Mr Macken, if it suits you I would very much like to accompany you to the Tate." The smooth voice interrupted him, efficient and crisp, Paul Macken detected an inference of sensuality.

"Mr Macken I will be having lunch at the Tate Restaurant at 2 o'clock should you care to join me. By then I will have had time to view the Turners and see the original sketchbooks and samples of Turners handwriting. Have you brought a high resolution sample of the wording for me to compare?"

"Yes, Yes I have it here,"

"2 o'clock then Paul, at the Tate Main Entrance Coffee Shop. I look forward to seeing you, bye for now."

Before he could say anything more the phone went dead. The fact that she had used his first name struck Paul to the exclusion of all else, definitely she had said, I look forward to seeing you, Paul.

Elated he felt like doing a lap of honour in the carriage.

"Nice one," he mouthed, making a fist and replacing the mobile in his pocket.

"Good news?" queried the fat man.

Paul turned with a look of distain.

"Are you still here? Hop it." He said.

"Big dinero Mr Macken," Tim stood up hitching up his waistband.

"€150,000 for your painting,"

He rocked back on his heels hands out, palms upward, shoulders hunched.

"It ain't exactly nuffin' to be sniffed at. I have a Dragon on board, the money isn't mine, only a small commission, but if you aren't interested go ahead meet your calligraphy expert, but don't think about it too long. I'm told the offer expires at midnight, two days. This pumpkin here turns into a prince. See you later Cinderella."

He placed a card with a number on it into Paul's hand. "€150,000 big ones, enjoy your picnic with Goldilocks at the Tate a Tate, Tate."

The Train came to a stop, the fat man swivelled and mingling with the other commuters disappeared from view.

Paul glanced at the card, cheap and nasty, one of the print-yourself ones. About to throw it away he changed his mind. The 150,000 big ones had registered and he had to admit to being amused by the Fat man's performance.

"She called me Paul," the thought drove the little fraudster and his crazy offer from his mind.

He looked at the Stations display on the opposite side of the carriage. Two stops and then Piccadilly Circus, he noted. Pity I have to wait until tomorrow to see her but it makes sense he reasoned. She's a pro, she needs to get prepared for the meeting.

Catching his reflection in the glass of the window below the underground map he adjusted his tie and lightly palmed his hair smoothing the grey bits at the temples.

The reflection, without the benefit of backlighting and also being slightly blurred, disguised the obvious thinning of what used to be an impressive mop. Paul, however, was satisfied with the image.

His slim document case on the seat beside him drew his attention. Apart from a toothbrush this was his sole baggage. In the case were the various high-resolution images Katherine had requested carefully copied and professionally reproduced.

The prospect of lunch at the Tate with Kathryn followed by furthering his quest to prove the "Turner" filled his mind, replacing any thought of the slightly amusing and somehow irritating fat man.

The train sped on its way rocking slightly on the rails, suddenly into daylight then back underground to be in Piccadilly Circus in the next few minutes.

"How did the little fella know so much?" Of course, Shelley had arranged the tickets and made all the arrangements. She had even advised him about Kathryn Thorndike. The same Kathryn Thorndike who had been instrumental in Tim Holmes, Shelly's ex husband's downfall.

The guy's a crook. She must have contacted her ex very soon after their conversation.

Settling back into his seat he let his mind drift away from fat men and onto more pleasant things. The prospect of meeting the owner of the delicious voice, the hotel booked.

What had she said when they'd spoken the previous day? I look forward to meeting you in London Paul, not Mr Macken, Paul, definitely there was an invitation in her tone he assured himself and now she had used it again. Professional women like Kathryn don't haphazardly use Christian names so early in a business relationship.

Tomorrow at two o'clock seemed a long way away. He couldn't wait to meet the owner of the voice. The fat man's business card was still in his hand. He turned it over *She'll eat you for breakfast* was written on the other side.

Obviously our mystery man doesn't like the lady, Paul thought, he seemed serious enough about the money, €150,000. What's all, this dragon stuff? What a load of rubbish!

He did not, however throw away the card, instead he placed it in his wallet. He had a feeling that he might very well see the fat man again.

The train pulled into Piccadilly station. He joined the commuters ascending the escalator. How I love London, he thought emerging from the underground station into the hustle and bustle of Piccadilly Circus leaving Eros to his right and making a beeline for the Regent Palace Hotel situated on the corner at the beginning of Soho. He looked up at the sky; fleecy clouds scudded by driven by a fresh breeze. Well-heeled commuters streamed each side of him as he took in the familiar sights, the centre of the world.

Feeling good, free, young, excited, and full of life, with a light step he headed for the familiar entrance to the relatively prestigious Regent's Palace Hotel.

The reception clerk greeted him with a courteous "Sir," from his position behind the rather old-fashioned reception desk.

"Welcome to the Regent Palace,"

Prompted by sight of Paul's credentials

"I see you are booked for three nights, Sir, Do you need assistance with your bags, perhaps?"

As Paul pocketed his room card he retrieved a toothbrush from his inside pocket and showed it to the not so pleased clerk,

"I don't think so. No I can manage," with a smile he looked over the top of his toothbrush at the desk clerk laughing at the incongruous flexible handle.

"I'm travelling light,"

With a, the customer's always right expression the clerk turned away. I'll have to buy some shirts and underclothes and something to put them in Paul thought to himself. Things are moving real fast, I've been offered €150,000 for the painting by a fat man who sees himself as Rocky Bilbao, I'm about to meet a very intriguing woman who from what my instincts tell me is available.

The familiar surroundings, the check in procedure prompted memories of times past when he and Susan had frequented the Regent Palace on a regular basis.

Taking him totally by surprise Susan's beautiful face suddenly invaded his good mood. They had stayed at the Regent so many times together. He glanced back at the entrance half expecting her to appear at the door looking as gorgeous and cool as ever. The room key, number 204, their usual room, Shelly must have requested it.

"Excuse me I would like a different room please,"

The clerk who was now attending to another guest turned, the professional smile slightly askew.

"I want another room please,"

Paul repeated with a slight impatience handing the card back to the clerk,

"Of course Sir," turning to a young colleague,

"could you please organise another room for Mr Macken."

The young girl in the white blouse and black pencil skirt lifted her head and looked straight at Paul. For a moment his mind did a spin. She fancies me he thought in a flash as she smiled at him.

"Yes Mr Macken, have you got anywhere special in mind?" The simple question to him appeared loaded with innuendo.

About to respond with a glib, "Your place or mine?" The foolishness of the words occurred to him just in time. Looking again at the expectant face this time he could only detect the demeanour of a rather friendly young woman just doing her job.

"Nowhere in particular, thank you, just a different room."

Having negotiated the room change he pocketed the key and headed for the door and Regent Street aware that his state of mind was precarious, aware that he was susceptible to misinterpreting even the slightest glance or word from a female, he would have to be on his guard.

Walking along Regent Street amidst the commuters and shoppers his resolve began to weaken as he caught the eye of girl after girl. They all seemed to be aware of him, he felt like a superstar.

The next move must be to get some clothes. He had only brought his document case with the better quality "Turner" pictures that Kathryn had requested.

After all as far as Susan was concerned he would be home this evening. It would not have been very clever had he packed an overnight bag.

Having acted on such a selfish impulse, doubts began to creep in. His feeling of high elation was becoming eroded by a quiet nagging feeling of guilt.

Catching sight of himself in a shop window as he strode amongst the well heeled shoppers, with the sun shining on a crisp autumn day at the heart of a great city, his feelings of guilt began to dissipate as he headed on his quest to purchase a couple of shirts and some underclothes.

He visited Hamleys famous toy store first to get some presents for his beloved grandchildren and flirted with the attractive shop assistant who received his attentions with a big smile. His mood was ever improving as he made his leisurely way back to the Hotel to have a shower and a change of clothing.

His mobile rang.

It was Susan. Paul still on a high from his imaginary success with the shop assistant was taken off guard. He had intended to ring Susan later with a really convincing alibi for staying overnight in London.

"Hello Paul, they didn't say it's not a Turner." Susan sitting in her car could not wait to tell him about the expert's reaction.

"They think there's a possibility."

She described her meeting at Sheridan's briefly.

"I knew it, I knew it," all else fleeing from Paul's mind.

"Wow! This is terrific. Look I'm really sorry I couldn't go to the meeting. Were they really impressed? Did they give any idea of its value?"

"It's early days yet, Paul. They think there's a possibility it could be a Turner but the real experts on Turner are at the Tate in London and they will have the final say. It's just as well you are over there though. Proving that it's Turners handwriting is really important. I'll fill you in on all the details this evening when you get home. What time is your meeting with the glorious Kathryn Thorndike?"

"Well that's the thing, Susan, I'm staying overnight. Mmm…. I met Peter Stevenson at Heathrow, you know Pete, and you met his wife last year when they were over for the ICAD awards. Well, he's set up a meeting for tomorrow and asked me would I go to it. You know, he's quite important to us. I didn't like to refuse…."

There was silence from the other end of the phone.

Susan, was already suspicious, that voice the quick words tumbling out. She remembered back to the last time.... she knew, Paul like a lapsed alcoholic… was up to his old tricks.

She was about to quiz him on the content of the meeting, put him on the spot and expose the lie but changed her mind.

"You can go to hell you little shit!"

She exclaimed, in a deadly quiet voice and cut him off.

Susan, if she could have seen her husband at that moment might very well have changed what she planned to do about Paul and his current foolishness.

She was pretty sure that his carry on was all bluff, he had never been unfaithful not even the last time. It was all about reassurance, a kind of male menopause, proving he still had it, none the less it was hurtful, supposing this Thorndike woman actually was attracted to him, what then. Either way she felt sick in her stomach. An end would have to be put to his antics.

Paul stopped in his tracks and looked at the dead phone in his hand. He knew Susan's strength and he had heard that tone on various occasions during their 30 years of marriage but never directed at him. Quite shocked at her deadly reaction he immediately rang back but she had turned off the phone.

Why did I make up that stupid story about a meeting with Pete Stevenson? He reproached himself, just because I saw him at the airport and the idea popped into my mind, it was so unnecessary. All I had to say was, Kathryn Thorndike is not available until tomorrow so I've decided to stay overnight.

"Hello anybody home?" The front door was slightly ajar and Susan's car was in the driveway. Jane Macken pushed the door open and headed through the hall towards the back of the house.

About to call out again, she saw her mother sitting alone in the garden. Her face was turned away but to Jane it was obvious that something was amiss.

"Mum, are you alright?" She called quietly.

Susan stood up and turned to face her daughter. It was obvious that she had been crying. Jane could not recall the last time she had seen this strong resolute woman shed a tear.

"What's the matter Mum? Are you alright?"

She watched the determined chin set and then the smile was there on the beautiful face. "How great to see you, I had forgotten that you were coming. Is Simon with you?"

The moment had passed, whatever had upset her mother may be revealed in time, obviously now was not the time.

"My is that the time she said looking at her watch, I was sitting in the garden and lost track. Are you staying for dinner? I'll book the Copper Kettle for an Early Bird." Susan now completely restored to her usual self became the organiser

"I'll make a cup of tea,"

"Where's Dad?" Jane enquired as the two women headed back into the house.

"I thought he might be here."

"He won't be here until tomorrow, something to do with a meeting in London." Susan had hesitated for a moment before replying

Jane detecting the slight hesitation decided to ignore it. It was obvious her mum felt a bit stressed.

"How did things go with the picture? You were going to the gallery today."

"Wait 'till you hear," Susan poured some tea for her daughter and pushed a packet of ginger nut biscuits towards her. They were sitting at the kitchen table. Jane always loved these alone times with just herself and Susan.

"Well, go on, what did they say?" Jane leaned forward as she dunked a ginger nut.

"They haven't said it's not a "Turner," Susan smiled

"Can you imagine that we have a picture that could be worth millions of euro. Of course it's only a start, it's just a possibility, we'll have to go to London with it. All kinds of experts will have their say."

"Your Dad is over there at the moment seeing someone about the handwriting. I was thinking I might fly over tonight. There are plenty of evening flights to London."

The thought had suddenly popped into Susan's head. Go to London, if he is up to something I could catch him in the act. Better than sitting here like a good girl waiting for my lord and master to return. He could do with a good shaking up. Yes, that would shake him up all right. Better to have things out in the open and not left to fester and become major problems. I'll go to London. I might even meet the famous Kathryn.

"Mum, mum, hello, hello!" Jane waved a soggy ginger nut in her Mother's direction. Susan's eyes caught the sparkle of the large diamond engagement ring on her daughter's finger. Looking past the ring she was more dazzled by the huge smile of joy on her daughters face. For the second time that day Jane saw tears in her mother's eyes.

"So that's your news." Susan dabbed her eyes, "tell me everything."

"Simon and I have bought a house and we hope to get married before Christmas." She held up her left hand with a flourish, gleefully and proudly displaying the ring.

"I'm so happy for you, for me, for us all," Susan held Jane at arms length and looked into her shining eyes. "Will I have to be the teenager's grandmother? How will you cope? What do you know about bringing up a family? Those teenagers are monsters, they don't even like me."

Jane laughed, "You really are incorrigible mum, they're great young lads. Wait till you get to know them."

"But…." said Susan with an incredulous laugh,

"I knocked the big one, what's his name into the flower bed? Oh my! This is terrible. Did Simon say anything?"

"He thought it was quite funny Mum."

"I knew you were looking at houses but I wasn't aware you were near buying. Where is it?" She searched Jane's face, the mother, anxious for her daughter's welfare.

"Not the one on the Clontarf road?"

"Yes," Jane nodded vigorously and quickly added.

"We got a good reduction on the price. I know it's a lot of money and we'll be stretched for a while," she shrugged and said with a candid expression,

"We just love the place and the location is perfect, don't look so worried, I can always go back to work if needs be. Anyway we discussed it with some of our financial friends and they all agree we couldn't turn it down."

"It's a beautiful house," Susan smiled her doubtful expression away, nodding agreement "I'm so happy for you. When are you moving in?"

"Soon, when we have all the details settled."

Jane glanced at the kitchen clock.

"Forget about the Copper Kettle. I can only stay for a cuppa and then I'm off. The teenagers will want their dinner. Vincent and Gerry by the way, Gerry is the one you knocked into the flowerbed."

She looked at her mother affectionately

"I just wanted to tell you and Dad the news. There's so much to do with the house and everything, you know, we can move things in at the weekend. Reaching for her bag, Jane produced her mobile."

"I'll just ring Dad and tell him the news."

Susan watched her daughter's expectant smile fade waiting for Paul to answer.

"That's peculiar, he always has his phone on," said Jane slightly perplexed. Then at the tone she spoke into the phone.

"What are you up to? You're always there when I want you. Here's my news," she continued excitedly.

"You know I love Simon, Dad. Well we're going to get married. Hopefully before Christmas." She looked across the table happily, her eyes moist.

"And we've bought a beautiful house in Clontarf. Simon is so good Dad. I am so happy and Vinny and Gerry are great lads. I love you and Mum, Dad. Ring me when you get a chance." She finished the message slightly tearfully.

With a feeling of pride Susan examined this mature confident woman's face knowing that whatever happened in the future Jane and Simon would, in their own way cope and her role would be minimal. Jane wasn't the only one with tears in her eyes.

"I know you're going to be a great wife to that Simon fella and a great mum to those two lads. C'mon, hop off home to your family. They'll expect you to be there. I'll tell your father all about it when I see him."

She ushered her happy daughter towards the door. Jane turned,

"Give me a ring later if you're lonely without Dad. Oh. There's some stuff in my old room I'd like to take, you know, for the new house, bits and pieces."

She stopped again. "Did you say you're going to London to join Dad? That's a great idea, did you tell him about the Gallery?"

Then with a serious expression she wagged her finger,

"You know you're crazy," indicating the painting on the wall. They both looked at it in its gold filigree frame looking every bit the masterpiece it could prove to be.

"That painting could be worth millions of euro and it's hanging on the wall and you're going to go to London. What if something happened? Is it insured? Someone could break in and steal it, these things happen you know."

The usual farewell hug and a kiss on the cheek followed.

"Oh I nearly forgot! Aunt Laura asked me to collect that black box for you. They got it down from the attic. It's in the car. I didn't have a chance to look in it, it's quite heavy but the two of us can manage."

Susan followed Jane out to the car and they retrieved the heavy black box from the boot bringing it into the house and eventually lowering it onto the floor of the studio.

"I really must go, good luck," Jane kissed her mother again and hurried away only to stop at the door. She returned quickly to where Susan was still standing looking at the box.

"I've only a minute," she said "Go on, open it, Mum,"

The square box was made from plain boxwood covered in a black leather-like material with a hinged lid. The black covering had come away in places. In the centre of the lid the initials JB were stamped, the gold of the lettering long worn away just leaving some shiny specks. Susan lifted the lid.

The contents had been piled into the box, documents, letters, photographs, some of them lay flat others were on their edges. It was easy to spot the framed picture amidst all the papers. Susan moved some of the old documents to one side and carefully retrieved the picture, standing up she stepped back holding it in her hand and without taking her eyes from it she reached behind her to feel for the sofa. She sat down without a word.

Jane sat down beside her

"Well? Say something."

"It's Abigail," Susan said at last transferring her gaze to Jane.

"I know," said Jane, pointing, "It says so, look, printed under the oval. "Abigail,"

"Yes, Jane, but who was she?"

Susan, with a puzzled expression looked across the room at the large painting hanging on the wall.

"She should be standing there on the shore in that picture,"

"Well she's not." It's just a lovely painting of a little girl that's been in the family for years and you played with it when you were five." Jane stated matter of factly.

"Now I have to go or I'll be in trouble."

She jumped to her feet. "I'll ring you tomorrow," Susan didn't answer instead she went to the big painting hanging on the wall and stood in front of it.

"There," she touched the painting,

"On the shore, she played on the shore I remember clearly."

"Yes Mum, I'll ring you tomorrow, ok,"

"Bye," Susan said vaguely

"Bye," and Jane was gone.

Susan gazed at the picture of Abigail still held in her hand and came to the conclusion that she must be mistaken it was such a long time ago. The figure of Abigail looked back from the oval shape, her name inscribed under the image on the gold card.

Susan turned over the squared gold frame, pulled out the hinged stand and looked around to find a suitable place to put it on display. The best place would be on top of the piano she decided. Moving a couple of smaller items she made space and placed the picture on the shiny surface. Standing back to admire her handy work the large "Turner" drew her attention. Susan realised that she had been avoiding close study of the painting, afraid of the memories that lurked in her mind. How silly, she scolded herself, mystery solved welcome home Abigail.

The black box stood open and Susan was soon lost in memories as she began to sift through its contents, marriage certificates, birth certificates, school reports, death certificates all in a bundle, cuttings from newspapers, old photographs, wedding photographs even pictures so faded that one could hardly make out the faces. The picture of Abigail looked down from the piano top, forgotten for now.

She eventually replaced all the nostalgic reminders and gently closed the lid of the black box. The house was quiet, everywhere memories, a picture, a small knick knack, a mark on the paintwork, every square foot of the house carried a reminder of the wonderful life she shared with Paul and the kids, a glimpse of the garden as she headed towards the back of the house a reminder of parties, of friends, the endless wonders of a loving family and the valuable years past.

Two raggedy dolls greeted her from the bed as she entered Jane's old bedroom. Lifting them gently she looked into their cockeyed faces as she sat down on her daughters bed. Sitting there the two raggedy dolls cradled on her lap she looked out into the garden with its lovely beech tree and flowerbeds looking so beautiful and familiar. How often had she sat up in bed, the floor to ceiling window framing the view, a cup of tea and a piece of buttered toast, the sound of Paul working at the computer or starting work on another painting filtering through from another part of the house.

"The stupid, stupid, stupid..." she mouthed the words angrily the raggedy dolls heads nodding vigorously in her tight grasp as she banged them again and again against her knees.

"What a fool to jeopardise all this for some kind of self-gratification?"

The phone rang. For a moment she considered not answering it. That's probably him now with some further wonderful implausible explanation. She could feel the anger mounting as she eventually went to answer the persistent ringing in the studio.

"Yes what do you want?" She snapped, her voice terse with annoyance.

There was a pause then a slightly hesitant voice answered,

"Hello, This is Sandra Stevenson, is that Susan," there was a pause.

"I'm so sorry, yes this is Susan Macken," she replied.

"We met last year at the ICAD. Awards. I'm married to Peter Stevenson, he's a colleague of your husband's."

"Of course, sorry, yes, hello Sandra, how are you, so nice to hear from you. How's Peter?"

"He's fine we're both in Ireland believe it or not. We saw Paul this morning at Heathrow he was in such a rush.

He just gave us a wave heading for the subway. I hope he got to his meeting on time,"

Susan imagined Paul all flustered and preoccupied with his silly little plan.

"Peter is meeting some people from the Printers Federation tonight, boring, boring. I thought it would be nice for us to have a girl's night out. Seeing Paul this morning put you in mind and I did enjoy your company last year. Are you free?"

"Oh Sandra that's such a good idea, exactly what I would like. Unfortunately I can't make it, I'm off to London tonight to join Paul. How long are you staying? We'll be back in a couple of days. Give me your number and I'll ring you."

Sandra confirmed that she and her husband would be spending the weekend in the West of Ireland and would be back in Dublin the following Monday, they exchanged mobile numbers.

"Have a great time, it's beautiful over there. I'll ring you then."

They said their good byes and Susan put down the phone resolving to keep her promise. Sandra sounded really nice.

The brief interlude and the pleasant exchange on the phone had not improved Susan's mood. If anything it had left her more annoyed than ever. That's where he got his excuse she thought to herself angrily. He saw Peter Stevenson at the airport and of course it was the first name to pop into his head when he was put on the spot.

Susan returning to Jane's room stopped in front of the "Turner". If they had not bought the picture none of this nonsense would have happened. In a way it would have been better if they had never discovered it. The picture is taking over our lives.

What if it disappeared or was stolen like Jane had said? No more trips to Thorndike land, no more arguments about its origin and no more Abigail. What if it disappeared? The thought persisted. Paul would be devastated.

Well a bit of stark reality is good medicine to bring people back to their senses. Perhaps the painting could disappear temporally to reappear again when things were on a more even keel.

The idea appealed to her more and more, but how? How could she make the painting disappear in such a way that it could reappear when needed and yet be safe and protected at the same time?

Funny thing about Ideas, they often have been working away in the subconscious. The answer had occurred almost simultaneously with the formation of the idea.

Vaguely in the back of Susan's mind she recalled a movie she had seen that had featured the discovery of a great masterpiece concealed and eventually discovered behind a worthless print.

Of course! In Jane's room there was a large print of a teenage girl, very moody, very 80's and very much the same size as the "Turner". Some boy had given it to Jane when she was a teenager. Susan hurried into Jane's room and taking the picture from the wall she carried it into the studio and laid it on the large worktable. Once in action she was revelling in the activity. In a couple of minutes she had the two pictures lying side by side on the large table in Paul's studio.

It did not take very long to remove the "Turner" from the frame, as all the fittings were quite loose. The back of the 80's print proved a little bit more difficult. It was held in place by a large wide band of adhesive tape. With the aid of a box cutter Susan eventually managed to get the back off. Now for the "Turner", gently she removed it from its frame and placed it face down on the back of the 80's print, being a bit smaller it fitted easily into place. Susan covered it with the backing card and secured the card with adhesive tape.

Back in Jane's bedroom she surveyed the result of her handiwork, the 80's print back in place looking as it had done since Jane was a teenager only now it concealed a secret. Behind the print lay the "Turner", safe and unlikely to be detected by anyone.

In the living room over the piano she hung the beautiful empty gilt frame now empty and forlorn, quite shocking in fact, its absence giving no clues to its current resting place. Susan in her present mood was quite pleased with the dramatic result.

She quickly packed an overnight bag satisfied with the ingenuity of her plan. The game of the missing painting could be played for as long as she wished. It wasn't long before she was ready to leave the house, her thorough practical mind raced, should I break a window to suggest the entrance of the perpetrator, the stealer of the painting? This would be a bit over the top she decided with a chuckle to herself at the thought. Perhaps the best thing to do would be to leave the back window, the access to the back garden, unlocked. Her quick departure and state of mind could be an explanation for the oversight. Yes, that's a better plan, anyway the thought of breaking the lovely big glass door didn't appeal to her. Slow up Susan, she cautioned herself, take a deep breath and consider the situation.

The painting is safe, I will produce it in time and the plan should stop Paul in his tracks. Before I head for London and a showdown with Paul I've got to ring Jane.

Her daughter answered almost immediately.

"Hi Mum, How are you feeling?"

The ever-solicitous Jane enquired, her tone anxious.

"Never better came the reply, don't worry about anything. Sorry about earlier I was just feeling a bit weepy." She sighed and then proceeded

"Your dad and I had a bit of a row and we didn't make up before he went to London." About to say goodbye Susan decided to explain a little further.

"Remember a couple of years ago there was a period when things were not going so well between us and I had to sort it out. Well it's time for some more strong stuff, that's why I'm going. If I don't come back with him he'll probably be found floating in the Thames." She laughed.

"I do love your news about Simon and yourself and I'm looking forward to seeing your posh new house. Don't forget to ring your brother and tell him all about it. Could you imagine Richard presiding at his sister's marriage? That would be so brilliant. Look I'd better get moving to make my flight."

Without waiting for her daughter to respond Susan said her good byes and put down the phone with a feeling of elation.

There's nothing like taking action to resolve a problem instead of sitting around waiting for things to happen to you. The break in, yes it would be so much more convincing if the back window was broken. The thought drove her to the kitchen where the hammer could be found in a toolbox under the sink. It was quite a heavy instrument with curved claw shape on the head for pulling out nails. Hefting it in her hand she returned to the back of the house and the large glass patio doors.

Hesitating only for a moment she took aim and delivered a blow to the glass right beside one of the large door-handles. The result was not what she expected. Instead of a nice neat hole appearing large cracks splayed out from the impact point however only a small portion around the door handle came away leaving a convincing gap.

Momentarily taken aback by the violence of her action she stepped back and viewed the damage. Well that's pretty spectacular. Oh! Well it's done now. She consoled herself with the thought of how convincing it would be to everyone, obviously breaking and entry.

Pulling across the large curtains to conceal her handiwork she returned the hammer to its place in the kitchen. With a last glance around the house she left and headed for the airport, a strong woman on a mission.

Sleep hadn't come to Paul easily, a late evening meal and a bit too much wine and Courvoisier contributing to his restlessness. He lay in the large double bed listening to the muffled sounds of London's nightlife. Unused to being in a double bed alone, at first he lay spread-eagled face down in the soft pillows wallowing in the sheer comfort, waiting for his excited mind to quieten down as it raced, creating and rejecting, anticipating the day ahead, the Kathryn Thorndike day the beautiful Kathryn Thorndike.

Her face swam into his consciousness and he sighed contentedly. Slowly but surely his paranoia began to infiltrate and spoil the fantasy. Right at the point where she looked up into his eyes and smiled, red lips slightly parted and whispered his name.

I forgot to get toothpaste! The thought flew into his mind. His eyes flickered open to be quickly closed again as he tried to retain the image of the beautiful face. "Paul." She whispered and he smiled into the pillow. A distant car horn sounded and the moment was lost.

What if I make a fool of myself, what if when I see her I behave in some ridiculous manner like some lovesick teenager? He turned onto his back wide eyed as he recalled the moment in the reception area of the Regent when he had imagined a response from the young girl behind the desk. With a slight smile he sank back into the pillows. I'm mildly paranoid, he reassured himself, and I have the edge. How ridiculous, it had been an instant and nonsensical assumption. He reassured himself. I did control the feeling and overcome the emotion of the moment he rationalized. This is the ultimate test, this meeting with Kathryn Thorndike. I have to keep my concentration keep it strictly business. Eventually sleep came to Paul interrupted through the night with haphazard dreams and moments of wide-eyed wakefulness.

He sat on the bed having arisen early, too early, for breakfast. He had gone for a walk in the Green Park with its early morning joggers, had passed through Piccadilly Square with its busy commuters briskly starting their day, returned to the hotel and collected the newspaper in the reception. Normally the full Irish would be consumed with relish but when the plate was placed on the lovely white tablecloth with a "Your breakfast Sir," he swiftly looked away and reached for the coffeepot.

It was another crisp bright day in London, instead of feeling elated he felt the opposite. Returning to his room after struggling through two pieces of buttered toast washed down with three cups of black coffee he now sat on the bed feeling a bit better with some of his confidence and optimism returning. The most important thing here is the "Turner". He opened the document case and spread the contents out on the bed beside him. Satisfied that he had all the elements needed he then replaced them carefully in the case. The thought of a positive outcome to the meeting helped him focus on the task at hand.

A call to Susan's phone was not answered, nothing unusual in that. She often leaves her phone unattended. Deciding it would be better to talk face to face he didn't leave a message.

The room phone rang, "Your taxi to the Tate Gallery, sir,"

Right at the appointed time Paul strode into the Tate Gallery Coffee Shop.

Angie Kiely's description of the cool Kathryn Thorndike, not stunning, could not have been further from the truth. The woman who stood up as Paul approached was quite exquisite. Her casual unaffected stance, her wide friendly smile of greeting as she extended her hand, Paul's resolve abandoned him. He looked into the candid eyes noting the slightest blue tinge accentuated by long dark lashes,

"Mr Macken, how nice to see you."

He felt her hand firm in his. Then releasing her grip she transferred her touch to his elbow.

"Please sit down I have taken the liberty of ordering coffee. I hope you don't mind. We don't have much time. The drawing office is allowing us just a short while for a preliminary appraisal." She smiled,

"I am afraid I have another appointment so my time is limited."

Paul, not trusting himself to speak, finding it difficult to take his eyes off the red lips, hefted the document case onto the table between them.

"I brought a professional quality copy of the lettering and some other samples of Turner's handwriting you may not have seen," producing the papers from the case he handed them across the table.

Her delicate well-manicured hands held the besotted Paul transfixed as she took the documents from him.

Selecting the copy of handwriting from the back of the picture,

"Deal, Hovellers going out to a wreck," red lips articulated the words as she slowly read the title to herself.

Mesmerised Paul could not take his eyes from her face. He watched as, without taking her gaze from the words her left hand searched in her black leather case producing some handwriting samples which she carefully placed alongside Paul's. He noticed the Tate logo at the top of the samples.

Donning a pair of spectacles she eagerly studied the lettering.

"It's a very beautiful hand."

She traced the letters with her fingers, noting every detail.

Eventually looking up.

"I have here some samples of Turners handwriting, quite good copies.

I contacted the Tate and had them prepared." She spread them out on the table.

Paul looked at the samples. They appeared to be the same as the ones he had already downloaded from the Internet, also a copy of a letter by Turner.

"Well what's your first impression?" He enquired, making a conscious effort to avoid direct eye contact. She looked up.

"Mr Macken," the candid formal voice was professional dispassionate.

"There are similarities between the original Turner handwriting and your copy," She gathered the sheets of paper together as she spoke.

"You must understand, Mr Macken, in the year 1825 those who were able to write, wrote in a similar fashion to each other, so I would expect similarities it is quite understandable how you could have been misled. My professional opinion is that this is definitely not Turner's handwriting and it would be a waste of time and money to pursue the matter further. I'm sorry, believe me. I would love to give you better news. You may want another opinion. Please take these samples they're yours. If you decide to pursue the matter further let me know, though I would not advise it."

She abruptly stood up, "I have another appointment Mr Macken, I am sorry you have had a wasted trip, Goodbye."

Paul hardly listening to the words grasped her proffered hand.

Preoccupied with his rampant imagination, confused, assuming in his temporarily besotted state that she was playing a game of some sort, he searched for something to say but the words evaded him, instead he just stared at her with a puzzled expression "I..." He began to say then changed his mind.

"Yes, Mr Macken?" she tried to withdraw her hand but his grip did not slacken.

"I.... wo..." he started to speak again inadvertently pulling her towards him.

She recoiled with a look of annoyance followed by one of puzzled incredulity mixed with distain.

"Let go my hand!" Paul looked down at the clasped hands in surprise. Then, looking back at the beautiful face in front of him he tried to apologise

"I'm so sor..." He was still holding her hand when the metal corner of her briefcase caught him flush on the mouth.

Recoiling he took a step backwards releasing her hand, off balance he was supported momentarily by the small ornate coffee table behind him. Making a grab for a chair it skidded away under his grasp across the polished floor into a surprised group of sightseers. For a moment the table supported him and then collapsed depositing him unceremoniously onto the polished floor of the Tate Coffee Shop.

The force of the impact drove the breath from his body. He rolled onto his side feeling the hardness of the floor against his cheek momentarily stunned. A reflex action drove him into a sitting position from which he tried to stand up only to fall backwards again. From this position he watched the retreat of his assailant as she headed for the escalator.

Shocked at the suddenness of it all, tasting blood in his mouth, he put his fingers to his lips and they came away with a red smear. The violence of the woman's reaction hit Paul with terrific effect. Incredulous, stunned, he sat in total bewilderment in the middle of the Tate coffee shop.

She hit me with the briefcase, he realised with a shock, his mind flooding back to sanity, all his romantic fantasies fleeing leaving behind only a tremendous feeling of regret and confusion.

How could he have been so stupid? Paul knew, knew at that moment, with a flash of mature insight, it had ended. Of course that beautiful young woman had absolutely no interest in him, the whole affair had been fuelled by ridiculous imaginings. He knew he would never play this terrible game again, risking all he loved most, his family his beautiful wife Susan. Susan! What must she be thinking?

136

Still sitting on the floor he fumbled for his mobile. I must ring her immediately. There was an unanswered message from Jane he activated the voice and listened to the message, imminent marriage, mention of a house, I love you and Mum, Dad you're always there.

There was a touch on his arm.

"Can you stand up please Sir?" a security man was leaning over him. Paul feeling that the man's attitude was not unkindly allowed himself to be helped to his feet.

"Thank you," One of the tourists had retrieved the chair. Paul gratefully accepted it and sat down with a "wince" feeling the effects of the impact when he'd hit the floor. He felt sure a lot of bruising had occurred especially to his ego.

The kindness of those around him was quite disarming. A white haired gent placed a cup of coffee in front of him while he could see others collecting his papers that had scattered dramatically.

"That's a feisty young woman you've got there. The younger ones are hard to handle old boy, I've got the scars to show." said the gent with a knowing smile.

"One lump or two?" Paul looked at his helper with a rueful smile, aware that the man was probably about his own age.

Paul now somewhat recovered, was standing in the Turner section gazing at the works of art. Meanwhile, in a nearby coffee shop, Tim Holmes nodded to the waiter and ordered another latte. The location, close to the Tate, suited him perfectly.

He toyed with the remains of his lunch, normal substantial appetite on the back burner, other things occupying his active mind, unanswered questions, assessing the situation he came to the conclusion that he was ahead of the game.

A lot depended on keeping Mackedy Macken off balance, sowing the seeds of doubt in his mind.

He looked out the window expectantly and then to the remains of his lunch, his mood improving as he anticipated the outcome of the plan. Calling the waiter again he ordered a banoffi with extra cream.

Patience is a virtue, he recalled his mother's words. "Patience is a virtue, have it if you can, never in a woman, seldom in a man." Well something like that.

The banoffi arrived and he attacked it with enthusiasm, head bent over the dish, eyes on the lookout, across the road.

From his vantage point he could see her approach, the blond head over the roofs of the parked cars, moving quickly, looking right, left and right again. That's my girl remember the green cross code. Now opposite to the coffee shop, between the cars she crossed the road, slim, stylish, spectacular, any mans fancy. I wonder what ole Paul thought of Kathryn Thorndike he mused affording himself a little smile.

She entered the coffee shop and came straight to his table. Standing up, Tim pulled out a chair. Smiling and animated she slipped off her lightweight coat depositing her briefcase on the floor beside the chair as she sat down.

Tim finished off his banoffi as the waiter approached and she ordered a coffee. He sat back and viewed the radiant young woman in front of him.

"Well how did it go?" He leaned forward

"How does Mr Macken feel about his Turner now?

Were you convincing, or need I ask?"

Jennifer Holmes, the apple of her father's eye, looked back with a broad smile as she delivered a very convincing impression of a precise, professional business woman delivering an impromptu speech ending with,

"Hook line and sinker."

Tim loved his beautiful daughter with all his heart. . What a classy lady, at 24 years she represented the benefits of all that Tim could offer. He had made and lost quite a

138

considerable amount of money in his time but no matter what, school, college, all fees were paid even that Swiss finishing school. Jennifer had lapped it all up like a prize pedigree cat with the cream.

He would have preferred had she done something more profound with her qualifications, maybe become a lawyer or a doctor. That particular dream was a non-starter. It very soon became evident that her headstrong individuality and innocent beauty were coupled with a natural flair for acting and a devious mind.

He looked across the table at the lively intelligent face of, what he considered regrettably yet with a certain tinge of pride, to be, potentially one of the best con artists in the business.

"Right," he said, rubbing his hands together

"So Mr Macken has severe doubts about the authenticity of the painting?"

"I would say so," came the reply. "He is relying heavily on the handwriting being Turner's to prove the case and now the eminent Kathryn Thorndike, handwriting expert extraordinaire has told him it is not Turner's writing."

Jennifer made a face.

"He's a bit freaky. At the beginning he was alright, then he seemed to become distracted and started to act funny," She looked at Tim collecting her thoughts, lips pursed.

"Like a boy with a crush," she continued, I hit him with my briefcase."

"You what, where?" Tim was a bit taken aback.

"Well kind of on the mouth, I felt that it would help him absorb the information by association. It's like a tactic, the shock of the impact underlining the information serving to help him remember the details."

Tim smiled, not quite following the logic of her explanation but prepared to go along with this smart lady.

"What about the phone number?" he asked. "Has he got your phone number?"

"Of course when he rings Kathryn Thorndike to apologise he gets me."

"You're pretty sure he'll ring to apologise?" Tim looked interested, his mind calculating the possibilities.

"Absolutely," Jennifer confirmed. "It's probably the foremost thought in his mind and when he rings I will further confirm his doubts about the "Turner".

"Where is he?" Asked Tim.

"He's at the Tate in the Turner section looking at the pictures. I hung around for a while out of sight to see what he would do."

"Ring him now," prompted Tim,

"I need to know his state of mind,"

Reaching for her phone she smiled devilishly.

"Poor ole Mackedy Macken is not having a very nice day, is he"?'

Tim watched her become Kathryn Thorndike

"Hello, yes, hello Paul, this is Kathryn Thorndike, I felt the least I could do was ring and apologise for my actions. How is your poor lip," she murmured.

"I'm so sorry, are you alright?"

When the phone rang Paul was standing before *The Fighting Temeraire*, a very large oil painting and one of Turner's most famous masterpieces. The last person he expected to hear from was Kathryn Thorndike.

"No, No, it's me who should apologise," he protested.

"Really my behaviour was not the best." Paul, who at that moment was feeling quite ridiculous and embarrassed, felt his lip smiling ruefully, aware that he probably deserved the smack with the briefcase.

"I'm sorry I was so abrupt about the handwriting. It's just that there were too many contradictions in the hand," the quiet voice continued.

Paul looking at the Turner painting in front of him, at that moment could detect very little resemblance between this masterpiece and the painting hanging on the wall at home.

"Well to tell you the truth I am looking at the real thing here at the Tate, it's called the Fighting Temeraire," he read the title.

"It bears very little resemblance to my painting. I'm pretty sure the whole thing is just a wild goose chase."

"Well," said Jennifer in a kind voice.

"I hope you're not too disappointed, I'm sure you have a very nice painting anyway. Goody bye Paul, sorry again about the briefcase," she rang off.

Tim watched his daughter's performance a slight smile creasing his lips, just the right blend of compassion, friendliness and regret and then the clincher at the end. He knew that she had manoeuvred Paul Macken into exactly the right frame of mind for the next move.

They both stood up, the young woman tall and quick bending for her briefcase and turning towards the door. Tim half a head smaller and a lot wider followed.

"While you're meeting with Mr Macken I'll do some shopping and head for the house. What do you want for your dinner I'll be staying tonight?" She said.

Father and daughter were now standing on the pavement outside the cafe. Jennifer bent down and kissed her father's cheek. "See you later she said."

As she walked away Tim looked after her for a moment and then headed in the opposite direction and the Tate gallery.

Exiting the glass revolving door of the Tate and out onto the high steps. Paul stood between the great pillars his mind in some turmoil. He now realised with a total conviction that he would never put his marriage in jeopardy again. The "Turner" subject, cause of his present predicament, had been resolved.

Somehow the fact that the painting was unlikely to be worth millions did not seem to matter quite so much, first things first, contact Susan. As he reached for his mobile phone a familiar figure caught his eye.

Across the wide Millbank road, on a bench under the trees beside the Thames sat the fat man from the train. He was looking directly at Paul and turned away as Paul looked in his direction.

Momentarily shelving his intention to ring Susan, instead of his mobile, Paul fished out the business card he had been handed on the train.

It might be amusing to hear what the little shyster has on his mind.

"Nice, nice, come to Daddy," Tim had a quick glance over his shoulder and saw Paul now at the bottom of the steps looking up the Millbank road, about to cross.

"We meet again," Paul stopped alongside the bench.

"Big Dinero, Mr Macken, big dinero." Tim didn't look around as he spoke. Abruptly he stood up and turned, beaming, friendly.

"I trust you got a positive reaction from the Thorndike bird?"

Paul hesitated for a second and then replied, "Very! Yes, very positive."

Tim noting the hesitation and then the lie felt a glow of satisfaction for the second time that day. A little porky pie, there, he thought to himself, Mr Mackedy Macken has entered the game.

"Tonight, this evening 8.00 in the Regent Palace bar, if that suits, we can take this matter further," He said extending a hand.

"Fine," Paul automatically accepted the handshake.

Before anything more could be added to the conversation the fat man stood up and turning away headed up the street. Paul stood and watched the portly figure walk away slightly taken aback at the abruptness of the encounter. There were some questions he wanted answered. Then he thought, he'd leave it till later. It's all positive, nice, I'm warming to this fella, and I might as well go along with it.

In the taxi heading back to the hotel Paul in typical fashion began to look on the bright side of the Thorndike encounter. Very brutal, very direct, well at least she's honest. Another person might very well have strung him along and made quite a lot of money on search fees etc.

Still this deal could be fun, this meeting with Mr Holmes. Paul's mind leapfrogged, strange fellow and pretty sharp, seemed to have the right connections. How did he know about the meeting with Kathryn Thorndike? Oh yes, of course, he had been there on the train when the call was made.

I wonder what Susan is up to, his mind skipped; I'm so lucky to have her. The little shit comment still plagued him. Trying her mobile again there was no answer. The home phone gave the same result.

Hamley's Toy Store, "Let me out here," he instructed the Taxi driver on realising he was in Regent Street.

Situated in a cul-de-sac in what was once quite a trendy part of London No 23 on the terrace was a small two up two down house. Its central location was its main attraction offering Tim Holmes easy access to his favourite stomping ground, the centre of London, Piccadilly Circus only a couple of stops away on the subway.

Jennifer Holmes pushed open the little green gate in the railings. The tiny grass area gave way to a couple of red brick steps with some tiling at the front door with its two stained glass panels. She shifted the bag of groceries to the crook of her left arm as she searched for the key and inserted it in the Yale lock and pushed the door open.

The violence of the blow between her shoulders drove her half way up the narrow hall, groceries and a bottle of wine flying in all directions. She landed on her hands and knees momentarily disorientated with the shock of the impact. Before she could gather her wits strong fingers cruelly dug into the back of her neck driving her to the floor, her supporting arms gave way.

Jennifer just managed to turn her head to one side as her face impacted with the vinyl floor, the full weight of her assailant pinning her.

She felt his spittle on her cheek as he pressed his face into hers.

"Not a sound," He lay on top of her on the hall floor.

Jennifer tried to move but her arms were pinned. Dazed, wild thoughts ran rampant in her head as she tried to regain control. The moments lying there seemed like an age. Eventually the face moved away from hers to be replaced by a large hand pressing her head into the hard surface. She managed to speak,

"My purse is in the bag, this is my father's house there's no money here."

The toe of a highly polished shoe appeared and landed lightly a foot away from her eyes quickly followed by its handmade glossy partner. Through the blurring tears in her eyes she watched as the owner of the shoes crouched down close to her, she could get the scent of expensive aftershave.

"I'm here for a little chat with you and your dad,"

The voice was very cultured and soft.

"I'm sorry to inconvenience you."

A pair of hands belonging to the owner of the voice came into view, long tapered fingers, pale, almost white skin, manicured. They moved mesmerically before her eyes crossing and re-crossing. A white mouse appeared like magic climbing and twisting within the delicate grasp passing from hand to hand. Transfixed, Jennifer watched the mouse, why? Who is this person with the soft voice?

"Let her up. I think she's frightened."

The voice was kind, compassionate. A hand was offered to assist her, palm up as the white mouse disappeared.

Jennifer's keen mind assessed the situation, her combating skills though considerable, and highly trained as she might be she decided to play for time and calculate her adversary's strengths, two against one, before betraying her own.

The heavy weight was mercifully released as the person pinning her to the floor adjusted his position and then stood away from her. She tried to move but miraculously her limbs wouldn't obey. In spite of her best efforts her body began to shake and she sobbed quietly.

"You'll be alright in a minute," a hand stroked her hair.

"Matt, find a kettle and make some tea."

Jennifer struggled to her feet as the gentle strong hands helped her to stand.

"Get away from me," she twisted and brought her elbows up fighting to free herself, indignation and anger flooding in equal proportions to no avail.

"Ssh, Ssh, the gentle voice continued, I'm sorry, I'm sorry, Matt is a clumsy monster." He released her and stepped back, one hand still supporting her by the elbow.

Head down she collected her thoughts, composing herself as she smoothed the front of her dress with now steady hands.

"My name is Alan Grant, I owe you an explanation."

Jennifer lifted her head brushing the hair from her eyes. For the first time she looked into the face, the source of the cultured voice.

Head to one side leaning slightly towards her he smiled apologetically.

"I'm so sorry,"

She felt relief that she was not going to be harmed further. Better play for time, find out what they want, she sensed that they were capable and determined the Matt one, dangerous.

Her wits now fully returned she slowly took a deep breath. Her agile mind raced through possibilities. This is not a random attack, they were probably waiting for Tim, I'm not what they expected, the way she was man handled was intended to intimidate. They know me and have probably done their homework.

Feigning more distress than she felt she looked at the floor bending forward as she clutched the bannisters taking long slow breaths and exhaling loudly playing for time. It was a convincing performance.

His eyes showed genuine concern. Jennifer couldn't help noticing how handsome he was. She now scrutinised every aspect of his appearance for clues, how to react, know your enemy. Mid thirties, lean build, tall, 6ft plus, immaculately dressed, self assured and confident. But the most notable aspect of the man were the eyes and his extraordinary face, the face of the hero in all romantic novels, almost too perfect and there was no denying the expression of genuine compassion and sympathy, the eyes the darkest she had ever seen.

The man displayed an amazing likeability. Her worst fears were dispelled as her feeling of apprehension eased.

"Here, sit down have a cup of tea, Matt will clear up the mess. I'll explain why we're here."

She followed him into the kitchen, Matt close behind eliminating all thought of escape. Her mind was working overtime on all the contradictions that were being presented.

Vaclav Janacec the man who now called himself Alan Grant sat at the kitchen table across from Jennifer and looked at her sympathetically over the rim of her dad's favourite mug as he sipped his tea.

In his jacket pocket he could feel the handle of the ornate ancient knife nestling snugly in the lining. His index finger caressed and played with the deadly instrument. There were two blades concealed in the handle one with a razor sharp edge for slashing and the other a needle pointed stiletto for stabbing.

"I'm embarrassed,"

He said, leaning forward towards Jennifer. Matt unenthusiastically clearing up the groceries hovered in the background. "You see I want you to tell me all about the Turner painting and your father's arrangements, and I'm sure you want to keep the information to yourself."

His friendly disarming expression remained exactly in place.

Jennifer smiled back,

"There's nothing to tell, my father keeps his business to himself, he tells me nothing." Her heart was racing as she leaned back in the kitchen chair assuming as casual a posture as she could muster.

The knife felt smooth, Vaclav Janacec's demeanour remained sympathetic and friendly as he imagined the deadly blade parting the white skin of her beautiful face.

Matt deposited the groceries on the kitchen table and spoke.

"I knew your Dad, we shared a cell in The Scrubs. How's he keeping?"

Jennifer looked up at the pale eyes, assessing the bulky heavy built man, ignorant and brutal.

"Fine," she said looking back at Vaclav,

"He's fine," she repeated.

"Look," she leaned forward earnestly. "The painting's worthless, the owner found out today at the Tate Gallery. I was there and heard everything."

"That's a pity, are you sure?"

Black eyebrows raised quizzically above the deep dark eyes.

"Absolutely, the owner met up with an expert today at the Tate and received the bad news."

Vaclav Janacec reached for the bottle of wine amongst the groceries on the table.

"Ah well," he looked at Matt who had moved to one side.

"We're on a wild goose chase Matt. The painting is worthless,"

"You heard what the lady said.... well now,"

He looked across the table and beamed at the girl opposite giving her the full benefit of his good looks and charm.

"Let's have a drink," he laughed with genuine amusement.

"Worthless," he shook his head from side to side.

"I'll get some glasses." Jennifer got up from the table, Matt stayed close to her as she opened the press beside the kitchen window, unnecessarily close. The other one was having a good time. He seemed highly amused at the news.

Jennifer brought the glasses to the table as Matt did the honours opening the wine and spoke again.

"Jennifer I'm sorry," he said filling her glass as she sat at the table.

"They said you could take care of yourself, you studied martial arts, that sort of thing. I overdid it with the strong-arm stuff. Are you alright?"

Holding his glass in his right hand Matt extended the other one with big thick fingers in a gesture of apology, indicating the side of her face where it had come in contact with the floor.

'There's some beer in the fridge, said Jennifer, trying to smile, maybe you'd prefer that."

"Much obliged," he said, placing his wineglass on the table.

Jennifer assessed her situation. The one who called himself Alan Grant posed a question that she had never encountered before and she was puzzled by many aspects of his behaviour. He didn't seem to present an immediate threat but was definitely the more dangerous of the two, she decided. Matt's capable of anything she concluded but she had encountered his type many times.

"Watch this," Vaclav was on his feet wineglass held aloft.

"A toast to art and honesty," he drank from the glass,

"Nice, a precocious little number with a delicate nose, a Chardonnay 2001,"

He mimicked the wine expert.

"Tesco, 4.99," said Jennifer with a laugh, trying her best to seem at ease.

"Please look at the glass of wine,"

Vaclav said, with mock gravity producing a perfectly white handkerchief as if from thin air.This he dropped over the glass.

"May I have a volunteer from the audience, how about you Madame?" He held out the concealed glass to Jennifer.

"Please take the handkerchief by one corner and remove it."

Jennifer with her best smile obeyed, whipping the handkerchief away.

Sitting in the middle of the glass was a white mouse the wine had disappeared.

"Behold the alcoholic mouse!"

Vaclav bowed. Jennifer, playing along applauded,

"Clever boy!" She clapped her hands together.

"Now for le piece de resistance,"

Taking the handkerchief from Jennifer's hand he covered the glass, the mouse still inside, and held his arm aloft dramatically. He was enjoying himself. Looking into Jenifer's eyes.

"Would the lady please remove the handkerchief once more?"

Again he lowered his arm. Doubt and apprehension invading her mind, Jennifer once more reached for the white material gripping it by one corner she gently pulled it away. The mouse, still inside the glass, now impaled on the cruel needle sharp stiletto blade struggled for its life. Jennifer stared in disbelief. Vaclav Janacec laughed as he watched the mouse.

"What time did you say your father would get home?" He asked, as the mouse's movements became weaker and a smear of blood stained the bottom of the glass.

Susan, refreshed after a good night's sleep stood at the window in the corner of the large lounge of the Regent Palace looking out at Eros and the commuters.

Tourists of all nationalities strolled amongst the bustle. Many famous streets and avenues converged here. To the left, Shaftsbury Avenue and theatre land. Over to the right were Regent Street and the beginnings of the Green Park. How she loved London especially the Regent Palace Hotel.

What a fool Paul could be. Everything in the world they needed, a great family, adorable grandchildren, money not a major issue and good health, he should be counting his blessings instead of making a fool of himself, again.

What the hell am I doing here? I should be at home awaiting his return like the good loving wife. I should turn a blind eye and wait it out knowing that eventually things would return to normal. Not this time, our marriage is worth fighting for, confront the issue and take the consequences. I'm not going through this again, she vowed. The stupid man needs to be told, but first some shopping and some fresh air.

She strode across the lush carpeted lounge past the reception and through the impressive entrance out onto Piccadilly Circus unaware that Paul as a result of the brutal treatment on his visit to the Tate had more or less come to his senses of his own accord.

The rather chastened Paul was at that moment making his way to the Regent Palace. The possibility of selling what in his opinion now was a rather valueless would be Turner occupying his mind. The handwriting did not match and none of the Turner paintings in the Tate looked remotely like "Hovellers going out to a wreck." Well I still have the fat man on board. I need not necessarily pass on any crucial information. All's fair in love and art transactions.

His step became lighter as he anticipated the evenings meeting.

Susan's number still indicated "no connection."

Walking amongst the commuters on Regent Street he rehearsed how, when he returned to Ireland he would tell Susan everything, leaving nothing out, about his wild imaginings and hope that his resourceful wife would make allowances. He reasoned that he hadn't done anything wrong but he could not in all honesty expect her to let him off lightly.

Life without her was unthinkable.

As he walked his eyes misting up with emotion all thoughts of Millions of Euro and Turner paintings were replaced with a feeling of dread at the dawning realisation that Susan would walk away from their marriage. He recalled how she had stated after the previous occasion,

"I won't go through this again, Paul, I'll leave you."

He stopped in his tracks, a pathetic dejected and dishevelled figure. Overcome with emotion he covered his face with cupped hands, the tears ran onto the white cuffs of his new shirt as he leaned dejected against a shop window, ignored by the busy London pavement traffic.

"Hello Paul,"

He jerked up his head, startled at the sound of the familiar voice. She was standing motionless about six feet away amidst the hurrying passers by.

"Susan! Where did you come from?" He looked up from his pathetic crouched position against the window at his wife in disbelief. Realising how wretched he must appear he straightened up to his full height but like a distressed child accepted the handkerchief from Susan's hand. Dabbing his eyes her scent invaded his senses.

"I'm sorry. Susan forgive me."

Susan had left the hotel and headed up Regent Street with the intention of doing some shopping in Hamley's Toy Store. Whenever in London she and Paul would always visit the famous store, on this occasion she felt that it would provide some light relief and of course she could buy something for the little ones.

She thought for a second that she had seen Paul further up the street coming towards her but immediately rejected the idea as too much of a coincidence. When she realized to her surprise that it was him she was taken aback at his appearance, he looked so dejected.

Resisting the temptation to immediately comfort him she had checked herself just watching his approach. When he stopped and leaned against the shop window her resolve had softened somewhat at his obvious distress.

With mixed feelings she offered him the handkerchief to give herself thinking time. Recovering somewhat Paul reached for her, anxious for her comforting forgiving embrace, relief and pleasure at the meeting diminishing as he sensed her hesitation.

All the familiar senses and feelings rising in him he held on until he felt her relax and respond. Then holding her at arms length he looked her in the face

"What are you doing here he repeated, you look terrific?"

His kiss was aimed accurately but missed its intended target as she turned her head to one side. Her smile of greeting was less than loving.

"Where are you staying?"

"The Regent Palace, I just booked for tonight, I didn't know what your plans were." She turned to him and they walked side by side up Regent Street towards Piccadilly Circus.

"What do you think of Jane's news?"

The question took him by surprise, for a moment he had no idea what she was talking about.

"Yea, great," stalling for time as he frantically searched his mind. There was something lurking back there in the recesses. What was it? It came to him. Jane's phone message when he'd been sitting on the floor at the Tate. He had been in a confused state at the time after the blow from the briefcase and the whole trauma of the incident.

"Yes great,"

"Is that all you have to say?" Jane stopped and looked again at her confused husband. "Are you alright, what happened your lip, there's blood on your shirt. Is that a new shirt...Paul... what's going on? Did you meet Kathryn Thorndike?"

Too many questions all at once Paul's mind spun and whirled completely thrown by the unexpected meeting with Susan and the barrage of questions.

He stood and looked at her, dumbstruck.

"Well?" she enquired impatiently.

"Your daughter's getting married, and that's all you have to say,

Yes, great!"

"Of course," he tried to smile,

"Jane and Simon are getting married and they've bought a house, it's great isn't it? I got the news, she sent me a message, and I forgot, no I was confused you see."

He stopped and looked at the ground, Susan waited.

When he looked up the tears were back.

"Susan we've got to talk." appealingly he put out his hand to her.

She turned away and the walk back to the Regent Palace Hotel at Piccadilly Circus was conducted in silence. Each occupied with their own thoughts and oblivious to all else. One looking ahead, head held high determined, a resolute set to her jawline, her mind resolved to the fact that she was no longer a victim in the relationship. The circumstances of the past few days had left her without any doubts. Unexpectedly she felt calm and relaxed and somehow relieved, a strong and competent woman who had somehow outgrown her partner.

She glanced sideways at her despondent looking husband. Head down, preoccupied with his thoughts, mind in a whirl walking beside her.

Aware of her attention he looked back with a rueful half smile and eyes that pleaded, at a loss for words he made a resigned gesture with his hands and shook his head.

"We'll get back to the Hotel and you can get washed up and change your shirt, Then you'll tell me all about it, obviously you've had a lousy time," She said, not unkindly.

The Very Tall Man was furious and feeling quite frustrated.

"Why can you not speak to me in my own language!" he bellowed in frustration. I make every attempt at yours, it would be easier for my people if you were more cooperative."

The voice at the other end of the line remained calm and unperturbed.

The Very Tall Man detected the word "patience" it sounded very similar in his own language and was easily understood. He cut off the car phone speaker and glanced at the man sitting beside him. The man had his head turned away as he watched Susan and Paul walking in Regent Street.

Back at the Hotel Paul sat in their favourite corner out of the mainstream of activity. Many a time he and Susan had relaxed here in the past. Today was a complete contrast, apprehensive, his lip throbbing, a reminder of what had ensued and the circumstances leading up to the incident of the briefcase.

He had hoped Susan would change her booking and join him in a double room but it was not to be. They had separated in the foyer with an arrangement to meet in the lounge within the hour. He was confused and at a loss, not knowing how to cope with Susan's calm purposeful detachment. When she joined him, now smiling, and looking very much her old self he felt a sense of relief, maybe things would be all right.

A waiter hurried over and they ordered a pot of tea, some scones and a double brandy for Paul. She seemed in good form and they discussed the imminent marriage, Jane's new house and how she felt. He responded and said how happy he was. Now and then she noticed his hand straying to gently touch his lip.

Any more nonsense from you and you'll get another one from me, she thought to herself and couldn't help smiling at the idea.

He smiled back and enquired enthusiastically about her visit to the Gallery in Dublin. Susan explained all in detail relating the positive comments of the lady from the National Gallery.

She didn't mention anything about hiding the painting, resolving to rectify that as soon as she would arrive home. It all seemed to her a bit foolish now. What could she have been thinking of, though there was a funny side to it, again she had a little smile to herself. Encouraged by her apparent good humour Paul threw caution to the wind and told all, with some omissions, mainly the briefcase attack, from the first contact with Kathryn Thorndike to the arrangement to meet the fat man from the train that evening at the Palace.

Susan listened, intrigued, and only interrupted on hearing about Kathryn Thorndike's rejection of the lettering.

"What? On the spot! Just like that at a table in a café?

No way Paul!" She exclaimed. "That doesn't seem like the Kathryn Thorndike described to me by Angie Kiely."

"No!" Paul protested, "I showed her the high resolution versions and she compared them thoroughly, she's an expert, she could tell immediately,"

"C'mon Paul lets face it, you were in no state of mind to judge that at the time. You were preoccupied with how she looked and thinking with your dick instead of your brain. There's more to this than meets the eye."

She laughed when her husband recoiled at the attack.

"Get a grip Paul, you're a smart bloke, start using that brain of yours."

Leaning forward Susan punctuated her words with an index finger stabbing the tabletop.

"The National Gallery believes our painting could be by Turner, I'm far from satisfied with your Miss Thorndike. We're going to see her tomorrow. Well I am anyway, whether you are or not. Now tell me about this meeting with your fat friend. I'm looking forward to it, what time is it at, is he coming here and how does he know all about the painting? Somebody must have told him, who did you tell apart from Terrible Thorndike?"

Cigar smoke and the whiff of good brandy filled the air in the private lounge of one of Prague's better hotels. The small select group of powerful men representing some of the higher echelons of Prague's trade, finance and politics sat and discussed their next move. Sir Geoffrey Fletcher had proved to be an invaluable asset in securing information and vital contacts essential to the success of their plans. Between them they controlled a large percentage of the countries organised crime and corruption, a tight knit group, each member an integral part of the whole. Trust in each other was generated by individual greed and a thirst for power. The ultimate penalty would be paid for any betrayal to the group.

Casually it was suggested that Sir Geoffrey was now, "Surplus to requirements." The slight inclination of the head from one member and the pursing of lips from another signed the Knights death warrant. He would be eliminated in time, not immediately, but at a later date, at the moment there were other more demanding matters to be dealt with.

It seemed that the Bellini List had yet again delivered up another potential masterpiece. The complex trail had eventually led to the Republic of Ireland and London. Their man had made contact and had started the process of securing the picture.

Ireland's immigration laws did not pose a problem. The organisation's network stretched to Dublin where people were already in place. It would be a simple matter for their man to return to Prague once the mission was accomplished.

On the coffee table lay a bundle of printed documents including an Internet picture of Susan Macken's painting, also samples of Turners handwriting and references to Deal and Hovellers.

There was an extract from the Bellini list referring to the probability that the great artist Turner had painted a picture of the Hovellers in action. The painting and two others had been passed on to a certain John Nash in 1827. The other two paintings now resided in private collections but the third had disappeared.

"A toast to Joseph Bellini," Glasses were raised in tribute to the Bellini List and its founder and to their good fortune in securing the extraordinarily important document.

Joseph Bellini an eminent art historian, a descendent of the great Renaissance painter Giovanni Bellini, a man who had dedicated his knowledge and most of his life to the discovery, authentication and preservation of so far undiscovered works of great artists. He gathered around him a group of international art experts. Only those with the greatest and most exceptional knowledge and dedication were admitted to the organisation. The pooled resources of these men resulted in an extraordinary compilation of information resulting in some outstanding discoveries over a period of seventy years. Eventually the group was forced to disband as a result of infiltration and misuse of information by unscrupulous individuals, organised crime and government intervention.

Contributors to the list had multiplied over the years and it had become somewhat unwieldy, interest waned for some years and the list was forgotten, to reappear at the end of the Second World War when there was an upsurge in the search for works of art, plundered or hidden away. In recent years a version of the list had found its way onto the Internet where it became corrupted by a deluge of contributors and had lost its credibility.

Pavel Dvorak, a Prague businessman acquired as payment for a substantial debt, some documents from a man who claimed to be related to one of the original founders of the Bellini List. This person maintained that the documents were authentic.

Pavel Dvorak's documents now lay on the table alongside the other Turner evidence.

"A toast, Thank you Mr Bellini,"

Glasses were raised amidst some laughter.

"Also a big thank you to Pavel Dvorak, where did he disappear to?"

More laughter as glasses were raised.

The list had made these men even richer. They had been tracking the potential "Turner Hovellers" painting for some time. The trail had led to Ireland and now there was the possibility of one of the greatest prizes of all, a Turner original.

The mood in the room altered abruptly when Karel Saudek, the most recent member to join the group, a man full of his own importance, put down his glass. With a raised voice he commanded attention addressing the group.

"In this matter I am most dissatisfied." He brandished his glass and glared around the table. "I have instructed my own operative to go to London and check this man out, this man you call Vaclav Janacec, the one who's looking after our interests in this affair, I don't know him. What are his credentials? Is he competent? We need the very best for this. Why not just kill this woman and take the painting. His tone, fuelled by alcohol was argumentative as he glared a challenge to one and all.

The other members of the group exchanged glances. One member of the group knew more about Janacec than anyone else. But would he speak? The silence held.

"Well?" Karel Saudek looked challengingly from one to the other.

"Vaclav Janacec is a very uniquely qualified individual." A quiet voice broke the silence. "A great deal of time and preparation has been spent resulting in a unique infiltration of the famous Tate Gallery and it's treasures. Your methods, Karl, like a blunt instrument may well secure this one painting but would jeopardise our long term ambitions." Saudek, about to protest was silenced by a raised hand. The soft voice hardened, the tone indicating no further interruption would be tolerated.

"Vaclav Janacec is highly educated, a qualified art historian who speaks perfect English, very acceptable socially and ruthless in achieving the success of all tasks. His loyalty to the group is above question. He is the best person. You should not have sent someone to, as you say, check him out. That, Karel, is a mistake you may live to regret." All attention turned to the speaker.

Karel Saudek, not used to contradiction stood up, fists clenched at his sides "That may be so but I was not consulted. The operative I have sent is at my own expense and is instructed to assess this man and report back to me personally. I prefer to be in control of such matters and I never have regrets, regrets are for people who fail. Your tone is not to my liking."

"Sit down Karel, calm yourself. I will tell you about this man, but only once. Do not ask me about him again."

He addressed the tipsy Karel Saudek with obvious contempt.

The speaker, a man called Magnito was known to them all, no other name had ever been provided, a well respected member of the group he headed some of the more lucrative businesses.

Karel Saudek looking around for support received some amused stares and some deadpan expressions. He remained standing, unimpressed maintaining an aggressive posture. "So, speak, tell me about my mistake."

Magnito sat back in his chair and fixed the belligerent Karel with a gentle smile.

"Vaclav Janacec was eleven years of age when he took his mother's and his father's life."

Karel Saudek sat down.

Most of those present were familiar with the story of Vaclav Janacec. His unique skills had elevated him to a very high standing in the group, in fact it was generally agreed that if they had to pick a leader it would probably be Janacec. It had been he who had brought the possible "Turner" to their attention in the first instance and had conducted much of the research. When the corroboration of the Bellini list had emerged and positive action was about to be taken, Janacec had insisted on pursuing the matter personally. Not one person in the group had objected.

Magnito continued, "His mother was a beautiful athletic woman, an accomplished high wire performer. His father was a magician. They spent most of their time with a travelling group. When the boy was only three years of age he took part in performances, astonishing audiences with his skills and courage. The boy's father exploited a financial opportunity with a magic act. The act attracted very rich people who paid large sums of money for special performances. The special performances involved a high degree of sadism and cruelty with audience participation. The young boy added an element of fascination, exposed to and taking part in the most sadistic of activities." Magnito went on to describe how, in some instances, victims were killed in front of an audience and what became known as "Snuff Movies" made a very lucrative activity.

He then explained how both parents had met their death, expertly assassinated. A trick knife, a stiletto, was the murder weapon. The boy, Janacec, was found by Magnito sitting between them with the bloody instrument in his hand. It was his eleventh birthday. At this point Magnito paused and looked around at his audience who though aware of most of the facts had never heard such a detailed account before. As the memories flooded back, memories of a time and events that were to change the course of Magnito's life, he had their complete attention.

"I'm a good boy. I did it the right way." Vaclav's great dark eyes searched his uncle's face for signs of approval and praise as he held up the knife for Magnito to see.

Just the stiletto part had been used; the deadly, long, pointed blade dulled by the blood of the eleven year old boy's mother and father. Their bodies lay where they had been professionally and accurately slain while they had slept.

"What have you done?"Horrified, Magnito's mind struggled to cope with the magnitude of the boy's deed.

"You killed them?"

The boy rose to his feet tall for his age, as tall as his uncle.

"Are you displeased with me Uncle Magnito?

I did it the way I always do," He demonstrated the swift action holding the knife lightly balanced in his hand.

"And I used the mouse,"

It was only then that the horrified Magnito noticed the small pile of wriggling white mice gathered at the blood seeping through the white bed sheet.

The boy's eyes still looked, searched, pleaded for approval. Avoiding their gaze Magnito taking a deep breath, hands clasped together looked to the heavens in a bid to find an answer from God.

"Will there be a funeral and can I wear father's black hat?" Came the unbelievable request.

"What?" Magnito could not believe what he was hearing.

"You will never see them again you have taken their lives away, your father and your Mother who loved you. Have you no remorse? Are you not sorry? Do you regret what you have done? Why did you kill them?"

Magnito looked into the big dark eyes, eyes that were now no longer pleading for approval.

Vaclav proffered the pig shaped moneybox.

"My Korunas please, I did two"

Outraged, grief stricken, Magnito sent the box flying with a backhand swipe.

Instantly his outrage was replaced by caution and fear.

The boy stood, balanced, the knife held forward the tip of the blade slightly dropped at an angle, ready, the fighter's pose. Magnito knew if he tried to strike the boy it would be his last living act.

"I will not kill you Uncle because you never hurt me."

It was a statement and a warning.

"But what if I killed you Vaclav, what if I caught you off guard and killed you with a knife what then?"

"It wouldn't matter, I might like it, I don't know," came the answer as Vaclav retrieved the moneybox and proffered it again.

"My Korunas please!"

Magnito reached into his pocket and taking out the coins dropped them one at a time into the slot between the yellow flowers on the pigs back. He spoke quietly to the boy.

"Say nothing of this to anyone. I love you. You are my son now. You did good and I will never hurt you."

Vaclav smiled and with a barely audible click the vicious blades receded into the handle of the ancient weapon.

The explanation of thieves in the night, organised disruption of the sleeping quarters and the authorities acceptance of several false eye accounts, plus the greasing of several palms resulted in no charges.

Time passed and Magnito and Vaclav formed a strong bond. The lucrative business resumed and grew under the control of Magnito and continued for over a year.

Vaclav's attitude to death persisted and he would talk in a friendly way about his deeds, even on occasion boasting about what he had done.

It was impossible to keep the rumours from the ears of the authorities. A thorough investigation ensued. Vaclav at twelve years of age freely gave evidence against himself;

His lack of a guilty conscience and even his pride in what
he had done made his conviction an easy matter.

"What happened the boy?"

Karel Saudek, fascinated by the account demanded more information.

In a voice devoid of emotion Magnito continued,

"He was arrested and convicted and then sentenced to fifteen years incarceration in Juvenile prison. Two years later when he was thirteen his special talents came to the notice of the military and the boy was moved to a military special unit prison. Here he came under the tutorage of experts in all aspects of undercover work and terrorist tactics. He was tested beyond all normal standards both mentally and physically, his tutors revelling in his receptive mind and his uniqueness.

It was a savage development of a child who was already immersed in such extraordinary behaviour. He flourished and developed.

At a very early age his reputation had spread within the force as an extraordinary gifted and coldblooded assassin with immense physical and mental strength.

In total contradiction he appeared to be a person of good humour and great charm, his affable manner and extreme good looks and stature belied the darker side to his nature.

On completing his sentence, choosing to stay in the military, he saw active service in the following five years, eventually leaving to become a mercenary for hire to the highest bidder."

"Where is he now, exactly?" Karel demanded, fascinated by the account.

"At our base in London came the reply."

"I want to meet him, when he comes to Prague, send him to me," Karel Saudek demanded, confronting Magnito.

"That would be up to him Karel, came the answer." If you wish to meet him you could make a request. But you would need to use a more polite tone."

"I certainly will make a request to meet him, who should I talk to?"

"I could approach Vaclav Janacec on your behalf,"

Magnito fixed the arrogant Karel with a steady gaze.

"Are you sure you want to meet this man? Your manners would irritate him and that would not be good for you," he said with a mirthless smile. "Are you sure you want me to give him your instruction, your demand to meet you," he continued with a quizzically raised eyebrow.

"Well maybe not," Karel, who, bluster deserting him was having second thoughts.

Magnito was not prepared to let him back away. "It's decided, you have demanded, no ordered, that he should meet you. I'll tell him."

Then standing up he addressed the room. "Good night gentlemen." At the door he turned. Karel was now standing arms outstretched palms upwards.

"It's alright, please don't ask him,"

Magnito, much to the amusement of those present made a horrible grimace, tongue lolling from the side of his mouth as he drew an imaginary knife blade across his throat never taking his wide eyed stare from the eyes of the unhappy man. Holding the position for several seconds.

" You're dead," he whispered, "sleep tight."

The "Base" in London occupied the entire top floor penthouse apartment of a large office block. Set back from the sides of the building the structure could not be seen from ground level. The lift stopped at the sixth floor and a discrete stairs behind a nondescript unmarked door led upwards to a small landing. Here a steel door barred the entrance to the "Base". Unless you had the combination you could go no further. The steel door when opened gave access to a very modern, three bedroomed apartment with ceiling high windows presenting an exceptional view over

London. At the back of the apartment access to the rest of the facility could be gained through a concealed door in the bathroom.

High windows on all sides of the building looked on to a wide balcony encircling the structure.

Inside was bristling with high Tec equipment and accommodation for up to twenty people. The facility could house and sustain a force for a considerable time with a fully equipped operating theatre, kitchen, refrigerators, cold storage, a dormitory, small well equipped gymnasium and five sound proofed cells. The smell of sanitising agent pervaded the air and the hum of a generator could be detected.

This evening only three people occupied the premises, two in the dormitory and one in the cells.

In the brightly lit dormitory Vaclav Janacec removed his jacket and opening the door of the slim locker beside the bed reached for a coat hanger. Meticulously he arranged the jacket, smoothing the shoulders and adjusting the lapel.

He was aware that his every move was under scrutiny by the only other occupant of the room, a tall muscular, broad shouldered man with a very steady insolent gaze.

Vaclav appeared to ignore him until the man rising to his feet moved to a position between the beds and stood legs apart, arms folded, staring.

The jacket now hanging in the locker Vaclav closed the door and turned, with a bright friendly smile.

"Hello," he greeted the man. No response.

His smile broadened as he made his way around the end of the bed. Catching his knee on the metal edge of one corner Vaclav's smile changed to a grimace of discomfort. Awkwardly he stopped to give it a rub before facing the man. "Alan Grant," he introduced himself extending his hand, which was entirely ignored.

The man standing watched every move. His brief from Karel Saudek had been succinct, contact the operative, assess and report back. They had said nothing about harming the individual or even killing him, the impression implied weakness, softness, a civilian, probably an observer, a technician of some sort, certainly not a physical operative.

Deciding to test his quarry further the man stepped forward in front of and very close to Vaclav.

"Choose another bed, this is mine."

The challenge was blatant and the threat obvious.

Vaclav Janacec looked apprehensive and apologetic for a moment and then, with a gentle smile said,

"Are you prepared to die for it?"

Trained military mind instantly sensing danger, aware of the vulnerability of his position and stance, too near, off balance, the man tried to adjust, too late. Something white flashed between them and out to one side, his eyes followed the movement. In the instant he realized his mistake the stiletto slammed in between ear and mastoid bone. The force of the blow pitching him sideways, dead before his body hit the bed.

Vaclav Janacec, alias Alan Grant, gently placed the white mouse on the muscular shoulder. It immediately began to investigate the trickle of blood coming from the small wound in the man's head.

Without a second glance at his victim Vaclav, the killer, turned and strode purposefully between the beds, out the door at the end room and through the adjoining dining area to the control room.

All around the base security cameras kept their continuous vigil. The control room housed the monitors and computers and it was a simple task to identify the monitors displaying the dormitory section.

Selecting a screen he watched the replay of himself taking the man's life. Close up and freeze, the exact moment, there right now he watched the man's eyes, the split second.

Vaclav leaned closer to the monitor and drank in the HD image. He examined minutely every detail savouring the exact moment when the man realized he was about to die. Replay the whole action close up, freeze, replay, and freeze. At last satisfied he pressed delete, the scene now forever stored in his mind to be called up and savoured at any future date.

Returning to the dormitory he retrieved the white mouse from its foraging. The dead man lying spread-eagled on the bed held very little interest for him. A quick check revealed nothing. All tags had been removed leaving no clue to identity, someone else's problem, to be disposed of. There was some cash in the wallet, this he removed and counted, seven hundred and twenty five pounds.

Slim, white fingers flicked through the notes with practiced slight of hand creating a fan. Holding the fan in one hand he made an open palm pass with the other. The money had disappeared and the white mouse had taken its place, sitting on his palm. Smiling he made a ladder with his fingers and watched with amusement as the agile creature wriggled and climbed up and down, in and out, going nowhere.

Tiring of the game Vaclav abruptly headed out the door and along the dimly lit corridor to the only occupied cell.

"It's only me," he greeted the terrified face of the occupant.

The cull-de sac had seen better days. Certainly the word character could be applied to the slightly crooked railings that protected small gardens in front of the two storied town houses.

Tim Holmes rounded the corner and hurried along the cracked pavement. He moved with the quick short strides his portly figure allowed. "Dum de dum eye of the tiger" he hummed, more Oliver Hardy than Sylvester Stallone.

Jennifer would have a drink waiting and something nice in the oven. What had she said? "Roast chicken?" Mmm… he sniffed the air in anticipation like a Bisto Kid.

Without breaking his stride he passed the parked cars lining the road and entered the little garden. At the door he transferred the bottle of wine from his right to his left hand as he retrieved keys from his trousers pocket.

"The master of the house has arrived wench and is demanding to be fed," he called to the awaiting Jennifer. No answer! No beautiful smell of roast chicken! Silence greeted him as he made his way down the short hall.

She's probably popped out for something he assumed pushing the door open into the kitchen.

"Hello Timmy boy,"

The vaguely familiar voice stopped him in his tracks filling him with dread and an overriding urge to run. Anxiety for Jennifer rooted him to the spot. His mind did cartwheels as he watched the big man rise to his feet and come towards him.

"Hi Matt, who's been eating my porridge?" Tim's attempt at humour and bravado fell short of the mark.

The big man smiled.

"Always the funny man, Tim!" A large hand clamped behind Tim's neck propelling him across the room. Matt followed up forcing the unfortunate Tim to his knees propelling him forward so that his face was jammed against the cooker and his arm twisted cruelly behind his back.

"Take it easy," he gasped on the verge of losing consciousness. Tim felt the pressure easing on his arm as his body was turned, the big man using his strength to manhandle him into a sitting position. Tim thought he heard a click.

Matt releasing him stood up and stepped back breathing heavily from the exertion. "A bit out of condition Tim, I'll have to eat more porridge," he said rubbing his hands together. "You don't seem very pleased to see me."

When Tim, relieved that he had no longer been manhandled, shakily made an attempted to arise he realized with a shock that his wrist was handcuffed to the Cooker door.

"Yes Tim my little porky friend. You ain't going no where!"

"Where's Jennifer, what have you done to her? Look, I can get you money if that's what you want." Tim looked up at the big man, "please Matt!"

"Won't you introduce us?"

The tall man at the kitchen door said in a pleasant voice casually leaning against the door jam his arm around Jennifer's shoulders. The speaker gestured towards the front door, "we're just popping out for a while."

"Jennie!" Tim tried to get to his feet.

"Are you alright?"

When she did not reply Tim switched his attention to the man.

"Who are you? What do you want? Don't hurt her, please! I'll give you anything you want. .... Is it the Turner? I can get it for you!"

He looked frantically at Jennifer, her head was resting against the man's shoulder and she seemed unaware of Tim's presence.

"What did you do to her you bastard?" He wrenched at the restraining handcuff trying to pull the heavy handle from the oven door.

"I'll see you later, we have a date at the Regent Palace I believe," came the pleasant reply. "We have to go now don't we Jenny," he stroked her cheek with the back of a forefinger and kissed her forehead. "Please hit him Matt, I don't like my parental credentials being questioned."

Matt obliged with an expert right hook from a standing position. The blow drove Tim back to the floor. He lay there watching the couple at the door as he struggled to keep focus. Jennifer still seemed unaware but he noted that she was capable of standing and walking.

Matt manhandled the semi conscious Tim and propped him up against the oven door. "Tim, Tim, Tim that one is not to be messed with," he said with a movement of his head in the direction of the door and the departing couple.

Regaining his composure somewhat,

"Where's that guy taking her?" The distressed Tim asked.

"I don't know and I don't want to know. What I do know is that he'll be back later to collect you my son and take you to this meeting with that Irish bloke."

"Well you'd better keep me in good condition," said Tim, "Lay off the rough stuff or I won't be able to go to any meeting. Look Matt, I'll cut you in on the deal; it's a great earner. All I'm interested in now is to get Jennifer back, safe. You can have my share of the deal. I've even got some loot in the bank. It's all yours Matt. Just let me go free and tell me where he's taken' her."

Matt stood up and looked down at the fat boy who had once shared a cell with him in prison.

"You don't get it Tim, do you?"

He hunkered down ant put his big face close to Tim's.

"I know you shopped me, telling porky pies to the G'uvner. Ole Matt here got an extra stretch and Porky boy got parole."

"It wasn't like that!" Tim protested, "I never did! You've got it wrong! Look Matt, this is a beautiful deal, big, big, big money! And I have it perfectly set up. Come in with me and you'll never have to worry about money again. There's a couple of million in it. You can have what you want. We jump that prissy lookin' boyo when he gets back. Put him out of action. Send him packin'. God help him if he's hurt Jennifer. What do you say?"

Matt who had been looking down at the floor slowly raised his big meaty head.

"You've no idea what you're messing with here. That bloke is something special." He looked earnestly at Tim.

"He doesn't want your face too messed up for the meeting tonight. When he gets back he won't have the girl with him. He's takin' her to some place in the city centre. I'm to go there later to be with her in case you don't behave yourself."

"We could take him Matt, there's no one better than you at the strong arm stuff, you're as strong as a bull and you know how to handle yourself. Think of all that money." Tim played every card in his hand.

"No chance Porky boy," Matt shook his head "This guy's something else. I never saw anything so quick and he's got this fancy knife. He had some kind of magic act, worked in carnivals on the continent and stuff. Says his name is Alan Grant, but he's foreign in spite of his posh British accent."

"The first time I met him". Matt looked to one side, remembering and then looking back at Tim, "It was in the car park of a pub in Vicars Street. He put out his hand for a handshake. When I reached to shake hands he stuck me in the shoulder with a blade. I never saw it coming it was so fast. He just stood there with this smile on his face."

"You know me Tim. I can handle myself and I'm big. I just wanted to knock the smile off his face. You wouldn't believe it,"

Matt, taken up with his story held up his fists.

"I took up the stance and showed him the size of me mitts. He never even moved, didn't get ready, just smiled at me, cool as you like. I know a thing or two about fightin' and for my size I'm quick. I showed him my left and brought up the right straight for his meat and two veg. He didn't seem to move but I missed. I was in close so I had him. I went for the bear hug and brought up my knee. It was like grabbin' something made of steel. It should have been all over when I got hold of him like that."

"Tim, he's something else," Matt shaking his head again, remembering, and dropping his fists said. "He easily broke my grip and pushed me back, all the time smiling. His fingers had me in some fancy Chinese Grip. I tell you, I couldn't move. The knife was still sticking in my shoulder. Now Mister Matt says he, reaching up with his lilywhite hand. You wouldn't believe it he was holding a white mouse. He put it on my shoulder and I could feel it creeping around where the knife was stuck in me."

The big man quivered at the memory. Obviously Matt had a horror of rodents.

"Then he told me that if I was going to work with him I'd have to do as I was told. He said, "Say yes Mr Janacec. I bleedin' said yes." Then said Matt, "He suddenly changed, nice as pie, sorry Matt, says he. He even offered to fix up my shoulder all nice and friendly like."

Matt shook his head again from side to side and looked at Tim.

"I can tell you I've seen that bastard do some terrible things to people. So ya see what I mean. When he comes back you're going to do whatever he says."

Tim listened to the account wide eyed with dread for his daughter. He was prompted to grab Matt by the arm. "You have to let me go, Matt!" He pleaded.

The big man pulled his arm free and hit Tim with the back of his hand then grabbed him by the collar pulling him close to his face.

"No deal ya little nark, ya shopped me and you're goin' to get yours. The foreign boy said I was to keep ya lookin' ok for the meetin' and when he's finished with you he'll hand you over to me."

He suddenly let go the collar and Tim slumped back to the floor.

"Now," said the big man, "Have you got a telly here, I'm goin' to watch the horse racin'? You sit here like a good boy an' behave yourself."

Rising to his feet he opened the fridge door. With a grunt of satisfaction he retrieved a six-pack of beers.

"Thanks Tim, these'll do nicely," he said and headed for the living room.

Tim sat on the floor his back against the oven door his mind in turmoil, every bone in his body ached. He could taste blood in his mouth and the side of his face felt numb, closing his eyes a feeling of despair overcame him and he slumped back resigned.

Exhausted he sniffed and his face creased as he sobbed.

"Jennifer! The bastard,"

His eyes flew open and tears of frustration coursed down his cheeks to be scrubbed away with the backs of both hands.

"Jennifer!" Appalled by his feeling of helplessness he began to feel angry.

The anger surprised him and fuelled his resolve. Get free and get them, make them pay, this cannot happen, I won't let it. He began to think more clearly about escape.

No amount of jerking or pulling would release him from the cooker door that was obvious. Painfully turning his body around he found it was possible to get into a kneeling position. The handcuff slid right and left along the metal bar, kneeling there facing the kitchen presses and the cooker he listened. He could hear the horse racing on the telly, leaning back and craning his neck he could see out into the hall and through the door into the living room. Just part of the sofa was visible and one of Matt's big size elevens.

The incredible hulk would rip the cooker from its mountings, go in and drop it on the fucker's head. Tim jerked the oven door open and examined the back of it searching for how the handle was attached. There was a metal panel covering the whole area held in position by screws. Two of these screws coincided with the long door handle.

Tim looked along the presses to the knife drawer. He knew that there was a screwdriver in there.

A quick lean back and a glance, the big size eleven was still there and he could hear the commentary.

Opening the door as far as it would go he slid the handcuff along the limit of the long handle. It made a rasping sound. Tim froze, lean back, glance, size eleven, ok.

Shuffling on his knees and reaching he could just touch the knife drawer with his fingertips but not far enough to grasp the handle. Physical endeavour not being Tim's forte the combination of stretching his body to the limit and fear made him gasped for breath. Frantically he reached out, feeling the metal of the handcuff bite into his wrist, just a fraction of an inch. The tip of his index finger reached the corner of the drawer, it opened slightly. He managed to prize it open further but lost his balance, jerking agonizingly, twisting his shoulder. His hand now nearer hit the side of the open drawer hard, propelling it out too far. It dipped and slid out and down spilling the contents onto the tiled floor. Knives, forks spoons and the screwdriver plus some other odds and ends spewed in all directions with a crash!

Tim was trying to regain his kneeling position when Matt came through the door fast and grabbed him by the collar. Wide-eyed Tim could see the screwdriver within easy reach.

"Tim, Tim, Timmy boy!" Matt's voice chided menacingly. "What's this? What's this?"

Tim tried not to stare at the screwdriver. Matt still holding his collar reached out a big hand and picked up the small sharp pointed kitchen knife that was lying beside the screwdriver.

"And what were you going to do with this you little fat fucker, stick it in me?"

He brought the knife up to Tim's throat as he spat the words through his teeth. The knifepoint pricked the skin, drawing blood. Tim, past caring tried to hit out with his free hand. Matt easily parried the feeble attempt and Tim cursed as his arm was twisted behind his back and his face pushed into the floor. The knifepoint at his ear drew blood that ran across his cheek dripping red and alarming.

"Next time Tim my boy, when the foreign lad finishes with you your mine. Why don't I keep this little blade until then."

The commentary from the living room signalled the final stages of the race. Matt pocketed the knife and hurried out of the kitchen.

The screwdriver, with its yellow and black handle lay where it had fallen on the tiled floor. Tim dragged his eyes from it as he checked over his shoulder twisting his body to see. The big size eleven was back in place.

Expelling air with a sigh of relief he grabbed the instrument that would set him free his heart racing.

"No! Shit! No!" he stared in disbelief at the Philips screwdriver in his hand, with its little star shaped head. He looked again at the screw head with its straight groove. The Philips would be useless!

Despair grabbed his heart and he slumped back, sitting on the floor head down with all the utensils around him, table knives and forks everywhere. He felt his ear, his fingers coming away with a smear of blood.

A knife! He reached for one of the table knives and turned his attention to the large headed screw. The knife blade fitted nicely into the groove. With a feeling of hope and desperation he put pressure on the blade but the screw didn't budge, some more pressure and the blade began to bend. That's Ikea for you, it moved and the blade slipped out of the groove but the screw turned slightly.

Heart racing, another quick check for the size eleven, attack the screw again.

This time, it turned easily. Holding the long handle in place lest it might slip and make noise as it came loose, he completed the task. Closing the door carefully it was easy to pull the end of the handle away from its housing and slide the handcuff free.

He contemplated for a moment the possibility of releasing the heavy handle completely and using it as a weapon to go in and smash Matt's brains in.

Too risky, he checked through the door. Matt was totally engrossed with the racing. Tim looked back to the oven handle. His instinct told him to make his escape, put as much distance between himself and the big man as possible *but what about Jennifer? He had to find her. Matt knew where she was.*

Tim scrambled to his feet. The big size-elevens were still in place. Fear of Matt drove Tim towards the back door and into the small yard. The red brick wall stopped him in his tracks but only for a moment. He scrambled onto the coalbunker and reached for the top of the wall, imagination-running riot now he looked over his shoulder at the open back door, half expecting to see the big figure of Matt come charging through.

Frozen in position, sitting astride the wall he watched the open doorway his heart thumping in his chest. *Why had he stopped? Escape, this is your chance save yourself.*

Then he saw it, left there by some careless workman, a heavy lump hammer with its short thick handle and square mallet metal head covered in rust lying in some weeds at the edge of the little path. *One blow.*

Tim releasing the top of the wall clambered down off the coal bunker, every sense on high alert, he reached for the heavy weapon and hefted it in his hand, the head was very heavy and it needed two hands to support its weight in a striking position.

"*One blow*" he repeated to himself. "*One blow*" and Matt would be at his mercy.

The handcuff dangled from the fat man's wrist as he stealthily made his way through the back door and towards the front room, the plan forming in his mind on how to save his daughter giving him strength and courage.

The sound from the commentary was at a high volume and the picture flickered as the crowd cheered louder, the crescendo of noise heralding the closing stages of the 4.30 at Chepstow, but Tim only had eyes for the back of the big head as he crept closer, hammer raised.

Knock him out, handcuff him to the radiator and when he comes too make him divulge where Jennifer had been taken.

"*Over the last its Lazy Henry and Delilah's Relish on the run in, with Magical Mystery coming fast on the outside!*" The big head shot forward as Matt suddenly leaned towards the screen "C'mon ya beauty!" He roared, "c'mon!, c'mon!"

Twenty pounds at seven to one would be a nice little earner. *"At the post it's Magical Mystery from Lazy Henry by a short head,"*

"Nice One!" roared Matt, drowning out the commentator's voice.

"Nice one!" he repeated sinking back into the sofa, head thrown back looking to the ceiling arms outstretched in victory.

He saw the rusty head of the heavy hammer just before it crashed down on his forehead, driven with all the panic-stricken force the Chubby Comedian could muster.

Tim, nerves jangling, his body convulsing with tension held the hammer aloft ready to strike again. There was blood in the curly grey black hair but he couldn't see Matt's face. Eventually, when he was sure the big head wasn't going to move he cautiously rounded the sofa, hammer still aloft, eyes fixed on the target ready to strike again, his mind playing tricks. The eyes were open and staring at the floor, hammer house of horrors. Tim looked away and stared at the big hands instead. They didn't suddenly reach out to grab him. Picking up courage he reached out and, avoiding contact with the man's flesh lifted a heavy wrist by the cuff of the jacket letting it drop quickly. It fell limply when he released it. Avoiding sight of the face he gingerly began to search, gently using his fingertips to take a wallet from the inside pocket, all the time gaining in courage as it became more and more apparent that Matt was unlikely to make a move. He found car keys and the key to the handcuffs.

Having removed the cuffs from his wrist Tim snapped them onto the right wrist of the inert unmoving man and pocketed the key.

Turning off the television he surveyed his handiwork. All that remained was to handcuff his tormentor to the radiator. Move quicker, the fear that his victim might come too spurred Tim to greater effort. Grabbing the thick wrist he hauled and pulled frantically until he eventually managed to hook the cuff onto the bracket that secured the radiator to the wall. During the struggle he had avoided looking at Matt's face. Now having completed the major part of his plan he stood back to survey his handiwork. Matt was lying on his side with his arm stretched to its limit eyes staring sightlessly the forehead collapsed, discoloured and misshapen.

It was not the first time Tim had been confronted by the sight of a dead person. It was certainly the first time he had been confronted with one he had killed himself. The fact that he had handcuffed a corpse to a radiator in order to prevent it from escaping, appealed to the fat man's sense of humour. The urge to laugh out loud was difficult for him to contain, however, he managed to restrict himself to a respectful grim smile.

He felt no remorse just regret that he had permanently silenced the person who could lead him to his daughter.

Suddenly he began to tremble uncontrollably collapsing into an armchair. For a while he lay sprawled with his eyes closed breathing heavily, beads of perspiration forming and rolling down his face, exhausted, spent, overcome with the emotion and unaccustomed frantic activity, his mind working overtime as his heart raced. Bands of pain raced across his chest and he gasped for breath convinced he was on the verge of a heart attack. How long he lay there he was not sure, immobile afraid to move. Eventually the pains subsided and his breathing became more normal.

"Bimma bam bimma boom I live to fight another day."

He laughed in relief and made an unsuccessful effort to stand up. Perhaps I'll take it easy for a minute or two, he cautioned himself but his watch said no time to hang about. With a supreme effort he turned himself in the deep cushioned chair and managed to put one knee on the floor. Matt's snakeskin wallet lay on the carpet where it had fallen, he picked it up, put both hands on the seat and pushed himself into a standing position.

Somewhere in the city centre, Matt had said, the foreign guy was going to take Tim to the meeting and Matt

*was going to hold Jennifer prisoner somewhere in the city
centre. Where in the city centre?*

Jennifer Holmes lay on her back and stared into what
seemed infinity. She knew her eyes were open but there
was nothing to see, closing her eyes and then opening
them again as wide as possible, moving her head from side
to side, still nothing.

Sitting up, she realized that she was on a narrow bed. I
must have been sleeping, she assumed. Her head throbbed
and her mouth felt dry, movement caused her limbs to
ache. Where am I? She felt dizzy and disorientated.

She and the bed seemed to be floating in mid-air.

With an effort she managed to move her legs
sufficiently to swing one foot off the bed and towards
where the floor should be. Her toes made contact.

With relief she put two feet on the white floor and
stood up.

It's an illusion her astute mind reasoned as she looked
around. There are no shadows; there is an equal
distribution of light coming from every side, even the floor
is slightly transparent allowing light through. Above her
head there appeared to be no ceiling, just whiteness.
Obviously the ceiling is very high and curved and the
room circular.

On further exploration of her cell she discovered where
the walls and floor met. The room was small, about ten
feet in diameter with a narrow bed in the centre.

Her eyes becoming more accustomed to the whiteness a
recess was revealed, which obviously served as a toilet,
there was a disc about one inch diameter. Jennifer pushed
it. With a loud vacuum sucking sound a hole appeared at
the bottom of the recess, rather like toilets on an aeroplane.
The sound stopped and the hole disappeared.

The only other feature in her white cell was a grill, which she opened, to reveal a small shelf holding a plastic cup of water, some cheese and a thick piece of bread.

The sight of the food tempted Jennifer, she felt hungry, thirsty, licking her dry lips she touched the water with her fingertips.

It might be drugged, that foreign guy is capable of anything. Should she take the chance and eat something?

Piece by piece the events of the day started coming back to her. The brutality of the attack, the sadistic smile as the mouse struggled and died, her dad handcuffed to the cooker. The memories served to strengthen her resolve.

I have to be strong and somehow survive this. I need to eat, I need to drink and I need my strength. She had not eaten since early morning.

Licking her finger, the water tasted good. Maybe some bread too. Breaking off a piece of bread she sniffed it and popped it into her mouth, thoroughly chewing the crusty morsel. It tasted good, another piece of bread followed and a sip of water. Deciding the water was ok she drank some more.

The cheese was tempting, cheddar.

On close examination it seemed ok. Suspiciously she broke it into pieces, examining each piece carefully. It seemed all right but Jennifer could not bring herself to eat it.

Taking the chunk of bread and the large plastic cup she returned to the bed and sat down. The dizzy feeling had gone and the movement had helped relieve the stiffness in her limbs.

I wonder if I'm being watched? Of course, he's probably watching me right now.

Allowing her shoulders to slump she dropped the water and let the bread fall to the floor making sure some water spilled on her hands. Putting her fingers to her eyes she began to sob letting the water to trickle down her face.

Raising her head, she looked around her cell with apparent despair showing on her tearstained face. "Help!"

she shouted, "somebody Help me!" She cried out louder and louder, looking around frantically. She jumped up and began to scramble at the walls as if trying to find a way out. "Help me, let me go! Please! Please!"

Eventually appearing to tire she made her way back to the bed and throwing herself down curled up hugging her knees, sobbing.

Dark eyes watched the distressed woman lying on the bed. Janacec had seen the pattern before, the sudden crumbling of the victim's resolve, the food forgotten, the protective position on the bed, the inert figure frozen into immobility. *The mouse stops its struggle and lies unmoving. The cat prods the mouse and steps back, then, prods the mouse again coaxing it into movement, the mouse runs, the cat pounces. The process is repeated until the cat tiring of the game kills and eats the mouse.*

Jennifer lay on the bed assessing her situation now totally convinced that she was being watched.

The whispering, coaxing, gentle voice when it came took her by surprise. *"Nothing stirred not even a mouse, nothing stirred not even a mouse."* She lay still and listened. *"Jennifer, Jennifer, you're safe now."* The gentle voice cajoled.

The figure on the bed remained unmoving. *"Jenny, Jenny, my fat hen lays her eggs for gentlemen. Let me introduce you to your new home Jennifer. It's called the killing cell with many attractive features, some experimental, some tried and tested, all effective and I have the controls."*

The voice sounded all the more sinister because of its gentle softness.

Jennifer did not react. She lay and thought of her Dad. I hope he's all right. She drew in a deep breath and exhaled slowly remembering how helpless he appeared crouched on the floor beside the cooker. I have to get out of here somehow. He's not strong, and his health is not great. She could feel real tears begin to come but they were for her father and not for herself.

A door opened behind her as she lay on the bed. "Hello Jennifer,"

While Jennifer had been examining the food she had noticed the hairline crack of the door. When she appeared to throw herself down on the bed in total despair she had done so orchestrating her position carefully.

She knew exactly where her tormentor was standing as he spoke. She lay still waiting for the prod, waiting for the cat's next move.

He was very close; she could hear his breathing, feel his touch as he stroked her hair.

The position of her body was correct, her hips turned, her torso twisted away from the target. She flexed her fingers and made a hidden tight fist.

Vaclav Janacec was off guard and taken by surprise at the ferocity of the attack.

Jennifer whirled with all the strength and flexibility of the trained karate player, the expertly delivered blow from her hard little fist impacted fractionally off target. Intended to shatter the septum of the nose, a lethal blow that renders the victim helpless, it glanced off Janacec's cheek but with sufficient force to knock him off balance.

The vicious kick that followed took his standing leg. He hit the tiled floor and rolled away avoiding the kicking feet as Jennifer came off the bed following up her advantage, trying to find a telling blow. She leapt through the open doorway pulling the door behind her, lock him in, quickly! The door would not close completely, two bolts protruded, obviously controlled by some electric device.

The door was wrenched violently from her grasp. Jennifer turned and fled down the white corridor.

"The mouse is away," Vaclav stood in the open doorway.

"Let the mouse run." He watched the fleeing figure until she reached the end of the corridor and then he strolled leisurely in the opposite direction to the fleeing girl.

Jennifer ran as fast as she could along the featureless corridor. There could have been doors on each side but she did not notice them in her headlong flight, through a glass doorway and another turn to the right, her heart thumping in her chest, looking behind, there was no sign of her tormenter. She slowed down, wide-eyed and watchful, listening for some sound of pursuit.

Satisfied that he was not close she looked around, for the first time taking in her surroundings. On one side a glass wall ran practically the length of the building stretching from floor to ceiling, on the other a white wall.

Putting her hands against the glass Jennifer looked out over London. The panoramic view stretched to the Thames, London's eye, government Buildings, so familiar so normal.

The glass felt warm against her palms, stepping back she searched for an opening. The balcony outside with its railing beckoned, surely there has to be an opening, a way out. Moving along the corridor Jennifer examined carefully and in vain.

Eventually, in frustration, taking a step back she leaped off the floor and hurled herself against the toughened glass, feet first with all her might.

Janacec watched the image on the monitor with amusement. How like a mouse she seemed in her feeble attempts to escape. "Jump little mouse, jump."

Obviously the glass wall was not about to give. A quick glance back along the corridor confirmed that there was no one in pursuit.

Surprise had been Jennifer's ally in her escape from the cell. She knew that skilful as she may be she would be no match for her captor in a head on confrontation.

Rounding another corner, another view of London presented itself, Big Ben, Tourists and Londoners going about their daily business, far below. How Jennifer wished she could join them.

"Hickory Dickory Dock," The cat watching her progress, crouched, ready to pounce.

Aware that she had been moving in a clockwise direction since leaving the cell Jennifer decided to explore elsewhere, not wanting to end up where she had started. Slow down, form a plan.

Looking at the other buildings she calculated that she was on the seventh floor obviously at the top of a modern office block. Taking a bearing from the position of Big Ben she knew, almost to the street, where she was. Not being able to see directly down because of the balcony she could still make an accurate estimation as to her location. If this is the building I think it is, the entrance should be on the other side, there has to be a lift, she reasoned.

Some doors in the corridor were ajar, try the first one, a quick glance inside revealed what appeared to be an operating theatre. Jennifer stepped inside in search of a weapon. Various medical instruments were neatly arranged in containers. Selecting the largest scalpel she could find, Jennifer returned to the corridor putting to the back of her mind the horrors the room might present.

Further along she found a kitchen but to her disappointment all the utensils were locked away. A nice big meat cleaver would be useful she thought to herself. The only thing to hand was a breadknife. Deciding to keep the scalpel as well she hefted the breadknife testing its balance.

"She cut off their tails with a carving knife,"

The cat noted the breadknife when the mouse emerged from the kitchen testing its balance and the flexibility of the blade as she walked along the corridor.

The next room was more promising, a dining area with tables and chairs and a counter on one side revealed nothing of interest. But a door at the far end would keep her going in the right direction. Sure enough the door gave access to a dormitory with beds.

As Jennifer opened the door a terrible smell assailed her nostrils. The centre aisle stretched to another door at the far end. Making her way quickly between the beds the source of the smell was soon revealed as she came across

184

the body of the man. Without a glance she hurried past, heading for the door, sure she was going in the right direction. Each bed had its own locker. Something caught her eye; she stopped and looked, then looked again, unsure if her eyes were deceiving her. One of the locker doors was open revealing its contents. There were some folded shirts and bathroom things. But on closer inspection it was obvious what had caught her eye, the glint of metal. Protruding from a yellow chamois cloth was the butt of a handgun, unbelievable.

Jennifer had no training in weaponry but the gun felt comforting in her hand as she withdrew it from the locker. The equalizer, the ticket to freedom, nobody can fight a gun. She allowed herself a little smile.

"*The clock struck one….*" Jennifer whirled holding the gun in both hands aiming it straight at her tormentor's midriff. *"The mouse fell down,"* He was standing four feet away smiling, relaxed, hands in his pockets.

Held in rock steady hands, the gun aimed at the middle of the target did not waver. "I'll use it," she said fiercely, standing up from her crouched position. "Tell me where my father is," altering her aim she pointed the gun at his abdomen.

"If you don't help me and do what I want I'll shoot you right in the stomach so you die painfully."

"The safety catch is still on," he informed her. If you pull the trigger it won't fire."

Still keeping the gun trained on him she twisted her wrist slightly, glancing to see where the catch was located.

"I could easily have disarmed you when you looked at the gun," he mocked.

His friendly smile seemed to display genuine amusement.

"The safety catch is above your thumb on the left side, my little mouse. Just flick it upwards and the gun will fire when you pull the trigger."

She felt for the catch, locating it as described.

"Take one step and I'll shoot." Her voice steady, she flicked up the catch her nerves shrieking and her mind in turmoil at what she was prepared to do.

"Good little mouse, now shoot me," His smile remained in place.

"I don't think you can do it,"

"Tell me where my father is. Take me to him now. I have no trouble about shooting you,"

"It's not loaded, now isn't that very amusing," he took a step towards her.

Jennifer pulled the trigger. There was an audible click as the hammer hit the empty chamber.

Vaclav Janacec kept coming. The cat had tired of the game.

Tim Holmes, feeling somewhat refreshed after showering and changing his shirt, examined his face in the bathroom mirror, his back aching from the unaccustomed physical activity, the side of his face beginning to swell from the effect of Matt's heavy hand. The blood had washed away from his ear revealing a substantial nick which he'd patched up as best he could with cotton wool and sticking plaster.

Killing people doesn't suit me, he thought to himself as he gingerly touched the bruising of his cheek, his mind carefully ignoring the memory of the near heart attack experience and his feeling of exhaustion. Adrenalin pumping, fuelled by the beginning of a plan, a possible way to solve the problem, he helped himself to some pills just to give himself a lift. He smiled grimly at the mirror.

Where are you Jennifer? How can I find you? That smiling freak has the answer. The face looked back from the mirror and he was not reassured. He still had a body handcuffed to the radiator in the living room, to contend with.

Fraught with doubts about the plan, sitting down on the WC the fat comedian began to go through the events that had brought him to this moment.

The foreign guy told Matt to wait for his return. Tim looked at his watch again aware that the foreign guy could return at any moment. The thought of confronting him didn't appeal. *I wouldn't be much help to Jennifer dead. He's sure to turn up at tonight's meeting. He wants the Turner. That's it, the Turner. I have a buyer, a powerful ally, the famous Dragon; I also have the ear of Mr Mackedy Macken.* Tim jumped to his feet and flushed the toilet with a vengeance and hurried downstairs tucking his shirt into his trousers, the half formed plan of action giving him hope.

Jennifer's capable, young, strong and smart. She can take care of herself. She'd Karate the fuckin' head off him if he tried anything.

The pain in his back forgotten Tim took the stairs two at a time with only a quick glance from the hallway at the big figure of Matt sprawled on the sofa. *Good riddance the world is one bad man less and now I'm after your boss* he reassured himself, anxious to get out the front door and away from the house.

His hand was on the door when Matt's phone rang. Tim's immediate reaction was to keep going. *No, No, wait* he paused, *it could be something to do with Jennifer.* He could hardly believe what he was about to do. Turning, he hurried down the hall and into the living room. The ridiculous refrain of *"Ole Mac Donald's Farm"* was coming from the dead man's inside pocket.

Ignoring, as best he could, the staring eyes in the blood drained face Tim reached inside the pocket. The intimacy of the dead body appalled him. He retched feeling the bile in his throat. His fingers made contact with the phone and he jerked it free from the pocket. The movement shifted the body slightly and the big head nodded forward "*ee, ii, ee, ii, o,* the ringtone played. Tim jumped away from the body clutching the phone and headed for the door, the tone coming to an abrupt end as he flipped the Motorola open.

He stopped and stared at the phone in his hand recognising the unmistakable sound of the foreign bloke's voice. *"Matt, I want you to do as I say... Matt are you there?"* Tim hesitated but only for a moment, "Yeah," he grunted, giving a reasonable impersonation of Matt's voice.

There was no hesitation as the voice at the other end continued. *"I am going to the meeting with Macken, you take Mr Holmes to the base, the girl is there. Put him in cell number four. Use the Vicar's Street entrance. I will not return to Mr Holmes house."*

With a growled "Yeah, right then," Tim closed the flap of the fancy phone.

The rotund comedian looked down at the big dead man

"Well did you hear that, Matt", Tim addressed the dead body,

"Get your arse moving."

Relief flooded through Tim with the knowledge that Jennifer was still alive.

She's at the base, Vicars Street. Tim knew Vicar Street. He tried to remember what Matt had said, something about being given an instruction.

Matt's snakeskin wallet revealed what he was looking for almost immediately, a piece of paper with Matt's scrawl, two words, Vicars Street and a six-digit number.

Janacec waited at the traffic lights on the corner of Vicar Street. In charge, in control, everywhere he looked he saw challenges, temptations. Opposite, at the other side of the street, in front of the Duck and Shovel Pub pedestrians waited for the lights to change. The call to Matt would put him and the fat man at the base together. Later, after the meeting in the Regent Palace, he would return to the base and deal with both of them.

The lights changed, he began to cross the road satisfied that he was achieving his mission, how impressed his uncle would be, the one called Magnito, the only person in the world worthy of his respect.

A young woman caught his eye as they began to cross the street. She smiled as she approached, he was used to that. They always smiled at him. He smiled back.

What a hot looking guy, nice smile, she thought as they passed. His fleeting thoughts were far more sinister. His smile remained in place as he contemplated the possibilities. He turned to look after her. She was looking back, her smile inviting. He was considering the possibility of following her when his phone bleeped.

The text message said "FAT MAN DEAD I KILLED HIM WHAT YOU WANT ME TO DO   MATT.

Vaclav Janacek looked after the girl who was standing feigning interest in a shop window. She turned her head to look at him. His eyes held her transfixed. A feeling of dread combined with an inexplicable urge to stand still invaded her mind.

Janacec transferred his attention to the phone, assessing the information he punched in the instruction. GO TO THE BASE NOW! STAY THERE.

The fat man's death didn't change things. Jennifer had supplied him with all the information he needed. But there was the matter of the Dragon. It was slightly regrettable. The Fat Man had been an introduction to a buyer for the painting. It would have been impressive to deliver the Turner and a buyer to Magnito and the group.

He looked to the girl who was standing as if frozen to the pavement.

"Damn Matt!"

He turned and strode past the pub entrance and towards the Subway, a connection to Piccadilly Circus and the Regent Palace Hotel. His focus now fixed on Susan Macken.

In her hotel room Susan sat at the large mirror and adjusted her make up.

Judge Judy barked at some unfortunate married couple on the plasma screen but Susan was not interested. She was busy trying to put thoughts of Paul to the back of her mind by concentrating on the meeting with the fat man, and of course, tomorrow's meeting with Thorndike, definitely there's something strange there, it doesn't add up.

She didn't realize she was crying.

There were no great sobs of grief, just some gentle tears running down her cheeks. Looking in the mirror she carefully dabbed with a tissue and blew her nose. I've got to look my best for the meeting she resolved.

Maybe I'll ring Jane for a chat later and see how plans are going for the wedding. I wonder has Geraldine followed up with that problem little Rachel was having in school.

"Pull yourself together."

She scolded her reflection in the mirror. There was a knock at the door. It was the boy from the lobby delivering a small envelope with the Regent crest.

Curiously she read the handwritten note.

Mrs Macken,

Could you please meet me in the foyer at 7.00 before your husband's meeting with Mr Holmes? I have your best interest at heart and am sure the meeting will be to our mutual benefit. Sincerely,

Alan P. Grant, Confidant and Advisor to Sir Geoffrey Fletcher, Downing Street.

The note revealed nothing more, no mention of a carnation in a buttonhole or anything like that. It did, however appeal to her.

Why not? It sounded very intriguing and could lead to something. She read the note again. Deciding to check the name out she switched from Judge Judy to the Hotel services and the Internet.

Sir Geoffrey Fletcher, retired Ambassador, Associate of the Tate Gallery and director of many high profile companies. Several pages carried his name with an abundance of information about his career. He appeared to be a person of great influence. The invitation to meet sounded very exciting and a long way from some fat man on a train. There was information on several Alan Grants but none tallied with the Alan Grant on the note.

At 7.00 she let herself out into the corridor and headed for the Reception feeling a bit guilty for not sharing this latest development with Paul. Normally they did everything together, especially important stuff. But her mood was influenced by the latest events and she just didn't feel like humouring him at the moment.

I'll check out Sir Geoffrey then go to Thorndike in the morning. Let Paul go back home, I can handle this without him.

She didn't bother with the lift. The carpet felt luxurious under the soles of her most stylish stilettos, catching a glimpse of herself in a full-length mirror she stopped for a quick check.

"You can't improve on perfection, if only I was ten years younger." The smiling comment came from a well-dressed man of about her own age as he passed her on the stairs.

Though the remark was made in humour it echoed how Susan felt at that moment, confident and strong.

"Thank you," she murmured.

The reception was a hive of activity. The well-dressed man from the stairs had joined a group of people obviously out for the evening, the delights of London at their disposal. Others were making their way to the dining room, some people at the counter were checking in. The chatter of voices was punctuated by the musical ping! as the lifts came and went.

Susan, a woman on her own paused and looked around. Nobody came to greet her, the clock over the door said 7.05. Several heads turned as she made her way across the floor.

"Mrs Macken? Thank you for coming,"

The voice was soft and enquiring, slightly hesitant, quite pleasing. Susan turned.

"I hope you're Susan Macken, forgive me if I'm mistaken."

The tall good-looking man appeared uncertain and apologetic.

"You're right," she said, putting out a firm hand, "I'm Susan Macken."

Stooping slightly he accepted the handshake with a relieved smile.

"I'm Alan Grant, sorry for the short notice but I only heard today that you were in town." His manner was so polite and respectful. Susan looking into the darkest eyes she had ever seen felt a need to put this nice young man at his ease.

But before she could speak,

"I don't make a habit of picking up …I mean meeting attractive women in hotel receptions," he said.

The attempt at a suave compliment was clumsy and he smiled ruefully.

Susan laughed at the expression on his beautiful face instantly assuming he was operating out of his comfort zone.

"Alan, this is quite simple. Please just tell me what this is all about," she encouraged.

"Of course," he straightened up running his fingers through his hair, hand pausing at the back of his head, a characteristic with which Susan was going to become more familiar. Giving her the full benefit of his smile he indicated the resident's lounge.

"I want you to meet someone."

To Susan's surprise he took her elbow, his touch was firm and guiding, his tall frame close. She did not resist, at five feet ten she had to look up at his profile as he guided her to the Lounge. The action suited her mood and felt quite pleasant.

Susan, for a fleeting moment hoped Paul would arrive and see her with this handsome young man.

"Well now isn't this interesting, one minute I'm watching Judge Judy on the television the next I'm being escorted by a strange young man to a meeting with a mysterious stranger."

"Touché," Alan Grant looked down into her face with a laugh. "I am at your disposal, the Ambassador must not be kept waiting, all we need is a pyramid of Ferrero Roche."

The large residents lounge at the Regent Palace boasted many quiet seating areas. Alan transferred his hand to gently touch her back with his fingertips as they approached one of these.

A small rotund man stood up to greet them. He beamed as he made his way around the coffee table.

"Susan Macken, meet Sir Geoffrey Fletcher."

Sir Geoffrey, feet together, back straight, raising his heels slightly as he drew himself up to his best height shook hands. Assured, confident and practiced, every inch the diplomat. He indicated for them to sit down, pulling out a chair for Susan.

A waiter hovered and Sir Geoffrey indicated with an outward palm for him to hold back until they were seated.

"Can I assume Mrs Macken, that you have eaten and perhaps would like a beverage of some kind, the coffee is excellent, or perhaps a refreshing cocktail?"

Susan had not eaten but the idea of a refreshing cocktail, as described by the pint-sized politician appealed.

Looking across at Alan Grant they shared a quick flicker of amusement.

"A gin and tonic would be nice, thank you, Sir Geoffrey."

"Alan, there's a good chap, could you summon a waiter."

But one was already at hand and the drinks were ordered, a gin and tonic, a beer and another double Courvoisier for Sir Geoffrey.

Pleasantries were exchanged until the drinks were served, Susan, all the while keeping a keen eye out for Paul, who was to meet the fat man at 8.00.

Susan's gin and tonic appeared to be quite strong, obviously the waiter assumed that on Sir Geoffrey's orders everybody drank double measures. She added some more tonic, keep a clear head, Susan sensed that she would need to have her wits about her.

Paul was in the doorway, looking around. No sign of the fat man. Susan was sitting with two strangers. About to go and join them he saw Susan stand up and move towards him. For the second time that day Paul was made aware of his wife's good looks. She fitted the surroundings perfectly and looked quite stunning.

"Why don't you have a drink and wait for your friend." She indicated the bar at the other side of the room with a casual hand.

"Who are those two?" he queried looking over her shoulder, taking in the contrast between the two people sitting at the table.

Facing him was the older man. Expensive suit, perfectly groomed, old school, Paul recognized the type.

The other man who was sitting side on to Paul had turned to look after Susan. This man was much younger, tall with an athletic build, long legs stretched out clad in designer jeans, casual sports jacket and open necked shirt. He greeted Paul's double take with a smile and a slight rising of his pint. Not beer commercials, more the Cinzano type, the adman's mind, at work.

"How do you know them?" Paul asked again, abruptly.

"The older guy is something to do with the Tate and the younger one helps him. I'll tell you more when I know more." She said quietly matching his mood.

"Look Paul, you're going back tomorrow. I've decided to stay on for a few days. I want to meet up with Kathryn

Thorndike and I feel I need some time to myself, we both need a bit of time," she added her expression serious.

"Well I have to go. I've booked an early flight and I need to catch up with things at the Agency. Susan, I'm sorry about all this."

"I know," she hurriedly interrupted him. "I probably won't see you before you go, by the way, the picture's not in its frame and the big back door window is broken."

Putting out his hand Paul grasped Susan by the elbow. They were now standing at the bar, holding her elbow quite tightly as if to keep her from escaping,

"A double whiskey and a gin and tonic" Paul ordered from the nearby barman. He turned back to Susan still holding on to her.

"Would you mind repeating that, what happened to the window and where's the picture?"

"The picture's safe, don't worry about it and I broke the window," she added casually. Incensed at her tone and seeming indifference his grip tightened on her arm as he turned and downed half the neat whiskey. Susan tried to resist the commanding hold.

"Why did you break the window you stupid woman,"

"Let my arm go, Paul, there's no need to be abusive." She looked around. People were beginning to take notice.

"It was an accident, I've been on to Jane and she's getting it fixed. So if you meet some workmen in the house when you get home you'll understand. OK?" She said, smiling as best she could. Taking up her drink she smiled again for the benefit of those around.

"Sorry," he said releasing her arm. "It's just. I'm a bit uptight about all this and you seem quite distant, aloof.

"This isn't the time or place Paul, see you in a few days when I get home."

Giving him a hurried kiss on the cheek she turned abruptly and headed back to the two men who were in deep conversation and seemingly oblivious to the confrontation.

Paul angry and confused watched her join them, the younger one, standing up and touching her elbow as he spoke to her, the older one half standing sat down again.

For a moment he considered crossing the room and introducing himself. Thinking better of it he downed his whiskey, ordered another one and scanned the room for the fat man. Of course, he must be in the lobby. This is the resident's lounge Paul admonished himself.

Drink in hand he made his way across the busy room. Susan didn't seem to notice his departure.

When Susan had excused herself to join her husband Sir Geoffrey had risen to his feet. The other man had remained seated head turned looking after her.

"Exceptional woman that, Sir Geoffrey," he said

"Not for the likes of you, laddie," came the caustic reply. The Knight sat down and, agitated, began to toy with his brandy, then taking a deep gulp of the golden liquid he swirled it in his glass, looked at Vaclav earnestly and announced.

"I'm not very happy with this situation, you know. It doesn't really suit me, misleading people this way, using other names, Alan Grant, indeed."

Vaclav Janacec looked back with a grim smile. When he spoke his tone was commanding with a threatening undertone.

"You have your instructions, Sir Geoffrey. You do not have any choice in the matter. Alan Grant is my name, art expert and your associate, consultant to your company for many years. You have a very high opinion of me and recommend my services without reservation. Would you like another brandy?"

The near empty glass made another trip to the diplomat's lips.

"Oh! All right, yes, yes, he said testily, I know, I know…. Look, Grant, or whatever you want to call yourself, straighten yourself up, stop lounging, you're not at some disco dance and really, those jeans, where's that smart suit you were wearing and the old school tie? I suppose that was a charade too." Not used to being on the back foot Sir Geoffrey attempted to assert himself.

"I didn't hear the lady complain," replied Vaclav with his best Alan Grant smile.

Susan returned. Feeling the effects of the double gin and tonic and the lack of food. She found it necessary to compose herself in the process of sitting down.

Alan stood up. "Perhaps a sandwich or something," he proposed.

"How thoughtful, no thanks. I have reserved a table for myself for 9.00". She felt his touch on her arm as she sat down.

"Now please tell me what this is all about,"

She looked at the two men in turn, the mood seemed to have changed, one relaxed and attentive the other seeming somewhat ill at ease.

"Mrs Macken", Sir Geoffrey took the initiative, "We would like to help you in furthering your interest in a painting which you have in your possession." He produced an extremely impressive looking business card and handed it across the table.

"How do you know about the painting?"

She took the card and looked quizzically back. "How did you know I'd be here, at the Regent? You seem very well informed."

She looked at Alan who was also looking at Sir Geoffrey, waiting for his answer.

"I am involved with the Tate Gallery," he continued after a slight hesitation. "In a capacity that is hard to define and at a distinctly senior level, I assure you. I am not involved in purchasing however…"

"You're not answering my question," Susan interrupted.

Sir Roger reached for his brandy.

"Tim Holmes" Alan Grant prompted smoothly. "Sir Roger was approached by a person called Tim Holmes. Apparently Tim Holmes used to be married to one of your husband's employees. In fact I thought he was coming here this evening to meet with us."

Susan looked over to the bar but there was no sign of Paul. The Fat Man must be Shelly Holmes ex-husband, she concluded.

"As I was saying before I was interrupted."

Sir Geoffrey glanced at Alan and then at Susan,

"I cannot be involved with the purchasing of art, or associate with a private collector because of my affiliation to the Tate. However, my colleague," he glanced again in Alan's direction, "can act on my behalf. He comes very highly recommended and represents a very sure path for you in your pursuit of the validation of your "Turner" Mrs Macken." He swirled his brandy and finished what was in his glass. It was immediately replaced with another one by a waiter who was hovering nearby.

New glass in hand he continued, "There is a list. It is referred to as the Bellini list. Have you heard about it Mrs Macken?" Susan shook her head but said nothing as the slightly tipsy Diplomat continued.

"The Bellini list was the brainchild of Joseph Bellini a scholar and an artist of the seventeenth century, he collected together a group of academics. Their mission was to explore the possible existence of missing works of art based on their knowledge and understanding of the great masters."

Alan anticipating a longwinded, boring account, interrupted.

"Through the years the list has been updated by like-minded people. There is a reference to Hovellers, Deal and Turner on the list. Susan, we have been tracking the painting for some time, it's very possible that you have the Turner we're interested in."

Here Sir Geoffrey interjected,

"Should this prove to be so it is our intention to ensure that the work of art ends up where it should properly be in it's rightful position alongside Turner's other great works at the Tate. A word of warning be watchful, there are some uncompromising people who would stop at nothing to get their hands on your painting." The little man rising unsteadily to his feet downed the rest of his brandy.

"I will take my leave of you now Mrs Macken. I believe that your hotel bill has been taken care of and Mr Grant is at your disposal, I am sure he will offer to go to Ireland to examine the painting, should you wish. Calligraphy experts and any other appropriate experts will be made available to you."

With a quick handshake and an unbalanced attempt at a gracious bow he made a very unsteady departure before Susan had a chance to reply. She looked after him and then at Alan, his face had a serious expression but the amusement was barely concealed.

Maybe it was the drink, maybe the tension of the day or the behaviour of Paul, certainly it had a lot to do with the pompous Sir Geoffrey's erratic course as he made his way out of the residents lounge. Susan, unable to contain herself, laughed out loud.

Alan's smile broadened,

"Oh my god," she laughed, did I hear him right or did he say he'd paid my bill?"

"Yes of course, Mrs Macken, should you need anything else, like your nails polished, a new handbag, a couple of bottles of Dom Perignon, just ask my associate he's at your disposal." Alan did a bad take off of the Ambassadors accent, much to her amusement.

"Join me for dinner," it was on impulse, she looked across at the laughing young man. "I hate eating on my own and we have a lot to talk about, you being so well recommended and at my disposal so to speak."

Without hesitation the offer was accepted.

"But your husband is he not joining you for dinner?"

"Well to tell you the truth I'm not a hundred per cent sure. He's meeting with that Holmes man, isn't he? Probably one of the uncompromising individuals after my painting that our tipsy friend was talking about."

Susan glanced at the card on the table.

"Quite impressive," she observed, "you know he is a director of eight companies and was Ambassador to three countries."

The attempt at seriousness failing, she laughed again. This time her dinner date joined in.

"You know he nearly threw himself off his feet when he bowed." The image made her smile even more. "It's not fair, we shouldn't laugh I'm sure he really is a very nice person." Susan, in an effort for composure remained seated.

"He is an important person in the London art world," Alan informed her "And someone who can help us with you're painting, now what about this dinner, I'm starving?"

He put out his hand and hauled her to her feet.

Paul, who, unnoticed by Susan had returned to the bar after a fruitless search for the Fat Man watched the exchange from the corner of his eye.

Susan had made it obvious that she did not want him to join her. Things had not turned out as he had expected. Aware that he had had a lot to drink he was quite happy to remain on his own. There were plenty of barstools available. Paul found a place to sit at the corner of the bar where he could keep an eye on the action across the room. "What'll it be sir?" The barman was Irish. Paul ordered a double whisky. Placing a small dish of peanuts on the bar, "How's auld Dublin?" The double whisky was placed alongside the peanuts and the barman smiled the greeting recognizing a fellow countryman. Paul stared him down without a reply before turning away, drink in hand preoccupied with his thoughts.

After all, he reasoned. I can't blame her for wanting some time away from me. I behaved badly over the Thorndike woman and I should have gone to the meeting in Dublin with Graham Roach. But what did she do with the painting and how did the window get broken? She said she'd been talking to Jane. That's it, I'll ask Jane when I get home tomorrow she'll fill me in on everything. Susan's great, she'll be back in a day or so and things will be back to normal. I'm a lucky man. He consoled himself. Turning back to the bar cradling his drink he helped himself to some peanuts with a rueful smile, feeling a bit better about things.

There were two attractive women sitting further along the bar. He had noticed them earlier. One of them accidently caught his eye in the mirror. She gave him a half smile and turned to say something to her friend who glanced at Paul and looked away again.

How I would have misinterpreted their intentions had it happened earlier the much wiser Paul thought to himself, regretfully.

His attention shifted to the other side of the room just in time to see Susan and the young guy heading out the door, his hand was on her back and she was looking up into his face. The sound of her laugh reached across the room.

Vaclav Janacec looked down into the face of his dinner date as they made their way to the dining room thinking she's not a bad looking woman, strong and resourceful. She would put up a good struggle. It would be amusing to test her before the kill. He licked his lips in anticipation of the time when she would become dispensable.

"This is fun," he said,

"I'm sorry, but I can't join you for dinner," He looked apologetic and crestfallen.

"I got carried away with having a good time, I have to work on some research I haven't completed. It completely slipped my mind. The report must be submitted tomorrow morning first thing. After 11.00 tomorrow I'm all yours if you want to pursue things further concerning your "Turner."

"Oh! What a pity I was enjoying myself too, of course your work must come first." Susan covered her disappointment with a gracious smile.

"Yes I would like to enlist your services." She put her hand on his arm as she spoke. "I'm going to see Kathryn Thorndike, the calligrapher tomorrow, would you come with me, I really would like your opinion on what she has to say."

"Of course," he smiled, "with pleasure, this is great, and you won't regret it. I'll organize everything for you. Your every need will be catered for. I'll be here at 12.00."

"Thank you Alan," she squeezed his arm tightly.

"See you tomorrow."

"Goodnight Susan." The dark eyes were friendly and warm, the smile, reassuring and enthusiastic.

She stood and watched him stride away. No harm, she thought, I'm doing no harm and it's flattering and rather nice to be on his arm. He looked over his shoulder as he reached the door and gave her an amused little wave.

Outside the hotel in the London night Vaclav Janacec looked up at the stars and took a deep breath, pulse racing, the closeness, the proximity of other people, their smell, breathing the same air in the close confines of a room with so many people, he felt nauseous.

The thought of sitting in a crowded dining room appalled him. Crisp vegetables and some fish, maybe some dark bitter chocolate he could eat and relish. Other than that all food turned his stomach.

Crossing hurriedly to the middle of Piccadilly Circus he sat down on one of the well-worn benches and waited for his pulse to slow and his breathing to become more relaxed. Night revellers passed back and forth to the tube station.

Satisfied with his progress so far he sat for a while considering his options, returning to the base and dealing with those waiting or strip joints and sleaze. Across the street down by the side of the Regent Palace the entrance to Soho invited. He allowed himself a mirthless smile and standing up crossed the road. At the door of the Regent Palace he checked the lobby, no sign of the Macken woman. Quickly entering he crossed to the reception desk.

"Yes sir, how can I be of help?"

"I would like a room for two nights please."

"Of course"

Having checked in with an explanation to the receptionist that his bags would be following on Vaclav Janacec, alias, Alan Grant left the hotel and headed into Soho where all things are possible, with no questions asked. He would return to the hotel later.

Vicar Street, in the heart of London, boasted a combination of private residences, some shops and business premises.

Tim Holmes was familiar with the street and aware of a pub on the corner. Matt had mentioned crossing the road and meeting the foreign bloke in a pub. The Duck and Shovel at the traffic lights, beckoned. This could be the place. Opposite to the pub was Clarendon House.

Tim liked pubs, this place was typical, warm and comfortable, lots of wood panelling, a few locals, the mandatory dartboard. Smoke stained memorabilia crowded the walls denoting all sporting activities, black and white photos, newspaper cuttings in a variety of frames and of course the signed shirt not immediately identifying for which sport. The barman detached himself from a conversation at the bar and a couple of heads turned to view the newcomer only to disinterestedly return to their pints. The waft of alcohol and the promise of food welcomed Tim through the doorway.

Selecting a table at the window, a good vantage point with a view of the entrance to Clarendon House, he sank into the button backed comfortable chair. Unaccustomed physical activity, Matt's fists, hauling dead bodies around, being handcuffed to cookers and anxiety for Jennifer were catching up on this normally jovial individual. The well-padded chair welcomed an ache in his back as he sat feeling the tension in his body begin to subside.

"What'll it be?" the Irish brogue was unmistakable as the lanky barman wiped the already clean table with a not to clean cloth.

"A pint and a chaser with a meat pie."

The picture of the meat pie dominating the little sign in its plastic holder on the marble topped table prompted the order reminding Tim that he hadn't eaten since morning, "And chips," he added noticing the tomato ketchup bottle.

This was a busy intersection and there was a fair amount of activity at the traffic lights outside the window and in front of Clarendon House. Tim had an urge to cross the road and enter the building in search of Jennifer, now, quickly get on with it, what are you waiting for? But reason prevailed, sit and observe, test the lay of the land, see what's what. Tim felt confident that he had the right place.

The pint arrived and shortly after, the pie and chips. Tim ate, drank and watched. Perhaps the foreign bloke would make an appearance.

He searched through Matt's wallet for the second time and then placed it on the table, the contents revealing nothing further. The six- digit number made no sense.

In all probability, Jennifer is somewhere in the building across the road. Making short work of the food he washed down the last of the pie and chips with the remains of the beer, downed the chaser, paid the friendly barman and left the warmth of the pub feeling somewhat rejuvenated.

Crossing the road he entered through the glass doors with the big grey lettering that stated "Clarendon House".

"Binga bam, binga boom!" The rotund gladiator entered the lion's den.

Quite a large, austere polished granite-floor reception area greeted, a bored looking receptionist hardly raised her head from behind a low wall of the same material as the floor.

Tim took a seat reaching for a copy of the Financial Times on the low table as he sat down. This he opened with a flourish as he glanced around, giving the receptionist a smile and a nod. She smiled back, with a business like. "Can I help you?"

Tim wanted to say, "Yes, did you see a tall well-dressed foreign looking bloke come in here today with my drugged daughter?" Instead he shook his head

"No thanks, I'm fine."

His position allowed him a view of the list of floor numbers and business names displayed above the girls head, black letters lighted on Perspex panels attached to the wall behind the reception desk, six floors six businesses. None of the names suggested anything. Of course any floor could house an apartment or a multiplicity of activities. The numbers on Matt's piece of paper bore no relevance, however, the view of the pub across the road and the traffic lights confirmed his belief that he was in the right building.

Ping! One of the two lift doors opened. Tim considered occupying the space vacated by the four people who entered the reception. About to stand up he changed his mind afraid that while he might travel in one lift the foreign bloke might enter or exit the other. Best to wait across the road and keep vigil from there he reasoned. Glancing around the cold reception his thoughts were of pies and pints and a comfortable seat.

The receptionist smiled as Tim returned the newspaper to the table and left re-crossing the road at the traffic lights.

Back inside the cosy pub he found his seat at the window, resolving to wait. The foreign bloke would have to turn up sometime.

The text he had sent in Matt's name should give him some advantage. The foreign bloke would assume he was dead and therefore out of the equation.

From his vantage point he studied the building opposite, six floors six businesses, people at computers, white shirts, business suits, nothing unusual, the lower floors displayed nothing of interest. Maybe higher up, he craned his neck but couldn't see much of the top floors.

"Back again? You're becoming one of our regulars. What can I get you?"

The barman enquired.

"A pint of Guinness, please,"

"A pint it is,"

"Yes", said Tim with a nod in the direction of Clarendon House,

"I just started working across the road," he offered glibly. "I suppose you get a lot of the Clarendonians in here?"

"You'd think so, but… no," he said in his Irish voice "Yuppies."

He glanced around at the few locals dotting the bar. "Yuppies" he repeated, "This place is not posh enough for them but sure that's the way of the world, it's all computers these days," He shook his head with a knowing smile.

"And foreigners?" said Tim

"I suppose you get lots of foreigners?"

He waited expectantly as the barman cupped his skinny chin between finger and thumb while he contemplated a retort.

"No, he said eventually, only me, I'm the only foreigner around here.

I'll get that pint for you."

During the exchange two doors to one side of the bar drew Tim's attention. One said Toilets and the other indicated another lounge upstairs.

While the barman busied himself collecting some glasses before the ritual of preparing Tim's pint, Tim headed across the floor and through the door marked lounge to find a stairs leading up to another level and the possibility of a better view across the road.

The second lounge was unoccupied and smaller, more of a function room. Tim, about to look out the window was attracted to a door marked private. Slightly open the doorway revealed the bottom of a narrow stairs.

Without hesitation he headed across the room in pursuit of a better view from a higher vantage point. Puffing slightly he made his way up to a small room with a tiny iron fireplace and bare floorboards, obviously it had served as a bedroom in the past but now as a storage room. There were some stacked boxes and out-of-date advertising pieces and a little cobwebby window. Moving a tubular framed sign with the legend *A double Diamond works wonders,* brushing some dust and cobwebs to one side Tim peered through the grimy glass across and up at the building opposite.

Craning his neck as far as possible, he could just see to the roof, there was a metal rail set back from the front façade, a seventh floor! Tim scrambled on some boxes to get a better look.

Sure enough there was the seventh floor, a penthouse, out of sight from street level.

"Your pint Sir, would you like it sitting on one of the crates or maybe back in the lounge with the other customers." The friendly barman, pint in hand enquired from the bottom of the narrow stairs.

Tim turned, losing his footing slightly and having to regain his balance with a hand against the cobwebby window. Having seen what he needed to see he was now anxious to get across the road. Jennifer had to be in that penthouse.

"Toilet," he said, forcing a casual air, hurrying down the steep narrow stairs.

"I was looking for the toilet."

"On the first floor under the big sign that says Gents,"

The friendly barman, no longer smiling, pint in hand blocked the doorway.

"You shouldn't be up here, its private,"

"Yes, I know, I'm sorry,"

The barman stood his ground and held the pint up for Tim to take it.

"We've been having some trouble lately, break ins and that. You look to me as if you're up to no good." The friendly barman well versed in assessing the public who frequented his bar detecting uneasiness in Tim's manner was leaping to conclusions.

Tim reached for the pint. He really wanted to get out of there and across the road to Jennifer. Feeling the frustration mounting, he had just killed a man, for a moment he considered smashing the glass in the bigger man's face.

Instead he reached into his pocket and withdrew Matt's wallet.

"I am sorry, I was looking for the toilet and at this moment I really do have to go."

Retrieving a fifty-pound note he held it up as he took the pint in his other hand. "Will this cover it or is it extra for toilet paper?"

"Well just about," the barman took the money with a disapproving look,

"Consider yourself lucky I'm not callin' the cops." He stepped to one side.

Tim hurried past down the stairs and through the ground floor lounge out the front door handing his pint to a surprised local on the way.

This time, as Tim entered Clarendon House he did so with a set purpose. Ignoring the receptionist he strode past to the lifts, preoccupied with the thought that the foreign bloke could be up there with Jennifer right now. I hope I'm in time. He's a bad bastard that one.

The lift arrived, the door opened and Tim stepped in. His anxiety for Jennifer overcoming everything else he rode up to the top floor.

Hastings & Hastings Solicitors, the large sign greeted him. He saw an opening to one side with a stairs.

Tim stopped, his heart beating frantically.

"Slow down Tim," he reminded himself. "Conserve your energy you don't know what you're going to face up there."

There were only ten steps with a metal handrail. He took them slowly, another landing, no carpeting, concrete block walls.

A metal door barred the way, flush to the wall with no handle or obvious means of opening it. To one side was a small computer keypad.

The six-digit number, Tim fished out the piece of paper and keyed in the numbers. With a metallic "clunk!" the door shifted slightly. He hesitated for a moment wishing that he had had the foresight to arm himself. Not knowing what to expect, he pushed the door. It opened inwards revealing a small brightly lighted square area with another door facing him, this door more ornate, mahogany and panelled. Tim stepped through the opening into the small area, no going back now. He stepped towards the second door. The first door closed behind him with a solid clunk!. He turned quickly, startled, locked in, no retreat. There was a keypad he saw with relief but when he tried the same numbers the door would not open. "I'll have to keep going."

Thoughts of Jennifer and fear of the confined space driving him Tim rubbed his sweating palms together and studied the ornate door barring his way, nice wood grain, no letterbox, I wonder how they get their post? No door handle. He pushed at it, solid, he stepped back. After careful studying, fingers tracing the wood panel for some opening device, eyes scanning the surrounding wall and low ceiling, Trapped! With the realization came an instant urge to panic, no escape! Small space, Tim's in big trouble, a phone box for superman, change, burst free and save the girl. Calm yourself Tim, deep breaths, search again for a way out. He hit the numbers again hoping to retreat. He tried them backwards, different combinations, frantically his stubby fingers flying. The metal door remained solid. How long? Maybe only a minute, it seemed like an age. He stood still to stem the feeling of nausea as his head began to swim and the space seemed to get smaller. He pressed his mouth and nose to the edges of the door hoping to find the slightest aperture. If I sit down I'm giving up. He sat down his back against the wooden door. His entire time in the small space lasted exactly 3 minutes when the timer activated with a low buzzing sound and Tim fell backwards through the door way. He lay on his back and took great gulps of sweet air-conditioned air.

The Foreign Bloke! He twisted around onto his stomach and launched himself to his feet taking a couple of quick steps to steady himself. A spacious and luxurious room with floor to ceiling windows on three sides presented a most impressive panoramic view of London. He crouched, eyes searching the room for danger, ears straining for the slightest sound, looking right and left expecting an attack, knowing that he would be outmatched.

Not a sound, nothing, the large room was definitely empty he returned to an upright position using both hands to support his aching back.

Of the three doors leading from the room, on the wall opposite, one was slightly ajar. Tiptoeing on the pale cream carpet, rounding a large low-slung couch and a glass coffee table he approached the slightly open door. All senses running riot, ears pricked for the slightest sound he stopped and waited, afraid, afraid of the foreign man.

Gaining courage he stepped to the door wiping his hands on his trousers, he pushed the door fully open, involuntarily jumping back at the same time. Silence greeted him from a beautifully furnished empty, bedroom.

The other doors gave access to a large bathroom and a corridor with two smaller bedrooms. Gaining confidence Tim investigated each room but there was no sign of Jennifer.

He returned to the large room, not sure what to do next, a fragile, sorrowful, rotund, overweight comedian, dwarfed by the height of the large windows and the magnificent view surrounding him.

She's got to be here, he agonized. I feel it but where?"

The windows on all sides looked out onto a wooden floored balcony bordered by white railings, the railings that had caught his eye from the attic window below. They ended at a wall coinciding with the back of the apartment. Obviously the pent house extended beyond the wall but there seemed to be no means of access.

Unaccustomed to such prolonged and tense activity, the out of condition Tim suddenly overcome with fatigue felt an intense desire to head for the bedroom and lie down on the beautiful bed. Resisting the temptation he began to wander aimlessly around the luxurious apartment at a loss for a plan, his tired mind unable to cope with the complexity of his situation. Obviously Jennifer was elsewhere, he was locked in and when he tried his cell phone there was no signal.

What action would Goldilocks take? The incongruous analogy brought a little smile to his dry lips. I better not be here when Daddy Bear comes home. I wonder if there's some porridge.

A discrete bar near the far end of the room beckoned, the prospect of a cool beer drove him in its direction. To Tim's surprise the bar concealed a screened off area with a console, swivel chair and a bank of 12 monitors. It was so subtly incorporated into the décor of the room one could easily have overlooked it. So Goldilocks tried the swivel chair, it fitted snugly, the activate pad was obvious, the monitors all sprang into life at the first touch. Tim whistled.

"We have lift-off."

He swivelled in the chair and surveyed the room, wondering. What is this place all about? Who is the foreign bloke? When will he get back?

Tim dreaded the thought of facing such a powerful adversary. About to go and find some sort of a weapon to defend himself, he changed his mind, swivelling he confronted the flickering monitors.

Each monitor was numbered. The console in front of Tim was obviously a touch screen. Number one displayed a black and white view of a room with somebody sitting at a desk. Tim was startled until he realized he was looking at himself. He touched the screen again and got another view of the same room. With mounting excitement, fatigue taking a back seat, "Jennifer, Jennifer," he mouthed her name excitedly as he touched all the numbers in quick succession.

Black and white pictures of locations sprang into view, a long corridor with a glass wall, more corridors, and a kitchen, a room with beds. He soon discovered a zoom in and out facility then left and right. Room after room sprang into view as he touched one after the other. No sign of Jennifer. She has to be here, he looked frantically at the console. Replay, he touched the symbol and recoiled in horror. Horrified Tim froze, at first he could not believe his eyes, every monitor showed the same picture, it was the foreign bloke and a girl, the stiletto blade rising and falling in deathly silence then turning to slash and stab. "Jennifer"! He forced himself to look not believing what he was seeing, his trembling touch ordered zoom in on the face, close up twisted and screaming, it wasn't Jennifer.

He hit the replay and the Monitors returned to actual time. Tim, wide eyed stared unseeingly at a blank screen the images of carnage vividly etched into his mind, the poor girl, the rise and fall of the murderous blade. Tim sat, struggling to cope with the memory, relieved that it was not Jennifer and at the same time feeling guilty at his relief. For a while he was powerless to do anything except sit in dread of what he had just seen and what might happen when the killer returned. Gradually the overwhelming desire to find Jennifer filtered through his consciousness spurring him to action with a renewed determination.

He began to scan the screens again this time with more control and purpose. The dormitory showed up again. On studying the picture he could make out what seemed to be a figure lying on one of the beds. Getting the hang of the system he zoomed in. It was a man lying spread-eagled, face down, head turned to one side, obviously dead. Move on move on. Tim found where the girl had died. Her body was half covered by a sheet. Black smears everywhere, obviously blood. Tim took a deep breath and rapidly moved to the next screen. Shimmering white, Tim about to move on instead decided to use the zoom control. He zoomed out to discover the camera had been focused on a close up of a white wall. The entire room now revealed, with a quickening pulse he could see a figure on a bed covered with a white sheet, head turned away from the camera. Dare he hope it was Jennifer? The figure moved slightly, but no amount of screen touching would reveal the face.

Maybe I can talk to her, there has to be sound? It had not crossed Tim's mind until that moment. Of course, he scanned the controls and there it was staring him in the face a sound and control option.

At a touch he activated the sound. At first there was silence, by increasing the volume he could hear her breathing.

"Jennifer! Jenny!" he shouted, "Wake up!" Jennifer scrambled round into a sitting position facing the camera.

"Dad, is that you? Where are you? Is he with you?"

Tim was unable to answer as the tears streamed down his face. Overcome by the release of tension and the sight of Jennifer he tried to speak but couldn't get the words out.

"Dad! Is he with you? What's happening?"

She was on her feet her face close to the camera.

"No, it's alright I'm here. We haven't got much time. Are you ok?"

"Yes, Yes, I'm ok he didn't do anything to me. He's very dangerous. He's a killer. He killed a girl and made me watch."

Dry-eyed, Jennifer looked straight at the camera.

"'Where are you now? Are you in the building?"

Tim could sense the strength of her resolve.

"Yes, I'm in the big room at the front, the one with the big windows. I'm at a desk with a whole lot of monitors," unable to take his eyes from her face on the small screen. She looked so appealing but in control. He felt a surge of pride for his brave daughter, what she must have been going through.

Her voice was steady,

"Look at the desk, don't switch from this room. Everything can be controlled from where you are. Because we can hear each other you are zeroed on to cell number 5." Calmly she looked expectantly from the small monitor and Tim knew her display of control was designed to reassure him.

Tim searched the console, there was a small pad blinking with the number 5.

He touched it and some panels appeared with options LIGHTING, GRILL, AIR and DOOR.

Tim touched DOOR with a trembling finger. OPEN, CLOSE. "Got it!" He hit the screen with the palm of his hand. Jennifer heard a click behind her as her cell door swung open.

"Go into the bathroom," she shouted excitedly, "I'll come to you."

Tim looked at the blank screen for a moment and then realising that she was free from the room he headed into the bathroom.

Jennifer sped along the corridor and through the dormitory passed the dead man and eventually to where she knew the entrance to the apartment was located. It just looked like any other door except there was no handle, just a keypad. Jennifer had no idea of the code.

Tim stood in the bathroom waiting for something to happen. He looked around, no door, other than the one he had just come through.

The entrance must be in here. He began to search for signs of a door. The wall at the back was tiled with large mirrored squares.

He waited, listening, expecting and then began to examine the wall, pressing glass panels. Jennifer was two feet away on the other side of the wall. Realising she could not be heard in the bathroom she had retrieved a metal chair from the dormitory. With all her strength she swung the heavy chair and hit the door, again and again.

Tim could just make out the sound, at first he was not sure and then he knew she was trapped on the other side.

Turning from the mirrored wall, aware that the foreign bloke could return at any moment he ran back to the control panel in the big room to find access to the rest of the building.

Twenty minutes of precious time had passed since Jennifer had left the cell. Realising the futility of her efforts she stood, the chair poised for another useless blow. The only thing she could hope for was that Tim could do something.

"I can't open the door," she shouted, as loud as she could "Try the control panel." Having hardly uttered the words, suddenly, unbelievably it opened. Throwing the metal chair to one side, she ran through the bathroom and into the big room.

Tim turned from the console to greet his daughter. When she saw him the tears came. She tried to brush them away.

"Are you ok, he didn't hurt you did he?"

He guided her to the big white sofa. Her lip trembled as she stared ahead.

Tim put a protective arm around her shoulders and softly uttered words of comfort until she became more composed.

"He's bad, he's a killer, and he could get back any time."

With a look of alarm she glanced across at the door as if he had just come in.

She was the frightened four-year old climbing into bed for comfort in the night, and Tim's heart went out to his daughter as he embraced her.

The portly comedian sat and held his karate expert, resourceful daughter, how often she had shown strength when he had faltered?

"I already killed someone today and I'll kill him if I have to," came the promise.

Susan was in two minds about dinner. Generally dining out was with Paul or else some friends. The idea of eating alone did not immediately appeal to her.

About to turn away from the entrance to the dining room, she stopped and considered her situation. Paul had been with her practically every night since she'd married, apart from when she was in hospital for that little job or the odd time he had a business trip and most of those times she'd been with him. Tonight I'm on my own. Changing her mind, Susan stepped through the doorway.

"Macken, table for one," it sounded a bit strange. The book was checked.

"Perhaps by the window madam?"

"That would be nice,"

It was exactly where she would have chosen to sit, a window table in the corner that allowed her a view of Piccadilly Circus and also of the rest of the room. People watching, at the Regent Palace could be an entertaining pastime.

The menu presented a wide choice and she was surprised at how hungry she felt. Stuffed Dover Sole for the main course, game terrine to start and maybe a glass of Chablis. The small round table was set for two. An empty chair where Paul would normally be seated faced Susan. The very delectable Alan Grant might have joined her.

It had been fun to flirt a bit, unusual to be with someone other than Paul.

Susan contemplated the vacant seat as she examined her motives. Conceal her feelings, punish Paul for hurting her, show her independence and compel him to think about her from a different point of view by paying attention to an obviously attractive younger man. Of course Alan Grant would have his own agenda, of course he was being attentive for a reason, after all there could be a lot of money at stake, but keeping her wits about her would not be a new experience to Susan.

Yes, she allowed herself a little smile, that's all this is, harmless enough in comparison to Paul's carry on. Well he seems to be getting the message, good enough for him.

Her starter arrived. The terrine looked delicious with some bruschetta.

The tablecloth was crisp and white, the table beautifully laid, and her surroundings elegant. Muted conversation mingled with the clink of bone china from all sides. Susan began to savour her meal with a feeling of personal contentment.

Reaching for the long stemmed wineglass she sipped the Chablis, aware that the one glass would suffice, have to keep a clear head for tomorrow. She looked around, an elegant and independent woman dining alone.

A group of people sitting at a table close by having finished their main course were discussing the dessert menu. Susan recognized the well-dressed man she had met on the stairs. He turned and said something to the woman beside him who smiled, as he slightly raised his glass in her direction.

It was a simple gesture but one of apparent appreciation which added to Susan's feeling of wellbeing.

She began to speculate on how she was being perceived by the other diners, about how she looked, how the well-dressed man perceived her, how Alan Grant perceived her, surprising herself at how seldom if ever, she considered the effect her appearance might have on men. The well-dressed man was still looking in her direction. Susan laughed and smilingly raised her glass to him.

The waiter reverently delivered the Dover Sole in front of her.

"Perhaps a snipe of champagne," Susan requested, "I'm celebrating,"

"Of course Madam, may I ask the occasion?"

"Me," she smilingly replied.

The waiter went to retrieve the wine menu and Susan turned her attention to the Dover Sole, stuffed with prawns and scallops with a crab mousse alongside.

I wonder does Alan find me attractive she speculated? The fish was beautifully cooked, the mousse delicious…. he seemed to be enjoying himself, those eyes, that smile, the texture of his jacket and the feeling of his bicep under the material when she held his arm. Susan couldn't help relishing her meal and thoughts of Alan simultaneously. Two rounded scallops lay side-by-side, deliciously waiting, she smiled at them.

"His butt in those well cut jeans," Yum…yum," she murmured reaching again for her wine glass with a quiet little chuckle.

"I know the food is good here but this is ridiculous," Paul's intrusion shattered the moment. She had not seen him come into the room. He was alongside the table swaying slightly

"Susan you're talking to your food and you won't even talk to me,"

"Not now Paul, I'm enjoying my meal and you've had too much to drink, go to bed. You have an early start in the morning."

With a clumsy hand and quite noisily he pulled out the Gold Framed cushioned chair opposite and turning it round sat astride it backwards, facing Susan and leaning very close to her face.

"I love you Susan," he slurred, loud enough for those around to hear. Come home with me, I don't care about the painting. You're better than any painting. You're more beautiful than any Mona Lisa."

Susan embarrassed by Paul for the second time that night, looked around at the other occupants of the room who were pretending not to take notice. She saw the waiter approaching with the champagne. The scallops deliciously waited.

"Is everything alright, madam? Have you got a reservation sir?"

218

The waiter placed the bottle on the white tablecloth.

She looked across at her husband, surprised at her own feelings.

"Mister Macken is just leaving. Aren't you Mister Macken? Good night Mister Macken," She said pleasantly and then more firmly. "Go to bed Paul!"

She turned her attention back to her plate. Paul stood up swaying slightly. He looked at the floor with a hand on the back of the chair to steady himself. Susan waited. He looked at her, she looked determinedly back, her knife and fork poised. Taken aback by her apparent indifference, at a loss he turned and left the room without a word.

Susan smiled at the waiter.

"Shall I pour madam?"

"Yes please,"

The cork made a satisfying pop as Susan eagerly returned to the enjoyment of her meal.

Recapturing the mood of the evening her thoughts returned to Alan Grant and the prospect of tomorrow's visit with Kathryn Thorndike, the briefcase wielding, Kathryn Thorndike. Paul had disclosed some further details and Susan now was aware of all the facts.

What must Paul have done to provoke such an attack from a civilized professional person like Kathryn Thorndike? He probably tried to kiss her right there in the Tate coffee shop, no he wouldn't, maybe, he would? But to hit him with a briefcase!

Her mind did cartwheels, poor Paul, maybe if he had been hit with a briefcase a couple of years ago he wouldn't be in the pickle he's in now.

The dining room was becoming less crowded save for quiet corners of the room where soft-spoken couples sat together. The sound level of the group at the nearby table had increased, not unpleasantly. They were on the brandies and more wine had been ordered.

The well-dressed man was enjoying himself, every now and again looking in Susan's direction. His wife, Susan assumed, shared his interest in her and Susan had inadvertently caught her eye on a couple of occasions.

A chocolate fondant beautifully presented with ice cream and caramel materialised in front of her.

"Would Madam like the coffee served now or perhaps in the lounge?"

The waiter enquired.

"Oh! I forgot I had ordered dessert it looks delicious, I'll have my coffee now, an Americano, please."

The fondant caved in at the touch of the silver spoon and dark chocolate oozed, to mix with caramel and the slightly melted ice cream. I wonder what Alan is like in bed Susan speculated as she lifted the laden spoon to her lips.

"She's famous, I know her face,"

The well-dressed man looked at his wife,

"Who?"

"The woman sitting on her own, the one you've had your eye on all night. The bunny boiler."

He looked at her. "The bunny boiler!" he laughed,

"You mean Glen Close, in Fatal Attraction?"

"Ssh, keep your voice down, she'll hear you."

The well-dressed man looked across at Susan considering her profile as she savoured her dessert, the blond hair with its casual style, the strong features and determined chin.

"It is Glen Close, I think you're right."

He leaned across the table to announce in a stage whisper

"Don't look now but Glen Close is sitting right behind you tucking in to a chocolate fondant."

When half the people at the table close by turned to look at her Susan was quite startled. Spoon poised she looked back. They were all smiling.

"Sorry," The well-dressed man smiled.

"But you're not Glen Close are you."

They appeared to be very nice people having a nice time.

"You're not even near never mind close," she said in her best Irish accent.

With smiling apologies they turned and resumed their conversations. The well-dressed man and his wife looked even more apologetic.

The beach was strewn with debris washed up from the storm. With Bowsprit and main mast gone, the cutter had been reduced to a wallowing hulk now at the mercy of the heavy sea. Her back broken by the might of the waves, she ran aground. Her cargo, timbers, canvas, bodies of her crew battered and cast mercilessly to litter the shore.

Men, women and children combed the beach, searching, finding and reporting. The authorities organising and observing as best they could.

Abigail Wakeley, nine years of age, scrambled amongst the salt soaked debris, agile and quick.

At first she paid no heed to the funny looking man sitting on the rock observing her.

Bent over her work she pulled and tugged at a large piece of canvas. Sometimes valuable things got caught up and wrapped tight in the strong material. As she pulled and tugged, I hope it is not a dead person.

Sometimes she'd find a deadder and she would have bad dreams. People don't close their eyes when they die, the living do that for them.

Abandoning her struggle with the cloth she stood up. The small man sitting on the rock was looking right at her. Abigail stood still, curiously enthralled, with that special focus especially reserved for nine year olds.

The man was not searching for things. He kept looking down and then at her again. His eyes were moving all the while, now on her face, next her arm and her feet.

Crouching down she pretended to search moving her hand brushing the sand, head down all the while watching from the corner of her eye.

His eyes followed her every movement, a small book with a leather cover was on his knee, his hand moving quickly as he sketched.

Again the eyes now slipped right and then left and back to the sketchbook. He perused a page rapidly moving his right hand magically recording everything he saw.

Unafraid and curious Abigail moved nearer looking at the trodden sand with scant attention, her aim now, not as much the search as to get a look at the sketchbook.

As she sidled closer she could see that the man wore good clothes, breeches and a long coat. He had a severe face with a big nose.

He looked at her and sketched some more, grimacing and grunting as he worked, now screwing up his eyes as he peered into the distance, then looking intently at her and the others as they searched.

Abigail moved around his shoulder and slightly behind the funny looking man.

He had lost all interest in her then as he looked along the beach. His eyes fastened on the luggers pulled up high from the waves, their russet square sails at half-mast, their strong clinker built hulls turned towards the sea ready for the next rush to salvage.

Abigail watched the lightening movement of his fingers as he sketched, magically and wondrously the shape of her father's boat appeared on the page not on the beach but in a stormy sea. With a child's awareness she noticed how long his thumbnail was, the other nails clipped.

With quick movements he ran the water soaked brush all over the page and then selecting another brush, made the waves look real. He put the sketchbook down carefully on the rock beside him and turned his head towards the girl.

"It has to be somewhat dry before I put any detail in. These are preliminary studies, sketches of elements for my next masterpiece," he said, with a smile though his voice sounded gruff and he mumbled the words. He wasn't

looking at her now but looking at the picture with a gentle expression.

"Show me more I want to see."

JMW Turner always liked an audience when he worked, even a nine –year- old Hoveller child.

Without another word he lifted the sketchbook and Abigail watched enthralled as her father's boat, with two figures crouching and a wreck in the distance appeared on the page before her.

"Put in the two," said Abigail, "on the sail."

"Abigail! Come away Abigail!" The tall woman called as she strode towards them picking her way along the debris-strewn beach. Abigail, do you hear me?"

"Look at the picture!" Abigail pointed as she reluctantly moved away from the man's side. The woman grabbed the little girls hand.

"Look at the picture it's a painting!"

"Excuse Abigail Sir, I hope she's not disturbing you,"

She addressed the artist who didn't look up but in a garrulous voice mumbled.

"To the contrary,"

Eileen stood holding Abigail by the hand as carefully putting the small palette and the sketchbook to one side he stood up and spoke, his voice gruff and his expression quarrelsome, though the words were politely delivered.

"Perhaps I should introduce myself I am Joseph Turner a friend of Sophie Booth to whom you are acquainted. You are Eileen Wakeley, I have seen you at the guest house."

Eileen, still holding Abigail's hand now recognised the man as the great painter JMW Turner, she had heard Sophie mention his name on several occasions.

"I am now Eileen Janacec and this is Abigail," she said adjusting a wayward strand of hair that had blown across her face.

From this chance meeting Turner had found exactly what he needed for the painting he was planning, the painting of a mother and child standing at the waterfront anxiously watching the Hovellers in their boats racing out to salvage a wreck in a terrible storm.

Sitting down and reaching for his sketchpad he began to work vigorously, sketching the two figures, at the same time enquiring if Eileen would mind him including them in his next masterpiece.

She agreed enthusiastically and struck a pose.

"No, as you were, please, just as you were, holding the girls hand and looking out to sea, if you don't mind."

The Very Tall Man was angry. This was mainly due to the lack of competence displayed by those entrusted to carry out his orders. Distance was posing a problem, as indeed was the inflexibility of some people who saw his inability to speak the language as an opportunity to avoid involvement and to postpone events.

Emails could be ignored and skype was out of the question. The mobile phone between Prague and London had become his main means of communication, however this too was proving unsatisfactory. Personally taking to the field did not appeal and he was becoming more and more involved, he hadn't enjoyed it when he was an operative and he certainly did not enjoy it now.

The man sitting beside him in the car did not improve the Tall Man's mood. Ignorant bloody peasant, he thought to himself, why should I have to put up with him. The man was staring straight ahead his face expressionless, dour heavy features set in an impassive stare. He sniffed and made the throat noise.

The full-length mirror in room 1125 at the Regent Palace faithfully reflected the room's image, identical to that of 1130 further down the corridor with one notable exception, its occupant.

Alan Grant, satisfied that he had secured a room on the same floor as Susan, examined his image in the mirror, sure in the knowledge that he was meeting all the requirements to satisfy and seduce his quarry. He smiled his Alan Grant smile, raising an eyebrow slightly.

How he hated the image, the simpering smile, the practiced movements and the apologetic manner. The portrayal of one so weak offended him.

Resentment smouldering, he longed for the savage existence of the mountain terrain north of Prague, at one with nature, where he could live and breath where he did not have to succumb to the will of others. Offended by the weakness and pallor of the image in the mirror his gaze dropped to the floor to the black leather, handcrafted, highly polished shoes surrounded by the floral pattern of the soft bedroom carpet.

When he raised his head to stare at the mirror his visage transformed, had become that of the killer, eyes colder, full lips no longer generous, but sardonic and cruel, a far more satisfying image.

Lying back on the bed and relaxing his body he invited the demons, familiar adversaries to be controlled and harnessed. All else fading from his mind, conjuring up a Kaleidoscope of images so grotesque, so bizarre, so arousing, his face contorted and twisted, no longer seeing, eyes rolled skyward he lay accepting the challenge. The challenge, to watch his own eyes fade in death watch his own eyes as he had watched so many other's die at his hand, the final stroke of the blade, the ultimate theft, the ultimate betrayal.

His breathing eventually steadying, he reached out for the I pad, heightened senses aware of its slim sensuality as it opened to his touch satiating his desires, his thirst, his eyes devoured the images it offered. How he marvelled at his ability to prolong the act of killing. *The cat loses interest when the mouse stops struggling.*

Eventually, leaping from the bed he began to pace the room his body agitated, hands clenching and unclenching.

The stiletto blade magically appeared and he slashed at an imaginary victim again and again.

In room 1130 nearby, Lyric radio played out some Chopin, a slight breeze disturbed the curtains at the open door leading out to the small balcony as Susan stood ready for bed, her thoughts inward, contemplating her day. The sounds and sights of a London evening, from her vantage point, normally hard to resist went unnoticed.

The intruding flashback invaded her mind stronger than before, more vivid, a cats face, white hands, an old woman the images cascaded together underlined with a horrible feeling of dread. She moved her head from side to side and grimaced, her eyes tightly closed. The images began to recede to be replaced by the face of Alan Grant. With a relieving inward breath she allowed her feelings full rein. He's a charmer there's no doubt and an extremely attractive one, she speculated on his intentions. He seemed to be acting on his own behalf with an end game in mind, obviously the securing of the painting and should it be a Turner original all the attendant publicity. Well that's fine, she mused, as long as I keep my head and my feelings in control. It is obvious that one so very well connected in the art world can be of great use to me.

Examining her motives and not without some feelings of guilt she questioned: Am I using my alleged admirer to punish Paul or am I encouraging the attention because I'm enjoying it and want to see where it takes me? As honest with her own feelings as she was with all things, Susan could only answer both. Well! The latter more than the former and of course there's all the help I'm going to get with the Turner.

Her mind switched to Paul and his male Ego. The term really irritated her, so many of her friends referred to their husbands and their delicate male ego.

The understanding of the male ego evaded Susan in spite of thirty years exposure to Paul and his sporadic fantasies. There was one truth that she understood. She had no wish to lose Paul or indeed to hurt him. But this indulgence this understanding of the male ego thing was becoming tiresome.

What about my ego, the female ego? I'm sure at this moment Paul is not considering my feelings or the probability that I may be hurting. Probably he's snoring his head off, full of good booze on the next floor. What if things had worked out the way he had wanted? I'd be at home feeling sorry for myself and he'd be hobnobbing with Thorny Thorndike.

Well I hope he and his fragile ego have a good nights rest and a pleasant trip home to Ireland tomorrow. I'm off to see Thorndike and Alan comes too. Maybe we'll have some lunch at a nice romantic location and a stroll around the Tate to view the Turners.

After that... Who knows? A lot depends on what we find out.

She felt nicely elated and sad, excited and apprehensive.

All the emotions coming together were replaced by a feeling of tiredness.

"I hope I don't have a hangover tomorrow. I'll need my wits about me to handle the Thorny Woman," she muttered to herself, her mind blurred from the effects of the alcohol. "Maybe I didn't need the Champagne," she smiled. "It was worth it."

With a shiver as she became aware of the chill in the night air she went back into the welcoming warmth of her hotel room leaving London to itself for the night. Closing the door behind her she drew across the heavy curtain to block out the pulsing lights of Piccadilly Circus.

The bed beckoned with its cherry chocolate liqueur and flower on the pillow, a fitting finish to an extraordinary day.

Lying alone in the comfortable bed with the distant sounds of the London night filtering through the balcony doors and with the soft changing multi coloured neon of

Piccadilly Circus on the curtain she drifted into a peaceful sleep.

Moving quickly and silently Janacec, revelling in the physical challenge had easily gained access to the roof.

No longer in the shelter from other buildings the welcoming chill wind touched his naked skin and blew his lank black hair as he looked down over the stone parapet to the street far below. Lowering himself over the edge, bare feet finding a hold in the pointed block work, his solo mountain climbing skills made short work of the decent to Susan's balcony.

He slipped through the high doorway into where she slept and paused beside the bed. Alan Grant or Janacec Vaclav, which persona should he assume? The white mouse played up and down the ladder of his splayed fingers. She looked so vulnerable lying on her back, one arm out-flung, her breathing heavy in sleep, gentle snores breaking the silence. Pulling back the bedcover he revealed her sleeping form. His eyes travelled over her body to the black triangle of hair, dark as his own. Exactly what he had expected to find. Crouching ever closer his face almost touching hers he inhaled her smell, his nostrils narrowing with the deep intake of his breath, his senses absorbing the essence of her body.

Consumed by the power, the knife in his hand held deftly, lightly, the surgeon's scalpel, the artists brush, he poised, the needle like point hovering above the exact location, death within an inch. Relaxing his fingers with an exhaling of breath he allowed the deadly point to prick the skin.

Susan's eyes opened wide as her hand flew to the spot where the knife had lingered a fraction of a second earlier. She sat up her senses dulled by slumber.

He stood in the shadows motionless, even the sound of his breathing could not be detected. "You must wait Susan, not now later, when all is done, later my victim, when you're aware and awake," he whispered.

The words penetrating her consciousness Susan stirred and murmured in her sleep as she sank back into the pillows.

Listening 'till her breathing became steady he left her side and slipped out through the balcony doors quietly closing them behind him.

The white mouse struggled as holding the knife out over the balcony, Janacec allowed the little creature to slide off the point and drop to the street below.

Katherine Thorndike had had a tedious, wasteful start to her day due to a major trauma concerning her partner. The cat had gone missing, Christina had freaked out. The cat was found in the fridge. It was still breathing though overcome from the cold and lack of oxygen.

Judging by the condition of the fridge contents, the Prize Persian had made a great effort to escape from its freezing prison and had eventually collapsed from exhaustion.

"Its dead!" Christina bursting into tears at the discovery grabbed the cat from its cold resting place and headed for the hot-press.

"They've got nine lives, you know," She informed Katherine wrapping the unfortunate moggie in one of Katherine's best white fluffy towels, not before wiping it's fur clean of yoghurt, mince and other debris from the fridge. She placed the bundle on the hot water tank in the hot-press and stood back anxiously viewing her handy work.

"If that stupid mouse catcher doesn't come back from the dead I'm out of a job as sure as night follows day, I'll get the sack, it's not fair! He asks me to mind the love of his life, his Prize Persian, and this happens!" She tearfully ranted.

When the cat suddenly coming to life leapt from the hot-press apparently none the worse from its experience,

Katherine, a large portion of her morning wasted went to work leaving Christina to clean up the mess.

Parking her car in the usual place she headed for the office a short walk away.

Looking at her watch she hurried, the wolf whistlers delight as she passed the building site. With bleached hair close cropped in a mannish crew cut, strong athletic figure, long, purposeful stride, some would say a beautiful looking woman others might find the jawline a bit angular and the figure too athletic. Whatever the opinion, whatever point of view one came from, the word "striking" would be the common conclusion.

Heads turned as she passed in her grey suit and calf length high-heeled boots. Everything about her demeanour stated, disrespect me at your peril.

The two steps to the front door of the modern office block were taken in one stride. In the reception two sets of eyes followed her progress across the floor as with a nod she indicated her office, a signal for the receptionist to follow.

"Well there goes Thorny Thorndike," Susan turned to Alan with a grim smile.

"Poor old Paul he couldn't have known what hit him,"

The secretary emerged from the office,

"Ms Thorndike will see you in fifteen minutes unfortunately she is running a bit late this morning, perhaps you would like some coffee?" She casually indicated the Wannamaker Coffee machine nearby as she returned to her position behind the reception desk. The clock above her head stated ten twenty five.

The offer of coffee being declined by both, Susan taking note of the time looked at Alan again.

"Well I'd prefer to have the Thorny One with me than against me, wouldn't you?"

Alan put up his hands and exhaled loudly,

"Terrifying, absolutely terrifying, that is one scary woman and you say that your husband tried to kiss her, that Ice Maiden?" He laughed incredulously. "She hit him with her briefcase! It's a wonder he's still alive."

At exactly 10.40

"You may go in now." The receptionist indicated the door.

They both stood up, Susan reaching for the document case as Alan buttoned his jacket running his fingers through his hair.

The door opened before they could reach it.

The last thing Susan expected was the bright smile, perfectly even teeth displayed in a friendly greeting.

"I'm so sorry to keep you waiting, Hello, Mrs Macken," she apologized as she shook hands.

She looked at his business card. "Mr Grant,"

Pleasantries were exchanged and they took their places on white leather seats at the beautiful pillared glass table.

"Coffee?" China cups and saucers were produced and the aroma of fresh ground coffee wafted across the room from where she stood coffeepot poised.

"Yes please," came the response in unison.

The casual informal style and pleasing manner, the clink of china-cups as the coffee was carefully poured and delivered with neat silver coasters and a biscuit barrel, all combined to calm Susan's mood, she began to relax and warm to the "Ice Maiden."

Alan observed as the two women sized each other up, his expression slightly amused and baffled at the same time.

"I've had the most ridiculous start to the day," Katherine, sitting down, stated in a chatty manner, looking at Susan as she helped herself to some sugar.

"I've had a pretty hectic couple of days myself." Susan sat back in the comfortable seat and lifted her coffee cup in both hands. Alan helped himself to a jammy dodger from the selection of biscuits.

"Yes," Katherine obviously grateful for the informality and happy to relax. "The cat got locked in the fridge and my partner nearly lost her reason, we spent an hour and a half looking for it. That's why I'm so late."

Both women laughed.

"Well, that's the best excuse I ever heard,"

The cat in the fridge appealing to her sense of humour Susan had not missed the revelation that Katherine's partner was female.

"By the way, never mind the cat," she laughed.

"Poor old Paul, that was some whack you gave him with your briefcase. Don't worry about it, I'm sure he deserved it, he's not been himself lately," she quickly added.

"What?"

Katherine Thorndike put down her coffee cup and looked across the table, her expression amused and incredulous.

"Is that what your husband told you? When, when did I hit him with my briefcase?" She quizzed Susan leaning forward with interest.

Susan, who was expecting some kind of apologetic response from the woman opposite, was taken aback at the question.

"Yesterday at the Tate?" It was more of a question than a statement.

"One, I was not at the Tate yesterday and two I have never met your husband,"

This revelation left Susan stunned into silence.

"Would anyone like a jammy dodger," Alan proffering the biscuit tin was ignored.

"Then who did he meet, how did he get the cut lip?"

The question was directed at the floor rather than to anyone in particular as Susan tried to make some sense of what she was hearing.

"I don't know but it certainly wasn't me, I did get a call from your husband to say he was in London and he was coming to meet me but we never organized a time. He rang off in some confusion," Katherine said not unsympathetically.

"I believe Sir Geoffrey Fletcher has talked to you," Alan interjected gaining the women's attention. "Concerning Mrs Macken's painting *Deal-Hovellers going out to a wreck* and the possibility of the title being in Turner's hand. We have the samples you requested." He opened the document case and proceeded to lay the samples out on the table.

"Yes, of course, I know Sir Geoffrey, I've had some dealings with him in the past and I was delighted when he called." She reached eagerly for the documents and began to study them intently one by one, the matter of Paul and the briefcase fleeing from her mind.

Susan was preoccupied with her own thoughts. What was Paul up to? Who had he met? Why did he say the lettering wasn't Turner's? He must have met someone. Probably it was a jealous husband or maybe a woman who objected to his advances, more like.

Putting all thoughts to the back of her mind deciding to concentrate on the business at hand she looked across the table. Katherine had donned a pair of reading glasses and holding up one of the lettering samples was studying it carefully. Her head held high, full lips pursed, porcelain white skin soft in the light from the window, holding the document in a long fingered hand, the pose unintentionally provocative.

Kathryn Thorndike had Alan's full attention. Susan was momentarily startled by the strange expression on his face. There was intensity in the look that seemed way out of character. His hand raised poised, forward. She was reminded of a cat watching a mouse, about to pounce.

Katherine began to speak diverting her attention and the moment passed but the expression on Alan's face remained in Susan's mind.

"I need to explain,"

Katherine put down the sheet of paper and removed her glasses. "On this evidence there seems to be a strong connection between Turner's hand writing and the hand written title on the back of your painting. I must stress that the samples have been specially selected and are limited in the amount of information they provide. There are similarities.

However, a further more extensive search needs to be made, more samples of his handwriting need to be examined, the paper dated and the graphite from the original tested. At the moment I would say it is worth looking into. The best way to proceed would be for you to leave these samples with me. As I said to Mr Macken on the phone I will check with the Tate and come back to you."

Her expression softening, "I can tell very quickly if it is *not* Turner's handwriting, proving it *is* his writing will take a bit longer. It is a very exciting and interesting case." she added.

"Please proceed Katherine and deal directly with me from now on," stated Susan "The painting belongs to me and my husband seems to have lost the plot."

With a polite cough Alan Grant attracted their attention.

"The Tate is at your disposal and Sir Geoffrey has promised full cooperation and access to all Turner's original sketch books and letters, all you need to do is ask. Mrs Macken must have everything she needs."

They discussed the painting for a while and the finances involved. Alan Grant proved to be very knowledgeable in all aspects of provenance and Susan was quite impressed with his performance.

"I hope you solve the problem of the briefcase attack," Katherine said in the reception, as they were about to take their leave.

"Well I hope your partner recovers from her cat ordeal," Susan riposted

"I think she has already," came the reply. "She's a very strong minded lady,"

Susan felt ill at ease. "Alan please could you, would you mind? I need to have a word with Katherine." Leaning close to him "It concerns Paul he's been making a bit of an ass of himself, I'll join you in a minute outside." She whispered.

"Of course take your time," shaking hands and with a nice to meet you smile he headed out the door and down the steps.

Katherine, drawing herself up to her tallest looked quizzically at Susan who with a smile and a glance indicated the office they had just left.

The two women returned closing the door.

"You're pretty sure it's not Turner's handwriting aren't you?" Susan said.

Kathryn sat down.

"It's a challenge Susan, in 1825 those who could write wrote very similarly, therefore there are of course similarities in the handwriting so the amateur eye sees them as the same. But you're right Susan, I don't believe it is Turner's handwriting as there are some substantial discrepancies. I was going to let you know as soon as I could be sure you were alone."

"I know, It's Alan Grant isn't it," Susan smiled, "he's very smooth, a bit too glib a bit too unbelievable."

"I can't say too much," Kathryn looked earnestly at Susan.

"Be careful, Sir Geoffrey Fletcher is not exactly one hundred per cent behind your Mr Alan Grant. I know him quite well and he is very ill at ease about that person. He hasn't said anything directly," she quickly added putting out a conspiratorial hand to grasp Susan's arm.

"Thank you Kathryn, I've come to certain conclusions myself but these people can be of use to me and I'm prepared to play along and see where it takes me. Frankly Kathryn, I'm enjoying the game, its quite exciting."

Out in the street Susan, spontaneously, took Alan's arm as they walked towards the Green Park. "Thank You for your help Alan I'm glad you were there. What do you think from what she said? Do you think it's Turner's writing?"

"She seems to be quite positive about it. Don't you want to ring Paul?"

Susan glanced at her watch.

"No, he's probably at the airport I'll ring him later." Her grip became a little firmer on his arm and she pulled him closer.

"Com'on smart boy show me the ducks in the park and then we'll have a bit of lunch."

"Sounds good," he said transferring his arm to around her shoulders looking down into her face with his Alan Grant smile. She snuggled closer and he kissed her on the top of her head. In the circumstances the kiss seemed quite appropriate.

Susan, feeling happy and in control, aware of her own feelings, matched his stride as they entered the Green Park

Above her head Vaclav Janacec's expression told a different story as his fingers touched the smooth handle of the knife in his pocket.

He kissed her again this time on the forehead.

"Quack, quack," his duck impression matched the apparent lightness of her mood.

"What did you think of Katherine?" Susan suddenly said, remembering the look.

"Scary, scary, lady. I wouldn't like to meet her on a dark night, I prefer Irish women of substance. Anyway she's a Thorny*dike* with a lady partner who keeps cats, no thanks!" He said with a laugh.

To Susan his attempt at humour was callous and ill considered, reminiscent of some of her own children's friends in their teenage years. Susan's instincts, her radar of experience zeroing in indicated that this thirty-five year old was not exactly all he was pretending to be.

For a while they walked in silence preoccupied with their own private thoughts. Susan cherished such moments visiting places in her mind, harbouring her own private fantasies.

Today as she walked and laughed with Alan, exchanging looks now and then, their hands touching, a fantasy. Yet he was being so attentive, she studied his face searching for a hint of cynicism but received only a look of genuine enjoyment, this puzzled the perceptive Susan. His eyes held hers with his dark all- seeing penetrating gaze.

Is it reasonable she conjectured to assume that a young man so handsome, likeable and sophisticated would want to be with her in this way? He was certainly flirting, that was obvious.

The idea appealed to her and there was no -doubting the attraction.

Men had never been a problem to Susan, she liked them and they liked her. Over the years there had been occasions when, for instance some of Paul's business associates had made more than just friendly overtures and some of them had been on the young side, she smiled at the thought. Well what's wrong with that? She rationalized. I'm a lucky girl.

Jane and Richard had often joked about some of their friends at school fancying their attractive mother. It was always something for her to take a certain pleasure in but always treated as a joke and passed off in a light-hearted manner. But responding, feeling the way she felt now, dropping her guard, allowing herself to weaken was exciting and very nice.

I can back off at any time she reassured herself.

Alan had removed his arm from her shoulders and taken her hand to cross the road. It was a natural simple gesture but somehow thrilling.

'Maybe I don't want to back away.'

They hurried across the road dodging the traffic laughing at the blare of a car horn, holding hands at arms length.

Susan felt her reserve waver, a teenager again, all resistance deserting, they reached the other side. He turned round pulling her towards him as she gladly went into his arms. They kissed, close intimate and wonderful. The commuters hurried by without a glance, just another young couple in love.

The Riverside Café for lunch, the perfect location, the aroma of fine Italian Cuisine, deep cushioned wicker chairs, sparkling white tablecloths, in the shade under stretched canvas awnings, looking over the wooden walkway with rows of daffodils and the Thames beyond in the bright spring sunlight.

Susan and Alan were guided to a table and made themselves comfortable amidst the celebrity sprinkled diners. As they studied the menu a waiter poured them two glasses of champagne placing the bottle in an ice bucket on a stand beside their table. Slightly surprised they looked enquiringly at the waiter who indicated another table where Sir Geoffrey turned to salute them with his customary glass of brandy and a slightly tipsy smile.

They smiled back, nodding their thanks as Susan noted the rather dour expressions of Sir Geoffrey's be-suited male companions.

"They're a happy looking bunch," she commented slightly sarcastically. "Poor Sir Geoffrey looks as if he's taking refuge in the brandy again."

She looked across at Alan who was no longer smiling as his gaze lingered on Sir Geoffrey's companions.

Abruptly he excused himself

"I'll be back in a moment," his Alan Grant smile slightly askew, betrayed his feelings.

Susan watched as he crossed to the other table. She could not see his face as he addressed Sir Geoffrey's companions but he seemed agitated in his gestures. The two men facing appeared to be foreign and one in particular seemed angry. Susan was unsure but she felt that his expression changed from anger to a look of what she could only describe as real fear. It was hard to be sure. Sir Geoffrey appeared not to take part in the animated conversation.

Alan turned abruptly, smiling broadly as he returned leaving the two in deep animated conversation one with, Susan noted, an "I told you," look on his face, the other who still seemed uncomfortable stared after the tall departing figure.

"Just some business I had to deal with, he apologized, sometimes people misunderstand their position and I need to put them straight, it's nothing." He gestured dismissively.

"Well you certainly had some effect, that man seemed terrified."

Susan looked across to the table where they were preparing to leave. Sir Geoffrey as usual hastily downing his drink gave them a casual salute the other two didn't look across.

"Would you like to order?"

The waiter hovered and Susan chose seafood while Alan went for the pasta with a bottle of Barolo, explaining apologetically that he didn't really like champagne very much.

Susan watched as her glass was topped up.

"This is really good champagne, Sir Geoffrey may not know where he is half the time but he certainly knows his liquor," Susan laughed, regaining the mood.

The glass of red and the glass of champagne met with a satisfying clink.

"To Turner and Hovellers." They drank a toast.

"To Sir Geoffrey and his taste in champagne," said Susan raising her glass.

Warm crusty bread rolls from a basket were placed on the table. Alan took several and said how much he liked them with lots of butter. The warm salad starter with crab and avocado had to be complimented with a crisp Chablis Alan insisted. They ate and smiled at each other a lot.

The seats seemed to become more comfortable. The other diners seemed not to exist. Susan, finding it difficult to resist the mood, aware that she was drinking far more than she normally would only had eyes for the beautiful attentive man across the table.

They discussed the painting and its potential, making plans, mapping out procedures.

239

"The original painting is the key, emails and scanned images are fine for the preliminary stages." Alan explained, "but the experts at the Tate have to see the original work. You cannot assume anything until they have had a chance to bring all their resources and skill to bear. You need to get the painting to London." He looked to Susan for a response.

"Your eyes are almost black," she responded, "You know they are the darkest eyes I have ever seen. Tell me about yourself Alan." She leaned across the table and reached for his hand. "What's going on behind those eyes, where are you when they go so black?"

"Right here," he said taking her hands and looking into her eyes.

"There's very little to tell. I was born in Europe near Prague thirty-five years ago. My parents came to England when I was three they had sold a profitable business and because my mother was partly British, they came here. I went to public school where I did well and then to Eaton where I excelled at sport and studied art history. Very boring really."

"Three, when you were three! I bet you were a beautiful little child. Tell me about your parents. Have you brothers and sisters?"

"I'm an only child," he looked down at the tablecloth and then to her eyes.

"Both my parents died in a car crash three years ago."

"I'm so sorry, you must miss them terribly." Susan's eyes filled with tears prompted by the sad story and the effects of the alcohol.

"I really do, Susan but enough of this sad stuff. Tell me when I'm going to visit you in Ireland, the land of saints and scholars? Why don't I go back with you, you could show me around and I could have a good look at the painting before it comes to the Tate."

Susan immediately responded enthusiastically. "Yes that's perfect we could spend a few days in London and then travel to Ireland together, then come back to the Tate with the painting. We have a very nice guest room; you would be very welcome to stay."

Alan Grant, looking at her all the while took her hand and kissed it.

"You're an extraordinary woman," he said. " I'm a lucky man,"

"And a bit younger than me," she prompted

He leaned back with hands linked behind his head and looked at her intently.

"I know one should never ask a woman her age but what age are you, forty, forty-one?"

"Why Mr Grant, you're good very good almost right, forty-three," she smoothly lied. "And beautiful," he added

Still leaning back Alan persisted "You know there are official channels we employ for transporting valuable works of art around the world, correct procedures, so to speak. The Tate is very particular but there is no reason why I cannot accompany your painting myself."

Leaning forward and taking a bread roll in his hand he held it up.

"I solemnly swear on this bread roll that I shall accompany and protect, at all times, the Turner painting entitled Hovellers going out to a wreck."

"And what about the beautiful owner, does she get to accompany the handsome bread roll swearer."

"Of course," holding out his arms in a magnanimous gesture, "to the ends of the earth."

The mood thoroughly restored, Susan feeling more in charge looked across the table earnestly.

"I'm enjoying myself Alan, I'm not ready to go home just yet. It would be lovely to see some of the sights together."

Aware that she was playing a game, aware that she needed to be in control, Susan took note of the amount of alcohol being consumed.

"And," Alan took her hand.

"The bread roll swearer and the beautiful owner could get to know each other a little better."

Nothing else mattered to Susan, his hand felt nice, this is what I want. She felt herself lean towards him wishing he was closer, for a while just for a while I'll take it all.

She studied his face, his gentle, sincere, slight smile. She trusted him in that moment. He really likes me she admitted to herself confidently ignoring the obvious warning signals.

"What about the young girls, you could have them all," She confidently tested.

"Young girls are tiresome, anyway they think I'm an old man. Susan I know what I want. You're a fabulous woman and there isn't a man in this room who wouldn't want to be sitting where I am now."

The smile was there as they leaned across the table to each other. She reached out and touched his face moving her hand gently upwards to brush his thick black hair with the back of her fingers.

"It is the law of the bread roll, the bread roll has spoken," he took her hand and closing his eyes kissed her fingers. Then looking up, "let's go," he said impulsively standing up and dragging her to a standing position.

"No wait a minute, don't move."

He looked out towards the Thames and then hurried away between the tables across the boardwalk to the daffodils. He returned with a broad smile on his handsome face holding the single bloom. Ignoring the amused glances from the other diners, full of fun, laughing at her embarrassment he presented her with the yellow trumpet shaped flower.

"Thank you,"

She stood embarrassed as she took the flower from his hand. With eyes averted she never saw it coming. He held her and kissed her full on the mouth. For a moment she felt the surprising strength of his arm as she was lifted slightly off her feet.

"The Tate awaits,"

He slowly released the tight grip around her waist allowing her to slide down his body and her feet to touch the floor. Holding her by the hand he led her from the restaurant.

Outside the popular Café stretch limos and cabs came and went. They stood on the path as a large limousine cruised to a halt at the doorway.

"Another celeb arrives," Susan bent to see the occupant of the large car.

The driver quickly exited from his seat and strode around to open the door.

"Your car Madam," he said looking at Susan and indicating the plush interior.

Wide eyed she looked at the smiling Alan

"What's this? Don't tell me you ordered a limo?"

"Courtesy of Sir Roger, it's at our disposal whenever needed."

"My Oh My I could get used to this!"

As she made herself comfortable in the spacious interior the warning lights flashed again and she laughed as she heard Alan instruct the driver.

"Take the scenic route." He slipped in beside her, nice.

"Is Madame comfortable? Let me see, perhaps champagne?"

The fridge revealed champagne and two frosted glassed. "Or maybe some Butler's hand made chocolates? Unfortunately we have to provide our own coffee," he indicated the espresso coffee maker.

The big car surged away from the riverside Café and Susan snuggled contentedly close to the extraordinary young man.

"Let's give the Tate a miss and see the sights. Tomorrow's another day," he said reaching for the Champagne bottle, aware of Susan's weakening resolve, "I thought we might take our time." He put his arm around her.

"What's the scenic route?" she enquired.

"Anywhere you want to go,"

They cruised around Trafalgar Square with its sightseers taking in London's famous landmarks, the Tate,

Westminster Abbey, Big Ben, the Houses of Parliament by Downing Street and Number Ten, up the Mall and Buckingham Palace, the Thames and London's Eye.

Susan looked out at the faces peering in to identify the celebrity in the stretch limo. She felt like waving but managed to restrain herself, keeping her cool.

Harrods was a must. The driver pulled in to return and collect them half an hour later, Hamleys Toy Store with floor after floor of every thing imaginable. A magician demonstrated a disappearing pile of coins holding out white- gloved hands. They stopped and watched. He held out his empty hand to Alan, closed it and opened it, a small pile of pound coins had appeared on his palm.

Susan clapped her hands. "Impressive!"

Alan taking the coins from the showman's hand examined them incredulously. The magician held out his hand with a knowing smile for the coins to be returned.

Alan placed the coins one by one on the open palm and closed the magician's fingers over them when the Magician opened his hand they had disappeared to be replaced by a white mouse.

Susan clapped her hands again.

"Isn't that amazing!" she exclaimed. "How did he do that?"

"I have no idea," as they walked away. Susan looked back. The magician was looking at the white mouse in amazement. She looked at Alan again quizzically.

"It only cost him six pounds for the mouse," he said showing her the coins.

"What? You did it, how?"

"Magic," he said

"No, where did the mouse come from?"

"If I told you it would spoil the effect,"

"It had to be somewhere?" she said, "Do you carry white mice around with you all the time?"

"No!"

"Where are they? In your trousers?" she laughed and made a playful grab to search him. "All magicians have secret pockets."

"No!"

The movement that swept her hand away was far from gentle. The look in the eye chilled her good humour. "No," he repeated more gently. "I sometimes bring a prop with me when I want to impress. I'm a keen amateur magician."

She smiled an uncertain smile, the effects of the Champagne still driving her mood. His explanation satisfied though the look lingered.

'Play the game.'

"I'm sorry, Alan of course, I didn't know. You're very talented. Did you see the expression on that poor guy's face?" She exclaimed. "How did you do it, show me another trick I love magic tricks?"

"We had better get a move on," he said with a laugh, grabbing her hand

"Or our Limo will have disappeared."

They headed quickly down the escalator towards Hamleys Regent Street entrance arriving as the car drew up outside. The good humour restored they bundled in with their carrier bags, flushed and slightly out of breath.

"The Regent Palace, please," Susan gaily gave the instruction.

"What about tomorrow?" We must go to the Galleries.

"The driver has his instructions. If it's alright with you he'll pick you up at ten thirty." Alan sat alongside, arm across the back of the seat as he spoke, casually looking out the window at the passers by.

"Are you not coming too?" She placed her hand on his knee and looked at him earnestly. "I'm sure you would be able to guide me on Turner. I really don't think it would be the same without you." The appeal was genuine.

Alan was thinking of the base and Jennifer in cell five. Matt also would have to be dealt with. He was well past his sell by date and of course the fat man, pity Matt had killed him. Three blind mice, see how they run, scampering in panic as he dealt with them one by one. He licked his lips in satisfaction. The action provoked a cruel expression of anticipation on Vaclav's face.

"Alan!" Susan shook his knee to gain his attention.

Realising his expression had betrayed his thoughts Vaclav gave her his best Alan Grant smile. He need not have worried. Susan was now waving champagne waves at the passers by.

They were circling Eros and Piccadilly Circus.

"We're here," he said as the big car pulled up smoothly in front of the Regent Palace.

The door was opened and Susan in some disarray had to make several attempts to extricate herself from the deep upholstery before they both made it out onto the pavement and into the reception. Susan, feeling giddy and light headed clutched tightly to Alan's arm unaware that the champagne was not quite what the label had indicated. He laughingly helped her across the floor, the driver following with the carrier bags and several items they'd left behind in the car including Susan's handbag.

"There are several messages for you Mrs Macken."

The receptionist informed with barley-concealed disapproval. "You were not contactable by phone."

She was handed several envelopes with the Regent Hotel Crest. Composing herself long enough to accept the envelopes, the effort required surprised her. The room swayed and she had to look to Alan for support as they entered the lift.

In the bedroom corridor on the third floor somehow Susan rallied enough to remember the room number.

"I'm 1130 just leave me to my door it's been a lovely day, thank you very much".

The driver stopped at 1125 unlocked the door depositing the bags inside.

Susan standing unsteadily in the doorway searching in her handbag for her room card heard Alan talking to the driver in a foreign language. The driver appeared very attentive while Alan was assertive and clipped in his speech.

"Is that Italian?" she said with a knowing look, pointing a finger. "I didn't know you were Italian?" Not waiting for an answer she entered the room and lay back on the bed with a contented sigh and closed her eyes. For a moment she lay there and then sat up with a puzzled expression

"I'm in the wrong room. I'm in your room." Alan closed the door as she struggled to a standing position, the thought having a sobering effect.

"Don't worry, relax," he took her hands "feel at home," he led her to the comfortable armchair in the window alcove. "Sit here I'll order some coffee from room service it'll help sober us up,"

"Thanks," she sat down looking around the room with an uncertain smile.

"Room service please," he stood at the small writing desk. "Could we have some coffee and….?" He turned to Susan smiling, "Would you like something to eat or maybe another bottle of champagne?" he said with a mischievous laugh.

"Just the champagne," she joked

Alan put down the phone,

"I'll just be a minute he said," heading to the bathroom humming a tune. "Don't go away," he said before closing the door behind him.

Susan beginning to feel quite sober looked around the room. It was exactly the same as hers, the drapes and the high doorway to the balcony, even the bed covers and the carpet.

The small computer on the table drew her attention. A touch screen Apple Mac I pad. "Nice," Susan ran her finger along the rim of the open lid her interest fuelled by the fact that Paul after a lot of thought had eventually bought himself a similar one.

I'm sure Alan won't mind. The screen, without sound sprang to life immediately at her touch. Alan's face swam into view, she smiled, how handsome he looks.

Her smile froze on her face in horror at the most hideous sequence of events that followed. At first her mind could not cope with the images on the screen. Her hands flew to her face to stifle the gasp of horror.

"It's not real!" she swung around wide-eyed. He was standing at the bathroom door with his Alan Grant smile. "It's a movie. You didn't think I was really killing someone, did you?" He laughed as he rounded the bed.

She had seen enough to know he was lying.

While her mind raced trying to cope with the images, her brain was telling her to keep calm and not to betray her real feelings.

"That's a relief," with an attempted smile.

"Yes it's a movie I took part in, a cheap thriller," his voice casual. "I wasn't proud of it. What was it called? That's it," he clicked his fingers and she jumped.

"The Killer Gets His Kicks," he laughed. "I can't even remember the name it was something like that."

His explanation so simple, his performance so smooth and natural, his amusement at the situation so real, she almost believed him.

Now acutely sober, the images had already begun to haunt her mind. Standing up quickly she felt lightheaded.

"It's the drink." She put her hand to her head. "I really had too much," her voice feeble. "May I use the bathroom?"

"Of course, I understand," he took a step towards her. "Here let me help you."

She brushed past him avoiding contact. The bathroom door was open. If she could get inside and lock the door, but he was right behind her as she crossed the room.

In the bathroom she was violently ill. He stood at the door watching with a concerned expression.

He's a killer! Was all she could think, no he can't be? It's got to be a mistake! She crouched there beside the toilet pan and knew he had done terrible things, the realization struck. She had no doubts. Still grappling with the images, the knife, the blood, the gaping wounds, the poor girls face drove Susan to her feet.

She flushed the toilet and forcing the terrible images from her mind with a supreme effort managed to rise to her feet. My handbag, she thought and my phone.

"Your handbag," leaning casually against the doorframe he held it out for her to take, his eyes never leaving her face, staring with an intensity that made her feel as if he might strike out at any moment. It was all she could do to will herself to take a step towards him.

"Thank you!" it was difficult to keep her hand from trembling as she took the bag. "I must look dreadful, I'll be alright in a minute," she said checking her appearance in the mirror her hand rearranging loose strands of hair.

"Booze, the demon booze, I don't know what came over me. It's a long time since I indulged in more than a glass of wine or two, you're a bad influence." Amazingly she heard herself laugh and in spite of her fear she felt steady and in better control.

"Just give me a moment and I'll be fine," she said taking a step towards him and indicating the door.

His stare didn't waver and he didn't move. *The cat watches the mouse.*

"You look fine," he suddenly smiled his whole face lighting up. "Beautiful, yes you look beautiful."

Concentrating on her image in the mirror, her mind racing to buy time she put her bag on the washstand and began to search through its contents.

Alan Grant watched from the doorway.

Susan could feel the anger overcoming her fear, anger at her physical weakness and frustration at her inability to meet him head on and defeat him.

"Out!" she said walking towards him with a dismissive gesture, "Out!" she repeated " A woman must be left alone at moments like this, Go!" She commanded with a dismissive backward flicking of her hand, Susan the mother, in charge expecting to be obeyed.

He stepped back as she came towards him slightly wrong footed by this aggressive and commanding stance. Sensing his hesitation she followed up her slight advantage imperiously sweeping past him bag in hand.

"I'm off to my room, maybe I'll get some privacy there," She blustered.

"No wait, I'm sorry it's just that we've had such a nice day and I do think you look great, please don't go!" He followed her, his eyes soft as he appealed, pure undiluted Alan Grant. "What do you say?" Head to one side smiling apologetically he reached for her hand.

"I have to get my beauty sleep it's been a wonderful day. You were so good to arrange the beautiful car and the lunch was wonderful, thank you, you're very nice and all that but we can do it all again tomorrow."

She let him take her hand and he raised it to his lips. His touch was, at the same time caressing and threatening.

Gently withdrawing her hand she managed to smile up into his face.

"You're such a nice boy but I really must go now."

"You're right he said softly," and turning he walked to the door opening it wide.

"The lady must get her beauty sleep."

With a sense of relief Susan viewed the beckoning corridor, bright and inviting. Janacec stepping away to one side walked casually to the window.

Susan calculated the distance to the open door. She would have to pass quite close to him to round the large double bed that lay between her and safety. Avoiding the temptation to clamber over the bed and rush out the door, for a moment she studied his broad back. He seemed disinterested as he stood at the window looking out through the open curtains.

"What a great city, I'm looking forward to tomorrow." He remained looking out the window. Deciding to pursue her positive attitude she moved along the side of the bed with a purposeful stride.

"Such a clear evening" he bent towards the window to look out and upwards. "Not a cloud in the sky."

She hurried around the bed without taking her eyes from his back. The open door was feet away. Relief and gratitude flooding her mind she dashed across the carpeted floor. *The mouse must make the first move.*

He came across the bed in one fluid motion. She felt his hand in her hair as her head was jerked violently backwards, her scream cut short by a smothering hand on her face making only a whimper possible. The bright light of the hallway receded as she was dragged back into the room and the door closed.

She tried to bite his hand, use her elbows, reach his face with her nails, and kick out. The more she struggled the tighter and more cruel his grip became, she could feel his strength as he crushed her body enveloping her in his powerful arms all resistance futile, her senses began to recede.

With a supreme effort of will she allowed her body to go limp.

With a low grunt of approval, blessedly relaxing his grip he let her fall back onto the bed. As her shoulders made contact with the bedspread she brought her foot up with all her might in a kick powered by anger, frustration and near panic. Her shoulders sinking into the soft bed added impetus and strength to the impact of her pointed shoe as it caught him between his legs.

Rolling off the bed she scrambled across the floor to the door.

His kick caught her in the ribs. It was well placed and spun her over onto her back. She tried to twist into a crouched position and he hit her again. He grabbed her and this time his grip was terrifyingly strong.

She felt herself being lifted off her feet and thrown violently onto the bed. Cruel fingers closed around her throat

"You're going to be killed by the knife," She heard the words as she struggled to breathe.

"Mrs Macken is going to die."

She tried to fight, her fists punching, her lips drawn back from her teeth in a rictus of pain and fright.

Laughing at her feeble efforts he slackened the grip on her throat, she gasped for air, he waited a moment and then with a smile he slowly increased the pressure again. Her senses began to swim but before she passed out he slackened the grip again.

"You brute, you animal," she heard herself gasp as she blessedly lost consciousness.

Vaclav Janacec sat astride the inert form. Susan, clothes in disarray, her facial expression losing its tension, looked peaceful as her high colour receded from her face. He checked her pulse noting the rise and fall of her chest as air began to course through her body.

Reaching to the bedside locker he retrieved a small rolled up cloth wallet and laid it out on the bed beside Susan's head, revealing various medical instruments including a syringe. Selecting an ampule he filled the instrument. Susan stirred slightly as the needle entered the vein in her upper arm.

For a while he sat astride her looking down into her face waiting for the serum to take effect. He felt anger at her resistance, anger at himself for his carelessness in letting her discover the video, thereby having to show his hand. The "Turner" would be valueless if attained by illegal means. Janacec was aware that if the correct channels were not followed it would amount to total failure. He would have to return to Prague empty handed. Anger the fuel, violence ignited, he could feel the sensations begin to stir and the knife flew into his hand.

At first the sound did not fully penetrate his consciousness, impatiently he looked to the source. His phone vibrated and bounced on the bedside locker.

Magnito, its Magnito the only man in the world that commanded his respect, without hesitation putting the knife away he reached for the phone.

Remaining silent he held the phone to his ear.

"I see you are making excellent progress with the Macken woman." The voice was slow and measured, "But your threat to Boris today at the restaurant was ill advised, he is in our control and at the moment your involvement with him is not required. When you return to Prague and the painting has been secured you may do with him as you wish." The phone went dead.

Vaclav looked again at Susan the source of all his problems, he slapped her face and she stirred slightly. The slap was calculated not so much to hurt as to rouse the woman.

Susan opened her eyes, her mouth dry and her head aching.

"I'm thirsty," She looked calmly up at her tormentor. But no words came. She felt she was speaking but she could not hear her own voice, he watched with satisfaction as her lips moved without sound.

"Water? Of course you're thirsty, they always are."

He went into the bathroom and returned with a glass of water. "Sit up," he instructed her with a slight smile. She tried but somehow her limbs would not respond.

"I said sit up!" he repeated

But no matter how Susan tried she could not change her position on the bed.

"Fine, in a few minutes you will be able to stand but you will not be able to rise into a standing position without help."

Now fully conscious, Susan looked at him, the beginnings of a realization of a personal horror beginning to dawn upon her.

He looked deep into her eyes in silence he studied her face. A wisp of blond hair had fallen across her eye. He traced the line of her jaw with a caressing finger and gently brushed the wayward strand from her face.

His eyes were soft and deep, all anger receding. His next words astonished and horrified her. "Susan Wakeley or should I say Janacec," he said softly.

"Yes Janacec, you are a Janacec." He nodded with a false seeming apologetic smile.

She could not respond.

"All is about to be revealed." Reaching to the bedside locker he retrieved a yellowed parchment page torn from a sketchbook and turned the image to face her. It was a watercolour sketch of a little girl with a blond lady holding her hand. The same little girl in the painting they had found in the black box only a much smaller picture and not as detailed. There was handwriting on the back of the picture. Her tormentor turned it for her to read.

15 may 1825
Dear Mrs Janacec,
Thank you for allowing me to use the study of you and Abigail in my latest work. Please accept this small sketch as a wedding gift. JMW Turner."

He looked down into the expressionless face knowing she could hear and understand everything he said. "Your maiden name is Wakeley, Susan Wakeley."

His voice a sinister whisper, "Shall I go on or is all this too much of a shock for you?" head to one side he mockingly quizzed. "Nothing to say? Are you sitting comfortably my poor pathetic little Irish housewife?" He paused, "Then I'll tell you about your family heritage, your blood relatives.

"Your ancestor, a woman called Grace Wakeley, married a man called Vojta Matej Janacec in 1825. The marriage only lasted a couple of years. He was eventually found guilty of murder, tried and hanged. They had two children, two boys. Grace stopped using the Janacec name but one of the boys didn't. He was my relative, my blood!" He smiled and then laughed out loud looking down at her. She remained unmoving, helplessly looking up into his taunting face.

"Hi cousin, give us a kiss!" He bent and kissed her viciously on the mouth. She could feel his breath as he withdrew to sit back, still astride her. As he studied her face, she knew with horror that he was capable of terrible things. His hand moved as he stared into her eyes. "We're the same! Susan Wakeley," he whispered as his magician's fingers began to caress, search and probe her helpless body in the most intimate manner. He smiled his satisfaction. His mocking dark eyes looked deep into her eyes of the exact same colour. As the endless moments of helpless mortification passed the sinister whispering voice continued.

"You are capable of killing, we are the same, I see it, you are a Janacec in your heart." In his free hand he held the knife an inch from her face tracing a path between her eyes and across the bridge of her nose. "At this moment you could kill."

Susan, in mortified despair, desperately wanted to escape from his control to contradict, to turn away, to cover her ears, to cry out, to scream.

"My name is Vaclav Janacec, and Vojta Matej Janacec my ancestor killed a man called Michael Wakeley and his two sons with this knife in 1825. This knife has spilled much blood. I killed my first man when I was three years old. I killed my father and my mother when I was eleven. It is fitting that this beautiful instrument will take your life as well. The picture links us Susan. This is no coincidence. I have been trying to trace the picture for many years. The Bellini list confirmed its existence and the Internet led me to you."

Susan knew she was crying, the salt tears stung her cheeks. Her deepest emotions stirred by the callous act and the words, she struggled but failed to put her mind elsewhere as she felt the bile rising in her throat, choking her.

"No! That would be too easy," he quickly turned her onto her side blessedly removing his exploring hand. She lay helpless while he talked.

"Yes in a sense you are paralyzed. Your muscles will support you but you cannot control any movement. You may scream as loud as you like but it will only be in your head. You have been injected with a drug. It's a drug that is still in experimental stage, you may or may not recover from it but that's incidental."

"Now Susan it's time we left. But before we go there's one more thing."

Taking her hand he purposefully wrapped her fingers around the handle of the knife. White hands, a cats face, an old woman, Susan remembered. She watched with horror as slowly he lifted her arm aloft. Still holding the knife clasped in her fingers he turned the stiletto blade to rest against his chest allowing the needle sharp point to slightly prick the skin drawing a trickle of blood. His eyes never left hers. Susan's eyes betrayed her extreme emotion as small threads of her memory stirred. Janacec continued. "You have taken life. You have killed, Susan Janacec."

It was an easy matter for a man as powerful as Janacec to lift her to a standing position beside the bed. He rearranged her cloths and her hair. She tried to collapse to sink to the floor but the muscles of her legs would not obey any signals. Putting his arm around her he smiled his Alan Grant smile.

"Now we will walk, Susan." He took a step and she could feel his hands manipulating her. Helpless to resist she found herself shuffling by his side. They walked to the door and back to the centre of the room.

"Good that was very good." She tried to move to strike him, anything to retaliate but to no avail. The only movement she could feel were the tears as they streamed down her face.

Vaclav stepped to one side releasing his hold on her allowing the full-length mirror to reflect her in her sorry state as she stood alone and horrified looking at the image, her face expressionless and pale. Move! Move! Her mind shrieked at her limbs. Not even an eyelid flickered, she stood powerless to do anything and still the memories ebbed and flowed in her own personal sea of horror.

Vaclav made three phone calls, abrupt and curt, in a language she did not recognise. He sounded impatient and authoritative. Obviously he was now in a hurry.

Without comment he effortlessly lifted her with one arm and carried her to the door. Having checked the corridor he walked her to the lift. Her knees unbending he held her very close turning her face away from inquisitive eyes and bending her head so she was looking towards the floor.

They stood waiting for the doors to open.

"Hello again,"

Susan's heart surged with relief and hope. It was the well-dressed man and his wife with some friends. The door of the lift opened, Vaclav's grip tightened and they stepped into the lift together.

"My husband is embarrassed about last night,"

The wife stooped to look into Susan's face. "That business about the bunny boiler you know," she noticed the tears, "are you alright dear?" concern was written on her face.

"Help me!" Susan screamed silently unable to lift her head.

"Please excuse us," Alan Grant spoke softly and solicitously his hand gently turning her head away. "We've just received some very distressing news about Susan's mother."

"Oh dear! I am sorry." A small hand coming into view gently squeezed Susan's arm and withdrew.

The well-dressed man and his wife stood in respectful silence as the lift descended. The doors opened into the busy foyer. Without comment they all stepped tactfully to one side to make way for Alan Grant and the 'grief stricken' Susan, to watch sympathetically as they walked slowly across the lobby to the exit.

It was obvious to all that Susan was deeply distressed and needed the support of the nice looking young man. In vain she tried to stumble, to fall, anything to make it difficult for her tormentor.

She could hear him with his Alan Grant voice, hushed and sincere as he accepted their quiet words of sympathy.

"She'll be fine, thank you." His voice infuriated her as she was manipulated to walk close beside him, her head turned into his chest, to play the part of the bereaved, her uncontrolled tears of frustration evidence of her distress.

Vaclav had contacted the hotel staff to advise them about the demise of Susan's mother and word had spread.

There were many sympathetic glances in their direction.

The Door Man, his face showing his sympathy opened the door and stepped to one side revealing the large black limo waiting outside. People free to walk and talk, smile and laugh thronged the pavement as Susan soundlessly screaming for help was guided amongst them.

Holding the door open the driver put out a supportive hand. With a feeling of despair Susan heard him and Vaclav exchange some words before solemnly helping her into the back of the car. Vaclav got in beside her and the doorman closed the door. The big car surged away from the front of the Regent Palace.

"Poor woman," the well-dressed man watched their departure. "She seemed so happy last night. You never know the hour or the day,"

His wife solemnly agreed.

How could this be happening? Susan, near despair slumped to one side unable to control her movement, helpless. This is the stuff of fiction, or news in the media of terrible deeds one may read or hear about. This happens to other people. So many questions and conflicting emotions, her head reeling from the sheer enormity of the situation as he sat in beside her, the violence of his presence invading every emotion at so many levels, her dread of the unknown. What would happen next?

But most of all there was the feeling of helplessness in her immobility. The car manoeuvred through the evening traffic and she was thrown, to lie, face pressed into the upholstery, her arm painfully trapped under her body unable to readjust her position. To the dispassionate Vaclav she had become a carcass, a large unwieldy piece of meat that needed to be transported to a destination. *The mouse couldn't move*

The only factor in Susan's favour was that he needed to keep her alive at least until he had his instructions from Prague. After all she was the owner of what he considered to be one of the most valuable paintings in the world.

The Driver, one of the Prague Operatives checked out his passengers in the rear-view mirror. He had not met the man Janacec or heard of him until three days previously. His orders had been specific. Make himself and the car available and follow all instructions without question.

The man who seemed to have lost interest in the woman and was looking straight ahead, his eyes staring unblinkingly, suddenly spoke

"There is clean up work to be done at a house at number 24 Cornmarket Road," he said, still staring straight ahead, "A total removal."

The driver knew better than to ask any questions, he repeated the instruction word for word and the man nodded approval.

The operative had a team of people at his disposal and they would take care of the details. "Leave us at Friar Street and don't wait. You will be contacted at a later date if needed."

Many deliveries had been made to Friar Street and the driver was familiar with the Base. He only got the chance to use the limousine when important visitors came. More often it would be the large van, sometimes with hopeful immigrants, sometimes with military types who didn't speak. In a period of five years he had transported an assortment of people to and from the Base, always without question.

In the back of the car, preoccupied with his thoughts of failure Vaclave could feel the anger mounting. There was work to do before returning to Prague. The base would be useful. There he could dispose of the people who were a threat to him, those who knew him as Alan Grant. He would have to confess his stupidity to Magnito, disclose how he had made videos of his victims resulting in the woman's discovery, thereby losing all credibility and causing failure of his mission. The painting would be worthless unless gained by legal means. Failure to Vaclav was the ultimate humiliation and the feeble woman was responsible.

Negotiating Central London Traffic requires concentration but the driver became distracted, his eye caught by the flash of reflected light. The man had moved and was now looking intently at the woman. The driver peering into the rear-view mirror failed to see the pedestrian light change until the last second. Swerving and braking at the same time he felt the back of the big car begin to come around. Releasing the footbrake and applying a reverse lock he managed to negotiate the space avoiding pedestrians and oncoming cars.

When he looked back to the rear-view mirror he could plainly see that the man had adjusted his position. The driver could clearly make out the long pointed blade of the knife held between forefinger and thumb. The man appeared to be unaffected by the manoeuver at the pedestrian crossing and was staring intently at the inert figure lying head down on the back seat.

After a quick glance ahead to make sure the road was clear he checked the rear-view mirror again in time to see the man reach out with a finger and prod the woman in the small of her back like a cat coaxing a mouse into action.

Vaclav turned Susan round to face him and prodded her again with his finger he wanted her to move so he could use the knife.

Her immobility was working in Susan's favour, as she lay helpless on the back seat of the car. Killing came easily to this man but he needed his victims to struggle to put up a fight, to attempt escape. The knife was in his hand. She perceived that he seemed ill at ease, in a strange way uncertain. With a feeling of relief she realized at that moment he was unlikely to use the knife.

His attention wavered, he seemed to lose interest in her and turning to the driver he began a tirade of abuse.

Perhaps there is reason for hope. Susan had detected a flash of uncertainty for the first time, emotion, and a chink in the man's self-control. Helpless though she felt and full of dread for what might happen, strangely and surprisingly she felt calm.

The small mercy of being turned onto her back had relieved a lot of the physical discomfort. With this relief the feeling of panic had ebbed to be replaced by anger and outrage. Her limbs began to ache, it was a slow nagging sensation at first but with the aching came a sense of movement, the drug was beginning to wear off. Experimenting she found it possible to move her head slightly.

"Mrs Macken we are near our destination, you will be able to walk unaided."

He spoke without looking at her as he reached for the small medical bag and withdrew a syringe. Susan struggled to control the feeling of panic, her movements feeble and trembling, the trembling uncontrolled.

"It's the effects of the drug wearing off," she told herself, her mind calming as she gained some control.

The jab in her thigh as he inserted the syringe was hardly noticeable. Within seconds the trembling eased and slowly her ability to move began to return as a feeling of warmth spread through her body.

"If you do not do exactly what I say, if you resist in any way," he showed her another phial. "I will inject you with this. It is more of the paralysis drug. It will control you absolutely but your system would not be capable of withstanding another dose. Eventually you would die unpleasantly."

Remarkably strength and vitality flooding through Susan's body, feeling extraordinarily elated she sat up and began to adjust her clothing, the powerful drug propelling her into action.

"A glass of water would be nice," she said. "May I?"

Without waiting for an answer she helped herself from the drinks cabinet and drank greedily emptying the plastic cup. At that moment the water seemed more important than life itself. She filled her cup the second time and drank more slowly her mind racing to find some means of escape knowing that he would make good his threat.

The car slowed down and came to a halt in a dark and lonely street. For a while they sat in silence and waited. His hand was on her arm gripping her elbow just above the joint. She knew there was no escape. The wall of the building seemed to open and the big limo moved forward its headlights picking up a bare concrete wall. As it came to a halt the entrance closed behind them. The driver got out and briskly opened the door at Susan's side of the car.

"Out and don't make a sound," Vaclav instructed. She was propelled from the car. The driver attempted to help her but stood back when Vaclav instructed him to,

"Leave her!"

He emerged behind Susan and with a strong arm projected her forcefully towards a doorway. They were now in a small hallway and then in a lift on their way upwards, giving her no time to collect her thoughts. When the lift stopped and the automatic doors opened they stepped onto a small dark landing. Quickly exiting, Vaclav propelled her at speed along a corridor repeating his warning. Afraid of the consequences and aware of her vulnerability Susan complied stumbling forward under the strong grip on her arm.

Eventually Vaclav pointed his mobile phone at a strong looking metal door in front of them. When it opened he pushed her through, stumbling forward she came up against a second door. His grip was strong on her arms as he held her with her face pressed against the cold metal surface. The door opened and she fell forward onto a cream carpeted floor.

"Up!" the command came, he hauled her to her feet. As she came into an upright position he released his grip causing her to lose her balance. She stumbled backwards against the back of a large cream sofa. Holding tightly to the leather surface Susan watched as the metal door closed behind them.

"If you want the painting," she said desperately, "you're going the wrong way about it."

Vaclav ignoring her completely strode past and began to check each of the doors leading from the big room. "Matt!" He called impatiently checking the rooms in turn, his anger increasing as it became apparent that Matt was not to be found.

Susan wearily sat down on the beautiful sofa with its black and white cushions. All around the floor to ceiling windows presented a magnificent view of London's night skyline. Incongruously it crossed her mind what a beautiful apartment, what a nice place to stay when she and Paul would next visit London.

Vaclav strode to the other end of the room seeming oblivious to her existence as he sat down at some monitors.

Knowing there would be no mobile connection he put his phone to one side and activated the landline through the touch keyboard, the code coming to mind immediately.

"Matt has not turned up at the base, have him picked up immediately!"

He barked the words.

Susan rose from the sofa and walked a bit unsteadily to stand and gaze out across London, arms folded in a protective self-hug. Way below people walked the streets, drove their cars and lived their lives in freedom but she was trapped and facing danger. It was hard to believe, to comprehend, the violence, the threat to her life, it all seemed unreal, a terrible nightmare that would disappear when she would awaken.

I'm not dreaming. It is real and I will have to cope, but how, how can I survive?

Deciding to explore she went into the kitchen. There was a large well-stocked fridge, an island with a marble top and high chairs, presses and deep drawers revealing pots and pans and a large collection of kitchen knives, even a marble rolling pin.

The rolling pin felt heavy in her hand as incredulously she considered the possibility of hitting Alan Grant, or whatever his name was, over the head and escaping back to Paul and her family, back to normality. Tears sprang to her eyes at the thought of Paul and how she had been so dismissive of him.

"Put it down and don't bother with the knife. I will not tell you a second time. It is futile to resist, if you try you will be punished."

Susan started as the harsh voice echoed around her and she quickly returned the "weapon" to its place in the drawer. Obviously there were cameras and speakers everywhere.

Her side ached from where he had kicked her, she had a headache and her throat felt dry, helping herself to a glass of water with ice from the fridge, she stood in the kitchen reassessing her situation surprised at her own calmness.

His voice carried through from the other room and though she could not make out the words, she took some comfort from its tone. It seemed that her tormentor was losing some control.

I may be becoming dispensable. The thought alarmed her. Also she was helpless against his strength. The cold feeling of despair began to return, beads of perspiration formed on her brow and her hands felt clammy as her feeling of calm began to evaporate. Taking a deep breath she resolved to wait her time, be patient even submissive, confrontation was out of the question. At this moment her captor was at his most dangerous, if provoked he would be liable to lash out.

Meanwhile Vaclav was busy at the controls, a frown creasing his brow at the discovery of two faulty monitors.

He tried re-booting the appropriate section on the control panel to no avail.

His main interest however was cell five, the cell that held Jennifer Holmes. Satisfied that she was healthy and well he had left her plenty of food and water to keep her fit and strong.

He smiled to himself remembering the last time he had visited her in her cell, how she had whirled delivering the karate killer strike.

Vaclav made an adjustment increasing the temperature of the cell and checking the food compartment, it was empty. Unfortunately he had not checked the temperature in the room before leaving. The girl must have been quite cold.

Intrigued by her courage and strength and her fighting skills, he savoured thoughts of how he might kill her.

He took the knife from his pocket. Holding the ornate handle he deftly flicked it left and right springing the two blades into view, it was an impressive weapon when held like a fist, stab and slice, stab and slice.

Lost in thought anticipating the conflict he planned his tactic. At first, hand-to- hand with one arm behind his back he would let her strike him, encourage her to attack, give her hope. In the confines of the cell she could not manoeuver too far away. Two strides would keep her in striking distance and then he would produce the knife.

Putting down the deadly instrument he rubbed his hands together in a washing motion and magically produced a white mouse onto his palm. Pricking his finger with the deadly point of the knife he watched with amusement as the little creature began to lap at the blood smear. With a last glance at the monitor he abruptly rose to his feet and strode across the room into the kitchen.

Susan turned as he came through the door the glass of water raised to her lips.

"Time to go to your room Susan Wakeley, put down the glass and follow me."

When she did not react immediately he took two quick strides and swept the glass from her grasp with such violence that it shattered against the wall on the far side of the kitchen.

"I said follow me woman!" He shouted.

Susan looked at the liquid running down the wall and then to the threatening Vaclav. Fury and frustration and outright indignation driving all thought of submission from her mind, with fists clenched at her sides, "How dare you! You're a first class bastard and you don't scare me!" she shouted up into his face.

The blow was intentionally stunning, a calculated, expert glancing impact to a point on her temple. He caught her as she fell forward and carried her out of the kitchen through the bathroom and into the Base.

Tim Holmes slept, his head cradled in his arms resting on the control panel.

Control Room 2 carried all the same equipment as the main room and here Tim had kept a vigil for hour upon hour eventually succumbing to sleep.

One of the four active monitors above his head showed the return of Vaclav Janacec, but Tim was oblivious. He did not see Susan's dramatic entry into the apartment or Vaclav at the monitors. He didn't see the discovery of the three non-functioning screens, monitors that he and Jennifer had sabotaged eliminating the view of certain locations in the base. It would have given him certain pleasure to know that the first part of their plan had been successful.

As he slept the monitor above his head showed Susan and Vaclav in the kitchen, Vaclav turning and striking out, the glass flying across the kitchen to shatter against the wall close to one of the concealed microphones.

Crash! Tim woke with a start, disorientated, alarmed. The monitor swam into view. Vaclav is here! He could hear Susan shout in indignation and then saw Vaclav strike and carry her from the kitchen. Glancing in panic at the other monitors he saw them head through the bathroom entrance to the Base.

No time to warn Jennifer! Control room two was on the same corridor as the cells and Vaclav would be there in a matter of moments. Tim realised that he could not leave the control room without being seen. There would be no time to reach their hiding place, a small storeroom at the other end of the long corridor. Jennifer would have no way of knowing the danger she was in.

Susan became aware that she was being carried along a white corridor. Struggling to free herself from his grasp she managed to stand when he stopped to release her. He opened the cell door and pushed her through. With a metallic click the door closed behind her leaving no evidence of its presence against the white wall.

Vaclav strode along the corridor with mounting excitement as he approached Jennifer's cell.

"Hello Jenny Penny, wakey! Wakey! It's the bad wolf come to eat you all up," he sang softly as he peered around the door.

She lay on the bed with her back to him the blanket pulled up around her shoulders. He stepped to the middle of the room looking, remembering her tactic on the previous occasion.

"How is my little karate kid today?" He taunted, wanting her to make a move.

"Leave me alone," Jennifer's voice was soft and muffled by the blanket.

Janacec took out the knife and flicked it left and right so the blades sprang into view.

"The door's open Jennifer, I'll step to one side, run rabbit, run rabbit, run, run, run."

His highly developed instincts flashed a warning and he whirled with speed and agility lunging with the stiletto in time to catch a glimpse of the fat man's face.

He threw the knife and it flew through the narrow opening as the heavy door slammed shut and the locking mechanism slid into place.

"Welcome to my cell," Shouted Jennifer triumphantly into the microphone from the safety of control room two.

Vaclav in that instant knew he was trapped. Enraged he wrenched away the bedcover. The body of the girl he had killed lay with her back to him, the small speaker on the pillow beside her head.

He knew every inch of his prison. He knew with total certainty that there was no escape. Slowly turning to the camera he became Alan Grant with soft eyes, smiling his smile. "Jennifer, are you there? I want to talk to Susan, there's something she needs to know and by the way, I just killed the fat man, I believe he's your father, so sad."

Jennifer's feeling of elation turned to dread, without replying she rushed from the control room into the corridor. Tim was lying on the floor outside the cell door.

Running towards the inert figure she could see blood, he was lying on his back. Slowing to a hesitant walk, fearing the worst she took the last couple of steps and knelt down beside him. His face was pale and there was blood on his lips, grabbing his jacket she pulled it to one side. The position of the knife buried deep in his chest left no questions to be answered.

Jennifer Holmes stepped away and stood, her mind jolted into confusion. The tears would come later. Turning she strode along the corridor. Janacec is trapped, there is no way-out of that cell, or is there? Does he have a means of escape? She stopped to look back half expecting to see Tim stand up and Janacec emerge from the cell.

Susan sat on the bed and stared unseeing at the white wall. Every part of her body ached and she was scared, scared for her life and what Vaclav would do to her on his return. Traumatised, her resolve weakened by sheer horror and the physical abuse, she felt unable to resist any longer. Drawing up her feet she lay on the narrow white bed and cradled her head in her arms closing her eyes. Immediately her eyes closed she felt defenceless, vulnerable, so she lay wide-eyed staring at the white wall.

"Click!" went the lock mechanism.

Susan scrambled off the bed and backed away to the farthest point of the cell as the door slid open. This is it! He's come, the knife, the blood, the mutilated body of the girl, a cascade of dreadful images. Terrified she cried out to be left in peace.

"I'm Jennifer Holmes you're safe!"

Susan stared past the beautiful young girl expecting to see Janacec, her mind unable to accept the possibility that she was indeed safe.

"You're safe," Jennifer repeated the words and took a step into the room but immediately stepped back when Susan flung out protective arms and shrank away.

"Janacec is locked in a cell, he can't hurt us, come and see," Jennifer stood and spoke softly, encouragingly holding out both hands.

"Who are you?" Susan straightened up but kept her distance and glanced again over the girl's shoulder to the corridor behind.

"My name is Jennifer Holmes, you must be Susan Macken, my mother works for your husband." The name registered with Susan and her lips trembled in a slight smile.

"Where is he?"

"You're safe from him Susan, he can't hurt you he's locked in one of the cells. I'll show you." She put a protective arm around the older woman's shoulders and attempted to lead her from the cell, but Susan staring at the open doorway resisted.

"It's all right, he's locked up, he can't hurt you now," Jennifer coaxed, and cradled Susan's face like a mother comforting a frightened child. The words began to filter through and the strong resolve returned.

"I'm OK." She made a grimace and tried to smile.

"C'mon, he's locked in his own cell and I am going to have my revenge on the evil bastard!" Grim faced the tall

269

girl turned and hurried from the room. Susan followed more slowly, hesitating at the door to check up and down the corridor. The figure of the fat man lay thirty feet away. The tall girl was standing at a doorway down the white corridor waiting for Susan to appear.

"It's alright! In here!" she called disappearing through a doorway.

In the control room the two women stood side by side. Neither spoke, each preoccupied with her thoughts as they watched Janacec turn and look coolly into the lens of the camera. He smiled and chanted in a whispering sinister voice… *Three Blind Mice see how they run…see how they run….two dead mice…..two more to die….*

Jennifer spoke. "He killed my father with that knife," She turned to Susan dry eyed, and continued "That's my father, Tim Holmes, lying in the corridor. Tim locked him in the cell. His name is Vaclav Janacec and I'm going to kill him."

Vaclav stared through the camera at the two women. He seemed quite composed and unperturbed. Jennifer touched the control panel turning up the volume. The sound of his breathing filled the room.

"Hello Jennifer, how's your Daddy?" he smiled the Alan Grant smile.

"Is Sensual Susan with you?"

Calmly Jennifer looked at the screen and then at Susan, her demeanour casual.

"Let me see now Vaclav Janacec?" she scanned the control panel. "Let's play a little game of cat and mouse. You're in my cell, the killing cell. Am I right?"

Janacec smiled,

"Be careful little mouse. Touch the wrong control and you set the cat free."

"You underestimate me", Jennifer's voice was calm, controlled. "If I touch the right button you die a very cruel and agonising death. What have we got here?"

Her hand hovered over the control panel. Janacec's eyes flickered.

"This one? This one? Or this one?" Jennifer, head to one side, hand to her chin may as well have been trying to decide what selection to make from a large box of tempting chocolates.

Curiously and apprehensively Susan glanced at the beautiful face, then quickly back to the screen. Janace had not moved but Susan sensed a tension in the normally confident stance.

"This one!" Jennifer reached for the control panel. Susan realising what she was about to do managed to get between the bereaved girl and the panel just in time, knocking her hand away.

Jennifer stepped back. "Out of the way Susan!" she said calmly fixing her with a cold stare. "I don't want to hurt you but get out of my way!"

"No, Susan stood her ground, No! You've no right, he's a monster but I won't let you kill him."

"He killed my father!", Jennifer shouted, "he killed my father with that horrible knife and he made me plead for my life, he told me what the killing cell could do, he locked me in there and told me how I would die." Tears of grief and frustrated anger coursed down her cheeks. "I want to kill him!" she screamed.

Susan reached for her but she backed away.

"We've got to get out of here," Susan protested coaxingly and gently. But Jennifer now wide eyed and frantic would not be deterred.

"I want to see, I want to see him suffer."

Susan grabbed the girl.

"No Jennifer we need to get out of here, calm down, relax."

Jennifer stepped back wide-eyed and frantic. Seeing that she was on the edge of hysteria Susan swung an open palm intending to slap her face. It was a half-hearted attempt, Jennifer instinctively swayed away to avoid the impact, and the tips of Susan's fingers brushed her cheek.

Readjusting her stance Jennifer delivered the perfect counter punch her fist mercifully stopping an inch from Susan's astonished face.

The fist unclenching, Jennifer's hand began to shake and the deadly strike transformed into an appealing embrace. She threw her arms around Susan's neck burying her face in the older woman's shoulder and sobbed in grief, for Tim her father, Rocky Balboa the fat little conman, her best friend and mentor. It was an embrace that Susan was grateful to accept. Her own tears ran onto the girl's shoulder. At last they separated, now with a common objective, to escape and advise the authorities.

As they left the control room Jennifer looked along the corridor.

"I can't leave him!" Tim lay outside the cell door.

"You have to, the police will take care of everything, there's nothing you can do for him." Susan sympathized.

Suddenly Jennifer ran without a backward glance until she reached the end of the corridor. Susan, not sure of the way back to the entrance followed as quickly as she could aware of how tired she felt and aware of the pain in her side, running was out of the question.

The fleet footed Jennifer reaching the door of the dormitory had stopped to look back.

Putting all though of her discomfort to one side Susan ran to catch up, spurred on by the thought of escape.

They hurried through the dormitory and the unbearable stench, into the bathroom. Susan grasped the heavy door and pulled it closed. It locked with a metallic click, the mirrored wall now in place.

"Well that's Mr Janacec taken care of," she stated, firmly. Jennifer was trembling violently. "We can't get away, we can't escape there's no way out!"

The two women stood reflected in the mirror. "Sshh," Susan putting her arm around her gently led her to the large sofa in the big room.

"There's no rush I'm going to make some tea and we'll work this out."

The idea of drinking tea seemed ridiculous to Jennifer but she followed Susan into the kitchen and at the instruction, "I'll put on the kettle while you search for some teabags," she found herself opening presses. "Sugar as well," said Susan, "and biscuits if there's any," The well-equipped kitchen had everything they needed. Susan talked as they busied themselves.

Back in the big room they sat together on the sofa. Jennifer sipped the hot tea with plenty of sugar and stared at the wall opposite.

Susan's heart went out to the distraught girl. Jennifer leaned close and accepted the mothers comforting embrace as Susan, putting aside all her own doubts and fears reassured and comforted. They sat for a few moments as the twilight faded and the evening lights began to brighten the London Skyline, the Karate Trained Confidence Trickster and the Irish Mother, all the while Susan's mind frantically trying to figure a way out of the dreadful place and away from danger.

Susan brushed her hand gently on the tear stained face resting on her shoulder. When had she last comforted one of her children in the same manner? When had she last really felt needed by her own children? She never let down the barriers and showed her feelings. Now Jane had met the love of her life. Time to let go Susan, time to let go.

She could feel the tension beginning to ebb in the girl.

"Come on Miss, we're going to fine a way out of this God forsaken place. If only we could phone, maybe there's a land line?"

"The phone, I remember now, he used his phone to open the door. The bedroom, it'll be in the bedroom with his things."

She strode purposefully into the bedroom, Jennifer following. His clothes hung neatly in an Ikea wardrobe with its cage drawers. Susan with total disregard for another's privacy searched thoroughly pulling out the drawers and opening the bedside lockers.

They found a cage with lots of white mice and the I pad which Susan brandished triumphantly.

"Evidence, evidence of a monster!"

The picture of the girl was there, the two figures looking out to sea. With a quick glance Susan thought, not now, later when she would get home and have time to think, then she would face the reality of her past life and her connection with the Janacec monster. There was however, no sign of his phone.

Having searched the other rooms, the bathroom and the kitchen they finally came to the conclusion.

"It's on him, he has it with him, we'll have to go back for it." The two women looked at each other. Out of the question!

"I'll go!" said Jennifer impulsively.

"No wait, think it out!" Susan grabbed her arm.

"We have to check, see if we can somehow reason with him."

"How do you work the monitors?" She strode purposefully towards the end of the room and the monitor bank. This I can do without, she was thinking to herself not relishing the prospect, while accepting the fact that it was the only course of action. She was no longer worrying about Jennifer who seemed to be more in control.

"I'll do it!" Jennifer offered but Susan was already at the controls searching, in her haste missing the obvious, the monitor was switched off and of course did not react. "How do you turn it on? "She looked at Jennifer

Both women scanned the controls left and right.

"There it is!" Susan couldn't believe her eyes. "There it is, the phone!"

It was where he had left it over to one side the control board and in full view. Obviously they overlooked it in their anxiety.

. "He used the phone but what's the code?" On examining the phone nothing was revealed, no combination of numbers or letters.

"He must have memorized it,"

Susan switched on the monitor to cell three.

No sign of Janacec, she moved the control left and right.

"He's not there he's out, Susan!" Jennifer clutched her arm swinging around to look fearfully at the slightly ajar bathroom door.

"Nonsense!" Susan could feel the short hairs begin to prickle on the back of her neck as she searched the picture on the monitor, left and right. Jennifer jumped up and ran to the bathroom door and slammed it shut. She stood with her back to it, arms outstretched.

"He's out! What can we do? Can we lock this door?" She looked around frantically.

"He can't be, that cell is like a vault," Susan her heart racing, as calmly as possible studied the picture moving the control slowly searching and then she saw the slight blurring at the bottom of the screen. There seemed to be a faint movement. She held the control still and watched and waited, there it was the movement again.

"Jennifer!" She cried with relief, "he's there, come and see. I think he's standing against the wall under the camera!" She scanned the controls and quickly located another camera giving her a different view of the cell.

Janacec's eyes fixed on the second camera. He stared into the lens and then spoke in a controlled quiet voice.

"You have my dark eyes Susan, that blond hair's a little white lie. Time is on my side. There's no way out for you," he smiled, "Anyone who comes to the Base will kill you and the girl or better still, they'll open the door to this cell and the pussy cat will have all the cream," he licked his lips at the prospect purr.... purr, the sound coming from deep in his throat, catlike and sinister. His eyes staring from the monitor still had the power to hypnotically hold Susan in their gaze. Furious at her weakness, revolted by the sound, she managed to look away. The purring continued. She wanted to eliminate him, to stop him, to punish the monster, her emotion so strong it astonished her.

"How do you want to die?" she said quietly and purposefully her tone leaving no doubt as to her intention. "Tell me the code to the door and I won't kill you."

She scanned the control panel. "There seem to be several lethal options here. I have no way of knowing which to choose. Perhaps I should start from left to right."

"Susan, Susan," he purred gently with a quiet laugh. "That would be such a bad thing to do, so unlike you my little mouse, of course you're not going to do it, Susan I know you. You're not like me."

Susan's hand hovered over the control panel. Just a touch and Vaclav would die horribly. "You're right, absolutely right, I couldn't do it but I know someone who is dying to kill you! Someone whose father you have just killed, perhaps I should walk away and leave you two alone! Now that is something I would do, you were not exactly gentle in your treatment of me. My ribs still ache!"

Vaclav laughed, "fraid not Susan, I know you too well."

She looked back to the mocking face on the screen.

"Nerve Gas, one of them was a nerve gas. When I was in the cell..." Jennifer explained, ".... and another is rodents. He said that he would set loose hundreds of starving rats into the cell with me." Susan, carefully watching Vaclav's reaction detected a flicker in his eye, a slight flicker of doubt, it was gone in a flash and the smile was back but Susan had seen it.

"Rats! Hundreds of starving rats! Vaclav, what's the code?" she demanded again. Vaclav laughed, "You couldn't do it Susan, the fat man deserved to die and you will too," he laughed again. Jennifer hit the control panel. It happened so fast Susan couldn't stop her.

For a moment there was no apparent change in the cell and then there was a noticeable movement. Vaclav turned to watch. His eyes widened with terror as a section of the wall slid to one side to reveal an opening about three feet-square. The opening was covered with wire mesh preventing the rats piled up against it from tumbling into the cell. There were hundreds of them they squirmed and wriggled and squeaked.

Janacec pushed the girls body off the bed, grabbed at the flimsy structure and wrenching it from its mountings frantically tried to use it to cover the opening. The rats scrambled at the wire. Obviously panic stricken, he looked into the lens of the camera.

"Don't do it," he pleaded in a horrified whisper. Neither woman answered, there was only the sound of the milling mass beyond the wire mesh and Janacec's frantic breathless voice. The overwhelming fear of rats, deep rooted in some past horror, overcame him and he retreated to the furthest point away from the opening his eyes never leaving the object of this personal nightmare. Susan spoke softly and reasonably.

"The code Janacec, or I'll let them at you. You know I'm a killer, you once told me so yourself." His ashen face turned appealingly to the camera and he understood the total conviction in her voice. "Watch them come for you, they're starving, pretty pussy," She lightly touched the control and the mesh door shuddered. "The hash key!" he screamed.

Susan grabbed the phone and ran to the ornate wooden door. Pressing the hash key repeatedly. The door swung open revealing the second door beyond, she pressed the symbol again and the door to the landing opened.

"Jennifer," she turned with a relieved shout, "It worked, we're out!" but Jennifer was not looking at her instead she was looking at the monitor.

"No!" Susan ran to her side. The monitor screen was blank. "You didn't?"

"I didn't know that would happen," Jennifer looked horrified. "I just wanted to scare him some more. I opened the door a bit and then I couldn't close it. I tried but the

277

rats jammed it with their bodies. I turned off the sound and the picture."

Susan dreading what she was about to see turned the screen back on. The cell, now transformed was teeming with rats. She couldn't see anything else. She tried the other camera with the same result. There was no sign of Janacec, just a mass of rats. They had been breeding for a long time behind the wire mesh. Susan turned off the monitor.

The two women looked at each other, unsure of their motives. Had Susan left Jennifer alone on purpose, knowing what she would do? Was Jennifer sure that she only wished to frighten him? Neither woman at that moment knew the answer. All they knew was that they were now safe from Vaclav Janacec.

"Sorry I have to leave you, I've got to go." The Very Tall Man, Chief Superintendent Gerard Viking regretfully addressed the beautiful piece of sirloin steak on his plate, the chips and onions were equally inviting. "Good bye," he said.

"What time do you think you'll get back?" enquired Julie Viking calmly from the other side of the restaurant table. In the Fifteen years of marriage to her beloved husband many a medium to rare sirloin had had to be abandoned.

"It's hard to tell," he said pushing back his chair and drawing himself up to his full six feet eight and a half inches, the size of the knife and fork diminished by his big hands as he bent to cut the steak in half and put the large fork-full in his mouth.

"Don't wait up for me, it's the Vicar Street business, there seems to be a breakthrough."

He looked at his wife with a broad smile.

"At last, it seems I'll be finished with this foreign fella Interpol assigned to me, no more wheeling and dealing with those Czechoslovakian half wits, no more of this diplomatic stuff, it doesn't suit me. No more foreign bloke in the car with me everywhere I go. I'm a simple man with a simple disposition. Wish me luck."

The rest of the steak followed the first half. "Apparently they can't do without me, these young ones…" the sentence went unfinished as he came around the table to kiss his wife goodbye.

Looking up at the towering figure, "you'll probably need these," she said, taking a packet of Rennies from her handbag and handing them to him. He smiled at her taking the pack and putting it in his pocket.

"The car's here to pick me up, you take the Toyota,"

Helping himself to a handful of chips The Very Tall Man headed for the door, his mind already working on the information received. Access to that building on the corner of Vicar Street had been denied again and again, international interests, protocol even embassy intervention. Now he had the excuse he wanted, a British citizen and an Irish woman had been abducted and held captive and there were a couple of bodies reported to be in the building.

"Go in," he gave the order, "I'm on the way, don't take no for an answer. Make sure the women are available for questioning."

He got into the back seat of the police car beside the foreigner and opened a big hand, "Would you like a chip?" The offer was turned down in a guttural foreign accent as the car sped off across London, siren at full volume.

The intersection at the Duck and Shovel had been cordoned off. Friar Street teemed with police and the emergency services, police cars, ambulances and two fire engines. Figures, silhouetted by the revolving blue lights stood in small groups or moved urgently in and out of the buildings

In contrast the atmosphere of the lounge of the Duck and Shovel was subdued and quiet. The usual customers having abandoned the premises for the excitement of the street stood in the doorway anxious not to miss any of the action, the proprietor amongst them taking orders for drinks.

Wrapped in a blanket, exhausted, Susan had been made comfortable on a corner seat. A young detective after interviewing her had then refused the medical people permission to take her to hospital. This had caused a major discussion eventually resolved by the arrival of an extremely large, quietly spoken member of the force. Susan took the opportunity to close her eyes and relax making herself as comfortable as possible.

At the other end of the lounge Jennifer Holmes was now being interviewed by the young detective sitting across from her, note book in hand, a female police officer nearby.

Once outside the Metal door Susan had used Janacec's phone to call the police. By the time she and Jennifer had negotiated the stairs and travelled to the ground floor of Clarendon House they had arrived in numbers, the young detective taking charge. Immediately she and Jennifer had been separated and a WPC appointed to each of them.

"Mrs Macken,"

Susan, who blessedly succumbing to tiredness had rested her head on the upholstered seat, opened her eyes to be greeted by the sight of the largest pair of feet she had ever seen in her life.

"I'm Chief Superintendent Gerard Viking of the London Metropolitan Police," he lowered his great frame to crouch beside her, elbows resting on his knees hands together with fingers entwined.

He seemed to fill her entire field of vision, momentarily unsettling her but she was comforted by his calm expression and big craggy face. His presence in her state of trauma made her feel safe, helping to provide a sense of closure on the horrific events.

"Mrs Macken," he repeated her name,

"You're safe now and so is your friend,"

"I've already given my statement to the young man," she said.

"I know, thank you, he'll soon be finished with Ms Holmes. There's just one question I'd like to ask if you don't mind. Could you tell me the last time you saw Sir Geoffrey Fletcher?"

It seemed such a long time ago since the lunch at the Riverside Café. She related the incident with Janacec and the two foreign looking men and how they had left so hurriedly. The inspector was extremely interested in the two men. Susan was able to give him a fairly good description of both.

"Thank you Mrs Macken, you have been very helpful. We'll probably talk again as our investigations proceed. By the way, when your husband arrives I would like to have a word with him." He nodded in the direction of the waiting medics and in no time at all she and Jennifer were on their way to the Hospital in separate Ambulances.

Travelling through the London traffic Susan took the opportunity to ring Paul. It was a difficult conversation with so much to relate but Susan managed, leaving much of the detail until he would arrive in London the following morning. Full of concern he had insisted on taking the first flight possible and Susan was surprised at how relieved she felt at the prospect of seeing him.

After 24 hours of police interviews and intensive hospital checks, Susan, relieved at receiving the all clear was looking forward to getting back to Ireland.

Apart from a slight discolouration on her temple and bruised ribs there was little evidence to be seen of the trauma and extraordinary circumstances of the last few days.

The police however, were interested in Jennifer at a different level to Susan and continued to keep them separated. Susan enquired but they were evasive. The only information she could glean was that Jennifer was helping the police with their enquiries.

The big Superintendent had turned up and was quite forthcoming about several things, reassuring Susan that

281

she need have no worries about Vaclav Janacec or people from Prague.

The London Base had given up its secrets in abundance, providing an extraordinary amount of vital and outstanding evidence. Many people in powerful positions, politicians and businessmen, some already under investigation, exposed. The crimes covered money laundering, people trafficking, drug dealing, prostitution and many other illegal activities with the centre in Prague and a network of bases spreading throughout Europe.

The facilities of the highly equipped Bases and their satellite services in so many major cities had attracted the attention of some very sinister and powerful forces. The ultimate goal of those involved, if allowed to continue, could have had implications for the stability of peace and the European money markets, security forces responding in Washington, Beijing, Tehran and many other cities.

"What are you saying exactly?" Jane Macken looked across the breakfast table at Simon. She could hear the spotty teenagers arguing in the other room and it did not help her mood.

"Wait a minute, I'd better sort those two out."

Putting down her coffee cup she left the table and munching on her toast headed into the living room of the two bedroomed apartment leaving Simon to gather his thoughts as he contemplated his boiled egg.

He had waited until this morning to tell Jane about the problems concerning their new house. She had been listening with some dismay when the kids had started to act up.

The deal on the apartment had fallen through. The prospective buyer, a victim of the current recession in Ireland, whose income had been substantially reduced, had contacted the Estate Agent the previous day with the bad news.

Simon cut his toast into strips. The boiled egg waited invitingly as he considered Jane's reaction to the news. Bloody recession, he sighed. Simon's own business had taken a few setbacks recently and it seemed unlikely there would be much relief in the near future, judging by the news and the morning's paper.

With their hearts set on the new house the deposit had been paid and contracts signed. He was relying on the sale of the apartment to clear the mortgage with enough over to reduce the repayments on a new mortgage.

There were no other prospective buyers and not likely to be as people, uncertain of the outcome of the recession were holding onto their savings.

The way things were shaping he could end up with two mortgages on his hands with very little prospect of getting rid of either.

Well Things could be worse, he thought to himself plunging the bread soldier into the boiled egg as he listened to Jane expertly and humorously dealing with the boys. We can rent the apartment and hope the business picks up, only option.

Jane returned with a smiling face, all was quiet in the other room. Simon sitting, soldier poised, looked apprehensive as she came through the door.

"I'll take them to school this morning," she said sitting down and reaching for her coffee cup.

"Two things, Simon," she stated firmly.

"One, the kids are at the age now when they can look after themselves to an extent. Gerry is almost fifteen." She looked at him encouragingly.

"And two?" he enquired.

"I can go back to work. I only gave up my well-paid job to mind the kids and because you were making plenty of money.

"It won't come to that,"

Simon reached across the table and took her hand.

"I really am the luckiest man to have found you,"

"I know," Jane grinned reaching for a toast soldier and dipping it.

"Did I tell you about Mum breaking the window before she went to London?"

"No! What window?" Simon laughed,

"The huge window in Dad's studio,"

"Why?" Simon looked incredulous,

"She had this crazy idea that if she broke the window Dad would think the picture had been stolen by an intruder."

"Where's the picture?"

"She hid it and went to London. There was some kind of problem, she felt Dad was misbehaving in London and wanted to confront him. I got a call from her about the window, Dad's on his way home but she's staying on in London for a while. None of it makes sense. I just have to arrange for the window to be fixed."

Simon, not that surprised with the revelations and generally aware of his mother–in-law to be's eccentricities smiled without comment.

Jane stood up from the table and called loudly,

"Are you two ready we're leaving in five minutes?"

The two boys trooped into the kitchen.

"I'm leaving these two to school then going to the house to meet the window man. I need to pick up a few things from my parent's house. After that I was thinking I might call to the new house and do some measuring."

Simon sat and watched her as she buzzed about full of energy and enthusiasm eventually he got up from the table

"I'm off too, another day another dollar," The four of them left the house together.

Not allowed to leave the boys to the school gate, "it wouldn't be cool," Jane dropped them off at the end of the road near the playing fields. She sat watching them for a moment as they strode away to join up with the other kids before taking the short drive along the coast through the village to the Macken House, her mind occupied with the predicament of finance. At least we are fortunate in that

284

we have options. Simon's business is reasonably stable but the recession casts doubts everywhere.

As she drove she reflected on the Ireland of a few years back, riding on the crest of a wave, the rampant Celtic Tiger, until banks and politicians dealt their hand with all the aces up their sleeves. The cranes had now stopped moving, the skyline frozen, unfinished see through concrete apartment and office blocks everywhere, monuments to greed and power.

Jane drove along the cliff road, unanswered questions skipping through her mind. Mum must have been in a weird state of mind to leave the house with a broken window. What could she have been thinking? Dad went off very suddenly and then came back without Mum and him not answering his phone?

She had called Richard but he had been quite off hand. "Don't be worrying, Dad's really into the painting and Mum feels she's missing out on a visit to London and the Regent Palace. He had to come back in a hurry because of his business. Mum's staying on to talk to the Tate gallery or the Calligrapher or something. You'll find there's a simple explanation."

"But what about the broken window?" Jane had persisted.

"An accident," he laughed, "she had the plane seat booked so she went, you know mum. She rang you to get it fixed didn't she?"

Richard had it all worked out logically.

He's probably right Jane concluded uneasily. But Mum was crying before she went and she never cries Jane thought as she opened the door and let herself into the house.

Obviously Paul hadn't arrived home yet, the house felt particularly cold as she walked through the big room feeling the draught coming from the back of the house.

Expecting to find a hole in one of the windows of her Dad's studio Jane was taken aback by the sight of flapping curtains soaked with rain, papers strewn and broken glass where the entire glass door had collapsed inwards, leaving a gaping hole allowing the elements to wreak havoc.

Jane looked at her watch anticipating the arrival of the window man, then started to move things away from the window and to clear up the mess as best she could.

When the window man arrived he took some measurements, leaving to return twenty minutes later with a large sheet of chipboard to block up the opening.

Relieved at the repair job, the curtains no longer flapping and things back in place, Jane began to relax a bit.

Obviously Susan in knocking out a small section of glass around the door handle had weakened the whole thing and the wind and rain had done the rest, she would never have left things the way Jane had found them.

A large box full of Jane's things had been put to one side in her old bedroom. The two raggedy dolls sat on top. Jane looked around, there wasn't much she wanted although the bedside light was nice and the hand painted rocking chair, plus the box of things. She could put down the back seat of the Ford Focus there'd be enough room to take them and the romantic picture hanging on the wall over her bed. Memories of teenage years came flooding back. On impulse she lifted the large framed print from the wall and placed it on top of the two raggedy dolls.

In London, Paul had arrived at the hospital all doubts and uncertainties between himself and Susan evaporating as they greeted each other.

They had waited together for the all clear. Sitting close, Paul kept looking for assurance that she was feeling no adverse effects. The attention was well received, Susan revelling in the TLC.

"Did you get the window fixed?" She suddenly enquired.

"Don't worry about the window, its fine, Jane had it organized before I got home. Someone came right away and boarded it up. They're coming today or tomorrow to fit a new one."

"What about the painting?"

"I don't care about the painting." Paul said, putting his arm around her shoulders and pulling her close.

"If I never see the damned painting again it wouldn't bother me. Look where it's brought us."

They sat in silence lost in thought of what might have been, both thankful for, and taking refuge in, the strength of their relationship and the worthwhile investment in all the years. "You know I couldn't be unfaithful to you, no woman comes near to you." He said looking at her appealingly.

"I know, don't worry about it," she said gently kindly patting his hand. With a sigh he relaxed back into his chair. Susan's thoughts were her own, not so sure what she might have done had Alan Grant not turned out to be Vaclav Janacec.

Turning his head he looked quizzically at her. "What are you thinking?"

"Nothing, it will be nice to get home and back to normal,"

"So that's why you had that little smile on your face,"

"Exactly." She replied now smiling broadly.

Waiting in the hospital afforded them plenty of time to chat and catch up. They discussed the impending marriage, Susan a bit surprised to hear that Simon's business was suffering a bit of a setback. "They may be somewhat extended on the new house, Jane can't think of anything else."

"We'll have to help out," Susan immediately reacted.

"Let's wait, see how things work out, Simon's a mature bloke I don't think he'd appreciate our interference."

"They shouldn't lose the house because of a little pride. I know what it means to both of them."

Susan was interrupted by the arrival of Superintendent Viking and the young detective. She introduced Paul who

287

stood up, to be dwarfed by the mountainous Super who, smiling broadly extended a large hand.

"Pleased to meet you Mr Macken, your wife is some strong lady, we've been pursuing our enquiries and a great deal has come to light, we're grateful for the part you played Mrs Macken," he said turning to Susan. "We're here to tell you you're free to go home, it's unlikely we'll need you further."

"What about Jennifer, is she ok?"

The two policemen exchanged a glance, Susan detecting a signal for the younger man to leave.

"May I sit down?" the big man enquired politely indicating that they should all take their seats. Waiting until the other man had left the room he spoke.

"Jennifer Holmes is a resourceful young woman, her father, Tim Holmes was known to us as a small time conman, who had served time. My personal opinion is that Jennifer is capable of great things given the right motivation."

His expression was solemn and sincere, his words carefully chosen but Susan could detect the hint of humour in his eyes.

"She is extremely intelligent and has suffered greatly at the loss of her father. I've decided not to pursue my enquiries into the fate of a certain Vaclav Janacec any further. We may never know what exactly happened. This is of course off the record."

He stood up. "Some woman you've got there, Mr Macken," he repeated with a smile before taking his leave.

That afternoon they left the hospital. Medically Susan had the all clear but she had been referred to her local GP in Dublin on the advice of a very serious faced young doctor. She was however, not impressed with some other advice he had to offer regarding her attending a Psychiatric Clinic. "Rubbish, I feel fine," she had reassured herself and Paul, as they sat in the Regent Palace reception awaiting a taxi to take them to Heathrow, brandishing the referral note in its white envelope with the St.

Bartholomew's Psychiatric Clinic logo. "I'll bin this when we get home."

On the way to the airport Susan tried to contact Jennifer Holmes but without success. Gerard Viking's office advised that she was still helping them with their enquiries. Susan persisted and eventually some extra information was forthcoming. Apparently the Superintendent had left a message for her. The efficient voice informed Susan that Jennifer Holmes would be released with no charges.

The flight home was uneventful. Uncharacteristically Susan had fallen asleep shortly after take-off. Paul had to rouse her when they arrived in Dublin.

Within a short time of arrival they were on their way, skirting the city limits taking the strand road going South with the twin chimneys of the Pigeon House Power Station on their left. They drove along the coast to eventually arrive at their local village, so nice to be home, and then out along the cliff road to the cul-de-sac. Susan was overcome with weariness as she stepped from the car.

The house was in darkness but nonetheless welcoming. The thoughtful Jane had left milk, bread and some cheese and a note.

I'm sure you're looking forward to a cup of tea. Welcome home. We're doing Sunday Lunch tomorrow. Everyone's coming and you're not to lift a finger. See you at about twelve o'clock. Love You both Jane.

"You get off to bed," Paul insisted, "I'll make some tea, would you like something to eat?"

"Tea will do nicely." Susan headed for the bedroom and collapsed gratefully onto her own sweet bed, at last able to relax completely and give in to the tiredness, aches and pains. Paul checked the back of the house. Richard and Geraldine had spent some time cleaning up and there was very little evidence of the havoc caused by the rain and wind save for the large sheet of chipboard where the window had been.

Tea tray in hand he entered the bedroom. Susan lay on the bed fully clothed and in a deep sleep. Putting the tea tray to one side, reluctant to rouse her, Paul stood studying his wife's face thinking how much he loved her and how vulnerable and beautiful she looked. He knew that she had held back on much of what had happened in London and he was in wonder at her strength and fortitude. Eventually she would share the experience and let him in, but at the moment he would hold back and wait, give her time and space. Doubts assailed his mind, doubts concerning his own capabilities, his own fortitude. Well time is a great healer. The clichéd phrase popped into his mind as he tried to brush the feeling of dread away but instead of receding the feeling persisted overwhelming him.

Overcome with emotion he sat down on the edge of the bed and buried his face in his hands. Eventually with a deep sigh he stood up and looked around the room juggling with his feelings and thoughts.

Covering Susan's still form with an extra duvet he turned off the light at the door and stood looking at the figure on the bed. With a deep feeling of resolve he gently closed the door.

Susan wakened with a start. The room was in semidarkness with a strong chink of light between the curtains. The Regent Palace, I'm going to the calligrapher, Alan Grant is calling, where's Paul? The thoughts tumbled through her confused mind, panicked for a second she reached out a protective hand pushing away the imaginary threat of white hands and cats. Slowly the familiarity of her surroundings began to penetrate her consciousness. I'm home, I'm home she realized, everyone's coming to lunch, it's over. Tears of relief rolled down her cheeks. She reached for a tissue from the familiar bedside locker.

Climbing from the bed she drew back the curtains letting the light flood the room, clasping her hands and raising them to her face she drank in the sight of her garden, the grass needs cutting and I have to make dinner she thought happily. What time is it? Her watch said eleven thirty she could hardly believe that she had slept for fourteen hours. In spite of her prolonged sleep, to her surprise a feeling of weariness overcame her as her eyes followed the progress of a neighbour's cat stalking a bird in the garden. The cat pounced, the bird flew, the cat sprang high, outstretched claws tearing its frantically fluttering prey out of the air, landing and pinning it to the ground. Susan's mind flashed and she remembered everything.

"Hello sleeping beauty, I was waiting for you to wake up," Paul walked into the bedroom. Susan lay on the floor beside the window.

After many weeks of treatment at the Highfield Stress Clinic, taking part in a complex programme devised by a team of specialists dealing in posttraumatic stress Susan was considered capable of getting back to her life and returning home.

There would follow regular attendance as an outpatient and a considerable time before she would hopefully be free of the past. She still suffered from flashbacks. In the meantime Susan could function pretty normally and get on with her life. There had been many factors in her recovery, the strength and support of her family, her own undoubted resourcefulness and the black box with its revelations.

In the box amidst all the old documents, birth certificates, Christmas cards and other odd and ends, an envelope containing sixteen photographs was discovered, sepia toned and some quite faded. On the front of the envelope had been written "*Janacecs.*"

Obviously at some time during the years the Wakeley family and the Janacec family had made contact. Maybe somewhere in Prague there's a similar envelope bearing the Wakeley name?

Susan was not permitted to see the pictures until the fourth week of her stay at the clinic. She had sat alone in her now familiar surroundings and removed the pictures from the envelope with some temerity, examining each one carefully. The first picture was of a group of people standing on the famous St Georges bridge spanning the Vltava River in Prague, men women and two children, two of the men in uniform, a very faded picture cracked and worn of two people with what looked like a circus tent in the background, some more pictures of Prague, a smiling group of people at the beach, several pictures of somebody's wedding and a severe looking man obviously posing in a photographers studio with a dog sitting at his feet.

Susan examined each picture minutely, noting the family resemblance between her own family and some of the strangers in the photographs. It was the picture of the two girls holding hands standing with Prague castle in the background that provoked a sharp intake of breath. The younger one was skinny with a severe face and about twelve years of age the older one with that unmistakable smile was a young Nana Eileen. Tearfully Susan replaced each one back into the envelope vowing to visit Prague and her relatives.

It was her first Sunday home.

Under Jane and Richard's instructions family lunch would be provided and Susan would not be permitted to raise a hand. How this was going to be achieved Susan and Paul had no idea

"They'll be here in an hour, what'll we do for lunch?" Paul looked over the Sunday paper at Susan.

"Lunch? What am I going to do for lunch? Absolutely nothing," she laughed. "I'm going to make myself look my best and enjoy being with my family. That's what I'm going to do. I might even consider cutting the grass."

"How do you feel?" The agitated Paul enquired, "You've had a hell of a time. I can put them off if you like?"

"Don't you dare, this is what's important to me, not Turner paintings or trips to London or monsters like Vaclav Janacec or whatever he called himself, you, me, the family that's all that matters." She stood up briskly, "Now I'd better get ready."

Richard turned into the drive on time as usual. Susan and Paul stood together on the doorstep Susan smiling and waving a greeting.

"She doesn't look the worse for wear, god help those baddies in London she must have given them a rough time." Geraldine joked.

"Behave yourself!"

Richard laughed as the kids piled out of the car.

"Well a least I didn't have to make a Pavlova. Hi Susan, Hi Paul!" she called smiling and waving.

"That's the girl," Richard encouraged following.

Simon, Jane and the teenagers made a more sedentary arrival. Jerry and Vincent dutifully bending their heads shuffled to receive unaccustomed hugs. Today was different there was a sense of relief in the air and the greetings were a bit more prolonged, the odd tear brushed hastily away.

In the house the "Hamley" purchases were produced and Paul slipped the teenagers a couple of notes. The football was put to one side and Gerry was texting but quickly put his phone away at a look from Simon.

No food in evidence, Susan noted but didn't say a word. The table set out, the oven was turned on, a couple of bottles of wine produced. The best glasses taken out, plates heated.

The mystery was solved on the arrival of a van outside. *Copper Kettle Catering* the legend in ornate gold and red with a smart motif stated.

Susan ordered to sit at the head of the table with a nice glass of her favourite wine was not allowed do anything while everyone fussed around.

She sat sipping her drink and enjoying the attention and the luxury of not being in charge.

With time to observe the family from a somewhat different point of view she was agreeably surprised and aware of how much she had missed. Paul had a very good rapport with the boys and she had not noticed before that they both reacted to Jane as if she was their mother. Also, Simon and Jane's relationship seemed to have matured, and Geraldine had a fair amount of banter with Richard. Revelation after revelation presented itself in the course of the meal and Susan felt grateful, vowing to be a little more aware.

Pork steak and all the trimmings on large serving plates in the middle of the table and everyone helping themselves, little Molly, wielding a large serving spoon, roast potatoes getting speared, there was plenty to go around.

"I don't like carrots. Well don't eat them. Can I have some of the burnt bits? Help yourself. What's that green stuff? Ask your Nana, I love chicken nuggets." On and on the beautiful chaos of an informal Sunday lunch a sharp contrast to previous formal affairs.

All serious discussion put to one side the Turner painting was not getting a mention though the subject lurked in everyone's mind. Where is it? Is it a genuine Turner? What happened the window? What happened in London? All questions were being tactfully avoided.

When put to a vote it was declared that The Copper Kettle's Pavlova wasn't a patch on Geraldine's. This provoked genuine laughter from all except Geraldine who thought she had been relieved of Pavlova duties forever.

Susan tapped her wine glass and stood up. In the resulting silence every head turned with expectation for a revealing statement.

"I would like to propose that from now on all Sunday Lunches should be provided by the Copper Kettle. I have decided to take an early retirement."

She sat down to applause from all.

"Where is the Turner painting?" Becky innocently enquired quite loudly, loud enough for all to hear. "Daddy said you hid it. Can we play find the painting?"

"Rebecca!" Geraldine chastised with a look.

But all eyes were on Susan. She had decided to leave the painting hidden, out of sight out of mind, until she felt ready. Now was the time. She hadn't ventured into Jane's old room since she had come home. This was the moment when all the hard work by herself and the amazing people at the clinic would be put to the test.

"No Geraldine its fine. I'm sure you're all wondering." Susan put down her glass.

"Paul and I had a big argument and it got out of hand," she looked at the tablecloth, taking a deep breath, then around at the expectant faces. "Paul went to London and I wanted to punish him so I decided to pretend the painting had been stolen. I broke the window, just a small break at the handle and I hid the picture in a place where I could retrieve it whenever I wanted to. I'm sorry Paul it was just an impulse. When I went to London I had no idea things were going to work out the way they did."

"But where did you hide the painting!" Several voices echoed the question.

"Behind that print in Jane's room I got the idea from a James Stuart movie."

"That's a good place," Becky agreed, "I'd never have thought of looking there!"

"Tell me you didn't say that!" Jane had everyone's attention as she clasped her hand to her face in dismay. "I took the print. I brought it home with some other things for the new house!"

Susan laughed, "well that's ok, I would have got a shock if I'd checked and it wasn't there."

"It's gone to O'Reilly's!" Jane spoke through her clasped fingers, I decided I didn't want it and I gave it to O'Reilly's with some other things for their next auction."

The second silence hit the table.

"No worries, you can withdraw it," Simon immediately consoled the distraught Jane. "No problem, people take stuff back all the time."

"Yes," said Paul "Call down to O'Reilly's tomorrow and withdraw it from the auction," he smilingly waved a dismissive hand.

Jane collapsed back in her chair in an exaggerated faint, arms hanging by her side, "Of course, that's a relief, for a moment I thought it was gone."

"When's the auction"?" Susan asked gently reaching across to console her daughter. Jane sat upright, "Tuesday, Tuesday afternoon two thirty, I'll call tomorrow."

"That's ok," said Susan, "Leave it to me, you've got things to do. I'll have a word with Mr O'Reilly and get the picture back."

"I don't like it," Becky was looking to the other end of the long open plan room where the ornate, empty frame hung on the wall over the piano. "Its spooky," she whispered, so quietly nobody noticed.

"The match is starting!" One of the teenagers said suddenly. "What match?" enquired Simon.

"Man United and Liverpool, Jane told us you have Sky,"

"Well watch it." Susan who normally frowned upon television on Sunday get-togethers watched them scramble to turn on the Television.

"Rooney's a waster!" the two boys tumbled onto the big sofa. Richard was just behind the lads taking a grandstand seat, followed quickly by Simon and Paul.

"I quite like the soccer myself," said Geraldine claiming one of the armchairs

"I think they're all, overpaid wasters," she said with a laugh.

"We'll have the picture back in its frame in a couple of days,"

Susan sitting at the table with Jane and her granddaughter reassured Becky who had remained seated her eyes still focused on the empty frame. The little girl turned her head. "It's still spooky," she repeated with an uncertain smile, her eyes wide and as dark as Susan's. She slid from the chair and went to join the others.

"That child has such an imagination," Jane watched Becky climb onto her dad's knee. Richard, eyes on the telly pulled her close to his chest and absentmindedly began to stroke his daughter's long black hair as she snuggled close. The two women watched

"She's in a world of her own," Jane looked at Susan.

"A very nice secure world," Susan nodded with a quiet smile then changed the subject, asking abruptly.

"Now, how are your plans about your new house? Paul and I can help you if you're stuck for money."

"No need," the independent Jane was adamant. "I'm going back to work and we don't really need two cars."

There was a time when Susan might have pursued the subject but she decided not to as she took into account the resolute set of her daughter's jaw. This time Jane changed the subject. She put out a comforting hand.

"How are you, Mum? I don't need details of what happened in London, maybe sometime in the future," She waved a dismissive hand.

"But how are you, you seem to be coping ok?"

"Everything's fine now," Susan reassured her concerned daughter. "Paul and I are solid as a rock and really the events in London have made me appreciate so much. It was a pretty extraordinary shock to the system. You're right, maybe sometime in the future I'll tell you all about it, give you all the gory details, so to speak."

She paused, her mind struggling with some emotion, silence, but only for a moment. She gripped the younger woman's hand and with an earnest tearful gaze, her voice slightly shaking.

"I need to tell you how much I admire you and how proud I am of you..." Her voice trailed off as she searched for the right words. Jane squeezed her hand comfortingly and reached out to brush her mother's cheek, much like she would to comfort a child. The gesture was received with a gratified tearful smile as a new understanding was realized.

"Life is good with the Mackens," they agreed "Turner or no Turner."

"The Turner," Jane fluttered her hands and exhaled audibly with relief. "That was a near one all the same. I'm glad Becky asked the hard question. What if the print had sold at the auction and we'd lost the picture? I know how you love that painting. Are you sure you can have it withdrawn?"

"Of course!" Susan reassured, "This is only Sunday, I have plenty of time between now and the auction to arrange it, don't worry!"

Mr Seamus O'Reilly, Auctioneer, climbed up the five steps to his lofty position above the heads of the attendant bargain hunters. Undoing several buttons of his gold embroidered waistcoat, he wriggled his ample buttocks on the well-worn cushioned seat and made himself comfortable.

Every Tuesday at 2.30, on the dot, he went through the familiar procedure, after cleaning his rimless spectacles with a big white handkerchief he would blow his nose vigorously then check the items on the small shelf in front of him, his antique gavel, his phone and his list. When satisfied he would look over the heads of all those present to the small square window of the office located at the far end of the long room. Here Sheila, his assistant sat awaiting his signal to begin proceedings.

The phone in front of O'Reilly was in perfect working order but never rang, it's presence justified solely for effect, only to be lifted occasionally to receive an imaginary bid.

Today could prove to be a very special day in the History of O'Reilly's Fine Auctions for today he had received a pre-auction phone bid of fifty thousand euro for lot 137, a romantic print in a white frame, probably valued at about thirty five euro. The print was nice enough, a picture of a boy and a girl and a rose. The caller had proved to be authentic and checked out favourably on all counts.

Lot 137 should be coming up at about 4.00, he licked his lips at the prospect and peered impatiently at the office window where Sheila, under special instructions had to ensure the phone in front of him was working today of all days.

Greeted by an empty window,

"Sheila!" he roared.

Her face appeared in the small glass square, phone to her ear, the one in front of O'Reilly gave a soft Brrr! Brrrr!

He picked it up.

"Thank you Sheila," he smiled genially for the benefit of his audience, regretting his momentary loss of composure.

With a keen eye he scanned the crowded room recognising most of the faces, small time dealers, housewives, young couples looking to furnish a child's bedroom, some local business people there for the better stuff, some dealers from the city he recognized. There were some faces he did not recognize but thirty five years in the chair had thought him how to measure a crowd and nobody added up to the kind of money already bid for lot 137.

He picked out Jane Macken the lady who had, along with some other items, submitted the picture.

After his usual statement on the conditions of sale and times of collection and delivery he announced lot number one. Quickly getting into his stride the various lots were dispensed of at record speed, his excitement mounting as he eventually neared lot 137. Glancing quickly at his watch he ran a chubby finger around his collar, lot 121, he checked the faces again and there he was.

Several people had joined the auction but there he was standing near the doorway. It was the aspect of the man that attracted the Auctioneer's eye, his sallow complexion, well dressed, his sense of purpose. O'Reilly could always pick out the ones who were here to buy. Then he saw Cecil Sheridan arrive and take up a position right at the back of the room. Cecil Sheridan, owner of one of the biggest Galleries in Dublin.

O'Reilly sat up a little bit straighter and delivered the remaining lots with professional precision, his voice taking on a new quality, playing to the gallery.

"Lot 137, a romantic print!"

Denis, the go-for, did not normally display an item but on this occasion the print was placed on the display shelf alongside O'Reilly's perch as he casually announced a starting bid of €50.000 euro. This brought an excited murmur from the crowd.

"Do I hear €55,000?" his auctioneer's eyes scanned the room but he knew where to look. It was a slight rising of a sallow finger but a bid all the same.

"Thank you!" looking right and left his eye picked out Cecil Sheridan but glanced off to a frantically waving Sheila at the office window as she pointed to his phone. He picked up the phone just as Sheridan appeared to raise his hand.

"€100,000," said the now familiar phone voice. O'Reilly nearly fell of his perch.

"Thank you, €100,000!" the noise level rose as the crowd reacted, some examining the innocent print for a clue as to it's value, others casting round to see who was bidding.

"Quiet please!" this was O'Reilly's moment.

"Have I €110,000?" he enquired

The sallow finger did it's bidding.

O'Reilly looked again to the window and an excited Sheila. He lifted the phone "€200,000," said the quiet voice"

"€200,000 to the phone!" There was a hush in the room, not a sound. History was being made at O'Reilly's fine Auction House.

"€275,000!" The accent was foreign but the amount unmistakable, the foreign looking gent had spoken, his hand now raised.

Sheila looked at the phone in her hand and shook her head in reply to the expectant glance from O'Reilly who lifted his phone anyway but it was dead.

"€275,000 for the romantic print," he scanned the room catching sight of Sheridan's back as he departed.

"Going, going, is that it?" a last look around, the foreign man was looking straight at him. "Sold!"

Amidst the crescendo of voices that followed O'Reilly climbed down from his perch and strode majestically across the floor. The crowd parted leaving the foreign man standing alone to receive the full impact of O'Reilly's bonhomie.

"Seamus O'Reilly, Proprietor, and to whom do I have the pleasure of addressing?" His great chubby hand was extended towards the man who stepped past him totally ignoring the proffered handshake.

O'Reilly did an about turn to follow. The man took lot 137 down from the display shelf. "Can we go to your office please I would like to conclude our business as quickly as possible?"

O'Reilly hesitated, but just for a moment as he turned to his audience.

"Excuse us please I am suspending the auction for ten minutes while I attend to this gentleman." He smiled and jostled his flabby jowls puffing out his cheeks and raising a fat hand brushed back an imaginary lock of hair. "This way!" The two men headed into the office, O'Reilly taking a bemused Jane in tow.

"Ms Macken I'll need you to finalise things,"

In the office the print was laid on the desk face down. The foreign man without a word produced a pocketknife and swiftly cut through the backing paper. He pulled it away enough to reveal, not the back of a modern print but the unmistakable patina of the aged vellum. With a grunt of approval he turned to face O'Reilly.

"I have talked to my bank, they have been in touch with your bank Mr O'Reilly," a phone appeared in his hand, "they are just awaiting my instruction as to the amount to transfer to your account. The transaction will be completed immediately."

"Sheila," O'Reilly blustered, "paperwork please!" Sheila was already at the printer, ready with the pink and white dockets.

O'Reilly carefully separated them and handed the white one over stabbing the document with a clumsy finger. "That's the total including commission."

The foreign man spoke into the phone giving the appropriate details.

After a short wait, during which time the only voice to be heard was that of O'Reilly who made some inane comment about the weather, the office phone rang and Sheila answered it.

"It's Andrew from the bank. The transaction has been completed,"

Without a word the foreign man headed out the back door carrying the valuable purchase.

"Sheila, a cheque for Ms Macken please," O'Reilly beamed, "I need to return to the auction." He strode through the office door to a crescendo of applause from his regulars.

The cheque safely stowed in her handbag, Jane left through the back door in time to see the foreign man being bundled into a police car. One of the officials was probably the biggest person she had ever seen, an extremely tall man in plain clothes.

"It's time we got ourselves a new mower."

Susan unscrewed the petrol cap and peered into the half full tank. She replaced the cap and removed the clip from the spark plug and blew on it. Expert mechanic, she laughed to herself. Replacing the clip she joggled the wire of the throttle moving the lever back and forth. Well that's all the tricks I know. Standing up and putting the lever to start she grasped the ripcord handle and gave it a good pull. With a bang and some smoke the motor stuttered into life.

Cutting the grass was something Susan enjoyed, letting her mind wander as she followed the curves of the flowerbeds.

Rain on the way, looking out across the lawn over the rooftops of the holiday homes to the sea and the distant horizon she could see an ominous cloud line. The sea was running with an incoming tide and the seagulls wheeled, the sight stopping Susan in her tracks. Ever since the traumatic events in London and her time at the clinic, especially since her return home, Susan's attitude had changed in many ways. She now stood contemplating the view prompted to dwell for a moment on the sweetness of life.

Better get this grass cut before the rain comes she thought. Those clothes are nearly dry, the wind had sprung up and the rotating clothesline had begun to move catching her eye.

"Mum!" Over the sound of the motor mower Susan at first didn't hear Jane as she came around the side of the house. "Mum!" Susan at the other end of the lawn saw Jane running across the grass towards her.

"The painting sold!"

"What?" Susan glanced out to sea at the approaching cloud and kept mowing.

Jane her face flushed "Turn it off," she stopped Susan with a firm hand on her arm. Susan afraid that the mower would not start again nonetheless did as she was told and looked at Jane.

"Sorry I couldn't hear what you said I wanted to get the grass cut before the rain arrives."

"I thought you said that you were going to withdraw the painting from the Auction?" Jane took the cheque from her shoulder bag and showed it to her Mother, "It sold for €275,000, a foreign man bought it and then was arrested by the police. There was a phone bid."

Susan took the cheque and looked at it with a smile,

"Wow! That's very nice!" For a moment she looked slightly perplexed and asked, "That's a lot of money, are you sure the cheque's ok?"

"Absolutely!" Jane explained the procedure in O'Reilly's office and how both banks were involved.

"That's perfect," Susan took Jane's bag and stuffed the cheque into it letting the bag fall back against her side. "It's made out to you, it's yours to make the house possible."

"No way Mum!" Jane exclaimed, ""that would be very nice but I couldn't take the money."

"Keep it Jane," Susan said smiling. "It's been worth every penny, would you like a cup of tea?" Turning quickly to avoid any further protest she headed into the house. Jane stood for a while and then followed.

Susan moving quickly was through the studio and into the big room when Jane caught up with her.

"Mum, you went through so much for that painting I really couldn't…" her voice trailed off.

Susan was sitting on the sofa looking across the room she was smiling.

"Come and sit down," She said without looking at her daughter.

Jane, as she was bid, sat down on the sofa beside her.

"What do you think?" Susan gestured to the wall opposite.

The turbulent sea merged with the fabulous sky. The sunlight caught the russet sails of the Hovellers going out to a wreck.

Jane could only stare in disbelief at the "Turner" back in its frame hanging on the wall opposite.

"Fabulous, isn't it," Susan laughed at Jane's expression. You didn't think I'd give it up that easily?" She took her daughter's hand. "You get the money for the house and I get to keep the painting."

"But how?" Jane stared, her head reeling with questions.

"The foreign man checked the back of the painting. I saw him?"

"Just the back of an old watercolour Sheila and I put there yesterday. That's what you saw."

"OK...?" Jane looked confused and asked the big question.

"How did the foreign bloke know the print was in the auction and that the "Turner" had been hidden behind it?"

Susan held up a mobile. "Vaclav Janacec's phone! I sent a text to all the numbers on his contact list."

Jane looked at the phone beginning to understand.

"There was someone making phone bids pushing up the price, that must have been someone from the phone list. You played them against each other," she said knowingly.

"No that was me," Susan laughed, "It worked beautifully."

"You?" But what if they had stopped bidding? You'd have had to pay for it."

"But you would have got the money," Susan countered with a little smile, and it would only have cost us O'Reilly's commission. Anyway, Sheila told me that high bidders had enquired about lot 137 including our Cecil Sheridan, the owner of Sheridan's Gallery. He must have been on Janacec's list, they were probably in touch all along."

Jane leaned against the back of the sofa and was quiet for a few seconds as she contemplated the ceiling letting the information sink in.

"You are something else," she shook her head in disbelief." The two women, mother and daughter sat back in the big comfortable sofa looking at the beautiful painting that held so many secrets.

"Do you think it really could be a Turner?" asked Jane eventually.

Instead of responding Susan stood up and went into the bedroom to return with two small water colour sketches, the painting from the black box and the small sketch with the note from Turner on the back that she had found amongst Janacec's possessions at the Base.

"I haven't had any time since I got home to have a good look at this. It's very exciting." She showed Jane, "There's a note on the back from Turner too."

"I haven't shown this to anyone yet Jane, not even your father." In answer to your question, do I think it's a Turner? No Jane I don't." Turning over the picture, the one with the note on the back from Turner, she traced the wording with a finger.

"The handwriting is not the same as the handwriting on the back of our painting, it's similar but definitely not the same hand. We were relying all along on the handwriting being Turner's." Her eyes went to the picture on the wall.

"It will always be a Turner to me Jane. The painting is very valuable to us all, its part of our past and I love it."

"Janacec, Vaclav Janacec." Jane said quietly, "During your time at the Clinic that name was mentioned." Jane studied her mother's face. "They asked us about him and of course we had never heard the name, apparently when you came round after your collapse you talked a lot about him, even the police enquired."

Susan, at the mention of his name could not prevent the memories. So much of what had happened she had put to the back of her mind, the revelation about her ancestors and her connection with Janacec, the fact that they were blood related, his comment about her eyes when she lay helpless on the bed in the hotel room, the terrible trip in the car through the London Streets all the time fearful of what was happening to her, afraid for her life and of the terrible acts of which the man was capable. But most of all the doubts and fears in her mind, the knowledge that she had done something very bad when she was a child, the haunting memory of how the knife felt in her hand, the fear of what she was capable of, that she was as bad as Janacec, the kaleidoscope of questions and doubts.

Thanks to her stay at the Clinic Susan now had an understanding and her doubts and fears had been put to rest. Her faith in the good in people restored.

Jane looked back, her dark brown eyes soft with concern at her mother's expression. "I'm sorry, I shouldn't have mentioned it, please forget what I asked, it doesn't really matter. I know you went through a dreadful time, just try to put it out of your mind."

Susan smiled broadly at her daughter's concern.

"You know Jane you have the most beautiful eyes," She said softly, "and you're such a really good person."

"Mum, where did that come from?" Jane laughed

"Nowhere really, I'm just grateful for so much."

They examined the small sketch of the little girl and the woman. It was a page, one side ragged, obviously torn from a sketchpad. On the back was a message signed by Turner.

15 may 1825
Dear Mrs Janacec,
Thank you for allowing me to use the study of you and Abigail in my latest work. Please accept this small sketch as a wedding gift.
JMW Turner."

"I'm Sure the Tate will be very interested in this and this," Susan picked up the other picture of Abigail, "to think this was in that old black box in the attic all that time," she held the framed picture in her hand and studied it.

A memory stirred, an image flashed, an image of herself as a little girl standing with her face inches from a beautiful seascape. She closed her eyes to maintain the elusive image in her mind and then began to speak, eyes closed, her head resting on the back of the sofa, reliving the memory while Jane listened.

"There were two grey haired old ladies, my Nana Wakeley and nana's sister, sitting talking," she whispered. "I was holding this picture of the little girl and the lady.

Of course!" she exclaimed excitedly "Abigail wasn't in the big picture of the Hovellers, I put her there, she was my imaginary friend and we played on the beach." She looked at Jane, "I was five and I was bored so I played with the picture of Abigail while my Nana talked with her sister, this is the picture I played with."

Quickly turning the picture over Susan twisted the little catches on the back and removed the painting from the frame. It was attached with some adhesive to the oval card frame. The card was much wider than the oval shape and was concealing a large portion of the painting. When this was removed Susan and Jane could see the entire picture. There was a woman standing holding Abigail's hand, she had been concealed by the oval frame, both figures in the painting looked out to sea, the woman's blond hair blowing across her dark eyes.

"Watch this! The mystery is solved!" Susan stood up with the picture in her hands and stepping to the "Turner" on the wall she placed the image of the woman and Abigail on the large painting, moving it around.

"I used to play with it like this and imagine Abigail talking to me, calling over the sound of the crashing waves." Susan beamed in satisfaction. "I remember now!"

She pointed to the sketch on the coffee table in front of Jane.

"Read what it says on the back again. It's a message from Turner to Grace Wakeley thanking her for allowing herself and Abigail to be included in his next masterpiece." She paused for effect.

"So you see, our painting is not the original, the original would have a woman and child in it. Look at Turner's handwriting on the note. It's not the same handwriting as on the back of our painting."

"Tell me all about it. Where did you get this?" Jane brandished the small sketch. "It's very beautiful and with Turner's handwriting and signature it must be valuable. I want to know everything."

Susan sat down.

"The woman in the picture is called Grace Wakeley and Abigail was her niece. They were friendly with Sophie Booth who lived with Turner, sometimes in Margate and sometimes Deal." Here Susan paused and took a deep breath.

"Now Jane, I want you to listen carefully. We are directly descended from Grace Wakeley. She was my mother's I don't know how many greats, grandmother. She married a foreign man and they lived in Deal, Kent. They had two sons. The foreign man was a bad character and was convicted of murder. He escaped the authorities and fled to Europe. One of the sons kept the Wakeley name. When I was in London I was given the picture by a descendant of the other son, a man called Vaclav Janacec."

"So that means that this Vaclav Janacec is related to us. What's he like? Where's he from?" Jane asked. She studied her mother's face waiting for an answer. For a few moments there was no response as Susan looked down at the picture in her hand. Then she looked up and her expression was resolute with a half smile.

"Let's say it's a closed book Jane."

Jane tactfully remained silent, as her mother obviously was not ready to discuss details. "He's dead Jane and he won't bother this family again."

1944 County Dublin

To the five-year old Susan her name was "Nana Eileen."

Nana Eileen Wakeley had never missed a Thursday visit with her sister Emma, at the old house. In all her eighty-seven years she could not remember a time when Emma, three years her junior, had not relied on her. Emma in a strange way always seemed unsettled, troubled. As a child Eileen found her younger sister to be manipulative and sometimes cruel, clinging to Eileen and always demanding her big sister's undivided attention. Many adventures were lost, as Eileen, unable to accompany her friends would remain behind with Emma. Teenage years duplicated the experience and on into adulthood, Emma always in tow.

With two failed marriages Emma seemed to invite disaster at every turn and Eileen would be there to pick up the pieces. After the break-up of her second marriage Emma travelled abroad typically advising no one of her intentions, she had gone from their lives. Eileen heard through a mutual friend that Emma had married again and was living somewhere in central Europe. Ten years had elapsed without a word and then one day she reappeared back into Eileen's life taking up where she had left off. No amount of probing or subtle discussion could elicit a shred of information.

Every Thursday Eileen would call to visit with her sister and unlike Eileen, who was outgoing and cheerful, Emma, as she grew older had become an embittered, cold, secretive and austere old woman. The only time Eileen ever saw her sister show softness was when her big black cat curled up on her lap. Then the cold features would relax and she would cluck and purr and stroke, her long blue veined fingers pure white against the cats black fur.

On missing a Thursday, Eileen would be greeted at the next visit with a truculent cross- examination. In spite of these reservations Eileen's natural kindness and love for her sister prevailed, she felt that one day a week was not too great an inconvenience knowing how much Emma relied on her.

These days Emma lived alone in the large old house except that is for the lodger. The mysterious lodger lived upstairs and Eileen had never met him. Occasionally Emma would disappear from the front room to appear again with a tray.

"Something for the lodger," she would say as she passed the doorway heading for the stairs. There would be a murmuring of voices from upstairs and then she would return without comment and Eileen never enquired.

On these visits Eileen would sometimes be accompanied by little Susan her five year old grandchild. The little girl had a fascination for the large painting that spent its time propped up against the wall between the piano and the dining room table. Emma normally paid scant attention to Susan. However on one visit, to amuse the child she had produced a picture of a little girl called Abigail, placing it on the large painting she showed Susan how it merged in and fitted to become part of the large dramatic seascape. From then on Susan would look forward to her visits and the opportunity to play with Abigail her imaginary friend. Placing Abigail's picture in different places she played a wonderful game of make believe as they swam in the sea and ran along the beach chatting and laughing, the five year old would amuse herself for the duration of the visit.

Mostly Eileen would arrive alone aware that her sister had very little time for children. She was surprised and pleased of late, that Emma had requested for little Susan to come on every visit and she even produced ginger nut biscuits, Susan's favourite.

Thursday 26 June 1944

"Today we will be unable to stay for the whole afternoon," Eileen had announced apologetically on their arrival.

"Leave the child with me, you can collect her later," Emma immediately made the unexpected request. In spite of Eileen's reluctance to leave the child, Emma as usual had her own way and it was agreed that Susan would stay to be collected later.

"Bye! Bye! Have a nice play with Abigail," Eileen waved from the bend in the drive at the tall austere figure of her sister standing with the little girl by her side on the step at the front door.

Had she detected a look of uncertainty in little Susan's eyes at her departure? Resisting a strong inclination to go back and take the little one with her she headed out through the high gateway with a nagging feeling of unease.

Emma waited until her sister was out of sight before she spoke.

"I have ginger nut biscuits, would you like a picnic with Abigail?" she said, her eyes still fixed on the bend in the drive? Without waiting for a reply she turned and headed through the doorway. Susan was also looking at the bend in the drive.

Not wanting to be left alone she quickly followed but stopped in fright just inside the doorway when she saw the big black cat sitting in the middle of the hallway looking at her. A mouse struggled in its mouth. The cat's eyes glowed in the dim light. Susan, frightened, called out but the old lady had already reached the kitchen at the end of the hall and didn't hear her or didn't want to. Lowering its head the cat placed the mouse on the floor where petrified with fear it crouched unmoving. Susan watched wide-eyed as the cat prodded the mouse with a paw coaxing it into action. Suddenly the mouse made a dart for freedom straight towards Susan. With one gleeful bound the cat pounced, its unsheathed claws trapping the mouse tight to the floor. As the little girl watched, horrified, the cat began to eat the mouse. Susan feet dancing in panic, arms waving frantically, crying out, rounded the unequal conflict and fled down the hall not looking back until she reached the safety of the kitchen, the grim smiling face and Emma's outstretched white hands.

The cat with a disdainful look after the tearful child having reduced the mouse to a reddish stain on the worn carpet, was heading for the kitchen.

Strong white hands lifted Susan aloft with no attempt at comfort. Glad of the sanctuary she hugged her arms around the hard skinny shoulders and buried her tearful face in the lavender smelling paisley material of the dress.

Emma, leaning back, reached to take two ginger nut biscuits from the kitchen table and handed them to the sniffing child in her arms before heading briskly along the hall to the stairs.

Looking over the old woman's shoulder Susan could see the large painting as they swept past the doorway of the living room.

"I want to have a picnic with Abigail!" she reached out with a biscuit in her hand but she was carried swiftly past and up the stairs across the uncarpeted landing and into the lodger's bedroom.

Out of breath from the stairs and the unaccustomed activity, the stern faced Emma lowered Susan to the floor and stood for a minute to gain her breath before guiding her across the floor with a firm hand.

The bedroom was smelly and Susan's nose twitched, the ginger nuts fell to the floor unnoticed as she swung to look behind her. The big black cat sat in the bedroom doorway licking its lips. It's unblinking eyes fixed on the little girl.

"So this is the child."

Susan shrank back grabbing a handful of paisley skirt as the old man lying on the bed turned his head and spoke, stretching out a long fingered hand to take her arm and force her closer to the bed. Holding the child in a strong grip he fixed her with a frightening unsmiling stare from dark eyes sunken deep under fierce frowning eyebrows. Susan sobbed with quick uncontrolled little breaths. She shrank away as he touched her face with his thumb and forefinger. It was not a gentle gesture more a pinch that left a mark on the tearstained cheek. Still staring into the child's eyes he took his hand away and slowly reached to retrieve an ornate handled knife from an open drawer in the bedside locker.

The five-year old Susan struggled but strong white-fingered hands held her fast. He moved a finger on the mother of pearl and black ebony decorated handle, the needle-point-stiletto blade sprang into view. He handed the weapon to the woman without a word. Taking up a hand mirror from the bedside locker he looked away from the child's face and began to minutely study his reflection.

Disentangling Susan's clutching grasp from her skirt Emma hastily wrapped the child's fingers around the handle of the viciously bladed knife. Holding the child's hands tightly, she forced the terrified five-year old up onto the bed. Susan's hands were still gripping the knife as the old woman pushed the deadly pointed blade into the man's chest. The old man named Janacec stared into his own eyes in the mirror as they faded in death.

4 June 1825 Turner's Gallery in London

"It's a very fine piece," The elderly gentleman carefully placed the painting on the worktable, a dramatic picture of two luggers battling against the storm in a race to a stricken cutter, the buildings of Deal in the background. "But where are the people, the woman and the little girl?"

"The painting doesn't need them," answered JMW Turner.

Picking up the study of the woman and child with a flourish he placed it on the large painting and positioned it carefully. "That is how I planned the picture originally but you see it becomes far too cluttered, this painting is all about the Hovellers in action, the sea and the sky, the figures are unnecessary."

Removing the smaller picture he stood back and the two men admired the work.

Gesturing with the picture in his hand, "This I will give to Mrs Booth. She's very fond of the child," he said

Then searching on the table he produced a smaller sketch of the woman and child. "This is for Mrs Janacec I'll write her a short note of thanks."

"What title shall we put on the painting said the old man?"

"Deal, Hovellers going out to a wreck," came the reply.

Carefully turning over the beautiful painting Turner's father began to write in a flowing script,

Deal   Hovellers going out to a wreck

CPSIA information can be obtained
at www.ICGtesting.com
Printed in the USA
BVOW08s1958021116
466751BV00001B/1/P

9 781787 190887